I0647836

TAKING HOPE

JAMES K. BURK

WOLFSINGER PUBLICATIONS

WolfSinger Publications Security Colorado

Copyright © 2014 by James K Burk
All rights reserved. No part of this book may be used or reproduced in any
manner whatsoever without the written permission of the copyright owner.
For permission requests, please contact WolfSinger Publications at
editor@wolfsingerpubs.com
All characters and events in this book are fictitious.
Any resemblance to persons living or dead is strictly coincidental.

Cover Art copyright 2014 © Mitchell Bentley
www.atomicflystudios.com

ISBN 978-1-936099-79-5

Printed and bound in the United States of America

For
Orion Salvador, Olivia Isabelle, and Scarlet Francesca,
the next generation.

And for Whitney,
who inspires me with her courage and strength.

CHAPTER 1

Morgan had ridden only a few paces from the cave before he stopped, staring at the bodies sprawled among the rocks. Mendarian stood in the cave's mouth, arms crossed. She'd have work enough fighting her own demons without having to confront the wolves that would come prowling after the corpses.

Hesitating only a moment, he slid out of the saddle. The horses were easy to gather. He decided to leave at least three of them for Mendarian, along with whatever the men had carried to this place. The bodies he stripped of valuables, tossing his finds onto a pile, and throwing the corpses over the backs of the nervous animals. He loaded most of the bodies two to a horse, although Forgren, even lighter by half a head, required a beast to himself.

When he glanced up during the work he observed Mendarian had disappeared, probably into the cave that had been his own home for nearly two months. They'd said everything they'd had to say, at least for the nonce. With a last glance around to be certain he'd forgotten nothing, he mounted again and led his procession of dead away from the cave.

The sun was nearing the horizon when he crested a low, rounded hill and saw, at its base, a stream fed by mountain runoff. Swinging stiffly out of the saddle, he cut the bodies loose, letting them fall in a heap, then led the horses down to water. At the stream he looked back once to see the pile of bodies, arms and legs at odd angles and beginning to stiffen, monuments to their own cupidity. He moved on, leading the horses, to a place where an outcropping offered protection from the wind.

He hobbled the horses, fed them a ration of oats from the supplies they carried, then looked to his own dinner. From the provisions of the dead men he dined on sausage, cheese, hardtack, and sour wine. These satisfied only his body's hunger, leaving him feeling a curious emptiness and lightness.

For perhaps the first time in his life, he had nowhere to go, nothing that needed be done. Mendarian was behind him, in more ways than the distance of half a day's ride. Seeing her again hadn't left him wanting only to be near her. He still felt some affection, some caring, but whatever fires had burned in him—love, anger, perhaps even hatred—had been banked. He hoped she'd use the opportunity to discover the gold in herself but, when next they met, they'd be two strangers who only looked familiar to each other.

He'd abdicated the thrones of Donradé and Glangurra and nothing drew him back to either place. At High Rage, in Valé Shanna, the walls had fallen and his brothers and sisters of the Winged Dagger Clan were all dead. If Forgren's men still ruled in Valé Shanna, they did so with a sword, not a scepter, and if they'd gone he was sure the people of the valley would provide respectful care for the bodies of his kin.

He had, without any thought of destination, ridden northeast, and he had to think for a moment before he recalled this was the way to Stag Mountain, a Dieri settlement. Mendarian, until her own abdication, had been the empress of Cerco, the mountain realm which included the Dieri, and he'd been her consort, later her husband.

Perhaps his choice of direction had been only a whim, but being guided by a whim was better than having no guide at all, and he wondered what his reception from the Dieri might be.

~ * ~

Two days later he rode through the Wolf's Gate at Stag Mountain, where he handed his weapons to a guard and was led through the tunnels and caverns to see the headman. Apparently, Stag Mountain hadn't been inhabited for as many generations as Crown; some of the caverns and almost all of the tunnels looked unfinished, and he saw little of the ornate carving that decorated Crown Mountain.

The headman was a typical Dieri; short and stocky with broad, clean-shaven features, blue eyes and blond hair, although the hair was paling to silver-gray. The familiar face required a search in a dim trunk in Morgan's memory to find the name. Morgan bowed slightly, then said, "Well met, Ergun. You fought well in the eastern wars."

There might have been some flicker of light in the Dieri's dourness, then he nodded in reply. "What have we to offer each other, Scarface?"

Morgan hid his amusement. The austere mountain home of the Dieri stamped its character on most of them. They were hard, laconic, and thrifty to the point of self-parody. He was known among these people by his use-name and the black scars that looked like the finger-marks of a demon at his forehead, temples, and cheekbones. "I'm seeking stable-places for the horses I brought, meals, and a soldier's cot. In return, I'll do a soldier's duties and train your younger men."

He was skilled enough with arms he could teach even Ergun, but thought it better to show respect for the man's well-earned pride.

"That seems an equitable enough trade. Perhaps you even ask too little."

"It's all I require for now, and if my needs change we can bargain again later."

"Well said." In the Dieri manner they struck the palms of their right hands together and Morgan was led to a barracks, a great hall containing a collection of wicker cots with straw-stuffed pallets, a wicker chest for each cot, and a low fire under a pot of stew.

~ * ~

He had his hair trimmed by another soldier and used a fine blade to clear the beard from his face, leaving only the moustache, and settled comfortably into a routine.

He thought he'd recovered from his madness for Mendarian but found himself, on guard duty, watching the trails to the southwest and, at other times, listening for any word among the other troops of anyone seen on the paths to Stag Mountain but, after nearly a month, he decided that whatever course she'd chosen had nothing to do with him or the Dieri.

At the beginning of his second month at Stag he joined a hunt to provide the settlement with fresh meat. When they returned with deer and mountain sheep they carried the meat to the common cavern, a large, almost circular cave which contained a spring-fed well.

Morgan laid down the deer carcass he'd carried and had just turned to go back to the barracks when a woman stepped in front of him. "Have you been avoiding me?"

Instantly he recognized Topaz. Despite her blond hair and emerald eyes, she reminded him strongly of Martina, his dead clan sister. Part of the resemblance was physical. They shared similar features; their faces were enough alike they could've been sisters, and both were slender with large breasts but trim waists and hips and long legs. And they seemed to resemble each other in temperament as well.

He considered the question carefully before he answered. "Perhaps. I think I'm a bit afraid of you."

Her smile drew his attention to her full, soft lips. "Knowing both your reputation and your nature. I don't know whether to be flattered or offended."

Again he paused to weigh his words carefully. "The truth should neither flatter nor offend. I'd wanted to see you but was afraid to, for several reasons." Her smile was contagious and elicited an answering one from him.

"Perhaps I could learn those reasons if I were to provide a meal and ply you with Shannan pomegranate wine."

"Only for the taste. Your company would be a headier potion than any wine."

She laughed and it was a sweet sound, like the ringing of a silver bell. "I see you still have the knack of turning a phrase prettily."

"Unfortunately, I have duties which demand my attention." He had no desire to close the door on possibilities. "I'll be training some men until sunset."

"If you're hungry then, my rooms are down that tunnel." She pointed to her left. "It's the fifth door from this cavern, and the door hanging is tan and green, with a red rose pattern."

"I'd be pleased," Morgan murmured, then strode to the armory to select his practice weapons. It was only a surprise he'd met Topaz then. He'd been told she was at Stag Mountain, and he wondered if that hadn't been the source of the whim that had drawn him here. He remembered having worked with her, long ago, casting a spell; remembered coming out of a trance kissing her.

He still wasn't sure his loyalty to Mendarian would've been enough to cause him to stop had Topaz shown any interest in continuing. And she very much reminded him of Martina who, had she not been kin, would have been his first choice as lover.

Remembering Martina was still painful. She was one of the Clan who'd died at High Rage, and her loss had been almost unendurable. And there was Poker, whose name, in Sinn, meant "proud." He'd lived with pride and, Morgan was sure, he'd died with pride. It was fitting that both of them had died well, but that brought him little comfort.

It seemed there'd been two Pokers to mourn. The first was the comrade in arms on the Das wars, who'd displayed a ruthlessness to match Scarface's own. In those days, he hadn't been Morgan, he'd been Scarface, and Poker had impressed even Scarface with his skill in interrogation and his boldness.

Then there was the Poker who'd converted to the church of Ianno. His blue-black hair and beard, tightly curled, and his canines, half again the length of the rest of his teeth, seemed incongruous in light of his gentleness and his devotion to the god he'd chosen.

Poker had been wounded in the Das war and had been rescued and treated by a follower of Ianno, but he hadn't simply converted out of gratitude. Morgan remembered his cousin's bouts of doubt, his careful study of religions, the deep thought he'd applied to his quest. And, apparently, the religious life Poker had chosen had brought him peace and joy. That was a comfort to Morgan.

Two glorious lives, both ended, leaving holes in his own life. His reflections had been dark enough that by the time he'd armed and armored himself he was as grim as the Dieri he trained.

The practice helped relieve some of his dark mood and, as he approached the tunnel Topaz had pointed out, anxiety had replaced the melancholy. He was afraid of rejection and afraid of hope. A small oil lamp in hand, he found the door hanging with the rose pattern and scratched at it.

"Come in."

The room was dim and fragrant with cooking smells. Besides a small fire for cooking, the only light was provided by the faintly glowing lichen that clung to the walls and which the Dieri spread throughout the caverns and tunnels they used.

Topaz wore a dark green robe that contrasted with her fair skin and blond hair. She gestured at piles of cushions flanking a low table, then carried a tray to the table. Morgan picked up the bottle on the tray, worked the cork loose, and sniffed. He recognized the rich scent of Shannan pomegranate wine and poured the deep purple liquid into two cups.

If Topaz had intended to impress him with her cooking, she'd succeeded. The venison was smothered in a thick sauce with mushrooms and a hint of dry red wine, while the bread had been mixed with vegetables and nuts before it had been baked. The venison and its sauce were hot, the bread still warm.

"Excellent," he pronounced.

She smiled. "I expect the conversation to at least equal the meal."

"I'm afraid I'll disappoint you. I'm coming more as a beggar than as a trader." He sipped at the wine, appreciating the rich, fruity flavor.

"I'd saved that wine for a special occasion," she said. She savored a sip of wine, then sampled the food. "All we know here in Stag Mountain is that a man who must've hated you very much, a man named Forgren, arrived at Crown Mountain with an escort of soldiers and Mendarian left with them, taking Orhan and a handful of Dieri warriors. Several days later, Orhan returned to Crown with the staff and crown of Father Wolf," she bowed at the name, "and the men with him said there'd been a battle. They said when they'd left, only you and Mendarian were still alive. Now you appear alone. You must admit the circumstances could inspire some lively assumptions."

"True. I hadn't thought about that." He ate slowly, appreciating the flavors of both the meat and the bread. "Forgren was the man who gave the orders that led to the deaths of Martina and several other of my cousins. I'm really not sure whether he wanted to take me alive as a hostage to trap Hadrian or whether he simply wanted me dead.

"He'd prepared a spell and used Mendarian to hunt me down. When they found me, Mendarian abdicated, giving the staff and crown to Orhan. I don't know what her motives were. In fact, I'm not sure she knows, herself. When Forgren raised his spell and it didn't kill me, he ordered his men to attack, either to kill me or to distract me enough that the spell could kill. My cousin, Hadrian, appeared, killed the men with Forgren, and left Forgren and Mendarian for me to deal with. Forgren asked my true name of Mendarian to use in a spell of binding. For whatever reason, she gave him a wrong name and Forgren died. I left Mendarian to find herself. I assume she's done so. It seems the way she's chosen doesn't lead into these mountains."

"Are you disappointed?"

He'd just taken another bite of meat and used the time he spent chewing to regard the question. "Not really. I believe her decision would've been mine, too, had I a choice."

Topaz had finished eating and sipped at her wine. "One always has choices."

He shook his head. "In the past, I've used some very presumptuous words; 'never' and 'forever,' but I still feel bound by them." He finished his meal while it was still warm.

Topaz stared at him. "But she's chosen to cut those bonds, and she has a right to make such choices, just as you do. So what do you choose to do now?"

"I'm not familiar enough with Dieri custom to know what I can do."

"You may ask the emperor to announce the death of the marriage, if that's what you want."

"Do you think I should do that?"

"I think you must make that decision yourself. It has nothing to do with me." She refilled both their cups.

His thin smile was a weak attempt to hide the bleakness he felt.

She watched him drink. "Was your being afraid of me a part of that?"

His nod was curt. "I found you...very attractive." He gazed at her in the room's half-light and found it still to be true. All the lines of her face seemed in perfect harmony; the oval shape; the slightly arched brows; the lustrous eyes; the nose, short and straight, broad enough not to seem pinched; the soft, generous lips. He looked away because it was almost painful to see such beauty and not touch it. She surprised him by chuckling. "I'm not going to tell you that I'm sorry. But that has nothing to do with your other decision."

Again he tried to hide his feelings behind a grin. "I like you very much. I was afraid I might do something that'd offend you."

Her lips took on an impish curl. "If we were friends, the friendship would survive my being offended or you being offended by my response, and if we weren't friends, you wouldn't have cared—nor would it matter."

This brought a laugh from him, one that was genuine, then he looked at his hands. "Are you friends with both of me? Sometimes I feel as though I were two people." He thought, momentarily, of the two Pokers. "I wonder," he said, "whether we aren't all two people; the person we want to be and the person we must be."

"At least all the interesting ones are," she replied. "The rest are either self-indulgent or unimaginative."

He laughed again. "You've given me a meal and much to think about. I thank you for both." He stood and, very carefully, kissed her forehead. "I'll hope to see you again."

"I'll hope for that, too."

~ * ~

Rising at dawn, he dressed, paced to Ergun's rooms, scratched on the outer door hanging, and waited anxiously until he heard "Enter."

Ergun had apparently just risen; his hair was mussed and his eyelids still drooped.

"I'd like your permission to visit Crown Mountain."

Ergun eyed him grimly. "If it's important enough for you to ask me at this hour, it's important enough for permission. Tell the emperor that all's well here." He dismissed Morgan with a wave and a yawn. Morgan paused only long enough to bolt down a meal, gather supplies for the three day ride, and see to his mount, then he was riding north, toward Crown.

~ * ~

Orhan was an old friend but a new emperor. Morgan could see he still bore lightly the air of command, still revealed those qualities of endurance and determination that made him a leader, but the lines around his eyes and the corners of his mouth seemed to have deepened slightly. He dismissed the guard who'd escorted Morgan to his suite of rooms. They were the same rooms Scarface and Mendarian had once occupied but the new furnishings had banished old ghosts.

"Morgan, it's good to see you again. Is this solely a friendly visit?"

Orhan had always seemed a little less taciturn than most Dieri warriors.

"Not entirely. I'm living at Stag Mountain and heard that I might ask you to pronounce dead the marriage between Mendarian and myself."

Orhan poured them each a cup of mead, then leaned back in his chair. "Crowns were joined as well as the two of you, in that marriage, but now neither of you wears a crown, and neither the new king of Donradé and Glangurra nor I seem to have anything to offer each other. If kingdoms can part..." He seemed to be looking into the past. "Sometimes I wonder whether Father Wolf," he bowed, "intended the crown for Mendarian, or whether he knew she'd find you."

Morgan sipped at the cup of mead he held. He disliked the sticky-sweet drink, but drinking it helped hide his embarrassment." If I'm accepted as a Dieri subject, my advice is ever at my emperor's command."

"Thank you. Nothing of importance has risen but it's always

better to look to the future. And what of your future? Is there a reason for this request?"

Morgan met Orhan's gaze. "Freedom is a great gift. And there's a woman...her name is Topaz."

"I've met her. It seems a good match. I'll announce the death of your marriage tomorrow morning. Until then, you'll be our guest."

~ * ~

Near sundown, three days later, Morgan rode through the Ram's Gate at Stag. Reporting to Ergun, he learned that for the next cycle he'd guard the flocks from noon until midnight and train the younger men for the two hours before noon.

Taking a bowl of stew from the pot in the barracks, he ate quickly, then followed the tunnel to Topaz's room. Battling an attack of anxiety, he scratched on the wool hanging, then she swung the curtain open. "Come in."

Stepping into her rooms, he experienced an awkward moment when he noticed a young man and a woman lounging on the cushions in the outer room. "I can come back another time."

"Why bother? You're here now." She introduced Morgan to the couple, although she gave his use-name, Scarface. He hardly heard the names of the couple, and didn't remember them.

Topaz lit a candle and examined the bottles in the corner of the room, carried one to the woman. "A sip of this before you go to bed, every night, for the full month."

The couple left with the bottle and Topaz sank onto the cushions. "Please, sit down. Have you eaten yet?"

"I ate in the barracks."

"Then you can watch me eat." She returned to the corner, came back with a platter of bread and cheese and a cup of water. "You smell of horse sweat."

"I've been riding. I was hoping to see you again but I just learned that for the next cycle I'll be on duty until midnight."

"I keep late hours. You may come by, if you wish."

He nodded, then cast about for something more to say. "We were speaking, before, of people being more than one person. Are you more than one?"

"Anyone who's studied magic has to be more than one person. Discipline is required. You should know the prices one pays."

He grinned and stroked the scars burned into his face. "I have some small idea."

"Have you been to the baths? The odor of horse sweat is really very distracting."

"I usually wash myself in the barracks. I'm not used to undressing before others."

"I'd forgotten that you're more solitary than we Dieri. Still, there isn't likely to be anyone at the baths at this hour. I have a robe I can let you wear."

He followed her to the baths—whatever they might be—with a mixture of excitement and reluctance. The baths turned out to be depressions in the rock, constantly filled and flushed by hot springs. Self-consciously, he turned his back to her to undress, stripping off his belts, boots, jerkin, shirt, and hose. When he turned around, Topaz was already in the water, only her head and shoulders above the surface.

He sat on the side of the pool and dropped his feet and legs into the water, which seemed scalding, but he slid into the pool. Adjusting quickly to the heat, he found himself relaxing.

"If one is two persons," he asked, "how do you reconcile them?"

"They must have some affection for each other. Or, at least, respect."

So that was how Poker had succeeded. The Poker who had come to be had accepted the Poker who had been. He laughed with the discovery. "That may not be easy. I'm still learning about Morgan—the man I want to be—and Scarface—the man I thought I had to be—could be a difficult man to like."

"Are you sure about that? I met Scarface, didn't I?" At his nod she continued. "I found much to admire about him. He had integrity. And loyalty. I believe he was somewhat self-deluded, though. He wasn't, for instance, the devil he pretended to be."

His knees suddenly felt weak as he suffered something like a blow to the soul. Martina had once said almost those very words to him and hearing them again had opened a wound that had never healed, never really scabbed over. He turned his face from her so she wouldn't see the sudden tears, or how grief twisted his features, making them ugly.

She put a hand on his shoulder. "It's all right to mourn her. I only met her twice, but she was someone worth mourning."

He thought he'd dealt with the loss but had never squarely faced its permanence. Feelings buried for too long shot to the surface and for several moments he sobbed uncontrollably; harsh racking sounds that came from feelings so deep inside him that he had hardly suspected their existence.

Finally he regained control of his breathing and, almost, his voice. Ducking beneath the water, he scrubbed his face before surfacing again. When he could trust his voice, he said, "I'm sorry."

"You shouldn't be. If you hadn't felt close to me, your feelings wouldn't have trusted me enough to appear." She climbed out of the pool. "Now we use soap and get back into the water to rinse off."

Climbing out of the water after her, he followed her example as she scrubbed herself with a coarse but pleasantly scented soap.

He was grateful that she seemed unaware of his arousal as she washed his back and, observing the apparent flawless beauty of her body, he had to force himself to simply scrub her back when his hands wanted to linger on her velvet skin, then it was done and they slipped back into the water.

By the time they'd finished washing, the hot water had so relaxed him he was barely able to drag himself from the pool. They returned to her rooms, he wearing the borrowed robe and carrying his clothing.

In her rooms, he stopped by the cushions, then drew the robe tighter. It was going to be difficult to sit in the too-small robe without some embarrassing gaps appearing. Topaz saw his dilemma and giggled. "I want to see how you solve this problem."

"I'll stand."

She assumed an expression of mock-severity. "So, you'd insult me by refusing my hospitality?"

He rolled his eyes, then drew the robe tight, carefully knelt, slumped to his right, and rolled onto his belly. Topaz clapped, twice.

"Well done. I'll be waiting to see how you get back up." She stepped beside him, knelt, leaned forward, and began to knead the muscles of his neck and shoulders. He sighed as the remaining tension in his upper back was drawn out of him. For several moments he lay in a state somewhere between light slumber and almost awake. Her hands moved down to the muscles just below and between his shoulder blades, and he moaned with relief.

Self-consciousness fled with the tightness in his muscles. Somehow, it no longer seemed so important that the robe stay closed. He rolled over and stared into her face. The harmony, the composition of her features seemed perfect. "I remember another time, very like this," he said. Slipping his arms around her, he drew her nearer, lightly brushed her lips with his, reveling in the sensation of the softness of her lips, then their mouths were pressed together.

Fearing at each moment she'd resist, his tongue probed between her lips, and she opened her mouth. He tried, with that kiss, to express all the tenderness he felt. When her ardor seemed to match his own, he surrendered to temptation, his hands finding the openings of her robe.

Topaz drew away from him, and he was afraid he'd assumed too much, then she smiled and drew off her robe. "Now, are you less afraid of me?"

For a moment he could only stare at her taut body with the proud, firm breasts, then he chuckled. "Less afraid than in awe."

Then he realized he was being offered something he desired as desperately as he'd ever wanted anything. He seemed unable to draw a deep breath, his heart hammered at his chest, and no words would come, He held her closely, momentarily unable to do anything more, as relief and gratitude and a great caring all came together.

Again he kissed her, then caressed her, first with fingertips, then his hands, then his tongue and lips. He could smell and taste the pleasant scent of the soap with which they'd washed themselves, and her body seemed to transmute the smell into something even sweeter and richer. Her breasts were soft, and warm to the touch, and he admired the fine ridge of her hipbone before stroking it with his lips.

What had begun as a gentle exploration became something approaching devotion, then grew into overpowering hunger, until he entered her. For a time he was unaware of anything but Topaz, almost forgetting himself as separate from her. Both breathed only in ragged gasps, as their bodies moved together until they shuddered together. After he withdrew from her, they lay together, their breathing slowing and deepening.

Her body was warm against his, and seemed to fit against him as though they'd been melded into one. Looking into her perfect face, he found himself silenced by his own tenderness. He couldn't even disturb the calm to tell her he loved her. As though feeling his gaze on her, she opened her eyes, and the almost child-like appearance became that of an urchin as she grinned at him, then she rose, drawing him up after her, and led him to the smaller room containing her bed. "Now that the edge is off the hunger, let's try it again."

For long moments he simply stared at her. Her pale body seemed to glow in the dimness and the contours of her body seemed endlessly fascinating.

He lay beside her and explored her with fingers and lips, becoming familiar with her sweet geography, learning all the routes and byways to pleasing her, trying to offer every trace of pleasure he could give. Controlling his urgency, he drew out the passion, lightly stroking, kissing gently, becoming a tender tormenter, denying release for as long as possible, and Topaz responded in kind, until, when relief came at last, it was beyond control.

Desire sated, he held her close, feeling as though they and the hours had become golden, until Topaz stretched like a cat, and they drifted together into slumber.

~ * ~

Morgan woke slowly, first aware of the sleek body lying beside him. With consciousness came memory, and a laugh of pure contentment welled up until it escaped him. Topaz made some small, inarticulate sound, and he mumbled, "I think I want to stay in this bed forever."

Again her laugh, like the chiming of a silver bell, and in a voice thick with sleep, she murmured, "Haven't you yet learned the danger of that word 'forever'?"

He smiled, then felt a rush of panic. "Do you know what time of day it is?" In the eternal twilight of the caverns he often lost his sense of time.

"It's still early enough for you to wash and break your fast before you have to leave."

He nuzzled her neck. "And I know what I'd like to devour."

She chuckled. "While I'd enjoy it as much as you, I doubt it'd keep you until the evening meal."

"May I see you again tonight?" Running his fingers gently down her back, he tried to keep his voice more casual than he felt.

"I'd like that."

He didn't even try to hide the grin that threatened to split his face.

~ * ~

That night he returned and, a week later, moved his few possessions into her rooms. A pleasant rhythm was established. He came to treasure even the time they were apart. In clear weather the skies were impossibly blue, reminding him of Sin Garlef, where he'd grown up. On other days, when storm stalked the mountains, he stayed in a sheltered outpost or in the caverns with the flock, grateful for the shelter. He learned to play the shepherd's pipe, not as well as some but well enough to entertain himself. Two of the horses he'd brought with him were traded for half a dozen sheep and he started a flock for Topaz and himself.

He learned to appreciate the stark beauty of the mountains; the broad pastures, the hidden glades, the crystalline water with its faintly metallic taste. In time, he came to enjoy each of the seasons in the mountains; the crisp mornings and golden afternoons of autumn, the howling blizzards and white stillness of winter when the long nights were warmed by the one with whom you lay, the sudden storms and resurrection of spring, the vibrant summer days so alive with light and color that one's senses were almost overwhelmed, He enjoyed them even more when he could share them with Topaz.

He often left with other hunters. Predatory by nature, he possessed all the qualities of a born hunter. He was, by far, the best archer in Stag Mountain, although he remembered that he'd never been able to match Hadrian, his adopted brother and once his rival. He sometimes thought of his kin and came to cherish rather than dread memories of Poker and Martina and the others who'd died at High Rage. Sometimes, idly, he wondered where Hadrian might be and whether he'd left the bloodtrail to find life again.

He also learned some of the differences between Scarface and Morgan. Scarface had always striven for leadership and command, while Morgan valued harmony. Scarface would probably have chafed at the lack of danger, the dearth of opportunities to exploit and manipulate, while Morgan found those absences a balm.

He also found similarities and began to appreciate them. Some of those qualities, after all, had made him a home among the Dieri.

Occasionally he regretted the lack of challenge at arms practice. He'd learned from masters, including Hadrian, and the Dieri he trained lacked the finely-honed skills he'd acquired. At other times he realized he was losing fluency in the several languages he spoke. Topaz knew some Gasgoran and he taught her more, correcting her accent, so she became adept while he, at least, slowed his loss of the language.

The passage of time was inexorable but the perception of it as unsteady as the gait of a drunkard. Sometimes it seemed as though it'd been yesterday when he'd first held Topaz in his arms, made love to her, could look forward to returning to a place he called home and finding her there. At other times, it seemed this life had been his forever, that it was well-worn.

One night he realized, with a shock, that they'd lived together for three years, and he asked her if she'd marry him.

"Aren't we already wed?"

"While I still have some gaps in my knowledge of Dieri custom, it seems to me there's a ceremony involved. Aren't you sure you want to marry me?" There was a pin-prick of worry behind the question.

"All our friends know what we are to each other. A ceremony isn't necessary, since it only puts in words what we already feel. There are couples who've never performed the ceremony who've shared their lives for decades. If you wish, we can perform the ceremony, but conditions must be correct. It's too late this spring. If you're determined to do this, then you'll still want it next spring."

"Why spring?"

"Because it's the beginning of the year, when life begins. It seems appropriate that a new life, one shared with another, should begin at the same time. Everything in its season."

He stroked her hair, then kissed her mouth. "This seems proper to every season."

~ * ~

Early the next morning he left on a hunt with some visiting Senshenni, the Cercans of the foothills to the west. Unlike the Dieri, who were a mountain people with little use for horses, the Senshenni seemed born to the saddle, and it provided Morgan an opportunity to keep his skills as a horseman.

They rode north and west, following the trail of a herd of wild cattle. Beef, Morgan decided, would be a welcome change from mutton and venison. They'd ridden from morning until, in the late afternoon, they'd found a wolf pack that led them to the herd. The Cercan hunters always left the entrails and several choice cuts for the wolves, and a sort of unspoken partnership had grown over the generations. The wolves led them by a circuitous route, so they approached the herd from downwind.

The Dieri used wooden bows almost as long as the warriors were tall, but the Senshenni horsemen preferred horn bows perhaps half the length of the Dieri weapons.

The hunters fitted arrows to bowstrings and, at a signal from the leader, rushed the herd at a gallop. The cattle, startled by the sudden charge, thundered away. Morgan chose a young cow, drew his horse beside her, and drew and released an arrow that buried itself almost to the feathers in the cow's side. The beast stumbled, then collapsed, rolling forward.

Before Morgan could choose another target, a large bull broke from the herd and charged him. Morgan's horse shied, nearly causing Morgan to drop his bow. He snatched at the horse's mane and clung to it desperately as he slid on the saddle.

One of the Senshenni shot an arrow that distracted the bull. Although it was a mortal wound, the bull would not fall until another Senshenni drove his lance into its side.

Morgan managed to right himself in the saddle and raced after the herd. He was able to kill a yearling bull before the leader of the hunt gave the signal to break off the pursuit.

Even with the offerings for the wolves, they gathered enough meat to load the pack horses they'd brought, but it was late enough in the day that by the time they'd finished their skinning and butchering they were barely able to pitch camp half a league away before the last of the light drained from the western sky.

~ * ~

The Senshenni rode south with him until midday, then turned their horses west to return to their own village, leaving him to make his way back to Stag accompanied only by his mount and two pack horses. Reaching the Stag's Gate in the late afternoon, he gave most of the meat and all of the hides to the garrison to distribute, keeping some ribs and a haunch, then began to tend his horses.

Ergun approached as Morgan rubbed the animals down. "Do you know a young man named Renay?"

Morgan paused in his work. "The name isn't familiar. Who is he?"

"He came to Stag yesterday afternoon. He called you 'King Daign,' but the description of you was close enough."

Morgan grinned. "There aren't that many men in these mountains with marks like these." With a fingertip, he brushed his black scars. "Where is he now?"

"With your wife. She's the only one in Stag Mountain who can make out those slurring sounds the Gasgorans make, so I sent for her to translate and, after talking with him, she said she'd take care of him until you returned."

"Thank you, Ergun." He finished tending to the animals, then hurried to the apartments he shared with Topaz. When he swung aside the hanging, he found Topaz in her herb corner, grinding something in a mortar while a young man sat on cushions across the room from her, gnawing on dried fruit and bread.

As Morgan strode into the room, the young man sprang to his feet and bowed deeply.

Morgan reached him in half a dozen paces and placed a hand on the boy's shoulder. "Stand straight," he said, in Gasgoran. "I've no crown, and I haven't learned to recognize the tops of people's heads." He peered closely at the youth's features. He could detect a certain familiarity, but it inspired memory of neither name nor occasion. "I'm sorry, I don't know you. I feel as though I should, perhaps, but..."

"After you'd abdicated, lord, just before you rode out of Hope for the last time, you embraced me."

The occasion came back to Morgan in a rush. "Sit down," he said, and sank onto the cushions across the table from the boy. This was one of the urchins of Glangurra he'd had brought to Hope, the capitol he'd begun to build in Donradé. The orphans had nothing in Glangurrach and he'd hoped Donradé could provide for them and that they, in their turn, could become the artisans Donradé so desperately needed.

"You're a long way from Hope," Morgan observed.

"That's very true, lord. Hope is scarce in Donradé now."

"Don't call me 'lord.' I wear no crown, nor do I want any. I've become happier without the weight."

"Yes, lor—Yes, Daign."

Morgan's lips twitched at the mention of the name he'd used so long ago in Donradé. Some element of caution remained and he found himself reluctant to give his true name. To give someone your true name, he'd been taught, gave them power over you. "Call me Scarface. Most of the people here do."

Renay simply nodded.

"You seem to bear bad news. You may as well tell it, although I fear I won't be able to do anything about it."

"There's enough bad news that I scarcely know where to begin.

Perhaps six months after you left, King Thienn replaced some of the lords of Donradé with men loyal only to him, men who began to demand more from their subjects. Wars between lords have become as common as they were in the days before you became king. Then the church of Mordach began to claim some of the lands in dispute and made slaves, in all but name, of the people on those lands. The church has become rich and powerful, and some think it may be biding its time, preparing to wrest Donradé away from Glangurra. There are even rumors the church has someone with a legitimate claim to the throne of Donradé."

"That sounds as though it might be for the best."

"Not so. The people are caught between fire and flood. Both are disasters."

"What of Duke Jonfré? I'd left him with a last command."

"He calls himself Earl and holds Linistia and most of southern Donradé, but if Thienn were to move his armies, it's unlikely Jonfré could survive. Two assassins tried to kill Thienn. The first one was luckier. He died in the attempt. The second spent two days dying in the square in Glangurrach. Thienn claimed the man had told him he'd been sent by Earl Jonfré. Thienn's already declared Jonfré outlawed but, so far, the people in southern Donradé support him."

Morgan stood and paced to the cupboard. Topaz was already preparing a meal and he was so absorbed in what Renay had told him he'd hardly noticed her. He chose a bottle of sour wine and two cups, then realized he'd neglected Topaz. He set the bottle down and stroked her shoulder. "I'm sorry."

She turned, her face grave. "I found this as disturbing as you do."

He kissed her lightly on the lips. In Cercan, he said, "I don't think you can. I'm responsible for most of this." He again picked up the wine, carried it to the table, and poured a cup each for Renay and himself.

The youth tried a sip, made a face, and set the cup aside.

"All that's serious news. What of Queen Ukena's kinsmen?"

"King Thienn has killed or driven into hiding everyone who might have a claim to the throne." He paused a moment. "There's worse. Queen Ukena bore Thienn a son. About a year ago they both disappeared. Thienn looked for them, but not very hard. Some say he had them killed, others say he's keeping them prisoners to force her few remaining kinsmen to support him or, at least, not oppose him. I realize he's your son, but he's ruining both kingdoms, and he must be stopped."

Morgan was startled but hid it, taking his time to answer. "You shame me. You came here to speak against a man I called my son, and you did it for others. I'm not sure I'd have that kind of courage, myself. Whatever I decide, you should know that I have the deepest respect for you."

Topaz carried a platter of food to the table, then seated herself beside Morgan. Her glance told him she expected some explanations.

When Renay started to speak again of Donradé, Morgan held up a hand. "Never bring unpleasantness to a meal. The custom here is to speak of nothing but how good the food is, and how well-prepared."

Most of the meal was eaten in silence except for the compliments to Topaz, then Morgan stood. "Let me take you to the barracks. The pallets there are more comfortable than a floor, even one covered with cushions." He led Renay to the barracks. "I'll see you in the morning. If you become hungry, you can always take food from the stewpot."

He returned to the rooms he shared with Topaz and they walked to the baths arm in arm.

"I wasn't aware you had a son," she said.

"I haven't." He undressed and slid onto the hot water with a sigh. "I was seizing power in Donradé and, to do it, I dealt with the church of Mordach, a war-god. I gave them more power and wealth than they'd ever known. I should've known I was mid-wifing a monster, but I was only interested in the immediate results. For the same reason, I made Thienn my son. He was an urchin from Glangurrach I used to gain control of Glangurra. He was to marry the princess, Ukena. The king was an old man and the Glangurrans pass the crown down the male line, but the only real claimant was the king's nephew. I was prepared to have him killed until he took care of that himself in a fit of heroic stupidity. Leaders have no business on scaling ladders."

Topaz, who'd been listening closely, laughed. "I can't speak to Scarface's morals, but he seems to have been an accomplished schemer. Did you go to sleep plotting, in those days?"

"More than once." He chuckled. "I rode the dragon better than most. Still, I gained each day at the expense of the next. Shortsightedness seems to be a requirement for that sort of power-grabbing."

"What are you going to do?"

"That's what I was asking myself. Of all the lords of Donradé and Glangurra, Jonfré was the best hope, but I believe he's over-matched. Since I'm the one responsible for this, I should be the one to deal with it. I'd told Jonfré if Thienn became a bad king, he should be killed. I had no right to ask that of Jonfré. It was my responsibility, not one I could wish off on someone else. Still, I have no desire to be a king. Nor do I wish to leave here. I've never been this happy before."

They climbed out of the stone basin and scrubbed each other, then returned to the pool. "Perhaps," she said, "it's a decision you should sleep on."

He nodded, then they hauled themselves out of the water, dried each other, donned fresh robes, and returned to their rooms. Morgan's need was greater than usual and their lovemaking had an edge of desperation. After Topaz had gone to sleep, Morgan lay staring up at the ceiling, trying to find patterns or pictures in the uneven glow of the lichen.

Had he been able, he'd have dismissed the problems of Donradé and Glangurra as matters to be dealt with by the peoples of those places, but he couldn't escape the onus of his responsibility in creating those problems.

Nor was he sure he could kill Thienn. In the old days, he could've assassinated the little bastard and been gone before they'd closed the body's eyes, but now, without his powers, such a killing would probably cost his own life, and that was a price he was no longer willing to pay.

Glancing at Topaz, he could distinguish only a shape. Love was perhaps the most dangerous emotion; it made one vulnerable, stole one's initiative, even when aggressiveness could be vital to success.

He was also hampered by the loss of magic from his scars. He'd accepted the branding in Sin Garlef to become one of the theocrat's elite soldiers, The Marked Ones. Later, after he'd escaped the country and learned magic, he'd discovered the anguish he'd borne, without thought of reward, had given him a reservoir of power on which to draw, allowing him to cast simple but potent spells quickly and without the draining that left most magi weak. Now, casting a simple spell of concealment would leave him hardly able to walk.

His life had become too rich, too valuable to himself and to others to waste on a simple killing. Besides, if he died killing Thienn, he'd be unable to do anything about his "son's" successor or the church of Mordach, which was probably an even greater threat.

There were far more questions than answers, but he'd grown to know himself well enough to know when a decision had been reached.

CHAPTER 2

When he woke, still tired and gritty-eyed, he realized Topaz wasn't beside him, then he smelled the aroma of fresh bread. He rolled from the pallet and drew on a robe, then stepped into the outer room.

Topaz looked up from the mutton she was cutting into strips. "I'll miss you."

His reply was simply to raise an eyebrow, then, "And I'll miss you. I'm only going to see what can be done—I'm not sure what I can do to make amends, but I must at least see."

He sank down on the cushions by the low table. "I'll have to ask you to cast a spell of disguise."

"I'm sorry, I can't do that."

"I thought you knew the spell. And, while I don't have the power I had, I'm willing to provide most of the energy."

She carried the food to the table, set it down, sat down beside him, and nibbled on a piece of cheese. "It's considered unwise for a pregnant woman to practice magic. There's a risk to both the woman and the child."

For a moment he couldn't quite grasp what she'd said, then he wrapped his arms around her. "Why didn't you tell me before?"

"I only became sure of it while you were gone. And after you returned I couldn't bear to add to your burdens. Your decision was hard enough to make without that."

"A decision made can also be unmade," he murmured into her hair. "You're the one who taught me that one always has choices."

"And you've made your choice." She moved away enough to be able to stare into his eyes. "It'll give you another reason to want to return."

"Believe me, I have all the reasons I'll ever need." He drew his embrace tighter.

"Besides, knowing this may make you more cautious."

~ * ~

Renay sat at a table in the barracks, dining on bread and stew. Morgan sat down beside him. "I have to ride to Crown Mountain for permission to go to Donradé. I should be back in no more than eight to ten days."

"May I ride with you?"

The question surprised Morgan enough that he paused before answering. The boy had never really seen an emperor's court, even one as rustic as that of the Dieri, nor had he seen the richly decorated caverns of Crown. "Wait here for me. I'll be back as soon as Ergun grants permission for us to leave."

He found Ergun in his quarters, arming himself for practice. "I must visit Crown. And, with your permission, I'll take the boy from Donradé with me."

"Take him. But be sure you take supplies for four. That boy eats as though he hasn't seen food for a month."

~ * ~

Morgan took the lead. The mountains were like some women; beautiful but treacherous. The spring thaw was well underway, with sudden floods a constant threat. The remaining snows hid depressions in the rocks and made the stone slick.

Still, the mountains had an austere majesty that acted as a clarion call to greatness of the spirit. To move among them was to confront one's actual place in the world; an ant crawling across the face of vastness, but an ant aware, and so, containing something greater than the mountains.

The pace Morgan set was deliberate, and the guiding principle was caution. He'd already decided that the journey to Crown would require an extra day.

At night they listened to the wolves, and Morgan explained that to the Cercans the wolves were sacred. The Cercans believed the gods were so far above men they had no conception of man's pains and terrors but, in their wisdom, the gods had made Father Wolf to intercede for man, and the howls were prayers for men.

If the gods of the Dieri were far above man and so neglected him, man was just as far from his deities, so they were seldom thought of or asked for guidance. Morgan could never tell if the religion of the Cercans was something very deep or very superficial. Perhaps, he thought, it was both.

~ * ~

Renay followed Morgan, wide-eyed and gape-mouthed at the

marvels of Crown Mountain, which had been the home of uncounted generations of Dieri. There, the tunnels had been squared and trued; stalagmites and stalactites and columns had been elaborately carved; there were even a few stone doors that pivoted at a touch.

Morgan was familiar to the guards, not only because of his past prominence but because he'd attended every Great Council since the tribes had been reunited and, at Orhan's request, had visited several times to offer his advice on relations with the neighboring kingdoms. A guardsman escorted them to Orhan's door and scratched on the hanging decorated with the wolf's head design, then left as Orhan swung the curtain aside.

Orhan had a trace more gray in his hair and another line or two on his face than when Morgan had last seen him, but he was still fit, still moved with a younger man's energy. "Morgan!" They embraced each other. "Come in. Who's that with you?"

Morgan had warned Renay the boy wouldn't be able to follow the conversation, so he gestured for Renay to follow him into Orhan's rooms. Lady Marikaa appeared at an inner door, holding the son she'd borne Orhan. She greeted them with a smile, then disappeared into the next room.

"This is my friend, Renay."

The boy bowed deeply at the sound of his name. Orhan nodded at him, then said, "The Ghiblins and the Abransans have agreed to open trade with us. It was as you said; both were trying to make allies of us, draw us into their war. But our agreements are limited to trade, and both of them agreed to let us trade with the other."

"Be sure you get your agreements in Gasgoran. There's enough imprecision in Ghiblin and Abarsa to turn a sheep into an elk." Morgan accepted the cup of mead Orhan offered both his guests, watched Renay sip from his cup, then sip again, obviously relishing the sweet drink.

"Renay's brought me some information that I'll have to act upon. I must return to Donradé for a time."

Orhan frowned. "What does Topaz think of that?"

"She's no happier about it than I am. It doesn't help that she's pregnant."

Orhan's frown deepened. "Do you know about her mother?"

Morgan shook his head. "Only that she's dead. It's something she's never talked about."

Orhan gestured toward stools, then sat down. "I'm not surprised. Her mother died giving birth. I think she kept that from you so you wouldn't worry."

Morgan felt a faint stirring of the scars on his face and immediately a pang of doubt, as sharp as a blade, twisted in his belly. Was that stirring an omen?

Orhan noted the swift shadows of emotions crossing Morgan's face. "It may be that she'll have no trouble, but I thought you should know the risk. Still, it's only a risk, not a sentence of death. You've taken greater gambles yourself."

That bromide didn't deserve a response. Any hazards he'd faced had largely been of his own making, and seldom had he been in danger of losing much more than his own life. Topaz meant far more to him than that. He realized the conversation had died while he was looking inside himself. "I also need to take a woman named Saril back to Stag Mountain, if you and she agree."

"I'd have suggested it," Orhan said. "She's the finest healer and midwife at Crown. If Topaz is pregnant, she'll need someone to assume her duties until she's fit again, as well as to assist her when her own time comes."

Morgan had observed the change in Orhan's tone and suspected some of his optimism was an attempt to allay Morgan's own fears. It had, of course, the opposite effect. After a brief conversation, which he scarcely heard and couldn't remember, he excused himself to visit Saril.

Saril was of middle age, with a broad-featured face and a bustling manner. She'd scarcely paused in her bottling of herbs when he entered her room.

"Topaz is pregnant with my child," Morgan said. "She asked me if you'd come with me to Stag Mountain."

That caused her to look up at him. She finished putting away the herbs she'd ground, then sat facing him. "I'll need to ask permission of Orhan."

"He's already given it."

If the woman was surprised, she didn't let it show on her face. "How soon do you wish to leave?"

"As soon as you're able. Preferably, tomorrow, at first light."

Her eyes lost their focus and he could almost hear her deciding what preparations would be needed for the journey. "I'll meet you at the Stag's Gate then."

~ * ~

The return to Stag seemed to take much longer than the ride to Crown, and the air felt charged with foreboding. The mountains appeared more forbidding than majestic and Morgan thought if there were something greater in men and women than the mountains themselves, it was also more ephemeral.

When they rode through the Ram's Gate he dismounted and helped Saril down from her horse. When she'd alit he said, "Please excuse me. I'll see if Topaz has prepared for your visit."

"I'll tend the horses, lor—Scarface." For once, Renay's eagerness to help was neither annoying nor an embarrassment.

"Thank you."

Morgan hurried to the rooms he shared with Topaz, found her waiting for him. He seized her and held her tightly to him, then held her far enough away that he could look closely at her face. "Why didn't you tell me what a risk you were taking?"

Her smile was faint. "Because it changes nothing. I want to have children by you. Do you think the risk would be less at some later time?"

"But, knowing the risk, I should be here when the time comes."

She stroked his cheek. "Again, it'd change nothing. Your being here won't make me live if I'm not meant to live, nor would it make dying easier. Death is a debt we all have to pay, and no one can stand in our stead. I know you would if you could. Believe me, I know it and I cherish that, but you can't do it. We each have our perils to face; me here and you in Donradé." Her smile broadened a trace. "Actually, it's probably harder on you than on me. Now, are you going to kiss me?"

He'd learned before her smiles were contagious. Some requests are easier to satisfy than others, and he complied with hers with a will.

Their kiss was long and lingering, but Morgan remembered other obligations. "I need to help Saril with her belongings. Did you want to have her stay in our outer room?"

"I've asked Meryem if she'd share rooms with her until after you leave, and she agreed. I intend to enjoy to the fullest the time I have with you."

~ * ~

Morgan felt rather like a dubious item of goods at a fair as Topaz and Saril helped discuss the disguise he'd adopt.

"I think it'd be best to travel as a peddler," he said. "I can't sing or juggle, and a mercenary would be too obvious. A Ghiblin peddler, I think. I still speak the language passably and I can use a Ghiblin accent when I speak Gasgoran."

Saril eyed him with a calculating gaze. "Besides the scars, we should change the black hair and those green wolf's eyes. Too distinctive."

Topaz seemed to enter into the spirit of the discussion with entirely too much humor and enthusiasm. "I'm rather fond of the eyes, although they do seem to intimidate some people. You're right, of course. Also, while I realize he's tall, it'd be uncomfortable for him to shorten him."

"Tall, but not remarkably so, especially for a Ghiblin," Saril agreed. "But we'll have to hide that warrior's body. Make him not so wide across the shoulders, add more of a belly."

Morgan winced. With the belly, he'd undoubtedly feel bloated, a sensation that would last as long as the spell did, and he anticipated being in Donradé for at least two months. He'd worn the spell before and found it confining. It seemed to change one's appearance but part of the cost was in the way it felt; it was like wearing ill-fitting armor that pressed and cramped the wearer. Still, it was necessary to the disguise, for one had to feel they wore another's body to move like another person.

"We'll cast the spell tomorrow," Saril decided. "I'll hold the change in abeyance until he's ready to leave. Oh, did you want to release the spell with a word or with an object?"

"Too many chances to need a word too soon, and too many chances for a slip of the tongue," Morgan replied. "I'd rather release it with an object. A staff would be best." The disguise would last until the staff was broken. "A plain staff should attract no attention."

"Until tomorrow, then," Saril said, rose, and left the room.

Morgan grinned at Topaz. "Since I'll only have the use of my own body for the next day or so, I'd like to make the most of it."

Topaz grinned in response, caught his hand, and led him to their bed.

~ * ~

Morgan was putting together a horse pack, part of his peddler's disguise. He'd assembled as many trade goods as he could find and afford. It hadn't escaped him that these dour, hard people were either offering the goods to him at a fraction of their value, or even giving them to him.

He'd always been a foreigner. His family had immigrated to Sin Garlef before he could walk and, since then, he'd lived in half a dozen places. Even High Rage, the Gascolan stronghold of the Winged Dagger Clan, hadn't been home. Now, he realized he'd found a home and, ironically, had only discovered that as he was preparing to leave.

He was trying to secure one of the straps when someone scratched at the door hanging. "Enter."

Renay ducked through the opening and strode into the room. A glance was enough to let Morgan know the boy had made some decision, and the way he opened and closed his hands revealed his anxiety.

"I want to go with you, lord—Scarface."

Morgan shook his head. "You've done more than your duty by reminding me of my obligations. If the situation in Donradé is as bad as you say, there's danger in your returning. Besides, I intend to travel as quickly as my disguise allows and, if I choose to take action, it'll be sudden and probably require a speedy escape."

Renay squatted, perhaps because he was uncomfortable standing above his former lord. "It's my obligation, too. As for speed, how quickly do you think a peddler can travel? And it's always better to have another pair of eyes and ears, especially when they're attached to someone not likely to be noticed."

"You argue very convincingly but I feel...uncomfortable taking you into danger."

Renay drew himself up. "I might have to take an order from King Daign, but you're Scarface, so I'll make my own decision."

His retort made Morgan pause in his work and look up. Determination had apparently won over deference. He considered a moment, then returned to his work on the bindings. "Very well. We leave the day after tomorrow. Be sure to pack enough provisions, and add a bow to them. You can use a bow, can't you?"

"Only indifferently."

"Then that's one of the first things I'll teach you on the journey. The very first thing to learn is to call me 'Halvar.' It's a common enough name in Ghiblein."

Renay grinned. "Yes, Master Halvar."

~ * ~

Preparing and casting the spell exhausted Morgan. He doubted he'd worked so hard or felt so drained since he'd arrived at Stag. At last it was done and he was lolling on cushions, staring at his sword. He'd have to leave it behind, of course. Like his scars and his pale green eyes, the weapon was distinctive. He stared into the naked sockets of the skull, horned and fanged, at the center of the guard. The sweep of the horns served as the upswept upper edge of the bat wings that formed the arms of the guard.

He drew the blade from its scabbard, his fingers and the scale pattern in the blackwood grip of the sword clutching each other. The hilt was long enough to allow the use of both hands and was topped with a silver falcon-head pommel. He turned the blade to catch the light. It was keen enough to cut through a dropped piece of silk and strong enough to hack through an iron bar.

The sword was the first thing of value he'd ever owned. It'd been crafted to his own design by a master smith in Bildesh, and it'd been his companion since, seldom more than an arm's reach from his hand.

He performed a few thrusts and slashes, ending, as was his habit, with a moulinet, then slid the blade back into the scabbard. Topaz swung the curtain aside and stepped into the room as the guard clashed against the sheath. "Is something the matter?" she asked.

"Nothing. Just deciding what to take and what to leave." He was suddenly embarrassed, as though he'd been unfaithful to her. This thing of wood and metal was only a tool, although one he'd used to save his life. Topaz was what gave that life meaning. It seemed to somehow diminish his feelings for her to care about a sword. He wrapped the belt around the scabbard and thrust it into a trunk. He had another farewell to make, and it wasn't to steel.

He rose and carried Topaz to their bed.

~ * ~

Morgan had used the spell before, years ago, so he knew what unpleasantness to anticipate. Saril raised the wooden figure carved to resemble him and, as she dripped wax onto it, he felt his features become set as something hot and heavy but invisible seemed to spread over his face, then his entire body. The heat became more intense as she moved it over the candle, softening the wax and making it more malleable, then he felt his head being gripped by a giant, invisible hand and his head and face were squeezed and drawn.

His disguise, the last time he'd used the spell, had been a greater change, and the agony of that change had wrung a scream from him. This time, there was only the heat and a little pain. The rest was mere discomfort. He grunted as something seemed to be drawn tight around his chest and shoulders, and grunted again at the bloating sensation at his waist and lower belly, then gritted his teeth as his legs seemed to bend.

Finally it was over. Rising required real effort, and he was able to raise his arms, although the feeling of constriction remained. Saril handed him a mirror of polished brass and he studied the reflection of a man of late middle age, with pale blue eyes and a short, hooked beak of a nose. His ginger-colored hair was thinning and his cheeks sagged.

Nodding, he returned the mirror.

All the preparations and farewells had been made. "Thank you," he said, resting his hand on Saril's shoulder, then trudged to the outer rooms, where Renay started at his appearance, then grinned.

"You'll probably have to help me into the saddle," Morgan grumbled. "These bandy legs and this belly—" he patted his newly acquired paunch with both hands—"make me feel like an old man." Together, they walked to where their horses and the pack horse were waiting.

Not trusting himself to leave Stag Mountain if he looked back at it, Morgan kept all his attention on the trail ahead. By pausing only long enough to favor the horses and, in the early afternoon, to eat a quick lunch of trail rations, they reached the foothills by late evening.

By noon of the following day they were within the territory of the lowland peoples, the Senshenni and several smaller tribes. No more than an hour later they observed three riders to the north. The strangers seemed to also be riding west, and the two trails would likely converge in less than half a league.

Morgan halted to string his bow, then climbed back into the saddle.

When the other three riders were near enough to be clearly seen, Morgan recognized them as Eripos, members of one of the smaller lowland tribes. The leader had a doe lying across the horse in front of him and carried a lance bearing a narrow white flag running from the base of the head to the butt. Victory stripes of several colors were painted on the flag. As the Eripo approached, Morgan recognized him from the games that were always a part of the Great

Councils.

A little more than the length of the lance away, the Eripo drew up his horse, leaned forward, his left arm draped across the carcass. "Besides the three horses, what else have you brought to trade for your lives?"

Morgan's lips twitched into a flicker of a grin, then he replied, in Cercan, "The last time we had business, it was all to your profit. We traded blows with practice swords at the Great Council, and you gave far less than you received."

He almost laughed aloud as the Eripo's face registered astonishment, then the man peered more closely at his face. "There's only one man who can claim that, and you aren't him."

"I'm Scarface. It's necessary to look different for a time, but I'm willing to do more trading with you, if that's what it takes to convince you."

The Eripo stared at him, then suddenly barked a laugh. "Our town's ahead and a little north. We'll reach it before sunset."

The man was as good as his word. The sun hadn't yet reached the tops of the hills before they topped a rise and saw the wooden fronts of houses built into the facing hillside. A group of children milled around in some game, chasing each other, and more splashed in the water of the creek that ran through the shallow valley. A few old people sat near their doors, and horses stood picketed on the lower slopes, cropping grass.

The Eripo who'd led them to the village gestured at the highest opening, decorated with carved and painted pillars. "That's where the headman lives. I'll take you there after I've left the deer."

They rode a couple of bowshots downriver to avoid muddying the town's water source, and splashed across the creek, then tethered their horses near the base of the hill. Renay remained behind to tend the animals, and the Eripo carried the carcass into one of the openings. He returned almost immediately and strode up the slope to the headman's dwelling.

Morgan trudged after him. He was tired enough, wearing the spell, that he indeed felt like a middle-aged trader.

At an ululation from the warrior, the headman stepped out onto his porch, his arms crossed, his hair and beard ruffled by the wind.

"While he doesn't look like him, this man claims to be Scarface, from the Dieri," the warrior said.

Morgan bowed with just the proper deference. "I remember you well, Kiral. You're a man of good reputation."

The headman peered at him as though trying to see through the disguise, then extended his right hand. After they'd struck their palms together, Kiral gestured toward one of the stools on his porch. "Sit." He turned to the warrior. "You may leave."

As the headman sat down on a stool facing him, Morgan said, "I have a friend who's tending our horses. I ask your hospitality for him, too."

The headman nodded, a brusque bob of the head. "What are you doing, looking like this?"

"I need to look like a trader. I'm visiting Donradé, where they know me, and I have enemies there." Morgan fidgeted on the stool. "It's difficult for me, since I'm accepting your hospitality, to remind you of your responsibilities. Orhan and the council have decreed that traders be allowed to travel freely across Cerco, but the man who led me here threatened to rob me before he learned who I am."

The chief scowled, and Morgan couldn't guess whether it was because one of his warriors had tried to defy a decree or whether it was because the man had been caught, making a decision necessary. Finally, the headman said, "Cahil is a great warrior."

"He may be a fine fighter, but a true warrior respects the wishes of his leaders and the needs of his people. It's not for me to tell you how to deal with this, but perhaps some time spent serving in some foreign army would make him a better warrior, as well as provide money for the tribe."

"I'll consider it."

Morgan and Renay spent the night in the headman's home. At the first meal the next morning, Kiral asked, "Would you be willing to trade your horses for a wagon and a donkey?"

Morgan decided it would be impolitic to enquire where or how the wagon and donkey had been acquired. "A good trade for us both."

By midmorning, Morgan and Renay had transferred their goods and supplies to the wagon and were again making their way toward Donradé.

Northern Donradé was so sparsely settled they often traveled two or three days between villages, and the lord's stronghold was over a week's ride east. The entire area could be ridden in a couple of days by a man with no concern for his horse, but a peddler's donkey and cart seldom traveled six leagues a day.

The villagers with whom they traded spoke a dialect of Gasgoran that was hardly Donradan, and few of the men wore the facial tattoos that were the mark of a freeman in most of Donradé. He was surprised to learn the villagers were much more interested in goods than in any news the travelers might also carry. Few of them even knew who was king: it was not a matter of interest to them. Their world was bounded by the seasons, planting, harvests, and weather.

A fortnight after leaving Stag Mountain, they learned of a town, four leagues south, large enough to have a temple of Mordach, the Donradan war-god.

~ * ~

The trader's wagon bumped and creaked across the heavily-wooded plain as the donkey drawing it and its driver tried to follow a track unworthy of being called a road. The high grass and brush had overgrown the path in places, and both snared the wooden-spoked wheels. The late morning sun beat down fiercely enough that Morgan and Renay were grateful for the occasional patches of shadow provided by the great trees.

Yellow and violet flowers clustered in patches in the grass, and a crimson butterfly seemed undecided which color it preferred, flitting back and forth between the clumps. A rabbit shot from the grass and scrambled away through the brush.

Ahead, the trees grew thicker, and after he'd found a way between them, the donkey stopped in a clear stream to drink. Morgan dismounted and he and the boy walked upstream to drink deeply of the cold, sweet water, then Morgan strode back to the donkey and led him up onto the far bank. "Renay, help me move the wagon. The bank's too steep for the donkey to manage it alone."

The boy set his back to the rear of the wagon and, with the two of them pushing and the donkey reluctantly pulling, they forced the wheels up the shallow bank.

Renay wiped his face with his sleeve. "Could we stop here for lunch?"

Morgan chuckled. "It's not noon yet, and you're wanting to eat already. No real merchant would keep you. You're too likely to eat up the profits."

Renay grinned ruefully. "Remember, this masquerade was your idea."

Morgan's smile expressed his satisfaction. It was pleasant to have Renay able to bandy words with him. He'd lost most of his deference, and Morgan was grateful to have a companion instead of a subject.

"I'll be grateful when you get your full growth and start eating like a human again." He nudged the boy to remind him it was only banter, then said, "We'll stop before long."

Renay pointed ahead to another arm of the forest in the distance. "Not before we reach the shade, I hope."

Morgan nodded. There was probably another stream among those trees and he, too, preferred shelter from the sun. "The next town shouldn't be more than two or three leagues from here, and we'll visit the temple."

"I've told you the priests of Mordach can't be trusted. They oppose King Thienn, but for their own reasons. They've had a taste of power and learned they like the flavor."

"I'm counting on no one, but gossip is always useful." Morgan shifted uncomfortably. Guilt was troubling him almost as much as the hard seat. He'd been the one who'd let the church of Mordach get its foot into the stirrup. He also found himself looking forward to the rest. His back and backside had taken a pounding and he wondered whether real peddlers developed calluses. The shade would be pleasant, and he'd also feel better with a bite to eat.

They'd just reached the trees, heavy forest redolent with the scents of growth and decay, and the donkey, smelling water, had quickened its pace when it suddenly lurched forward, then sagged in the traces, an arrow jutting from its side. The beast collapsed and kicked feebly, then died.

From the deep shadows of the trees swaggered four men, all with drawn weapons, and the archer appeared a moment later, another arrow nocked and pointed at Morgan and Renay.

"Well, trader, it's a lucky day. Good luck for us and bad for you." The man who appeared to be the leader advanced to a spear's length from the wagon, gestured with the sword in his hand. "Get down."

Renay glanced at Morgan, and Morgan nodded, then they climbed down from the seat. Morgan trod slowly to the donkey, whose eyes had already begun to glaze. "That wasn't necessary," he told the bandit.

The brigand shrugged and his slightly rusty mail shirt jingled. His hand snaked out, whipped the knife from its sheath on Morgan's belt. "If you're able to leave, you'll be able to carry everything you own. Besides, it's a meal or three for us. You're a bold one, though, aren't you? It'd be wise for you to learn who rules here. Move over to yonder trees." Again he gestured with the sword.

Morgan ground his teeth as he walked to the trees. It'd been decades since he'd been addressed by any other man as less than an equal. By adopting this disguise to protect Renay and himself, he'd left them vulnerable to every bandit and footpad in Donradé. The irony didn't escape him, it only made the present danger more bitter. Alone, he might've tried to fight them, but he was responsible for Renay, and the lad wasn't likely to survive any battle here.

His only hope was the safe-pass he'd written for himself. "I have a safe-pass written by King Daign himself."

One of the other bandits hooted a laugh. "Peddler, even if we could read it, it wouldn't mean shit to us. Kings come and go, but the forest is always here, and us in it."

Morgan's temper flared and he cast a glance at the trees overhead. "A good choice. Enough limbs to hang you all a dozen times."

"You've already provided food and entertainment for us," the leader said. "What else have you got?"

"I suspect what you really want is under the seat."

One of the bandits, a balding, coarse-faced man carrying an iron-bound club, strode to the wagon. Renay stepped out of his way, but apparently not quickly enough to suit the brigand, who seized the boy and hurled him to the ground. The thief rummaged under the seat, then held up a small leather bag, tossed it to the leader.

Morgan had clenched his fists and his teeth, but felt the taste of fear rising in him. He should never have let Renay come with him; it had made them both vulnerable. He realized then, to his fingertips, he was unarmed, and the scars hidden under his disguise had long since lost their power.

He tried to use the fear to waken the scars, but they'd been drained for so long.

The bandit leader pulled the drawstring of the pouch open and shook a handful of coins into his hand. "Twenty marks of silver, maybe ten of copper, most of it in foreign coins. You'll have to do better than that."

"The rest of the money's in the goods," Morgan said. "If I'd had anything of real value, I'd be in a caravan."

The leader sneered at him. "You'd better hope the goods pay us for our time and trouble, or we'll take the difference out of your hides. What's he got, Arman?"

The coarse-faced thug was already digging through the items in the bed of the wagon. "There's a sword here. It's plain but looks well-made. There's some bars of iron—"

"That's Bild steel," Morgan interjected. "Smiths use it for weapons and the best tools."

"—and cloth, some jars of spices and herbs, and some bottles." He uncorked one of the flasks, sniffed at the mouth, then tilted the bottle back and drank. He made a face and his voice was strained. "Good stuff. Whatever it is, it has more kick than wine."

"Ghiblin rye brandy," Morgan said, "better for sipping than guzzling, unless you're a Ghiblin."

The bandit leader struck him with the back of his hand. "Don't be telling us how to drink our liquor."

The archer found it amusing enough to laugh, then drew the arrow from his string and slipped it into his quiver. "Well, they won't make us rich, so the least they can do is entertain us."

Morgan concentrated on the hidden scars, trying to will them back to power, but felt nothing but fear and anger. Being overpowered by these bullies was insufferable. Another bandit had climbed onto the wagon and began to argue with the man with the bottle, and most of the rest of the brigands had relaxed. He caught Renay's attention, shouted, "Run!" and threw himself at the leader.

He snatched at the sword in the man's right hand but the thief extended his arm, keeping the weapon just out of reach. Morgan drove his fist into the man's left side, just below his ribs, then swung his elbow up to catch him in the side of the head.

Glancing back to see if Renay had escaped, Morgan saw the boy had been tripped by the archer and the bandit had fallen on him and was holding a knife to his neck, under his ear. "No!"

He'd allowed himself to be distracted and saw the man with the club beside him, swinging his weapon. He tried to duck, then the world was red and black.

~ * ~

He heard rough voices in his head, it seemed, felt rough hands on his arms. The world was a confused jumble of shattered impressions, and he was lost among them. He felt himself being dragged, and he had no strength with which to resist. His body had failed him.

He became aware he was being held up and his arms were drawn out roughly, then something was being wound around his wrists. Suddenly his arms were jerked upward, pulling him erect.

Feeling chilled, he realized he'd been stripped. His head throbbed, and even breathing seemed to cause more pain. He struggled to open his eyes, but that brought even more anguish, wringing a moan from him.

The sound attracted the attention of the bandit leader, who strutted across the glade to face him. "You've had enough rest."

Morgan realized most of the daylight was gone; it was almost dusk, and a fire blazed behind the brigand.

The bandit grinned at him. "You must have more money, or at least some way of getting it. You'll stay tied to that limb until we find it, or you entertain us as much as you can."

Morgan stared at the thief. As torturers, these brigands weren't as accomplished as some he'd met, or the man he'd been, but they were promising amateurs. Such men enjoyed inflicting pain; it gave them pleasure and a sense of power.

"Why don't you do something for our guest, Micklis? Swat those flies off him."

The archer stood, fished in his pouch, then strode to where Morgan hung, shaking the loops out of an extra bowstring. He grinned at Morgan, then began to lash his face and body with the sinew cord.

Refusing to give these cowards the satisfaction of hearing him scream, Morgan set his jaw. The pain was too much to consider, so he turned inward. To save Renay and himself, he needed power from the scars. Perhaps all that was left of the previous fire in him was ashes, but if a spark remained, perhaps he could fan it to life with his pain.

He tried to focus the agony, to feed it to the scars like kindling, but felt no response. He'd become one raw, aching wound, barely able to do more than suffer, and was scarcely aware of anything outside himself. Only new pain let him know when the archer began to lash his genitals. He shook against his bonds but only added to the anguish in his wrists. His struggles had been greeted with hoots and laughs from the bandits, and had only proven to him how weak he'd become.

The whipping stopped and the leader faced him again. "After we've used you up, there's still the boy. Something more for you to think about." He grabbed Renay by the strips of coarse cloth binding his arms and by the back of his neck and swung him around to face Morgan, brandishing him like a trophy. Renay's face was cut and bruised, with one cheek swollen and purple. Fear and determination waged a constant battle across the boy's features.

Rage and hatred welled up in Morgan, stronger than the pain, and he felt a faint stirring in his hidden scars. He was only vaguely aware of voices, arguing, then realized one of the bandits had suggested killing the boy before him.

"No!" he screamed, and opened his eyes to see the leader draw his sword from Renay's side. The body fell and lay jerking, the legs feebly kicking.

"Something more for you to think on, peddler," the leader said, then walked to the fire to take another drink from a stolen bottle.

The sudden stab of agony felt as though Morgan's face were being branded again, as the hidden scars burned. His body jerked like a suddenly-drawn bow and he ground his teeth against a scream, as fire seemed to shoot from the scars throughout his entire body, then power and fury raced after the pain. It was as though a forgotten dam had blocked a watercourse within him, but a flood had swept down the riverbed and the raging elements had burst over and through the barrier, sweeping it away. And Morgan was Scarface again.

With his hands bound and no spells prepared, he was unable to precisely direct the torrent of power, but he tried something he'd done once before, many years before. He transmuted the raw power into physical strength.

One of the bandits turned and noticed him as he drew himself up, then let himself fall, but catching the bindings in his hands. He twisted his body enough to let him exert force on the strips of cloth that held him.

The bandit broke free of the fear-trance enough to shout a warning as the bonds broke. One binding snapped an instant before the other, so that, instead of dropping onto his feet, Scarface was swung to the left and fell awkwardly onto his side.

That clumsiness saved his life, as an arrow hissed over him. The man with the spear rushed him. Scarface rolled and sprang to his feet. Slapping aside the spear shaft, he struck, driving his fist in just below where ribs met breastbone. The spear fell from limp fingers as the bandit went down, kicking, fighting to draw breath.

Scarface snatched up the spear, lashed out with it, leaving a gash across the chest and arm of the man with the club, then leapt to his right, driving the spear's head into the chest of another bandit.

The archer was trying to nock another arrow with fingers made clumsy by panic. Scarface drew the spear back, then hurled it, catching the bowman in the belly. The archer collapsed, screaming, clutching at the spear shaft jutting from his abdomen, his legs pumping as though he were running.

The man with the club was staring, wild-eyed, at Scarface as he stumbled back, while the leader stood several paces away, his sword bare in his hand, afraid to attack but determined not to flee.

Scarface sprang at the man with the club, taking advantage of the bandit's hesitation. With one hand he twisted the weapon away while he drove the other fist into the brigand's throat. He could feel the cartilage collapse as he struck, and he shoved the man, already choking on his own blood, into the fire.

The thief tried to escape the flames but he was already dying, unable to breathe through the ruined throat. He rolled away, his clothing on fire, and died as he tried to struggle to his feet.

Scarface side-stepped to the spearman, who was still fighting to breathe, and slammed the metal-laced club down on the man's head.

The leader snarled soundlessly at him, muted by fear, and Scarface, rendered inarticulate by the rage and the power suffusing him, could only growl, then he stalked forward. The bandit swung his sword up but Scarface closed suddenly and lashed out with the club, smashing the leader's sword arm. Scarface struck again, breaking the man's left leg, then, still driven by an icy fury, backed away to where the archer had dropped the bow.

Scarface tossed away the club, broke the bow, and strode back to the crippled bandit, the bowstring in his hands. As the man struggled under him, Scarface rasped, "When you get to hell, tell them Scarface sent you. Many better men than you will know the name."

He released the cord when it was drawn tight around the killer's upper spine, then staggered to his feet. He could hear the sounds of water running between banks and lurched that way, staggering into a tree in the darkness, then falling into the knee-deep stream.

The cold water eased the pain of his wounds and he drank greedily. When he'd drank his fill he turned around and crawled out onto the bank. The fire that still blazed in the place he'd left was a beacon, and he shambled toward it.

The contents of the wagon were strewn on the grass around it. He found a blanket, wrapped it around himself, then fell down beside the fire.

~ * ~

He woke screaming and struggling with the blanket. He vividly remembered snatches of the dream. Over and over, he killed the bandits and, each time, they rose again and stabbed Renay before attacking Scarface.

Looking around wildly, he could see, in the daylight, all the bodies as they'd fallen. He tried to get to his feet and found the pain so intense the trees seemed to dance around him. After resting, letting the agony in his head subside to a sullen throbbing, he tried again, this time moving slowly and carefully. He found some food and forced himself to eat but stopped after the first three bites. Chewing made his head hurt more and his stomach felt as though another bite would make him vomit what he'd eaten. Tossing the remainder of the morsel into the ashes, he dug into the mess around the wagon for clothing, took a leather jerkin from a dead bandit, and dressed himself.

Returning to the stream, he peered down at the face in the water and, for several moments, failed to recognize it. He'd almost forgotten he still wore the spell, and the strange face was made even stranger by swollen, bruised features and a network of fine cuts made by the bowstring.

After drinking his fill, he returned to the ashes of the fire. The wagon had contained a shovel, and he found it under bolts of cloth.

Digging Renay's grave was painful for both soul and body. The boy had been harmless, wanting only to do what was proper, and now he was only a lifeless husk. Unbidden, memories came back to Scarface and tears mixed with the sweat running down his face as he finished digging, wrapped the body in a blanket, and dragged it into the hole, then covered it with dirt.

The exertion helped. He still felt the aches and sharp stings of his wounds, but the stiffness had been worked out of his muscles.

He ate again, a little more this time, then rested.

Nightfall's chill wakened him and he finished the destruction of the wagon, using the wood to build a fire. When the flames rose he found more food and a leather bottle of sour wine the bandits hadn't drank. The throbbing behind his eyes had lessened. He stayed awake as long as he was able, fearing ghosts.

~ * ~

He gazed around the glade. He'd marked Renay's grave with a wagon wheel and a piece of planking with the boy's name carved into it. The bodies of the bandits swayed gently from the ropes around their necks; all but the leader. Hauling his body up had pulled off his head. Morgan had put the noose under the corpse's arms and used the hair to tie the head to a wrist.

"You bastards cheated me," he said to the cadavers. "I could only kill you once." Carrion birds had already started on the faces. "Feast well," he told the birds, then worked his way into the straps of the pack he'd assembled. Taking up the staff, he started walking toward the town he and Renay had been riding to three days earlier.

His being Morgan had been the cause of Renay's death. In this place, at this time, Scarface's ruthlessness was needed. He felt a sense of loss at abandoning serenity, but Renay was a greater loss.

He slowed at the sight of tilled fields ahead. Without the wagon, his disguise was worthless. Staying hidden in the woods, he circled the village, in case he needed to make an escape.

The temple was easy to distinguish; it stood east of the village, separated from the other buildings by nearly a spear's cast, larger than any six houses. A stable stood south and east of the temple.

Finding a likely spot, he hid the sword he'd recovered, along with the pack. He sank down onto the grass, his back against a tree trunk, and waited. As dusk descended, squares of yellow light appeared within the dark boxes of the log and plank houses, and he could even catch the scents of cooking. He still hadn't recovered his appetite, but at least the smells didn't revolt him.

When he judged it dark enough, he rose and strode to the temple and rapped on the painted wood door. After waiting for what seemed far too long, he knocked at the door again, louder.

Footsteps approached, then the door was jerked open by a man who wore the yellow robe of a monk. For a moment Scarface felt something was wrong without being able to understand exactly what it might be, then realized the monk had green whorls tattooed on his cheeks as well as the red lightning bolts of Mordach that ran down the sides of his face to almost meet at his chin. The monks he'd seen a little over three years before had been marked only with the lightning bolts, without enough standing to wear family tattoos. The church seemed to have begun to attract a higher class of monk. He also observed the man was well-fed and the yellow robe was of a good quality cloth.

"Yes?" The monk carried a shortsword but, from the way he held it, seemed not to be familiar with its use. Another difference from the monks of three years ago; those monks had been poorly fed but well trained.

"I was a soldier in the war in southern Donradé. As I traveled here, I was set upon by bandits. As a veteran, I ask a place to sleep, and a meal."

The monk tried to shut the door but Scarface's left hand shot out and held it open. "A tenth of my pay went to the church of Mordach, and King Daign and the church agreed soldiers had a claim on the church."

"Go beg elsewhere. Daign is gone, and the worshippers have learned to serve the church, not expect the church to serve them." The monk swung the blade of his sword up.

Scarface shoved harder on the door and thrust the head of his staff into the man's belly, just below the breastbone. The man staggered back, dropping his sword. Scarface stepped inside, then slammed the door shut behind him. The monk lay moaning and rocking from side to side, holding his belly with both hands.

"Daign may be gone, but Scarface isn't," Scarface rasped. He brought the staff down on the monk's head and heard something crack. As the disguise remained, apparently it was the man's head, not the staff, that had been broken.

Another monk, probably warned by the sound of arguing voices, appeared at another door, a spear in his hands.

Scarface wasted no more words. The monk advanced on him holding the spear with one hand about a third of the way down the shaft from the head and the other about a third of the distance from the butt.

Scarface shifted the staff in his hands to use the spear style he'd learned in The Marked Ones, his right hand gripping the butt, the left about a third of the way up the staff. He tapped at the spearhead, then ran the staff down the spear shaft until it slammed into the monk's knuckles.

The man swore and the spearhead jerked out of line. Scarface lunged and drove the end of the staff into the monk's throat. Instantly, before the man could fall, he struck again; a fast, vicious thrust to the forehead. The monk fell, as limp as if he were boneless.

Scarface stepped over the body and found himself in a corridor with two doors to his right, one to his left. Kicking open the nearest, the first door on the right, he peered into a dark and empty room. He'd just begun creeping farther down the hallway when the door to the left was slowly opened. A face appeared and glanced down the corridor, then the door was slammed shut.

Scarface sprang forward and drove his shoulder into the door, then fought to keep from falling as it tore from its hinges, carrying a man in a priest's red robe down with it, partially covering him. Scarface chuckled and stepped onto the door, trapping the fallen man and keeping him from retrieving the sword he'd dropped.

A glance at the bed showed a woman, her hair awry, hiding most of herself with a blanket. He gestured for silence. "I've no intention of hurting you. Actually, I came here for a meal and some conversation." He stepped off the door and kicked the sword into a corner. "I hope you're feeling talkative," he said to the priest, who'd finally crawled out from under the door.

The priest rolled over and sat on the floor, rubbing his left wrist. "You'll pay for this."

"I already have," Scarface replied. "Dealing with the church was one of the worst trades I've ever made." Looking around the room, he saw the woman's dress lying on a chest. He crossed to the chest and tossed the robe to the woman cowering on the bed. "Put that on."

He found a chair and sat down, facing the priest. "You seem to be doing well. Mordach appears to be very generous to his priests. You should've been prepared to share that bounty with the soldiers from whose wages most of that money came."

The priest spat. "I answer only to the archpriests and the high priest."

"I think you've forgotten Mordach, which tells me something about the depth of your devotion. Is old Cruach still the high priest?"

The priest's eyes widened momentarily at the mention of the name, then he nodded.

"What's this about archpriests? I don't remember the church of Mordach having archpriests."

"With the flourishing of the church, it was necessary for the high priest to appoint priests under him to help lead the church."

"I think I liked it better when the church was smaller and poorer. I've noticed your monks no longer perform devotions as they once did. Neither of the two I met seemed to know the use of their weapons. For monks of a war-god, that must be a sacrilege. It may be some comfort to Mordach that he's had his retribution. How about you? Do you know how to use that sword you dropped?"

"Let me pick it up and we'll see."

"In good time. I'll pray to Mordach with you in a little while, but we haven't finished our conversation, and I haven't had my meal. I also noticed the monks came from families of standing. I suspect the church has become a place for younger sons of some of the lords." He thought about the ramifications of what he'd learned and what he could guess.

"Who else is here?" he demanded.

"Just the three of us and the woman."

"No, just you and the woman." He paused to let the priest understand what he'd just said, then, "Who is the person with the church who has a claim on the throne of Glangurra or Donradé?"

"I don't know."

Scarface smiled. "I believe you. I wouldn't trust you with anything of importance either." He stood and paced to the sword, picked it up, and gestured with it. "Let's all go to the kitchen and have that meal. The woman first, you to follow her by four paces."

They filed out of the room and to the kitchen, at the end of the corridor. He motioned for the priest and the woman to sit on a bench by the table while he examined the shelves. The churchmen ate very well here. He carried food and a bottle of wine to the table. "Good appetite," he said.

The priest glared at him. "I won't share bread with a man I'm going to kill," he growled.

"Then don't eat the bread," Scarface said mildly. "There's plenty else here to enjoy."

He found his taste for food was improving, and ate with a will, although he only sipped at a single cup of wine.

"Who should I tell Archpriest Bennas I killed?" the priest inquired.

Scarface considered the question. This priest almost certainly knew no magic, and he doubted he'd have any sort of amulet or other trinket that'd let him commune with his superiors. Such objects cost too much of the magi who could empower them to waste one on a minor priest in a backwater temple, so he needn't worry about the church being warned before he was safely in southern Donradé.

On the other hand, his sudden appearance could cause ill-considered action by some of his enemies. That was always preferable to waiting for them to make mistakes. And the scene that would be played out struck him as amusing. He took up the sword in his left hand, the staff in his right. "Let's find you a sword."

"Brother Ondé had one in his room. It's the nearest door off the corridor."

"Get it," Scarface said to the woman.

She hurried out of the room. He followed her to the kitchen door, waited until she came back out of the room, the sword in her hands. He took it from her and examined both weapons. The monk's sword had a plainer hilt; otherwise, there was little difference between them.

"I presume you're more familiar with your own sword," Scarface said. Kneeling, he slid the priest's sword across the floor, then strode to the fireplace and brought the staff down on the stones in a whistling blow.

The room seemed to spin and he staggered a step as the relief struck him like sudden drunkenness, then he stretched his arms, exulting in the sudden freedom of movement.

The priest's jaw dropped. "Daign!"

Scarface laughed, partly at the pleasure of wearing his own face and body again, partly at the shock on the priest's face. "Are you still willing to make that offering to Mordach?"

The priest slid across the bench, then stood. "I've heard you were a wily leader, but there aren't any legends about your skill with a sword. I think I can beat a man who ran away from a crown and turned against the church that handed him that crown." He suddenly stooped, snatched up his sword, and faced Scarface.

Scarface laughed again. "The church gave me nothing. I bargained for everything I got from old Cruach. It seems I should've dealt with someone who'd have kept all his agreements." He glanced at the woman. "I suggest you leave, or get to the door. Things may become a bit exciting and perhaps dangerous here."

The priest sprang forward, whipping his blade around with a flick of the wrist. Scarface parried. "Very good," he said. Steel rasped as he slid his blade up the priest's and stepped forward so his weapon was between the priest's sword and his body.

The man leaped back, clearing his blade, then lunged.

The point was coming in to the right of Scarface's blade, so he moved his hilt to the right while keeping his point aimed at the priest's face.

Unable to halt his lunge, the priest's sword passed to the right of Scarface's arm. Scarface dropped his own point and ran his blade half a finger's length into the priest's chest. The man screamed and recoiled from the pain, dropping the point of his weapon, and Scarface moved with him, thrusting for the priest's right leg, just above the knee. He drove the tip of his blade a finger's length into the leg.

The priest's leg folded and he fell heavily. Scarface stepped back from the fallen man. "Perhaps you'd like to start a legend about my swordsmanship. Let's cheat Mordach this time, shall we? I'd rather have you alive to carry a message to your superiors. Just tell them I've returned. They should be able to deduce the rest."

Darting past the priest, he snatched up an oil lamp and trotted to the stable. He could hear the woman screaming and pounding on the door of one of the houses. In the stable, he quickly saddled and bridled one horse, bridled three more, then drove the last horse out into the night. It'd no doubt return but not, he hoped, until well after he'd escaped.

He put together two torches and lit them from the lamp, then led the horses out, mounting the one he'd saddled. Riding to the temple, leading the other animals, he tossed one torch into the open door and kicked the chapel door open and threw the second flambeau inside. Even wounded, the priest should be able to escape the burning temple, but he doubted the fire could be put out until the place was only ashes and a few charred boards.

Kicking his mount into a trot, he rode to where he'd cached his sword and supplies, reclaimed them, and rode away.

He realized he'd just begun a war with the church of Mordach, and knew he'd need allies. He recalled the game he'd often played with Poker, the game of Gods and Kings, and he remembered that gods could only be fought by gods.

To oppose Mordach, he'd need another god

CHAPTER 3

The ride to Donradan Linistia required a dozen days. His only ally on the ride, the only one on which he relied, was speed. In a few places he threw back the cowl of his cloak and let his scars announce him but for the most part he kept his face hidden. His manner and bearing may have inspired curiosity but they also discouraged questions. Twice he traded horses for fresher mounts.

What he found was a kingdom that had died in the cradle. Only once did he see a trader's caravan, and it was escorted by well-armed guards. No peddlers' carts traveled alone. Each town had become a fortress, and inns at crossroads had become the hangouts of thieves. He'd had to cut his way out of one of those, leaving two men dead, several wounded, and the place in flames.

The country through which he rode was gently undulating and heavily forested, with patches of cropland surrounding small towns. There was far more forest than cleared land, and what crops he saw were in fields rarely larger than half an hour's canter. He found only two towns of more than a couple of dozen houses. From what he could learn, the more populous western region of Donradé was in little better shape. Rumors of battles had become so commonplace that only clashes between confederations of nobles commanding hundreds of men had become worthy of interest.

On the seventh day of his ride, near noon, he halted just south of the Forest of Omaire. Beyond tilled fields and fenced pastures, he could make out a great fortress, once an outpost of the Sazian empire. Taking this fort had been his first conquest in the war with Sazia for southern Donradé. A glint atop the stone wall would be a guard, turning as he marched his circuit. A peddler's wagon seemed to crawl along the road to the open gate and Scarface kicked his mount into a trot, pulling two more horses after him.

From the road, he counted a dozen men and women in the fields and he could discern a sizable herd of cattle in a pasture bounded by a pole fence. He followed the trader's cart through the gate and into the central square.

A row of booths, all but two of them empty, stood along two sides of the square, and he could guess that on market day they'd be filled. A double handful of men and women walked through the square, a few of them speaking with each other, the rest hurrying, as though on errands of importance. Few of the men were armed, and it was one of the armed men, in light armor, that he approached, his cowl drawn up to keep his face in shadow. "Who commands here?"

The soldier barely glanced at him. "Baron Anjular."

There'd been an Anjular who's served him well at Hope. Scarface decided the stakes were right for a gamble. "Where may I find him?"

"He's out chasing some raiders from the north." The man shrugged. "He'll be back when he's done. When he's here, his quarters are—"

"That building?" Scarface pointed. At the soldier's nod and sudden searching look at his face, he added, "I was part of the army that took this place. Where can I get a cup of wine? It's been a while since I was here and some things have changed."

"There's a dramshop in that building at the far end of the square."

"Thank you." Scarface nodded, careful not to let the cowl slip, then led his horses to the stable. The stablemaster was a man rapidly approaching old age, assisted by two boys who couldn't, between them, raise one creditable beard. Scarface doled out a few coppers, then strode to the dramhouse.

The place was cool and dim, with a long wooden counter, several plank tables surrounded by rough chairs, and benches against the wall. The wall opposite the door held a large fireplace holding a blackened iron swivel-bar and flanked by stacks of wood. The shop appeared to be empty. Scarface rapped on the counter with a couple of coppers until a man appeared at the doorway behind the counter. Seeing a customer, he bustled out.

"Soldier's wine," Scarface said, and accepted a clay cup of sour red wine. Most of the southerners preferred a wine too sweet for his taste. He sipped, careful not to tip the cowl back. "Is the Anjular who commands here the same man as the Anjular who served King Daign in Hope?"

"You know him?"

"If it's the same man."

"He's the one. Got kicked out of Hope when the church took the place over. Earl Jonfré sent him here."

Scarface walked to one of the tables, sat down, and held up two more coins. "Why don't you have yourself a cup and sit down? It doesn't look as though you'd be neglecting any customers."

"Kind of you." The man poured himself a mug of ale, trudged around the counter, set his drink on the table, and dropped into a chair. "I've usually got more business than this, but Baron Anjular's taken most of the cavalry and all the footsoldiers he could find mounts for after the raiders."

"Is that a common problem?"

The man shrugged. "It's to be expected. This is a border post. Earl Jonfré might as well call himself king. This part of Donradé is free of that whoreson, Thienn."

"May it remain so, but I hope your business picks up."

"It will, as soon as the baron and his men return. Those soldiers will've grown a thirst."

"Where can one find a room and a meal?"

"I can provide the meal. There's rooms in the building opposite the market stalls. The southwest corner."

The room darkened as a man stood in the door, then entered. Scarface glanced at him, recognized the peddler he'd followed through the gate. The barman rose. "Lon, what can I get for you?"

After nodding to the peddler, Scarface continued to nurse his wine. The trader and the barman seemed well acquainted, and talked at the counter.

Scarface listened only enough to be sure the conversation held nothing of interest to him. He hadn't really considered the possibility his arrival might not be welcome to those who opposed Thienn. He'd pronounced the guttersnipe his son and abdicated, leaving both crowns on Thienn's head. That abdication might not set well with many who'd once supported him, and he had no church in his pocket to use as a bargaining chip.

It wouldn't help that he had no desire to remain as king once Thienn was deposed. He drained his cup. Noticing a lull in the conversation at the counter, he said, "I'll take that meal, and another cup of wine."

The barman disappeared into the back room and soon returned with meat, cheese, bread, and a couple of small green apples, and poured more wine in the cup. "That'll be five coppers."

Scarface handed the man a mark of silver and accepted his change. Eating slowly, he enjoyed the first time since dropping his disguise that he'd been able to linger over a meal.

When he finished eating he left, found the rented rooms, and paid for two nights' lodging. He'd have paid more for a bath, but bathing was held in low esteem by the Donradans, who seemed to take pride in the odors of honest sweat and dirt, and who seldom washed past their wrists, unless they were caught in the rain or fell into a river.

In the room, he fell into a reverie. He wished he could be with Topaz and tried to guess what she'd be doing at this moment. It was midafternoon, so she'd probably be visiting someone, or perhaps she'd be out picking herbs. If he closed his eyes he could almost see her, almost smell her scent, hear her voice. Unfortunately, there was more between them than a few dozen leagues. He'd again become what he thought he'd rid himself of; a creature of blood and strife.

Whether he sought it out or not, he had to admit there was an excitement in battle that almost matched that of lovemaking. Perhaps it came from facing the ultimate challenge; to prevail over your enemies or die. That was a test one failed but once. And that, too, was part of the excitement,

His pallet was under a window, on the second floor, and a breeze swept in over the fortress walls and though the window, one that cooled him just enough for comfort. From remembrance he slipped into drowsing, so softly he couldn't know when the change was made. He was seeing Topaz in exquisite detail, feeling again the smoothness of her skin, almost tasting her lips, when he was snatched from the precious slumber by the babbling of many men, the stamping and blowing of tired horses, and the jingling of harness.

Cursing, he rolled off the pallet and stood beside the window, peering out without showing himself. He watched a man with a red horsehair plume on his helmet dismount. For a moment he wasn't sure, then the figure turned, took off his helmet, and mopped his face with the end of his cape. It was the Anjular he'd known in Hope.

Scarface reached for his cloak, then hesitated. Anjular would need some time to himself, have a cup, perhaps several cups. Scarface lay back down on the pallet to rest a bit longer.

Rest wasn't easily taken when he couldn't escape fearing for Topaz. He still hadn't decided how he felt about having a child. He'd never seen himself, thought of himself, as a father. In three years he'd almost become a part of Topaz, but now what was between them would have to change—if he were lucky. It seemed Topaz was pleased to be bearing his child, but if having that child meant her life, he'd rather it'd never been conceived. That trade—a life for a life—wasn't one he was willing to make.

After half an hour of worry, he snarled another curse, rose again, donned his cloak, and drew up his hood. He paused then. If Anjular were less than pleased to see him, it'd be better to have a means of escape planned. He took time to recall the concealment spell. It required real effort. In three years he hadn't used a single spell, and now he had to remember one precisely.

The spell also required wetting his forehead. He'd used his own saliva in the past, but had learned that mouths could dry out at the most inopportune times. Now he'd have to count on his own calmness or the chance that Anjular had water in his quarters.

Leaving the room, he crossed the square and strode to where two men with spears stood before the door to Anjular's quarters. "I wish to see your commander," he told them.

"The baron is resting," one of the guards replied.

"Tell him an old comrade is here."

"I'm telling you, he's resting." The guard took a step toward Scarface. "And we wouldn't let a man in who wouldn't show his face."

Scarface recalled what Donradans lacked in cleanliness they more than made up for in stubbornness and a love of disputation. Now his decision was being made for him. He could expose his face or, in another step, the guard would shove his cowl back. That he would not permit. "There may be a price to be paid for seeing my face, but… "He pushed back the cowl and stared at the guards, ready to draw his sword if it were needed.

The younger guard almost dropped his spear. "King Daign," he said, and bowed.

The other man, a veteran by his appearance, was less easily impressed. "The baron is still resting."

"Tell him who's here," Scarface snapped. "I suspect he'll find it worth getting up for. Tell him I have urgent matters to discuss with him."

"What sort of urgent matters?"

Scarface barked a laugh. "If Anjular wants you to know, he'll invite you in to tell you himself. Might even offer you a cup of wine." Suddenly his tone became peremptory. "Tell him."

For a moment the guard only stared at him, then he lost the

contest of wills and turned to rap on the door. "Baron!" They could all hear movement in the room, and a voice, too muffled for Scarface to hear distinctly, spoke. The guard replied, "Baron, Daign is here."

In the time it took a man to spring out of a chair and hurry five paces, the door was jerked open and Anjular stood in the doorway. "Come in," he said, and stepped back into the room.

The room had no windows and the only light was provided by a couple of candles. There was little enough to see. Anjular had hung his armor on a stand in one corner, the center was occupied by a table and three chairs, and a bedframe stood against the wall. The bed was a cloth-filled pallet resting on a web of ropes strung along and across the wooden frame. Beside the bed was a small table on which stood an ewer and a basin, along with a bottle of wine. Anjular stood beside the armor stand, his sword within reach, his stance revealing wariness.

Scarface nodded at him, received a nod in reply, then gestured at one of the chairs. "May I sit down?"

Anjular seemed to relax slightly. He nodded again. "How may I serve you, Lord Daign?"

"No 'lord,' and that's my question to you. I'm bound for Linistia to join Earl Jonfré."

"Are you going to take up the crown again?" Scarface couldn't tell, from his tone, whether Anjular approved of the idea or not.

Scarface shook his head. "'King Jonfré' has a nice ring to it. I came only to offer Jonfré whatever support I can give."

"Does that mean you're opposing your whelp?"

"I'd kill the little bastard myself if I thought that'd end the problems, but I believe the earl has more dangerous enemies."

Anjular did relax then, and took a seat in a chair facing Scarface. "I'm afraid you're right. Mordach's church has grabbed everything its priests can lay their hands on. Since Cruach disappeared after appointing a handful of archpriests, the church's become a greater threat than any king in Glangurra."

Scarface raised an eyebrow. The priest he'd chatted with had omitted the information Cruach wasn't personally ruling as he once had. "How long ago did that happen?"

"About a year and a half, two years ago. There were rumors he was ill, or maybe dying. He might be dead now, for all I know. The church took over Hope, made it church property. All the lords around the place are in the church's purse, or they've been replaced by priests."

"Hasn't the church sided with Thienn?"

"The church is like a haggler at a bazaar. They make their bargains but don't grant anyone their custom. We've tried to keep them out of the south, but they have hands and ears everywhere. Many of the soldiers still respect or fear Mordach, even if they don't openly worship him. I've heard stories about the arrogance of the churchmen in the north, but in the south they're careful to honor their responsibilities and give lip service to Jonfré."

"Well," Scarface mused, "we can guess what happened to some of the priests and most of the monks I knew." He stretched. "With your permission, I'll stay another day to rest, then ride south."

"I'll have Rihar vacate the room next to this one. It won't hurt him to share quarters with the troops for a couple of nights."

Scarface almost argued he'd already taken a room but, since the two soldiers outside had seen his face, every soldier in the fortress would know by sunset. "Thank you. I suspect some of your men might think I'm here to take up the crown again, or to support Thienn." He permitted himself a flash of smile, which he quickly suppressed on seeing Anjular's cheeks redden and noticed the man's sudden concentration on his folded hands. He pretended disappointment. "Anjular, I'm hurt. How could you think that?"

Anjular glanced up, then returned to studying his hands. "No disrespect, Daign, but you're a hard man, and a hard man to know. I've never known what you'd do next."

"I suppose. By the way, did you catch those raiders?"

"Caught'em and hanged'em. We may have problems with others, but those won't be back."

"How much of a problem are these raids?"

"No single raid does much damage, but it's like being stabbed to death by needles. I lost two men when we caught up with them, and the peasants aren't sure we can protect them. That leads to hard feelings between the peasants and the soldiers."

"Perhaps you should send some of your own raiders north. That might do more good than all the patrolling you could do."

"I've considered that. I just need to be very careful who I send." Anjular rose, slowly. "Have you eaten yet?"

"A couple of hours ago."

"Long enough for you to have grown another appetite. I'll have food and wine brought here." He plodded to the door and spoke with the guards, then returned and fell back into his chair. They shared reminiscences of "the old days" through dinner and most of a jug of wine, until Anjular almost fell asleep in his chair.

Scarface stood. "We can talk more tomorrow." He left, allowing the younger guard to escort him to the room he'd been given.

Between the wine and the wear of hard traveling, he was just able to undress before he fell onto the bed.

He was wakened by the crash of nearby thunder and heard a heavy rain pelting down. He listened for a while, found the sound soothing. It'd been less comforting when he'd been caught in a storm five days earlier, drenched by cold rain and fearing each bolt of lightning, but unpleasantness regarded from a haven gave a sense of warmth and security. He wrapped the blankets tightly around himself. Had Topaz been there to share the bed with him, it would've been perfect.

If he concentrated, he thought he could feel Topaz's presence, almost feel her beside him.

~ * ~

The rain continued to fall the next day. Scarface granted himself the luxury of rising late but he could still hear rain driving against the door. Groping in the dark for his clothing, he found his pouch with flint, steel, and tinder, and groped again for a candle. When he had the candle lit, he looked around the room. It was similar to Anjular's room, but the armor rack was bare.

A shelf on the wall opposite the bed was lined with figurines of soldiers, peasants, and animals, carved of several kinds of wood. Whoever Rihar might be, he had skill in his hands and a sense of humor. Not a bad recommendation. Like the table in Anjular's room, Rihar's was without parchment or quill.

As Scarface dressed, he compared the fortress as it was and as it'd been when he'd seen it the first time. The Sazians had garrisoned over a thousand men in this post. He doubted Anjular had a fifth that many, and the place had been opened to farmers and tradesmen. Neither the dramshop nor the bazaar had been here when it'd been under Sazian control, nor had there been pastures or tilled fields. This fortress had once been a parasite. Now, without a subject people to tax, it seemed to be self-sufficient.

Indolence and hunger were drawing him in different directions. From the sound of the wind moaning at the door, the frequent rumble of thunder, and the pelting of rain against his door, he could guess that it was unpleasant outside; probably cold as well as wet, but he'd developed an appetite and was debating with himself when a fist hammered on the door.

Scarface opened the door and Anjular charged in, then slammed the door against the storm. He threw back the hood of his cloak. "I thought you might be hungry. There's a kitchen in the barracks."

"There's a place across the square that I visited yesterday—"

"Jacré's place." Anjular thought for a moment. "The food's better there, and there'll be fewer soldiers. Most of the troops will stay in the barracks, where they have food and wine and no need to go out into the weather."

Scarface donned his own cloak and followed Anjular out, turning to draw the door shut behind himself, then they dashed across the square, splashing up plumes of water with each step. The door, under an overhang, was kept open. A fire blazed in the hearth and a large pot on the swivel bar filled the room with an aroma that brought saliva to Scarface's mouth and made his stomach rumble a counterpoint to the thunder.

He glanced around the room. Only a handful of men sat at the tables or on the benches. The tables nearest the fire were occupied. Anjular unclasped his cloak and let it hang over the back of his chair, and after a moment, Scarface did the same.

Jacré bustled out from behind his counter. "May I serve you, lords?"

"Bread, some of that stew, and soldier's wine." Anjular looked at Scarface. "You?"

"The same." Scarface tried to ignore Jacré's sudden attack of manners.

The bread was only an hour old and the stew was hearty and well-seasoned, loaded with onions. Scarface wiped the horn spoon Jacré had provided on his cloak and tasted the stew. "Excellent."

The other men in the room had fallen silent, the conversations beginning to die when Anjular and Scarface had removed their cloaks. Now one of the men rose to his feet and raised his cup. "To Thienn's funeral. May it come soon."

Wordlessly, Scarface raised his cup to the man and took a drink, then ignored him. The soldier scowled, then slowly returned to the conversation he'd been having with his friends.

Scarface and Anjular finished their meal and had another cup of wine, then Anjular leaned back in his chair. "When you abdicated, where did you go?"

Scarface explained, in as few words as possible, how he'd spent the last three years.

"What's the chance of hiring some of those Senshenni to raid for us? They fought well with our army, in the war with the Sazians."

"I'll ask Jonfré, when I see him."

Scarface quickly became bored and begged leave to return to his room. He took with him bread, cheese, and a bottle of sour wine. The weather had begun to affect him. His earlier sense of well-being had been drowned by the pouring rain. Back in his room, he lit a fire in the hearth and sat staring into the flames.

For the first time he could remember, he felt himself truly a foreigner. One of his earlier sources of pride had been in being complete unto himself. He had a gift for languages and an opportunism that allowed him to adjust quickly to strange situations. Others had probably perceived him as an outsider, but he never had. When one lived everywhere, or nowhere, he supposed, one was equally at home anywhere. Now he was in a place that was not home. It was a new experience for him. Before, he'd yearned for the company of certain people, but no place had called him back to it. Now, he missed Topaz terribly, but he also felt a longing for Stag Mountain and the Dieri who lived there. Now he had a home, and everywhere else he was a foreigner.

Some of this identification with the Dieri was a matter of depth. Never before had he given himself to a place or a people. Even in Sin Garlef he'd held at least a part of himself aloof. And, although he had family and acquaintances in half a dozen nations, he'd never before become a part of any culture or nation. He'd simply used what was accepted as a handle, to manipulate situations to his own needs.

The rain had slackened several times, only to return each time with increasing fury. He'd eaten some of the bread and drank half the wine and was preparing to finish them when someone rapped on his door.

He looked to be sure his sword was in hand's reach, then, "Enter."

Anjular ducked in and slammed the door against the rain and the wind that whipped the fire into a frenzy. "I wanted to tell you I appreciated your restraint."

"Mmh?"

"That soldier was trying to goad you. He's one who resents your having abdicated."

"It's his right to resent it. And I must bear the onus of not having finished what I started."

Anjular sat down in the chair across the table from Scarface. "As I've said, I never know what you'll do. No disrespect, but you fight like a woman. Most of the men I know roar and pound the table. You don't often show anger, and even then it's on a short rein. You never threaten, but when you decide to act, you're merciless, and it's usually a single, devastating attack."

Scarface snorted, almost a laugh. "I've a cousin who's even more like that. I never fight for pleasure. I prefer to give a single, soft warning to make my stand clear but not to inflame the argument, so the other man can back down and still salvage his pride. Beyond that, any other warnings or threats only serve to put your enemy on guard. If I have to kill, why should I risk more? Does a quarrelsome fool deserve a chance to show off his skill with a weapon?"

Anjular pursed his lips, considering the different perspective, then one side of his mouth turned up in a lop-sided grin. "It sounds reasonable as you say it, but it's still odd." He sat staring at the fire. "Were you still planning to leave tomorrow?"

"If the weather permits."

"I'll have a score of men escort you."

"That isn't necessary. If you feel I need an escort, how about the two men who were guarding your quarters yesterday? I've three horses, so I won't eat into your garrison strength."

"As you wish. Edou, the younger man, is one of the orphans of Glangurrach, but Aovalyn is one of those who resents your abdication. He's a veteran and a good soldier, but he's been soured."

"All the better. If I can't convince him my return is for the best, he might be right, and if I can convince him, there's no firmer believer than a convert."

Again Anjular thought a moment before he grinned. "As I said, I never know which way you'll jump next." He rose. "I'll see you in the morning," he said, and went back into the storm.

~ * ~

Sometime during the night the storm exhausted itself. Dawn was clear and rose-colored as the rising sun dried out the last few small clouds in the east. Scarface reclaimed his supplies from the rented room, ate heartily at Jacré's, and strode to Anjular's quarters, where his escorts were waiting. They carried saddle pouches of provisions and, after he'd made his farewell to Anjular, they followed him to the stables. Both his guards were silent; Edou awe-struck, Aovalyn sullen.

The gravel road they followed to the south was Sazian-built and well-drained. The horses, not having to plod through mud, were able to make good time. A breeze from the south kept the heat and the moisture in the air from becoming oppressive, and Scarface soon removed his cloak and tied it to the saddle in front of him.

They'd ridden through two small towns before noon, and shortly after passing through the second town they encountered a wide band of forest trying to reclaim the land it'd lost to the road. Scarface drew rein. "This is the first likely place for an ambush I've seen. Edou, you have the youngest eyes. Take the lead. Walk your horse to rest him, but be prepared to ride. Aovalyn, you follow me. We'll also walk our horses to give them some rest. Keep your sword bare in your hand."

As Edou moved ahead, leading his horse, Scarface and Aovalyn dismounted. Though it took an effort of will, Scarface turned his back on the veteran and began to walk. He heard the rasp of Aovalyn's sword being drawn from its scabbard and continued to walk, slowly and steadily. The best way to ensure the veteran's loyalty was to show complete trust in him.

The shade from the great oaks and maples was a respite, and the rustle of the leaves was almost soporific. A creek, swollen and brown from the storm, snaked through the forest, and Scarface stopped beside the bridge to let his horse drink. Aovalyn stuck his sword in the ground as he watered his own mount and Scarface waited until the soldier had pulled his horse's head away from the creek before he resumed his walk through the woods.

Across the bridge, they quickly reached the southern end of the woods, where Edou waited for them. "Thank you," Scarface said to Aovalyn, as he gripped the saddle and set foot to stirrup. Aovalyn's only reply was a nod, but it seemed to reveal more friendliness than he'd shown before.

By early afternoon they'd arrived at another fortress, this one much smaller than Anjular's post. When the Sazians had held it they'd garrisoned it with a single sixty-man *seymana*. Now it held a dozen Donradan soldiers, more farmers, and an inn.

Scarface approached with his face hidden. They ate and drank at the inn, leaving their mounts to be tended by the stablemaster. They ate slowly and lounged, drowsing until the hottest part of the day had passed, then rode on.

The character of both the land and the people had begun to change just south of the Forest of Omaire. The areas of tilled land were larger than in the north, the towns more numerous and larger. Here, the wooded areas were mostly strips between the fields surrounding the towns.

The Sazians had laid out their major north-south route well, with small forts placed eight leagues apart, so travelers, whether they marched or rode, could stay each night at a fort. The Sazian army was made up primarily of footsoldiers, and they measured their distance in *cheymenna*, a thousand double-march strides representing a *cheymenna*, and three of those was a league, or close enough it didn't matter. As proud as the Sazians were of their seamanship, they seemed at least as proud that their army, in a day's march, could cover twenty-four *cheymenna*, eight leagues.

By early afternoon of the fourth day out of Anjular's holding they could see the spires and towers of Linistia, the great port city at the mouth of the River Bromron. They shook their reins and quickened the pace, and the sun still stood above the horizon when they rode through the massive iron-bound gates of the city.

Scarface hadn't seen the city since he'd entered it at the head of an invading army. He left it to Aovalyn to arrange an audience with Jonfré, and Edou to take the horses to the stable, while he waited at an inn.

Edou was the first to return.

"May I see your sword?" Scarface asked. Wordlessly, Edou drew the weapon and laid it on the table. Scarface picked it up and examined it. It was indifferently smithed of local steel, with the balance of a club. He unhooked the scabbard from his own belt. The sword he wore was plain, but the blade was exceptional and the balance was very good. He handed Edou the sheathed weapon, "A good soldier needs a worthy weapon." He waved away the stammered thanks. "I know it'll be well used."

Aovalyn entered as Edou was replacing his old scabbard with the one Scarface had given him. The veteran dropped into the third chair at the table. "Earl Jonfré will see you as soon as we reach the palace."

"Well done." Scarface fished in his pouch as he stood. He had a few copper coins and three marks of silver. He left the copper on the table and handed the silver to Aovalyn. "I've never seen the army that overpaid its soldiers."

"I can't take this."

Scarface laughed. "Of course you can. If Jonfré is pleased to see me, I won't need it, and if my presence displeases him, well, I won't need it then, either."

They made their way through the streets, which were already becoming dark. Scarface knew the way well; he'd been in this city for several days, had lived in the palace during that time. Beggars still prowled and squatted in the alleys, imploring and cajoling, but the urchins were gone.

Torches marked the entrance to the palace. Just inside the gate, two soldiers in burnished mail met them. Scarface turned to his escorts. "Please express my gratitude to Anjular, and good fortune to you."

He turned on his heel and followed Jonfré's guards down a corridor and up two flights of stairs to a small room, bare but for a rug on the floor, a table, and two chairs. Two candles on the table were lit, although the dim luminescence they provided was almost lost against the glow of the hearth. A man stood in front of the fireplace, visible only as a silhouette. The figure dismissed the guards with a wave of the hand and paced to the table.

In the candlelight, Jonfré's face had aged more than three years; his beard had gone all white but for the moustache and the corners of the chin. Lines were deeply drawn from the corner of his eye and the black patch that covered the empty socket, and more lines ran across his forehead. All his features appeared to have been dragged down by care and exhaustion. He gestured at the chair facing him but stood leaning on the back of his own chair. "I failed my last command," he said.

"I'd no right to issue it," Scarface replied. He sat, again aware of the wariness his presence seemed to inspire. "The task was mine to do. And, from what I heard, you did your best."

Jonfré nodded, slowly, then rounded the chair and fell into it. "What brings you here?"

"What passes for a sense of obligation. I'm here to offer you my support, even to help make you king."

Jonfré did manage a laugh. "I'm not even sure I want to be a baron." He settled into a more comfortable position in the chair. "When first we met, I saw you as a man who could make himself king. I was willing to be your...left hand, let's say. You were your own strong right hand. But I was willing to serve you to earn some small domain where I could grow old in some measure of comfort. I'd sold my sword often enough to know there's damned little money in it, and that soon spent. Sooner or later, I'd be a little too old, too slow, too weak, and that'd be the end."

He poured a cloudy liquid from a glass decanter into two silver cups and offered one to Scarface. A sip was enough to remind him this was the liquid fire the Donradans brewed and distilled from tubers.

Jonfré leaned back in his chair. "So I served. I like to think I served well." He didn't seem to see Scarface's nod. "It was the first time I'd seen the making of a campaign from the leader's tent and learned about the scheming that goes into taking a crown and keeping it. I also learned that if the rewards of leadership are greater, so are the prices paid. Now, I've begun to wonder if I weren't better off as just another sword for hire." He took a drink from his cup, cleared his throat.

"It's good to see you again." He lapsed into silence while they both sipped at the liquor. "And I have a selfish reason for being glad to see you—I'm facing more problems than solutions. It's the sort of thing you seem to enjoy dealing with.

"The lords on the northern border are all loyal to Thienn, or they've been replaced by churchmen, which amounts to much the same. I know there've been raids from the north. So far, Anjular and his men have dealt with them well."

Scarface grunted, then said, "He and I were wondering why you didn't order him to raid in his turn, or to hire Senshenni to do it for you."

"If we raid north, Thienn is liable to use it as an opportunity to gather the nobility behind him and march south. Our friends among the northern lords, Glangurran or Donradan, are few and quiet. They all know Thienn is only looking for a pretext to seize their holdings to award to his friends, and what he doesn't grab the church will take. And there are no living former lords still in the north, although a few have joined us here. I suspect many of the other lords, who spit at any mention of Thienn's name, would join his army just for the plunder.

"As for the Senshenni, there are other problems. As I understand it, your marriage to Mendarian sealed a treaty between Glangurra and Donradé and the empire of Cerco, which the Cercans and I would both be violating. Thienn would then use our hiring foreign troops as an excuse to attack us, or even to attack Cerco. Finally, to hire Senshenni, I'd have to send a message through northern Donradé—we have no common border with Cerco—and the Senshenni would have to come through the north to join us."

Scarface sipped again at his cup, shook his head when Jonfré offered him the bottle. Jonfré had emptied his own cup and refilled it carefully.

"I presume," Scarface said, "the Sazians are less than pleased at having this unrest on their border."

"They're very concerned," Jonfré replied. "Who'd have thought, when we took this country from them, that we'd be looking to them for help against our own people in the north? Come to think of it, you might've. I remember your leaving a bridge a few days' march north of here."

Scarface shrugged. "Nothing is forever, and politics changes allies with the seasons. Have the Sazians offered troops?"

"Up to ten *seymana*, five of them from the Elites, but it's the same problem as with the Senshenni. Even worse. If I brought in Sazian troops, I'm not sure how many southern Donradans would turn against us, and all the northerners would fight out of panic."

"What part does the church play in this?"

"The same part a vulture plays when it sees two bulls glaring at each other. That's another reason an open war would be disastrous. We wouldn't be able to field an army as large as the one that took southern Donradé. Thienn would have us outnumbered and could fight where the land favors him. And the church would have a third army waiting to fall on the exhausted victors."

Jonfré drained his cup and stood. "If you announce you've returned, we might be able to gather an army that would give us a chance."

Scarface shook his head. "The time hasn't yet come for us to move in that direction. I'm at least as eager as you are to have this finished, but moving too soon would be a mistake. The church knows I've returned, as do a handful of soldiers and a few peasants, but it'll be just another rumor to most. If I announce myself, everyone will expect us to move immediately, while the rumor of my return may give some hope and, in the right places, fear.

"I'd like to sleep on what you've told me. I may have a few ideas, but I'd rather have time to turn them over and see what's on the bottoms of them. It's obvious we'll have to fight both the church and Thienn, and I think the church is the greater threat and should be dealt with first." He paused. "Have you learned anything useful? I've heard old Cruach hasn't been seen in over a year and might be dead. I've also heard the church has someone with a legitimate claim to the throne. Did Terralyn's brother, or Terralyn himself, have a bastard?"

"Not that I know of. I've heard the same rumors you have, but nothing specific."

"I need a place to sleep, and I'd prefer not to be seen any more than I must. Do you have a room I can use?"

"We have a chamber for visiting dignitaries. We don't use it much." He slowly produced a smile. "Few dignitaries are eager to visit a half-kingdom under siege. I'll show you the room."

They walked together, Jonfré a trace unsteadily, down the corridor to a large room containing a bed, chairs, and a table with candles, parchment, and a quill in an inkstand. One of the candles was lit. A tapestry graced one of the outside walls, although the room was too dark to be able to make out the pattern.

Scarface embraced Jonfré, then stepped into the room, closing the door behind him. Removing his cloak, he tossed it across the back of a chair. Sitting down, he sighed as he pulled off his boots, then stood and moved the chair to the window so he could sit and look out over the street. He could stare out over most of the other buildings in sight, and noticed people sleeping on the rooftops of neighboring buildings, enjoying the mild weather.

Something as nagging as a doubt tugged at him, an uneasiness he'd felt before and had learned not to ignore. The door to his room opened outward, into the corridor. He leaned another chair against the door, so the chair would fall at the slightest movement of the door.

Scanning the room, he memorized the location of each stick of furniture, then returned to the chair at the window. The candlelight was sufficient to let him just perceive the shapes of the tables and chairs and the dark mass of the bed against the pale wall.

Although he was tired, the dangers facing Jonfré kept his mind busy, turning over the difficulties and examining them from every angle. The manipulations gave some strange perspectives, probabilities, and possibilities. Some might even be useful.

He rested his head against the smooth, cool stone of the wall. It reminded him of the caverns of Stag Mountain. The longing to see Topaz, to hold her again in his arms, was like a hunger. As he'd told Jonfré, he was eager to resolve this dilemma as soon as possible.

The stars winked conspiratorially at him. He didn't often see them, living with the Dieri, unless he was outside on night duty. The stars here in the lowlands seemed paler. Or perhaps they only seemed that way because everything seemed to lack the flavor and sharpness of home.

The chair crashed to the floor and his door swung open, although he saw no one. Suddenly, the sight of that empty doorway caused his hair to stir, then there was no time for fear, only time in which to act. He'd used the spell himself, before, and he'd thought about how to defeat it. Springing to the wall, he tore the tapestry free, then swung the heavy cloth in a wide arc, saw its edge distorted by an unseen body, and flung it.

A shape struggled with the heavy fabric. Scarface's hand clawed for the hilt of his sword, then he remembered he'd given it away. He snatched out his knife and, in two steps, stood beside the chair where he'd tossed his cloak. Catching up the cloak, he swung it at the shape that seemed to be crawling out from under the tapestry.

He surprised himself: he laughed. Cloth ripped as something tore the cloak. Twisting the cloth, he jerked it to his left, then struck with his knife, felt resistance as the blade hit the tapestry, then it grated on bone before plunging into something softer.

Backing away, he tried to remember a spell he once knew. He advanced again, keeping the cloak in constant motion and, when it revealed a form he crouched and slashed with the knife, cutting low, at knee level. He felt the blade drag and heard something fall. Again he retreated.

The words and gestures required for the spell came to him and he performed the casting, feeling power being drawn from his scars, then he saw a dark shape in a darker pool on the floor.

Watching the form, he sidled to the table and seized the candle, then turned to face the man lying on the floor.

The assassin looked into his eyes, realized Scarface could see him and, without hesitation, drove the point of his dagger into his own thigh.

"Guards!"Scarface shouted. "To me!"

Feet pounded in the hallway and two guards burst into the room, one of them stumbling over the chair by the door. "Get to Jonfré. This assassin was concealed—invisible. Surround Jonfré with guards if you must, but protect him."

He glanced down. The man on the floor had sagged as though his bones had turned to water, then twitched. Suddenly he emitted a gurgling sound, and the odors of excrement and urine seemed to roll up from him.

Trying to ignore the stench, Scarface cut away the man's robe. His thrust had slipped past the collarbone into the muscle above the shoulder blade, but the wound hadn't been fatal, nor had the hamstringing. He pulled the dagger from the corpse's thigh. The part of the blade still unbloodied was stained. He'd seen a stain like that on a blade before. It was poison.

He held the candle near the body's face, but didn't recognize the features, wasn't even sure he could've, had he known the man. The face was tattooed almost solid black, effectively hiding whatever tattoos he'd had before. Scarface would've bet his right arm that among those hidden tattoos had been red lightning bolts.

Shouts echoed through the halls, and he heard the clatter of running feet. The guards had closed the door behind them and he used the blanket from the bed to make sure the assassin had been alone.

After he'd assured himself there were no more concealed enemies, a fist pounded at the door and one of the guards shouted, "Daign, Jonfré is safe. He's coming to your room."

Scarface frowned in thought. An assassin, specially prepared, able to use the spell of concealment, was hardly as common as an alley thug. He doubted there'd be another like this one soon. He and Jonfré should have time in which to take precautions.

Someone else rapped, more lightly, at the door, and he said, "Enter."

Jonfré walked in, half a dozen guards at his heels.

"Only a couple of guards, please," Scarface said.

Jonfré posted all but two of the men in the corridor, then knelt beside the body. "Who do you think it was?"

"A church assassin. No one else knew that I'd returned or, if they knew, they wouldn't have had time to arrange this. Also, the church is the only group that profits by keeping the present balance.

One should never underestimate the possible speed of an enemy." He pointed to the dagger and the wound in the dead man's thigh. "Also, money won't buy that. He was a believer."

Jonfré rose slowly to his feet. "What do we do to prevent more such visitors?"

"Make sure every guard has a dog. What a dog can't see, he can hear or smell, and if he hears something and can't see it, he becomes annoyed and barks.

"You want us to bring curs into the palace?"

Scarface had forgotten few Donradans kept dogs, they were generally regarded as scavengers, little better than rats. A few beggars kept them, probably as a hedge against starvation. He'd heard the Sazian court used cats as guard animals. "Cats would be better, if you had enough of them. They're curious, and tend to stalk the faint sounds of someone trying to creep, but they sleep too much for just a few of them to be reliable."

Jonfré, obviously reluctant, finally nodded. "I'll send men out to get dogs tomorrow." He gestured at the body. "I'll have that hung over the city gates as a warning."

Scarface shook his head. "My advice would be to have it burned with the rest of the offal. It'll make our enemies more nervous if they don't know what's happened. And I think I'd like another room." He nodded at the corpse. "He's stunk up this one."

They stepped out into the corridor and were immediately surrounded by guards. "You're sure it was the church who sent him?" Jonfré asked.

"As sure as I can be. I don't think Thienn knows I'm here. As I said, the church profits the most by the present situation. Perhaps they're afraid of me. Certainly I've given them personal reasons enough for them to want me dead. I think the best thing now is to watch and see what moves our enemies make."

Scarface slept on a pallet brought into a guard room next to Jonfré's chambers. As he closed his eyes, more possibilities swirled through his mind as he remembered a similar episode in the past.

~ * ~

Two days later, as Scarface and Jonfré returned to the palace from a ride along the coast, a guard saluted them, then said, "Lords, a priest of Mordach wishes to speak with you. He carries a parley cloth."

Jonfré chuckled. "That's the first time the church's admitted the true state between us. One only calls for parley with an enemy."

They strode into the palace and Jonfré ordered his guards, after they'd searched the priest for hidden weapons, to escort the man to an audience chamber where Jonfré waited, sitting behind a table and wearing his crown. Scarface sat on the broad ledge of the window, one leg drawn up into the opening.

The priest entered and stared at the two of them. "It's unusual to search a man for weapons when he carries one of these." He tossed the parley cloth, a piece of red cloth bearing the pattern of an open hand in white, onto the table.

"It's not often someone employs an assassin to kill one of my guests, nor to provide the assassin with an envenomed dagger."

The priest's face and blue eyes were as bland as if Jonfré had told him the sun was shining outside. "Has that happened?"

Scarface laughed. "He said you'd say that." He watched the priest closely and had to admire the bastard's gall; he never turned a hair.

"You're the one I was to address," the priest said to Scarface. "My superiors desire an opportunity to speak with you. If it's agreeable to you, they'll meet you in Sazian Linistia. They'll require a Sazian order of safe passage."

Scarface glanced at Jonfré, who stared back at him, then Scarface nodded. "Your leaders should understand the Sazians will make the arrangements, and they're more…sophisticated about magic and far more accustomed to the methods of treachery than we Donradans."

"My superiors will accept that condition."

Scarface nodded to Jonfré. "Please ask the governor of Sazian Linistia to provide an order for safe passage for two, to give to an emissary of the church." He glanced at the priest again. "How soon can your superiors be in Sazian Linistia?"

"Two days from the day I receive the safe-passage."

Jonfré stood. "I'll have it sent to you this afternoon. I presume you'll be at the former temple of the Sazian wisdom-goddess?"

The priest bowed and swaggered from the chamber.

"May I go with you?" Scarface swung out of the window and dropped lightly to the floor. "I've still got a cloak with a cowl, although I'm not comfortable in boats."

"We'll ride across. The bridge between the two sides of Linistia was rebuilt last year. But why take chances?"

"Because, if I may have the money needed, I'd like to send a courier to Cerco with a message." He thought a moment. "Two messages. And I think I'll need to book passage on a Sazian ship."

"Going where?"

"To the Empire of The Book, to look for the right god."

Jonfré considered that, nodded, then he asked, "Why are you bothering to speak with whoever the church sends?"

Scarface grinned. "Don't worry, I don't expect them to give me any more of the truth than I can pry out of them but, whatever they say, they'll tell me more than I know now, and there's nothing they can get from me. I might just find out the name of the claimant to the throne who's hiding in the church. I have a feeling I already know who it is. If my guess is correct, I don't think I'm going to like it very much."

CHAPTER 4

Scarface sat on a bench in a Sazian cottage. The pale, plastered walls were bare. He'd considered sitting behind the table, but if treachery were planned, he preferred to be free to move. He guessed the hour to be near noon, the time selected by the Sazians for the meeting.

He'd sent a message to Topaz, and another to Orhan. Both messages had been in Gasgoran, since Cerco had no written language. In his message to Topaz he'd tried to express all his longing, his tenderness, and the urgency of his desire to return to Stag. To Orhan, he'd simply tendered a report. He'd like an alliance between Cerco and southern Donradé, but that would be a decision for Orhan to make.

He'd also booked passage on a Sazian ship bound for Myslan, but which would stop at two ports in the Empire of The Book, one of them near the Myslan border. The ship would sail in a little more than a fortnight, after the contrary winds had abated.

A church, even one as corrupt as Mordach's, couldn't be defeated by an army in the field. The only way to successfully oppose a church was with another church. None of the other Donradan deities, nor all of them together, had been able to oppose the church of Mordach, so he must search abroad for a holy ally. The war with Sazia was too recent for Donradans to accept a Sazian god, even had one been worthy. From what he'd learned of the Sazian deities, they inspired more contempt than awe. Even the goddess of wisdom was jealous and petty.

Father Wolf was a worthy deity, but too limited and, from what he'd seen, was a nature god who was too much like nature itself; unforgiving. That wasn't a trait he'd remained fond of. Also, Father Wolf seemed to bestow his blessings only on Cerco.

Scarface had learned a hard lesson about gods; even the false ones had real power. When one dealt with them, the gods received their due—or more. What the mortal received was seldom worth the effort or the gifts he lavished on a god. He'd learned that Mordach was a god of blood and war, but he was also utterly selfish. What his worshippers received in victories they more than paid for in blood, and then needed to continue to fight to keep what'd been gained. He hoped to prove to the priests of Mordach their god was also a cheat; that the price paid in blood for victory was nothing compared to the price of defeat.

Perhaps Mordach's followers only worshipped because it gave them an excuse to fight. If so, they might lose much of their zeal when they learned how it felt to lose a battle.

No, if he dealt with a deity, he wanted one who was giving and forgiving. There was only one of those he knew of that had the power, in worshippers, to defeat Mordach without becoming another oppressor. Poker seemed to have found peace, even contentment, through Ianno.

There were problems. Ianno couldn't be bought, at least, not with gold, and he wasn't sure he could give what Ianno might require. Still, Ianno was their best, perhaps their only, hope.

He realized he'd heard the sounds of horses walking, and the sound had stopped outside the cottage. Harness creaked and he thought he could hear two people dismounting. Two voices carried on a brief conversation, low enough he couldn't distinguish the words, although one of the voices seemed familiar, then a figure, robed and cowled in red, stood in the doorway.

Scarface rose, strode to the table and stood behind it, the fingertips of his right hand resting lightly on the wood. The priest at the door stepped just inside the cottage and waited for his eyes to adjust to the change from the harsh brightness outside.

The man said something to someone behind him, then a second figure appeared, this one dressed all in black. The two of them paced, together, to the table.

Scarface stared at the shape in black, almost as tall as he was, trying to recognize the stride or find some other clue. The black-robed figure halted across the table from him, then threw back her cowl and shook her head to free her dark brown hair.

"Mendarian," he heard himself say, "I half-thought it was you, but didn't expect you to meet me like this." He studied her face, searching for some quality that had once inspired so much devotion in him, but saw in the gray eyes only the calculating coldness that had driven them apart. The faint stirring of emotion in him was only that of recognition.

She drew out the chair across the table from him and sat down. After a pause, the man with her did the same. He also shoved back his hood to reveal a narrow face marked with the red lightning bolts and a triangle of blue dots on his cheeks. Scarface sat down facing them.

"So," Mendarian said, "the counterfeit coin appears again. It seems you can't give them away."

Scarface only smiled. Once, such a comment would've cut, but he was armored in indifference. "I had a feeling you were involved. Ambition would draw you to power like offal draws flies. The invisible assassin with the poisoned dagger should've made me certain." He stared at her again, trying to see in her detached gaze and stiff manner some trace of the woman who'd nursed him back from only a step short of the grave after another assassin had tried to kill him the same way. She'd helped save his life, that time. "I presume you decided to renege on your gift"

"It seemed appropriate." She leaned forward, resting her arms on the table. "I've learned from many, including you. You want your piddling little kingdom in the south? Fine. You have it. But if you set foot north of the Forest of Omaire, I'll use your guts to string a harp, and I'll hope it pains you every time it's played."

A grin slowly spread across Scarface's features. "You're very free with land claimed by Thienn. I suspect he might have something to say about ceding southern Donradé."

"That's between the two of you," she snapped.

The grin remained. "You never seem to weary of being used, first by the Union, now by Mordach's church. I suppose that sort of tenacity should be applauded."

Some of the coldness left her eyes, burned by rage. "You mean, because you tried to use me and failed, I should avoid seeking allies, especially if they're your enemies." He voice had become louder and harsher.

His grin disappeared. "I never tried to use you. I advised you when you ruled Cerco, and that advice was for your benefit and the good of Cerco. But you refuse to see anything but what you've chosen to see."

"Always it's words with you." Her voice took on an even harder edge. "You think fine words can put a gloss on anything. No, I'm not being used. The church and I are allies. You threw away your crown to Donradé; I didn't. And with the crown to Donradé and the power of the church, I'll be able to make Thienn dance to the tune I choose."

He laughed. "If castles could be built out of hope, your last pronouncement would be a walled city greater than Linistia." He stared at the priest. "I'll wager if I were willing to deal with Mordach's church, they'd hand you to me on a leash. The church doesn't want allies, it wants tools—like the assassin you sent. Ask him what an alliance with them is worth."

For a moment the priest paled, then he slammed the table with his fist. "We didn't come here to trade insults"

"You probably would've if you'd thought you could win the trade," Scarface replied. "Mendarian, call your puppy to heel. He hasn't the teeth to match his snarling and barking."

The priest sprang to his feet but Mendarian put a hand on his arm and said, "Relax, Arbalyn. I'll see to it you can personally turn the screws on his rack."

Scarface laughed again. "More cloud-cities built of hope. I must say, Mendarian, the years have been kind to you. You seem not to have changed at all."

"I can't say the same for you. There's gray in your beard and you look older. I'd say you don't have long to live."

"Never underestimate the value of change," he said. He stood. "I believe we've all said what we came here to say—perhaps more than that." He remembered something from when they'd first met, and he couldn't resist saying, "Do you say it, or do I? We'll meet again."

Mendarian rose and glared at him. "Not if you're lucky." She turned on her heel and stalked from the cottage, followed by the priest. Scarface watched them go, a smile playing about his lips. Mendarian had made a beginner's mistake. She'd indulged herself with this meeting, needing, for some reason, to announce herself as his enemy. Perhaps she'd even believed she could again reach him, cause him pain.

As he'd said, he'd begun to suspect she was the shadowy figure behind the church, but she'd handed him certainty. The only thing she'd gained from the parley had been annoyance. Her assurance the church had no designs on southern Donradé obviously wasn't worth the spit in her mouth, but perhaps she believed he could be duped.

He waited as the hoofbeats outside receded, then climbed out the window and strode to the thicket where he'd hidden his horse. Staying cowled, he rode through Sazian Linistia, across the bridge, and back to the palace.

Jonfré sat waiting for him in the room he'd given Scarface. "Did you find out anything useful in your meeting?"

"A little. Mendarian's with the church. She's apparently waiting for the right moment to step out of the shadows and onto a throne. Her wait may be longer than she anticipates."

"Don't underestimate her. I've heard wives are the most dangerous enemies."

Scarface chuckled. "Is that why you've never married? Rest easy. Mendarian and I are no longer married."

Jonfré grinned. "Who has time to be married? Opposing a king takes all my time. And how does it happen you're free?"

Scarface explained, in as few words as possible, how he'd lived among the Dieri for the last three years.

"So," Jonfré said, "you've taken up herding sheep. That somehow seems appropriate for a former king. At least you came to the task with experience." He poured a cup of the cloudy, corrosive liquor and offered it to Scarface, who shook his head. Jonfré shrugged and sipped at the cup. "Did you learn anything more about Queen Ukena, or her son, Terralyn?"

"Nothing." Scarface was ashamed to admit he'd forgotten them in the rush of recent discoveries and immediate problems. "Have you?"

"Only a peasant's rumor. There're stories about a hermit-magus living in an old holding about fifty leagues north and west of here. It's less than a league from our border with southern Glangurra. The story is doubtful. The peasants in the area claim the place is haunted, and ascribe any misfortune to the spirits in the place, or to the hermit."

"Do the rumors provide any reason for the spirits or the magus to want to steal away the queen and her son, or how it was done?"

Jonfré leaned back in his chair. "The old holding was supposed to have been the capitol of a kingdom that encompassed Donradé, eastern Glangurra, and southern Gascolin. That was before the Sazian empire conquered southern Donradé. I don't know how true the story is, but it's ancient. The country around the holding is hilly and remote, and the people there have an atrocious accent. The joke goes that the men there marry their sisters because nobody else will have either of them."

Scarface frowned. "Were you going to do anything about the rumor?"

"I was thinking of sending four or five men. It'll be difficult to find soldiers who'll go. There are also stories that few go into that region, and even fewer come back out."

Still frowning, and tapping the table with his fingertips, Scarface considered. The ship he'd take wouldn't sail for a fortnight. If he could find the holding, it shouldn't take more than six or seven days. Also, the annoyance of having to keep his face hidden in Linistia was beginning to make him feel like a prisoner. "If I may borrow two horses and have provisions, I'll go."

Jonfré shook his head. "Too risky. Like many such stories, there's a kernel of truth in the bushel of exaggerations. I believe travelers are waylaid there. Were our situation more settled, I'd lead an army in and clean out the place."

"So far, I've come out of every place I've gone into. And while I'm gone I'll be out of the reach of Mordach's church."

Jonfré studied Scarface for a long moment, then took a deeper drink. "At least let me send some men with you."

"Just give me the mounts, the provisions, and directions to the ruins. Too many men might stir up a storm. If you don't mind my wearing out the horses, I can go more quickly and attract far less attention."

Jonfré finished off the liquor in his cup. "I never seem to learn. I can't win an argument with you, nor can I keep you from whatever madness you have in mind, short of having you clapped into the dungeon, which wouldn't do my reputation for hospitality much good. You do have a knack of crawling into a pile of horse apples and climbing out holding a crown and smelling of flowers. Let's just hope your luck runs true."

"Thank you. I'll leave just after sunset. That should keep my going sufficiently discreet."

~ * ~

A league from Linistia, Scarface drew rein in a strip of forest. The moon was only a sliver, and traveling at night on horseback was risky. He hobbled the horses, unsaddled his mount and hauled the pack off the other, then found himself a soft place to lie down. It was a relief to be away from the city and the necessity of remaining hidden.

Mendarian's siding with the church troubled him. She was probably doomed. Her thirst for power could never be quenched, and that thirst would likely lead to her death. She'd deal with dangerous men—had dealt with dangerous men—to gain power she'd never learned to use.

His hatred for her hadn't outlived his love—if that's what it had been—and all that remained was regret at the waste. She'd never be satisfied, would likely die still thirsty.

He woke several times during the night, although he couldn't remember the dreams that had disturbed his rest.

He arose at dawn, loaded the horses, and set as fast a pace as he could manage without wearing out the animals. The day was hot, and he rested himself and the horses during the early afternoon, then pushed on until it was too dark to see the obscure trails he followed. Avoiding most towns and villages, he'd seen only a handful of people, and they only at a distance.

His was a cold camp, with no fire to attract curious eyes, but he seemed to see deep shadows flitting through the starlight, and again was troubled by dreams that vanished but left him in a cold sweat. And, although the next day was hot, he still seemed to feel a chill.

Had he not felt so strong a sense of obligation to Queen Ukena, he'd have returned to Linistia. He knew enough about magic to know there was even more about magic he didn't know. It was difficult—and dangerous—to try to guess where the line between truth and tale lay. All the power in his scars had barely been enough to save him from a spell Forgren had loosed, and the cost had drained the power from those scars. If the tales were even close to the truth, he couldn't guess at the power of the hermit-magus.

By sunset he was in different country than the gently rolling plains and low hills that made up most of Donradé. Ridges of bare rock rose steeply from the grass, and shallow canyons showed where rivers had once run. The changes in the watercourses had been so long in the past that the depressions had largely been filled in by deposition.

The evening camp was, like the others, comfortless. Barring misfortunes, he should reach the ruins in another day. He ate sparingly of the cold rations, his appetite gone. Again his sleep was restless and he could only, each time he woke, put himself back to sleep with difficulty. At first, he'd tried to think of Topaz to help himself relax, but he found himself worrying about her.

By dawn he was again riding to the northwest. As much as possible, he stayed in the forest, riding wide around any signs of habitation or possible ambush sites, and avoiding skylighting himself on the crests of ridges. Midafternoon found him at the tributary that ran past the holding and into the Bromron. He followed the river west until he found the ruins.

He almost missed the holding. In the fading light, what was left of a castle looked very much like a natural rock formation. After a cursory examination, Scarface guided the horses to a copse, where he tethered them. A trickle of water ran through the clump of trees, forming a pool only slightly larger than a puddle, before finding its way to the creek that ran north of the holding.

He forced himself to eat, knowing tomorrow he'd need all the energy he could demand of his body. Eager to get into the castle and be gone, he knew he'd need both a fed and rested body and enough light to let him pick his way over and through the rubble.

The horses seemed to share his uneasiness and, even in the faint light, he could see them rolling their eyes at the dark blot upslope. Only with difficulty could he get them to rest, and finding rest himself was even harder. Twice he woke with a start and managed to get back to sleep but, near dawn, he woke to the sound of maniacal laughter and saw two balls of green light playing about the remains of a tower.

He shrank from the sight and tried to forget the stories about spirits haunting the holding. Or had the hermit turned Ukena and her son into the glowing forms? He tried to steady himself, exerting his will to force back the fear.

The sky was beginning to lighten and he considered how he wanted to approach the place. With the sun at his back, he might have an advantage over an enemy with the sun in his eyes, but that also meant he'd be silhouetted. Although it was the shortest way, he wasn't about to come in from the west. That would put the sun in his own eyes. He decided to make his way south of the holding, to approach from that direction.

He gnawed a piece of dried meat and a biscuit, washed them down with a long drink of water. A cloak would likely be a hindrance, so he removed it and left it beside his saddle. He didn't want his scabbard tripping him, but he'd likely need both hands for climbing, so he secured his sword across his back, the hilt just over his left shoulder.

Recognizing the signs of reluctance, be began to move south by southwest, trying to always keep a screen of foliage between himself and the holding.

South of the castle, the land rose in a gentle slope littered by boulders. From what he could see of the ruins, most of the walls had fallen and the rest leaned and sagged like drunkards. He began to work his way up the slope, taking advantage of any shrub or boulder along the way. He stayed concealed for as long as possible, and several times he stopped to peer over or around his cover to study what he could see of the buildings. From this angle he could barely see the ragged top of the tower around which he'd seen the lights dancing.

The boulders around him, he suddenly realized, had been shaped. They'd once been part of the crumbling wall, and he realized some were tan limestone, some were gray granite, and the one behind which he crouched was black basalt. It was as if the builders had chosen stones for the wall for their color, and not their hardness.

Another thought kept him hidden behind the stone. If this hermit were mad, then he could be at least doubly dangerous. Scarface had learned some magi became mad, and as they lost sanity they gained power, as though they'd traded their hold on reality to more fully inhabit that place of dreams and intuition that were the insubstantial substance of magic. If there were a hermit, and if he were mad, he might well be more powerful than Hadrian, or even Harma, the dead archmagus of the Union. And in this, his place of power, he'd be like a deadly magical spider in the center of a web of spells.

Furthermore, the hermit would know each stone, every rathole, and his madness wouldn't only make him more liable to attack, but the attack would probably be unusual, and so, unexpected.

Scarface growled a curse at himself. The time to consider all this was long past. Now it was time to act, not to be paralyzed by fear.

He unstoppered his canteen and took a deep drink, then crept forward. Only a single stone, turquoise-colored and with streaks of what looked like rust, and a rise in the ground stood between him and the ruins. If he were casting spell-traps, he'd leave one behind that rock. This wizard probably didn't think as he did, but it wasn't worth taking the chance. He dashed past the stone and scrambled up the slope.

Reaching the crest, he threw himself to his belly in the short, wiry grass and looked into what had once been a courtyard. Like part of the wall, the tower leaned at a precarious triple angle, like a broken limb. Also like the walls, the tower was built of different kinds of stone and he could almost discern a pattern, although it was a strange, unbalanced one. The stones of the wall that hadn't fallen down the slope had tumbled into the courtyard, lying in a jumbled heap.

He saw no door at the base of the tower, then perceived an opening in what seemed only another pile of stones. Studying it more carefully, he realized it'd once been a building.

He chose a route—not the easiest way—knowing when he made his dash for the opening he'd be visible to anyone in the tower. He considered using the spell of concealment, but not being able to see his own hands and feet made the rush more dangerous. There was also the strong chance using any spell this near the magus' seat of power would be like carrying a beacon.

He ran his forearm across his face, saw the blotches of dampness on his sleeve, then gathered his legs under him and darted forward. He raced to where two stones stood nearly together and sprang over the stone to his right, dodged left past a block of granite, then angled right. If someone were up there with a bow, he had no intention of making it easy for them.

He bounded over a boulder so covered with moss he couldn't guess what sort of rock it was, spun right, ran four paces, then broke left. Clearing a last boulder, he raced for the wall beside the opening.

He paused for a moment to recover his breath and let the trembling in his legs cease, then gripped the edge of the doorway.

The scream seemed to come from right beside him and he recoiled. Again he paused to steady himself, let his heart have a moment to stop trying to hammer its way out through his ribs and his lungs to get the air they seemed to need.

Trying to understand what had happened, he cautiously reached out again to the doorframe. This time he was prepared but the scream still unnerved him. It was an alarm spell. Stealth was no longer a choice.

He rounded the doorframe and dashed into the building, trying to ignore the third scream. Despite the open door, the air seemed stale. Crouching against the wall, he tried to see into the darkness.

As he peered into the ruin, something tickled the back of his right hand. He frantically tried to shake off whatever had crawled onto him, then stopped, straining to hear.

Something had scurried away into the deeper darkness. At least, he hoped it was moving away.

He had the sense of being stared at by lurking shapes, could almost make out their misshapen forms. This damned place was turning him into a child again, afraid of the monsters just outside the circle of firelight, fearing the things that moved in shadows and made the shadows move. This ruin was turning his own best weapon, his imagination, against him. He'd relied on that imagination to give him advantages or to seek them out, and now it was searching for the means to his own destruction.

Gradually his eyes became used to the darkness and he swore. Whoever had built this holding must've been part rabbit. He could see five openings, any one of which might lead to the tower. He remembered the tower was to his right from the entryway, and upslope. He chose the opening to his right and crept that way.

In half a dozen paces he felt the floor slant upward and was sure he'd taken the right passage. Suddenly he stopped again. He couldn't see his footing, and even a small hole in the floor could cause trouble. There had to be some way to be sure of what he couldn't see.

There were no sticks inside the building, nothing but stones and dust, then he saw a way. He unbuckled his belt. He unhooked the knife's sheath and slipped it into his right boot, then drew his sword. He made a cut in the belt, near the end, then hung the belt from the point of his sword and thrust it ahead, into the darkness.

He could hear the rattle of the buckle on the stone floor, and raised the blade until only the edge of the buckle scraped across the stone, then, probing ahead, he followed the tunnel. The floor became level and, in a dozen paces, he found the tunnel widening, to form a small room. Following the right wall, he found where the tunnel narrowed again, but it turned sharply left and began to slant downward.

The tunnel sloped downward for a dozen paces, Scarface had to resist being hurried by the grade. Suddenly the buckle touched something with an almost musical sound.

Stopping, he knelt and began gently probing ahead with his fingers, extending himself until he was on hands and knees, then his fingers brushed the wire. The wire was either ancient or very new, since he couldn't feel any rust on it. Pushing himself back onto his heels, he considered.

Obviously, whoever lived here didn't use this passage. One doesn't trap the corridors one walks—too many chances for an accident. Knowing this, there was no reason for him to continue down the passage, but it might be an opportunity for him to regain the element of surprise.

Stripping off the thin leather jerkin he wore, he used his knife to make a series of lengthwise cuts. Relying on his sense of touch, he made a series of small cuts, so he had a leather thong long enough to let him trip the wire from the top of the incline.

Gently, he tied one end of the thong to the wire and carefully backed away, playing out the thong as he went, until he'd reached the leftward turn. Using the wall as protection, he knelt on one knee and tugged at the wire. A groan was followed by a roar, and the wall against which he leaned trembled. Dust rolled in a smothering wave up the tunnel and Scarface crept back through the room to wait at its outer entrance.

He had to struggle to keep from coughing, and took another sip of water, then continued to wait. He was hoping the hermit would come to see the body but, after waiting a quarter hour, he stretched cramped muscles and crept back to the main passage.

Knowing these passages had been laid out to an incredibly complex plan—or to no plan at all—one tunnel seemed as good as another. He chose the passage next to the one he'd just left. Again using his belt dangling from the tip of his sword to probe ahead, he crept onward.

This tunnel began with a downward slope, then took a sharp turn to the left. As he turned with the passage he saw dim light ahead, then halted as he could see shafts of sunlight lancing through gaps in the wall and, by that light, the heap of stone blocking the tunnel. Only a few motes danced in the beams of sunlight, so he guessed this tunnel had collapsed long ago.

Again he retraced his steps to the entryway. With three tunnels yet to be explored, he decided simplest was best and slipped into the next passage to his left. Again he probed ahead.

Three paces into the tunnel he heard a loud groan and cowered, sure the wall was falling, then realized the sound was another alarm spell. He cursed aloud, knowing silence was worthless, and heard a shrill laugh echoing down the passage. The high-pitched laughter was more threatening, and more chilling, than a battle-cry.

Again, all his choices had been snatched from him, and the only thing to do was to press ahead. He continued to probe his way ahead, through a turn, then saw a flickering light ahead.

He reclasped his belt around his waist and crept forward, the sword in his hand offering less reassurance than he thought it should. The passage took another turn, in the opposite direction, then light filled a doorway, and beyond it he could see another small room with two openings and a blazing torch in a wall sconce.

He'd turned right each time he'd had a choice. It was better to continue the pattern as a hedge against getting lost in this damnable maze. The right-hand passage led downward and curved right, and he could see light from another torch ahead.

He suspected the hermit had lit the torches to show his way to the place of execution, but there was no point in following a path leading away from his quarry. He continued moving ahead.

The light came from another flambleau thrust between two stones in the tunnel wall. Just beyond the torch, the tunnel widened again. He ducked under the torch and investigated the room. It was bare, with only one other exit. Once, it might've been a guard station. He crept through the exit and the corridor, which ran straight for twenty paces, then turned left. At the corner, he could see another flickering light ahead, perhaps a spear's cast away. A dozen paces into the tunnel he noticed an opening in the wall to his left. He also observed that a ledge, a little higher than he was tall, ran along the left side of the passage. From what he could see, he guessed the ledge to be not much wider than the length of his arm.

The light at the end of the passage seemed to come from an opening to his right, and he assumed that it was cast by another flambeau, then the light became brighter, as though someone bearing a torch were walking toward the tunnel from a room to the right.

Retreating back to the opening to his left, he slipped into it, then peered around the corner to see who was carrying the light. What he saw made his feet suddenly feel icy. It was no torch carried by a man; the light was a beast made of flame. Scarface ducked back into the passage, sweat starting from his face and body.

"Find him, Bootsi-pet." The voice was thin, perhaps that of a child, or an old man, and the language wasn't Gasgoran. Scarface could read Oldtongue, and he'd heard it spoken, although he didn't speak it himself. He could understand it because it was similar to Gasgoran, and he guessed this was the "atrocious accent" Jonfré had mentioned.

He pressed himself against the stones, trying to keep his sword from clattering against the wall, wishing he could press himself through the stone. The crackling and hollow roaring of a fire was coming closer. He tried to make his breathing slow and shallow, and seemed to be able to hear his own heartbeat.

The light grew brighter and the sounds louder, then a hound, or a living fire that looked like a hound, stalked past him.

Heat accompanied the hellbeast, and Scarface held his breath, afraid even the faintest sound would attract its attention and an immediate attack. He let the breath slowly, silently leak out, then side-stepped into the passage down which the thing had come.

The hound had continued down the corridor and stood at the corner of the turn.

A thin, high cackle sounded somewhere to his left and above him, but the echoes in the passage made it impossible to trace the sound. "Good Bootsi. If he comes back, you can eat him. Now we listen for the groan alarm again, my pet. If he doesn't get that far, we'll go hunting him."

Scarface could guess the hermit was somewhere to his left and above him, but it was safer to try to slip past him than to try to find him before the hermit could have the hound on him. Every side-step seemed to take an hour to complete, and the passage seemed to have grown longer.

"He's not past the alarm, Bootsi, so he's somewhere in that— ah, how silly of me. I'd forgotten the old ways to the mews. Come back, Bootsi, and we'll look down that way."

Scarface couldn't look at the beast with flames for fur. He was afraid it could see him if he saw it, or perhaps it could feel his gaze on it, and it would be on him instantly. With his eyes tightly closed and his head turned away, he continued to creep down the passage certain that, at any moment, the thing would spring on him.

Even through his eyelids he could see the passage had darkened, and he cast a glance back. The light was receding down the side passage in which he'd hidden moments before.

He moved his feet slowly and carefully, wary of traps and carefully placing his feet level on the floor, wondering if another beast from hell would appear, fearing that Ukena and her son were indeed here, afraid that he'd find them. This place had to be some outpost of the land of the tormented dead, and he was afraid to see their agony; afraid, too, that he was trapped here forever, that he'd never see Topaz again.

The thought of Topaz seemed to lend him strength. He'd nearly reached the door when he heard another shriek of mad laughter.

"This one is rare sport, Bootsi."

He ducked into the room from which the beast had come. It seemed to be a kitchen, with a great fireplace, two large tables, bundles of what he hoped were vegetables hanging from the low rafters. Beside the fireplace lay bundles of wood and a large crock of water.

Staring around the room, he sought a place to hide, but the room was too open. Something rattled and he spun to see a piece of wood had fallen from the black irons on which the logs rested. He took a step toward the fireplace and realized the logs were slowly turning black and scaly, with a powder of white ash spreading over them, although the fireplace was dark and silent. Another step closer and he could feel warmth, as though there'd been a fire in the hearth, but it'd been extinguished some time before.

He heard a scuttling, scuffing sounds of footsteps approaching, then the voice spoke again. "Let's wait for him in the kitchen, Bootsi, where we can both get something to eat."

There was a connection Scarface could sense but not understand, but he knew the logs scaling to ash were important. He unslung his waterskin and dashed the cup or two of water remaining onto the logs.

The scream from the passage made him wheel, then footsteps scurried toward the kitchen. A twisted, dwarfish figure leaped to the floor, and the firehound raced into the room. It seemed smaller, but sprang at him with the speed of thought.

Remembering the crock, he leapt for it, thinking to throw it at the hound, then realized the idea was right but the target wrong. He was beginning to feel the heat of the flames as he caught up the crock and flung its contents into the hearth.

The flames around him vanished, replaced by steam and a hissing sound, and he wiped his face with his left arm, astonished he hadn't been badly burned.

The little man fell to the floor as though struck, then moaned and stumbled to his feet. He screamed, "Bootsi! My pet!", then rushed at Scarface, his hands raised and his fingers hooked like talons. Scarface drew his sword and slashed over the madman, striking with the pommel rather than the blade. The dwarf fell and Scarface leaped atop him. A hand clawed for his eyes, and he struck with the pommel again, then held the base of the blade under the hermit's chin.

"Close your eyes," Scarface shouted. "Shut them and be still, or

I'll saw off your misshapen head."

Just before the little man closed his eyes, Scarface noticed one eye was a pale gray and the other as black as obsidian.

A closer look at what he'd caught repelled him. The hermit's body wasn't only dwarfish, it was twisted and uneven, with mismatched limbs, as though pieces of four or five men had been thrown together. The features looked as though they'd been molded in clay, then smeared by a careless thumb. The crooked head was bald on top, with a fringe of unkempt greasy tendrils of hair and, although both the hair and the scanty beard were dark and the face was unlined, there was about it some quality of great age. Tears appeared from under the lowered lids, and one dropped to the floor.

"Where are Queen Ukena and her son?" Scarface demanded.

"Who?"

"The Queen and Crown Prince of Glangurra."

The little man's voice trembled but grew stronger. "Upstarts. What has the King of Caramuega to do with petty nobility? Those of our line were kings while they were still following an ox and a plow. If they were here, they'd be tending my stables." The tears began again. "Bootsi, I'll never be able to bring you back again." He began to sob uncontrollably.

Scarface was caught between pity and revulsion. Once, he'd have, without hesitation, nailed this pathetic creature to the floor, but Morgan was a more reluctant killer.

"End it now," the little man sobbed. "End the line. Spill royal blood." He shuddered as his nerve seemed to break, then whimpered, "I don't want to die."

Scarface raised his sword, then stood and fumbled the weapon back into the scabbard across his back. "Kings shouldn't kill kings," he said, and extended a hand to the wretch cowering on the floor. "I regret I no longer have a domain, and the only tribute I have to offer is my absence and my silence."

The dwarf looked up, then accepted the hand. Once on his feet, he screwed at the tears in his eyes with his fists, then drew himself up. "Do you acknowledge, then, my rule of Caramuega?"

"What's left of it."

"Kings should also pay their debts," the magus said. He muttered something, then stretched out his hand. The hand disappeared as though he'd reached into a hole, then reappeared, clutching a globe of green light. The hermit tossed the light into the air, and the kitchen was transformed. Cooks and scullions hurried on errands or kneaded dough or carved meats, and two of them cleaned the fireplace while others marched into the room with armloads of firewood.

Scarface blinked and rubbed his eyes, but the scene remained, and he could hear the murmurs of voices and smell the aromas of food being prepared.

He decided it was safer to continue to play to the hermit's madness. "I beg your leave to depart, lord."

"There's time enough for that after I've paid my debt. The tribute you've given, paltry as it is, is the first we've received in six generations. Our line was renowned for our generosity. Follow me."

Scarface followed, his hand ready to flash to his sword if the hermit decided that the demise of Bootsi required another sort of payment.

The hermit scrambled awkwardly across the room, his mismatched legs and twisted back giving him a queer, rolling gait. They followed another passage out of the kitchen to a great hall dominated by a throne and lesser chairs behind a broad table, with other tables, flanked by benches, running almost the length of the hall. Rich tapestries billowed slightly in the spring-sweet breeze that made the flames of the hundreds of candles dance and flicker.

The hermit tugged at Scarface's sleeve. "This way."

They trod across a bright carpet as fine as spidersilk and through another arched doorway. A dozen paces from the hall, the hermit opened an elaborately carved door and led the way into a room containing shelves of books and bins of scrolls. If this library wasn't greater than the one at High Rage had been, it rivalled the other.

The magus stopped, his index finger against the side of his nose. "What would be a worthy gift? I have it! The scroll to make firepets!" He moved a chair over to a rack of scrolls and retrieved a piece of parchment rolled into a thin scroll and tied with a flame-red ribbon. He jumped down from the chair, the scroll in his left hand, and handed it to Scarface. As Scarface bent down to accept it, the hermit's right hand shot out, snake-quick, and his fingers pressed against the black scars.

The sensation was like lightning and fire, and Scarface felt as though he'd been branded again. He was unable to move, as if he'd suddenly turned to stone. A light flashed, perhaps inside his head, then everything was black.

~ * ~

His scars still burned and his head ached fiercely, each heartbeat causing a throbbing. He tried to concentrate on drawing power from the scars to relieve the pain and, almost instantly, the ache receded. He opened his eyes, found himself outside in the twilight. Or thought it was so. He had a sense illusion and reality were far more difficult to distinguish than he'd thought. He turned his head and saw the dark blot of the ruins but, for the merest flicker of a moment, thought he saw the building as it'd once looked, and he could almost make sense of the patterns of different-colored stones of the wall.

Raising his left hand to his chest, he felt a scrap of parchment, as dry as an autumn leaf, tucked into his shirt.

He remembered approaching the building, and flashes of memory returned, but they refused to fall into a coherent sequence. It were as though his memory was, if not rejecting some things, refusing to make them a part of his life. It all seemed as disjointed—and almost as nightmarish—as a dream, and it seemed to be slipping away like a dream.

He did remember, or thought he remembered, that he'd spared the life of the magus and had promised his silence. His fingers brushed the parchment and the part of him that was Morgan thought perhaps mercy had been rewarded. The darker part of him that was still Scarface argued that, had the hermit left him a statue in the hall or killed him, the moral of the story would've been quite different, but he wouldn't be taking instruction from it.

He hauled himself to his feet. From where he stood, his horses should be to the left. Moving as quickly as possible in the gathering dusk, he set out for his campsite. He stopped often, looking back at the ruins to judge his location, until he heard a whinny to his right. The horses had grazed circles around their tether pegs. He led them to water, then saddled one and loaded the other, and was able to get almost a league away from the holding before he had to halt because of darkness.

Even that far from the ruins, he was reluctant to light a fire, and he recalled what Jonfré had said about bandits. He ate cold rations and curled up in his cloak and a blanket. He thought of Topaz as he drifted into slumber.

He felt stronger in the dawn. It was as if his scars had grown more powerful, and a sense of well-being suffused his entire body. He was ready to ride as soon as there was enough light for the horses. The steady pace he set, and the solitude, granted him the opportunity to consider some of the things he'd learned or guessed.

If his intuition were correct, magic was a sharper weapon than any sword, and one more likely to cut its wielder. If the deep study of magic and its frequent use indeed led to madness, it was even more important to live fully in the world around one. Or perhaps only some magi were so affected. Harma had seemed sane enough, though unpleasant. Hadrian was the second most accomplished magus he knew, and Scarface wondered if he'd been affected by magic. With Hadrian, it was almost impossible to guess. The man had always exercised an iron control, never revealing his own feelings, always apparently unmoved. Scarface had noticed that only with his wife and children had Hadrian dropped his air of reserve. He wondered if that, in itself, weren't a form of madness. Certainly the revenge his adopted brother had extracted from the Union for the deaths at High Rage and elsewhere had verged on madness.

A sudden insight occurred to him. Perhaps the danger was greater when magic was studied for its own sake, as an end in itself, rather than simply learned and used as a tool or a weapon. Or, perhaps, when it was used to escape from the world rather than to affect changes in it.

He'd had enough of magic in the last few days to sate his interest for a long while. It was better to be alive in the world that could be seen, weighed, savored. Although the day was hot, he enjoyed the heat and even his own sweating, appreciated the creak of the honest leather of the saddle, the steady gait of the horse under him. He'd come too close to dying not to realize that life was sweet, that even the discomforts and annoyances were precious.

Nightfall found him camped beside a creek. Desperately needing a bath, he watered the horses and refilled his waterskins, then undressed and washed himself in the stream, using sand to scour himself. The water was chill but not bitterly cold, and he also washed his travel-stained clothing. Finally, he started a fire, hanging his wet clothing on bushes near enough the fire that they'd at least be warmed. Perhaps it was the bath that caused him to think of Topaz, and he hoped she was well.

~ * ~

Two days later, at noon, he rode through the gate to Donradan Linistia. The horses he left at the stable would need a least a week's rest, but they'd recover.

He arrived at the palace while Jonfré was at table. Another platter was brought for him, and he seated himself and began to eat.

"I presume your quest was unsuccessful?"

Scarface finished chewing his bite of mutton and swallowed, washed it down with sour wine. "Ukena and her son were never there. It was only a peasants' rumor. One that might've been started by an enemy. I wonder whether Thienn or the church played a part in concocting the tale. I suggest you and your men stay away from that area."

Jonfré looked a question at him but didn't put it to words. Instead, he said, "We received answers to your messages, and a bundle. I've left them all as we received them for your return."

Scarface sprang to his feet. "Where are they?"

Jonfré dispatched a guard to bring the messages and the bundle, then said, "Sit down. Enjoy the food."

Scarface sat, but only fidgeted with his food, his appetite gone, snatched away by apprehension. As desperately as he wanted to hear from Topaz, he was almost afraid to read the message. After what seemed an hour, the guard returned with a bundle that was obviously a sword wrapped and bound in soft leather and two scrolled parchments. One was bound with a ribbon of royal scarlet and bore the wolf's head seal of the emperor. The other was tied with a pale blue ribbon, Topaz's favorite color. He opened the scroll from her immediately.

> *My dearest Morgan,*
>
> *I am well. Saril tells me we're going to have a daughter. I should like to name her Cari, after my mother.*
>
> *Life is still precious. And busy. My only regret is that you're not here to share it with me. I confess I sometimes forget about you. Yesterday, Saril and I delivered a baby. It was a difficult birth. At the time, I was too busy to think of you, but later I wished I could show you the baby and tell you how exciting it is to be part of the new life. Experience is better savored in the company of those we love.*
>
> *The messenger said you'd dropped your disguise, so I sent your sword and your knife. I've made a wish on them that*

they serve you well and help bring you home hale and sound.
I look forward to sharing my life with you for many more
years to come.

All my love,
Topaz

Scarface's eyes stung and he felt a fullness in his chest. For several long moments he couldn't trust his voice, then he laughed, a release of tension and an expression of complete satisfaction. When he was sure of his control over himself, he cut the thongs wrapped around the bundle and drew out his sword and knife. He laughed again as he held the hilts. He could almost feel Topaz's wish and the power it gave him.

Standing, he drew the sword from its scabbard, whirled it through a series of practice slashes and thrusts, then sheathed it with a clash and placed it on the table to pick up the message from Orhan. It was also written in Gasgoran, and Scarface was certain it'd been written by a scribe, who'd translated for the emperor.

Scarface,

I've carefully considered the question of alliances with Donradé. It's not in Cerco's best interests to be allied with a king of doubtful legitimacy. Whatever benefits the empire might gain would be temporary, and, should the king be deposed, the empire would suffer for its support of an unpopular regime.

For those reasons, I'm sending a message to King Thienn renouncing the treaty between his court and ours. I doubt he'll try to attack Cerco. If he's fool enough to try, he'll break his army's teeth trying to bite a stone.

If you wish to hire Senshenni or warriors of other tribes, you may do so with my blessings.

The war between Ghiblein and Abaransa is still in a state of truce. They're discussing peace—as they have, off and on, for the last hundred years. We're presently trading with both countries, and neither has made another demand for an alliance.

We're all well here. I'm keeping a bottle of mead for you.

Orhan, Emperor of Cerco

Scarface was momentarily distressed that Orhan had addressed him by his use-name, then realized that if he were speaking to a scribe, Orhan was simply exercising discretion. He read to Jonfré that part of the message that concerned Thienn, then began to eat again. The messages were like spices, improving the flavor of the meal.

After finishing, he stared at the ruins on his platter and suddenly thought of Renay. He experienced a pang of remorse and stronger regret, but realized there was nothing he could do for the boy now but to see the kingdom was in worthier hands than Thienn's or the church's.

After excusing himself, he returned to his room, where he read again the message from Topaz.

~ * ~

In the days before his ship was to sail he composed a brief reply to Orhan and a longer one to Topaz, sending them by another courier. He also visited tailors, jewelers, leatherworkers, and cobblers in Sazian Linistia, where he had dress crafted to his tastes, so by the time he boarded the ship he had, in a trunk, garb that fit both his body and his temperament.

He'd decided he'd visit a nephew in the Empire of The Book before going to the church of Ianno, and it was appropriate he dress so Damon would know him by sight.

CHAPTER 5

Scarface was never comfortable aboard a ship. He adjusted to the motion of the sea without losing more than a meal or two, but he always felt vulnerable on water, where he had not a vestige of control over his fate. He was at the uncertain mercy of the sea and the wind, kept from drowning only by a flimsy wooden vessel and confined to an area smaller than some inns he'd visited.

Once out of sight of land, he donned the black shirt and leggings, the black leather jerkin that extended to the upper thigh, and the black boots that ended in points on the outsides of his legs, points that just touched the bottom of the jerkin. He wore again his own good blades and pretended to power the sea would not quite allow him to believe was his.

He learned the ship as a prisoner learns his cell. He appreciated the irony of naming a merchantman *Zarin Hestaprin*, which, he learned, meant "*The Lady of Hestaprin*," and the crew referring to the merchantman as "she." If the name were at all appropriate, he had no desire to meet the lady, who would be stout, pot-bellied, and weatherbeaten. The vessel was twenty-five strides long, eight wide, and the tallest of the three masts was almost as tall as the vessel was long. There were ports and benches for oars but they seemed little used. The Sazians took pride in their seamanship and, to them, oars on a merchantman seemed an admission of failure.

A sort of cabin stood on the foredeck and a larger one on the afterdeck, where the crew hung their hammocks. Above the aft crew cabin were three tiny cabins; one for the captain, one each for passengers. Scarface presumed the other cabins were as small as his. He had only room enough for a hammock, with his trunk stowed beneath it.

The ship, with its lateen sails the color of saffron and its weathered gray hull, ran with the wind and the current past the coast of southern Glangurra and Pitlahsa. As intensely as he disliked traveling by sea, he was forced to admit that, under favorable circumstances, the oceans were swifter and more tireless than any horse. The voyage from Linistia to Pitlahsa had been accomplished in but six days.

He stayed in his cabin when the ship docked at Wimarik, in

Pitlahsa, to on-load exotic woods, and again at Sarma-Nala, when they took on loads of the fine cloth of Shatilla.

The northern current had borne them swiftly along the coast of Shatilla but, once clear of the port, the captain headed his ship westward, well out of sight of land. North of Shatilla lay Bildesh and, while the merchants of Shatilla were renowned thieves, the reavers of Bildesh took more avidly without even the weak balm of oily words or making any bargain sharper than a sword's edge.

Decades before, the reavers had sailed in great fleets and harried the coasts to the south, even raiding inland by as much as two days' march, but the Sazian empire had its own fleet and they'd taught the raiders circumspection if not honesty, and now it was rare to see more than one or two of the corsairs at a time, and they kept to their own waters, although they were quick to attack any single ship they found in those waters.

Two days out of Sarma-Nala, the lookout shouted a warning and pointed landward. The captain swore fluently in three languages and ordered his men to arm themselves. Men dashed belowdecks to return with crossbows and short, heavy swords, some donning armor. In half an hour Scarface could see two sets of square-rigged sails on the eastern horizon.

For all her ungainly shape, the merchantman ran like a hare, but the two Bild ships chased her like greyhounds, and steadily gained on her. The captain ordered the ballistae readied and the crew pulled the canvas covers off the war engines mounted above the fore and aft cabins and assembled a springal amidships.

Scarface watched the preparations with great interest—his life was part of the cargo they were trying to save. The merchantman had one advantage; while the reavers would be reluctant to sink their prey until after it'd been plundered, the ship's crew could and would use any weapon or tactic to damage or destroy the corsairs.

When the crew set a brazier near the springal, Scarface remembered the scroll he'd acquired and dashed to his cabin. The parchment was still in the pouch he'd worn boarding the ship.

The vellum was dry, and cracked in places and the directions and the spell itself were written in faded ink in a spidery scrawl. The fire required several kinds of wood, and pitch as well. The incantation was an invocation to the fire to give birth to the power within itself. The creatures of fire had no life or will of their own; they were totally subject to the will of the magus, and if the fire were extinguished before the creature returned to it, it would be impossible to conjure that particular creature of fire again.

When he returned to the deck the raiders were nearer. He could see they were shallow-draft vessels, and so, rode higher in the water. In the bow of each ship stood a tower with a ramp that could be dropped or raised, like a drawbridge. At the tops of the raised planks were steel fangs. When they closed with their prey, the Bild would drop the ramp, driving the spike into the deck of their victim, holding it fast while fighters would swarm up the tower and across the ramp.

Scarface strode to where the captain stood on the deck above the aft cabins. "If I may use that fire and some of your cargo, I might be able to rid you of those ships."

The captain stared at him in obvious appraisal. "What do you need?"

"Two billets of pine and one of blackwood. The pitch you have already. And something of value to sacrifice. A bolt of Shatillan silk should be enough."

The captain looked at his crew, grimly preparing for battle, then at the two ships. "Very well, but those Bild devils aren't going to wait long."

While the first mate scrambled into the hold for the cloth, Scarface gathered the wood he needed from the lumber stored on the deck. He fed the wood and the cloth into the brazier, added the pitch, and watched as the flames leaped higher. He began to gesture and invoke the power in the fire.

A flame leaped, snake-like, from the brazier, and he seemed to see in it a scaly, serpentine neck. It collapsed into the brazier, then shot upward again. Now the neck ended in a head with long, fanged jaws, and two more pennons of fire gave the appearance of folded wings. The figure seemed to be fighting its way out of the brazier as a chick struggles out of its egg.

Unbidden, a name leapt to his mind and he shouted it, knowing it was the name of the dragon he'd conjured. The form in the blaze shot upward once more, then its bat-wings of fire clutched at the air and lifted it higher.

Scarface knew he must concentrate on this beast, keep it on the leash of his will. He commanded it to attack the nearer ship, still out of range of the ballistae. The dragon soared higher, then stooped and struck like a hawk, clung to the mast, and began devouring the leather-reinforced sail. Scarface was only dimly aware of the screams of the Bild raiders as bits of burning sail fluttered to the deck, and more fire raced up the sail and rigging.

The ship heeled over as it turned away, and Scarface willed the dragon to rise again and attack the second vessel. Again the dragon clung to the mast, this time clawing its way up as it set the sail afire. As soon as the sail was engulfed, Scarface called it back. It shot upward like a hurled flambeau and hovered, seeming to resist his summons, then, slowly, spreading its wings, it began to descend. Scarface heard the scream of one of the merchantman's crew and, for an instant, was tempted by the power of his ally, then he commanded it to return to the brazier.

Lashastur the dragon vanished into a mass of leaping flames and Scarface flung a bucket of water onto the burning wood, then crewmen scrambled to throw more water into the brazier. He couldn't tell if their fear was that the leaping flames would endanger their own vessel or that the dragon would return.

Without a word to anyone, Scarface strode to the rail and watched the pirates fight the fires on their ships. As he watched, a flaming pitch-soaked line fell into a crowd of reavers causing more screams and even more frenzied activity.

He'd identified with the dragon. It was as though the spell had allowed some part of himself to find or assume shapes in the fire, to take on a life of its own; a part of him that reveled in power, and needed all the discipline he could muster to control.

He'd learned well that a taste for power was a trap. Power wasn't an addition to self, it diminished the self.

He scowled, not wanting to become again what he'd been before. Having power confined the soul rather than freed it. Each choice one made precluded other possibilities, turned them into impossibilities. He'd chosen to turn away from the illusion of freedom to embrace responsibility and harmony, where true freedom lay.

Now he was being drawn back into the trap of illusion. For the rest of the voyage, he and the sailors would distrust each other. He had a power they feared, one that made them feel weak in his presence, and led to envy and suspicion on their part. He'd need to be on his guard, and he resented the sailors for the enforced aloneness,

He'd been alone enough to know the difference between aloneness and loneliness, between solitude and isolation. Aloneness was part of being one who makes his own choices, for good or ill, answering calls only he could hear. It had nothing to do with the presence of others. He'd been as alone in a hall with a score of men sitting at his table, ready to leap to his bidding, as he'd been when he'd lived as a hermit in a cave. Loneliness was also a quality of the mind, independent of the presence of others, but included a bitter longing for contact with others.

Solitude was an acceptance of aloneness, of using it as an opportunity for reflection and growth. Isolation was imposed by others, or by circumstances. Ironically, it was a form of confinement, in which the one shunned is cut off from a sense of community. He had to choose whether to resist the isolation or use it to achieve solitude.

When he looked for the Bild ships again they were already beyond the horizon. He smelled food being cooked. Taking a platter of food and a cup of bad wine, he returned to the rail, staring at the empty horizon as he ate.

~ * ~

The captain took his ship wide around Bildesh, not returning to within sight of land again until they could see the boggy coast of Ianesk. Two days later they reached the port of Galkar, at the mouth of the Vanaktor River, which led to the Great Inland Sea between Ghiblein and Porcash. There they unloaded the Shatillan fabric and took on a cargo of Ghiblin brandy, Bild steel, and polished gems from Ianesk.

The wooden buildings of Galkar were unimaginative, stolid blocks, which seemed to suit the temperament of most of the Ghiblins he'd met. Wit and subtlety were wasted in Ghiblein, where most of the inhabitants seemed unable to appreciate anything more refined than a kick in the ass. Their sole relief seemed to be drunkenness, and they had a reputation as guzzlers. Even their brandy was more noted for its potency than its flavor,

Another day's travel up the coast, they were caught in a sudden summer storm, and for most of a day Scarface had to tie himself to a line and endure being tossed about like a die in a cup. The ship was whipped and battered by lashes of spray and mountains of water, and the rigging whined in the wind like a frightened giant child.

He thought often of Topaz and his unfinished mission in Donradé, and it was terrifying to realize that, if the boat were swamped or shattered, neither love nor duty could save him from the ocean.

He'd always had a sense of his immortality. He saw his life as a tale, and felt he was just reaching the middle passages, the most interesting part of the story. He was, himself, the teller of the tale and felt that, while the ending was in doubt, it'd be appropriate. Now he was forced to see the story might end anywhere or at any time, and the only point might be that some stories need not have a point.

At last the storm blew itself out and he spent the night and half the next day in his hammock, recovering from the exhaustion caused by enduring hours of terror. When he emerged from his cabin he had to endure the glares of the sailors, who appeared to believe that if he hadn't caused the storm, he'd at least had the power to stop it. When one of the Sazians started fingering his dagger, Scarface ostentatiously began to whet his sword and his long, double-edged knife with its section of jagged teeth near the guard. This accomplished little, save to make the glares more furtive.

It seemed the sky had lost its breath trying to blow them under the sea, and they were becalmed for two days. Scarface was beginning to try to find a way to help at an oar and still be ready to defend himself when a breeze finally rose from the west.

As the ship slowly sailed past the coast of Porcash he stood at the rail, staring. By the afternoon of the second day he could see the promontory at Cragsness and knew they'd reached the "neck" of Porcash, and his voyage was nearly half over. Perhaps a hundred leagues to the south lay Sin Garlef, and another ninety more the Harsherf Sea, where he and Hadrian had grown up, and where he'd been given his scars. There were other scars, too, and, while they were less visible than the ones on his face, they were more tender.

Having learned to know the members of the Winged Dagger Clan at High Rage, and at a few other holdings, it was as hard to imagine his father being related to them as to imagine a sheep as part of a wolf pack. His father had hidden himself in Sin Garlef and lived like a rabbit, always ready to flee.

That life of cringing at every shadow made the man covertly vicious, and any feat Scarface had accomplished that had attracted attention had also attracted a voice hissing reproaches and a beating. Even Hadrian, who'd been adopted by the family had felt the sting of a belt more than once.

Scarface wondered if Hadrian still bore scars. Nothing seemed to affect Hadrian; it would be like supposing that whipping marble with a feather would raise welts. Still, while Hadrian was an enigma, Scarface had come to understand the man had feelings, and they were no less intense for being hidden. Perhaps they were even more intense because they were hidden. Certainly, the Union had paid a hideous penalty for its treachery and Hadrian had exacted the greatest share of that price. Was probably still exacting it, Scarface supposed, unless he'd killed the last of them, or had died.

Sin Garlef was a hard land of hard people. The Marked Ones had fought incursions from Porcash in the west, from Doss in the south, and from the Pednor nomads to the east. He'd fought three pitched battles before he was twenty, two of them as one of the Marked Ones. It'd been a harsh schooling, and the tuition had come high, but the reward had been to know that from Sin Garlef to Pitlahsa and Shatilla, only the Sazian Elites were as capable and only the reavers of Bildesh, and they only when the bloodlust was on them, were as feared in battle.

~ * ~

The wind picked up and, by the late afternoon he could make out the rugged hills of the Herrask Wastelands. The Wastelands were the skeleton of a region. The wind and the flinty sand had scoured away everything softer than the rocky bones of the land. He'd heard there were hidden valleys where enclaves of the old race of Niphtenic still lived. A small number of them also lived in northern Sin Garlef. Poker's mother had been one of those, and had bequeathed him the legacy of tightly curled blue-black hair and black eyes, slanting eyebrows, and pronounced canine teeth.

The old race was feared and, therefore, resented by many of the Sinni. From the little Scarface had been able to learn about them, they seemed similar in all but appearance to the rest of the Sinni.

In the south of Sin Garlef lived the descendants of the old aristocrats. They were equally different; white-haired and fine-boned, but didn't inspire the same dread or hatred, perhaps because they were far fewer. Hadrian's wife, Vornarei, had been one of that race of the old lords of the Harsherf Sea.

The ship, following the coast, turned southwest, then left the coastline to follow the chain of islands of the Tu Chicen archipelago. Most of the islands were little more than bare rock and hardly a bowshot long or wide, but a handful of the larger islands supported fishing colonies. For a full day they sailed eastward from the last island in the chain before the lookout sighted the shore of the eastern continent, where they followed the coastline to the Bay of Bayang Lon.

The captain announced he'd go ashore to bargain with the merchants and that, with the exception of the first mate and another man, the crew was free to visit the port.

Scarface took advantage of the opportunity to regain his land legs and strolled through the foreign quarter, looking for a place to purchase something more palatable than the meals prepared by the ship's cook.

The foreign quarter of Bayang Lon was inhabited by the peoples of many nations. Squat, swarthy Ianeski rubbed shoulders with blond Porcashians, olive-skinned Shattillans, and Dossmans, Myslans, Gascolans, and Glangurrans, as well as peoples from nations he'd never visited; people with skins like blackwood and others the color of old copper.

He found himself striding the street of the Dossmans and smelled something familiar. Turning his face to the breeze, he saw a small, open court only large enough for a couple of tables and some benches. Stepping closer, he realized the patio was actually part of a cottage, and could guess the cook and her family lived in the dwelling.

A middle-aged woman approached him, accepted a dozen copper coins, and led him to a table already occupied by another man. Scarface sat down across the table from the stranger, who appeared to be about his own age, nearing forty. The stranger glanced at him, nodded, and returned his attention to the meal before him.

The woman brought him a farrago, heavily spiced, bread made with cheese and peppers, and a cup of *akvad*. The *akvad* was even more potent than Ghiblin brandy, but held a hint of flavor.

It'd been years since he'd eaten such a meal, and the tears in his eyes weren't from sentiment. The spices also caused sweat to bead on his forehead, and his sinuses were suddenly clear. He ate and drank, savoring the spices and the faint plum taste of the *akvad*, and he remembered Poker had favored the cooking of Doss. He wondered if his cousin had ever eaten here.

Finally he sighed and leaned back from the table, sated. The meal had been excellent and, partly for sentiment, a payment for Poker, he handed the woman a small silver coin.

As he stepped out of the court his sense of well-being was shaken by a shrill whistle. He tried to locate the source of the sound, but half a hundred doorways and windows opened along the crowded street. Several other people in the street stood looking about, but no one seemed to respond.

Within three paces, one of the sailors from the *Zarin Hestaprin* staggered around the corner, obviously deep in his cups. He was a large, balding man, one of those who'd glared and fingered the hilt of his dagger on the voyage.

Scarface was instantly on his guard. The sailor staggered toward him but seemed not to see him until he was almost within arm's reach, then suddenly the Sazian drew his knife and sprang at Scarface.

Scarface was ready for the attack. He whipped out his own knife and threw himself forward, spoiling the sailor's attack by moving to his right. He spun and dropped into a crouch, his left hand forward and open, the blade of his knife pointed at the seaman's face. The sailor had also spun to face his opponent and he feinted, trying to draw Scarface out of his defensive stance.

Scarface cursed himself for a fool for forgetting that dogs hunt in packs. He feinted, using the maneuver to shift his knife to his left hand, drew his sword, and side-stepped to put his back to a wall. That whistle meant the attack had been coordinated and at least one other man was also a threat. He'd let the big man hold his attention, when others might, even now, be creeping toward him.

A hurled stone struck him in the ribs on his left side, and the sailor lunged again. He swept his knife hand around in a swirling attack to deflect Scarface's sword blade outside. Scarface had played that game before, and whipped his point around in a fast circular maneuver that left it inside the other man's attack, so that, as the sailor rushed forward, he impaled himself.

The sailor's eyes went wide and desperate, and he screamed. Scarface slashed with his knife from low to high, cutting the Sazian's wrist, then stopped the scream in his throat.

Ducking and side-stepping to his right, Scarface heard another stone hit the wall beside him. Another sailor, dagger in hand, rushed forward. As Scarface freed his sword from the corpse, the second sailor halted his rush. For a long moment they stood staring at each other, weapons bared, then, as Scarface stepped to the left, the sailor's nerve broke and he took to his heels. Another man also ran, and Scarface considered giving chase.

He decided it was more important to protect the chest on the *Zarin Hestaprin.* He wiped his blades on the dead man's left sleeve, then examined where he'd been hit by the stone. His leather jerkin had spared him worse injury than a bruise. It'd be painful but not dangerous, and he'd borne worse pain before.

He strode through the narrow, winding streets to the quays. In the maze of bales of goods and piles of sacked grain, it was easy enough to find a place to hide himself and cast the spell of concealment.

Hidden by the spell, he wove his way through the cargo stored on the dock to where the *Zarin* was tied and studied the ship, No one seemed to be on deck, although the first mate and another sailor sat on the afterdeck atop the cabins, passing a bottle back and forth.

He crept up the ramp and across the deck. The sailors had raised their voices, like most men who'd drank too much, as though their companions were deaf as well as drunk. The greatest danger of discovery came when he reached his cabin. He glanced up to see both men with their backs to him, pissing into the bay.

Opening his cabin door, he winced at the squeal of the hinges, slipped inside, closed the door softly, and examined his chest. It seemed not to have been disturbed. He took the key from the thong around his neck and opened the lock, but had to struggle with it. When he raised the lid he realized that the lock had been picked. Someone had pawed through his clothing. They'd left the fine blade he used for shaving, but the parchment was gone, as well as the pouch in which he'd carried most of his money.

A great rage began to well up in him. They'd stolen from him, tried to kill him and leave him in a strange city over two hundred leagues from his destination.

The fine blade he slipped into his purse, then stood and flung open the door of his cabin. He sprang outside, wheeled, and leapt for the afterdeck rail, almost missing it because he couldn't see his own hands. Drawing himself up, he hooked a leg over the rail and gained the deck. As he drew his sword he dispelled the concealment.

The sailors quailed at his sudden appearance and he swung his sword up to the *en garde* position. "Where are my possessions?" he demanded, glaring at their horrified faces, then looked directly at the sailor standing beside the mate. "Where are they?"

"I...I don't...know," the man stammered in heavily accented Gasgoran.

"Then I don't need you," Scarface snapped. He lunged, the point of his blade taking the sailor in the chest. He jerked back the sword and, as the dying man fell, kicked him over the aft rail into the bay.

He whirled, fixed the first mate with his glare. "Where are my possessions? I know you speak some Gasgoran."

The man could only gape at him, his mouth working but no sound coming from his throat.

"Don't try to lie to me. Who picked the lock on my chest?"

"Tavarin. It was his idea."

Scarface was able to match a face to the name; Tavarin was a small, rodent-faced man. He suspected Tavarin was the one who'd flung the stones at him. "When will the captain return?"

The mate replied with a shrug.

"Then we'll wait for him. In the meantime, hand over your purse."

Very slowly, the mate unbuckled his belt, handed it and his purse over in a hand that shook. Scarface snatched the purse from him, shook the contents out onto the deck, tossed the pouch back, then swept up the coins. Among half a dozen coppers and two marks of silver was a Donradan gold coin. "You were well paid for your part in the theft. It'll cost you all this, and perhaps more, if you give me cause. I don't think you'd swim with a hole in your chest any better than the other man did. Turn around."

The mate turned his back to Scarface, who cut a section of line and bound the man's hands behind his back.

"Now we'll go down and wait for someone to return." He prodded the mate in the back with the point of his knife and followed him down to the deck. They sat on the deck beside the rail, so they couldn't be seen from the pier.

"If you make a sound," Scarface said, "I'll kill you first, but not quickly. There are eight or nine places below the waist alone where you can be stabbed or cut without killing you quickly. I know them all. Remember that, if you're thinking of warning your accomplices."

The rail cast only a narrow strip of shadow and it was difficult to keep from slowly roasting in the heat but by the time they heard furtive steps on the ramp, the shade had crept halfway to the mast.

"Veramin? Shadin?" The voice was soft but urgent.

Another voice hissed something in Sazian and the sounds of footsteps on the ramp stopped, then began again, even more quietly. Scarface waited until both men were on board, then he reached out and slashed the nearer man on the inside of the knee.

The man screamed and his leg folded, then Scarface sprang at the other sailor, hacking at the wrist of his knife hand. He heard another scream and a knife clattered onto the deck. Dark eyes stared, horror-stricken, from a rat-like face.

Scarface grinned. "I doubt you'll pick any more locks with that hand, Tavarin." He glanced down at the mate. "If this little rodent doesn't speak Gasgoran, translate it into Sazian for me. I hate to waste my wit."

The mate spoke in rapid Sazian.

"Now, tell both of them to take off their belts. The one I hamstrung can toss me his purse. Tavarin can kick his to me."

Again the mate rattled off a few phrases in Sazian. The man he'd crippled moaned and whimpered, while Tavarin simply clutched his slashed wrist, glaring at Scarface. Both men unbuckled their belts and the pouches were shuttled across the deck to him. The cripple still had his gold coin with silver and copper, while Tavarin's purse was heavy with silver.

"Spent part of it already, eh?" He took the contents of the other man's pouch, stuffed Tavarin's purse inside his jerkin. He'd had a dozen marks of gold and had recovered a little over a third of that. He might've had more if he hadn't kicked the sailor's body overboard before taking his purse, but satisfaction usually had a price.

"Did the captain know about this?" he demanded.

"No," the mate replied. "We decided to rob you after the captain had gone ashore."

"How many of you were in it?"

"The whole crew."

"How many sailors will you need to man this ship?" The mate seemed not to be able to grasp the question, and Scarface repeated it.

"A dozen men."

"It looks as though you're going to have to recruit." Scarface regarded his prisoners. The others had stolen from him, but the two he'd wounded had tried to kill him, and failed through cowardice rather than compassion. Suddenly he stepped forward and, using both hands, swung his sword, nearly taking off the head of the man he'd hamstrung. Even before the body fell to the deck, he'd spun and slammed the flat of his blade against Tavarin's head. The little man dropped to the deck in a heap.

If Tavarin had picked the lock, he was the one most likely to have taken the scroll. He probably hadn't sold it yet, or he'd have had much more money in his purse. Also, something like the scroll would be difficult to sell, and would've taken more time than Tavarin had. Using his knife, Scarface cut the clothing away from the man and found the parchment in his canvas trousers. He carefully tucked the scroll into his jerkin.

After a moment's thought, he picked up the two belts from the deck, left a loop in one belt, buckled its end to the other belt. On the seaward side of the deck he tied the end of the second belt to the rail, then dragged Tavarin to the rail, lowered the loop over his head, and drew it tightly around his neck. Finally, he picked the man up and hung him over the rail, his face inboard, his legs hanging out over the water.

A bucket of fresh water stood beside the mast. Scarface picked it up and dashed the water into Tavarin's face. He had to catch the robber, as he almost fell from the rail.

"Listen carefully," Scarface said. "Your right hand is useless, but you can catch the rail with your left, but I don't think you can hold yourself up by one hand for very long. The longer you hang on, the longer it'll take you to hang. You decide." He shoved the sailor over the side.

Ignoring the sounds of the man struggling and battering himself against the side of the ship, he dumped the other body into the bay, then stalked back to where the mate sat. Even with the man sitting in the shade of the rail, Morgan saw his face had gone white.

"I'm going to assume you knew nothing about Tavarin and his friends trying to kill me. Otherwise, you'd be kicking beside Tavarin. Now, we wait, quietly."

The sun was half hidden by the bluff above the bay when they heard several unsteady pairs of feet on the ship's ramp, and rough voices trying to sing. Scarface signaled silence to the mate. The footsteps halted at the end of the ramp, then feet slapped against the deck, and Scarface watched as three sailors stumbled toward the afterdeck. Suddenly, one of them slipped on the blood. He began to fall, caught one of his fellows by the arm, and both of them tumbled to the deck.

Scarface struck the third sailor with the flat of his blade, sending him sprawling atop the other two, then struck the two who'd fallen.

One of them still had a Donradan gold coin. The other two purses were heavy with silver. Scarface trussed the sailors up with a rope from the deck, tossed their knives overboard, and returned to the rail.

He'd begun to wonder whether the captain was going to return before full dark when he heard heavy steps on the ramp and could just discern the captain's bulk against the lights of the port.

Scarface stood, his sword bare in his hand. "We have to renegotiate."

The captain recoiled from the sight of the blade. "What—?"

"Your crew told me you didn't know they were going to rob me, or that they'd try to kill me, but a captain is responsible for the crew under him. Let's discuss this in your cabin." He gestured with the sword, and the captain trod to his cabin as though afraid it would be his place of execution. With hands that shook, he struck a spark and lit a candle.

"Your men stole twelve marks of gold from me. I've recovered three of them, and these—" He tossed the five pouches filled with silver on the captain's table. "You'll make up the difference, of course. Also, you charged me five marks of gold for this voyage. Since you won't be delivering me to Tong Celuay, I expect one of those back."

The captain seemed to have recovered some nerve, probably at the mention of gold. "This is robbery," he sputtered. "I won't be—"

Scarface got the man's attention by waving the point of his sword a finger's length from the captain's face. "You should discuss it with your crew. They seem to be well acquainted with the concept of theft. I'm only making sure I leave this boat with most of what I had when I boarded it." As the captain opened his mouth, Scarface gestured again with the blade. "You've seen my power, and you have some notion of the degree of my annoyance. Beyond burning this scow to the waterline, you don't really want to know what I'd do if I became really angry. I could lay a curse on this tub that would have you welcoming a sword thrust. No more haggling. Hand over my gold."

At the mention of a curse, the captain's face had gone as pale as the candle. He reached behind him, slid out a small chest, and opened it with a key from his purse. He removed a handful of coins, counted out ten marks of gold, and slid them across the table to Scarface. His hands still trembled.

"Very good." Scarface's expression could only be called a grin because it showed his teeth. "I don't expect word of this transaction to be bandied about, especially in this port, since it might make it complicated for me to find passage to Tong Celuay. I'd find such a nuisance very annoying." He stood. "Good evening to you, captain."

He ducked into his cabin, snatched up his cloak and some other clothing, then strode across the deck and down the ramp.

Walking away from the pier, he returned to the foreign quarter. The clan had enjoyed good relations with the merchants of Gascolin. While he wasn't personally acquainted with any of the merchants, he knew them to be generally honest, though not fanatical about it. Their ethics had never kept them from overcharging.

He continued to walk until he reached a street where Gasgoran was spoken, and found an inn. A room to himself cost a mark of silver, and a meal, fifteen coppers. It was late enough he was the only one eating, but several men sat at another table, drinking. After half-listening to their conversation, which identified them as merchants, he stood and strode to their table.

The merchants stared at him cooly.

"I'm seeking a man of enterprise," Scarface said. The stares shifted subtly, from cool to calculating.

The man across the table from him leaned forward. "What sort of enterprise?"

"I'm bound for Tong Celuay. I need a translator to hire a boat. I have two ounces of gold to spend. I'll cheerfully give both of them to a man who can arrange passage for me and pay the ship's master." He let them work out the elementary arithmetic. He knew he was paying too much for what would probably be a bad berth on a worse boat, but he was paying for convenience.

The man across the table from him steepled his fingers. "I might be able to secure passage for you on a boat. Let's see the color of your money."

Scarface dug two marks of gold from his pouch, set them on the table. "I wasn't aware gold had more than one color."

"Ah, yes, there's red gold, white gold—myself, I'm fond of the yellow variety. Now that we've established that you have what I want, how soon do you want to sail?"

"I've rented a room here. I only paid for one night. I should stipulate that I'd prefer not to sail on a Sazian vessel."

The merchant raised his eyebrows. "The cost may be higher for such quick service and discrimination."

"We've already discussed the price." Scarface reached for the coins on the table. "If you aren't able to—"

"I didn't say that." The man covered the coins with his hand, then slipped them into his purse. "I presume I can find you here at the inn."

Scarface nodded. "I'll be here." He purchased a bottle of indifferent wine from the innkeeper and carried it upstairs to his room. Closing the door, which opened inward, he placed the bottle on its side beside the door. If someone tried to enter, the sound of the bottle rolling across the floor should waken him.

He undressed and lay down on the pallet, reflecting on the day's exigencies and deciding he'd done nothing of which he was ashamed, nothing he'd hesitate to tell Topaz. That seemed as good a guide to behavior as any he'd found.

Seaports were lawless places, even here in the Empire of The Book, but he'd done something to, perhaps, make the voyage safer for the next traveler. He tried to imagine Topaz in bed beside him, then slapped at an insect and decided he wouldn't want her in a place like this.

~ * ~

The ship on which the merchant had arranged his passage was a Batian fishing vessel. Although the fishing ship ran faster than the merchantman, the crew played out their nets at least twice each day, selling their catch to villages at which they stopped on their way down the coast.

Scarface had never developed a taste for fish, and a steady diet of fish for the first day, and having to sleep on a deck that reeked of fish, were enough to convince him to spend the second day fasting. It was a real relief when he saw the golden light of sunset gleaming off the stone towers of the port city.

Tong Celuay was noticeably different from Bayang Lon. There were fewer foreign ships in the port. He'd learned that *Bayang Lon* was Thani for "Gate of the Empire," while *Tong Celuay* meant "The Open Hand of The Saint." Bayang Lon was an imperial port, while Tong Celuay was more like any other city in the empire, with a *fali* ruling the city in the name of The Saint.

Scarface handed the ship's captain two more marks of silver, then strolled along the wharf to the foreign quarter. As before, he simply kept walking until he recognized the styles of dress and the language spoken by the street venders.

Even many of the foreigners wore the common dress of the empire; tunics, trousers, and low boots, with men of importance wearing short, circular capes. He found an inn, hardly more than a tavern, on the street of the Gascolans. The inn was primarily a gathering place for locals and saw few strangers, and so kept only a single room in the back of the tavern. He paid for the room and a meal.

The meat was chicken, adequately prepared, and the dark amber wine was surprisingly good. As he ate, he listened to the conversations around him but heard nothing to interest him. After he'd eaten he leaned back on the bench, his back against a wall, and sipped at another cup of wine and tried to understand what he remembered of the empire, and what he'd learned.

The Empire of The Book occupied an area half as large as the western continent, and with as many cultures. The threads that bound the empire together were a common language and a common religion. Thani was, like Oldtongue, a "father" language, from which many similar but different languages had been derived. Almost a thousand years ago The Prophet had preached and The Book had been written in Thani. The Book was the center and the heart of the faith of Ianno.

The Thanitur had spread the word of The Book by conquest, from their northern plains to the Batian coastal villages, to the mountains of Kesh, eventually expanding to the borders of Myslan in the southeast and Falvush to the northeast.

When The Saint appeared, six hundred years later, the first empire had already collapsed under the weight of swords. The second empire had grown from the first like grass on a grave.

The common language, forced on the subject peoples, allowed those peoples to coordinate their revolt. That language remained, even after the destruction of the Thanitur, as a means of trade, and the faith had, however unwillingly, been learned. Then The Saint had preached brotherhood and tolerance, and the religion had changed, had been transmuted into something accepted, rather than a yoke laid across the shoulders of subject peoples, a reward rather than a humiliation.

The church of Ianno continued to grow, although more slowly. Parts of Myslan, and even Falvush, had converted, even as the church was being persecuted in those places. A few people of the western continent had traveled to the empire and converted, and some of them had returned to the west. Iannists in the west were few, but had had an effect out of proportion to their numbers.

Somehow, in the inn, Scarface seemed to feel Poker's presence.

It seemed he no longer faced the world alone; he had a brother beside him.

~ * ~

The innkeeper, a gregarious man, was delighted to offer his help in assisting Scarface in buying a horse, gear, and provisions. Scarface learned the breed of horse favored in the empire had shorter, slightly stockier legs than their western cousins, and a more pleasant or, at least, more steady disposition. The innkeeper also taught Scarface a few of the more useful phrases in Thani and was able to give him directions to Tong Shavath, "The Shield of The Saint."

Tong Celuay was built up on terraces, forming, with the bay, a huge bowl, so the first part of his ride was up a series of switchbacks, making the way less steep but several times as long. Near noon he reached the crest of the ridge above the city, where he stopped to let his horse rest and enjoyed the view.

The city, largely built of stone, was tan in the sunlight, with roofs and garden patches of vivid green, receding down to the brilliant blue of the bay. Distance lent beauty to the ships in the harbor, although most of their sails were furled. To his right soared the highlands, and snow gleamed on the nearest peaks. To his left lay vast fields of grain around an orchard and a town. The sea moderated the region's weather, so it hardly seemed like late summer.

Turning his horse's head to where the road dwindled on the horizon, he clucked his tongue and nudged the animal with his heels. Most of the ride was to the northwest, on a road running parallel to the highlands. Even anticipating the inevitable saddlesores, Scarface was grateful to be again riding a horse instead of a ship.

He was hardly carefree. He'd once renounced his membership in the Winged Dagger Clan, and he had to wonder what his reception might be at The Shield of The Saint. Neither Hadrian nor any of the other brothers and sisters of the clan at High Rage had treated him as other than kin, even after his self-exile but, until he arrived there, he'd have no way of knowing whether word of his renunciation had reached The Shield of The Saint, nor how Damon would view it.

Solidarity and mutual support had been the basis of the clan. He'd heard the elders had once been the highest nobility in Pitlahsa but there'd been a war, then a revolt. The elders had been maimed and banished, been forced into hiding, but they'd sent their children to foreign lands all over the western continent, where the children's children were to grow and to learn until they received the order to gather.

That order had gone out in the Das wars, when the clan had supported the revolutionary theocrat. If the elders had forgotten about the dubious durability of a leader's favor, the theocrat had quickly reminded them. After awarding the clan a holding, the theocrat had made demands the clan was not prepared to accept, and they'd left Doss, ready to fight their way out.

The elders had made agreements through clan members who'd settled in other places, and other holdings had been established. Hadrian had been the visible leader and executioner of the clan, and he'd ruled High Rage in Gascolin, until the attack by the Union.

That had been another bitter lesson in the instability of alliances. The clan had encountered the Union in the Das war and had forged an alliance, albeit an uneasy one. Scarface had opposed the alliance from the beginning. He wasn't easily inspired to trust, and the members of the Union he'd met hadn't favorably impressed him. Even the name of their holding in Gascolin, Gain, had seemed to him a warning. He'd believed the Union interested only in Gain, both in wealth and in power.

To Scarface, neither wealth nor power had ever been an end in itself. He'd made the mistake of assuming power meant security. Despite his power and that of the clan, the Union's treachery had wiped out the clan at High Rage, and he guessed other clan strongholds had also been attacked. So much for finding safety in power.

Scarface had ample time for reflection. The Shield of The Saint lay almost a hundred forty leagues from the coast, a good ten days' ride. He'd come this way almost a decade earlier, had found ruins in the mountains, and had discovered an artifact, probably from the Age of Building. He'd learned the hard way the truth he'd taken for superstition: powerful artifacts from the ancient past carried a curse. Or, perhaps, the curse was simply being human and having great power—something envied by others. The effect was the same.

He rode through villages and small towns but never tarried. It had to be obvious from his dress he was a foreigner, but he rode unmolested. Since he'd forgotten most of the Thani he'd learned on his earlier visit and had never learned the local dialects, conversation was impossible. He did purchase supplies twice—the innkeeper had taught him the words for his needs—and was mildly surprised the prices asked for the provisions seemed fair.

The sight of the highlands reminded him of Cerco, and especially of Stag Mountain, and he was afflicted with homesickness. Two months had passed since he'd left Cerco, and it seemed even longer. It was as though he'd angered some malign, vindictive god. All he wanted was to return home and hold Topaz in his arms, but it seemed deposing a monarch or conquering a continent would be easier.

He desperately wanted Topaz to be well. If she died, there'd be nothing for him to return to, nothing but memories, and they'd be painful. The child she was bearing was his, but he'd be afraid to hold it if its birth caused Topaz's death; afraid the anger and pain would drive him mad and cause him to smash the child's head against a stone.

His emotions drove him one way, his mind another. No, it was even worse than that; his emotions drove him in two different ways. Topaz wanted the child, wanted it enough to risk her life giving it birth. It was hers as much as his, and to resent the child was to resent her. Had her father felt the same way about his daughter after the death of his wife? Everything was in flux, and peace was not to be found. He growled a curse and slammed his fist into the cantle of his saddle. If power weren't security, if it were only an illusion, it was at least a comforting illusion. Powerlessness offered no comfort at all.

~ * ~

By the ninth day of the ride from the port, the trail had moved nearer the mountains, which had become even more rugged. The peaks beside him were even more intimidating than the worst mountains in Cerco. They seemed an unbreachable wall protecting that part of the empire.

The chill wind from the peaks caused him to wrap his cloak tightly about himself, and he slept fitfully that night, shivering in his cloak and a blanket.

Before dawn he mounted and pressed on. The last fields and orchards were far behind him. The land through which he now rode was largely arid; the cold, dry wind leeched of moisture. The little vegetation he saw seemed hardly enough to support the herd of goats he saw in the afternoon, and he remembered The Shield of The Saint was one of the few clan holdings that hadn't been self-sufficient. It stood at the mouth of a pass, and the empire provided supplies in exchange for the defense it offered. At one time, the clan had provided some of the necessities and all the few luxuries the garrison there enjoyed.

Near noon of the eleventh day he could clearly see the fortress of The Shield of The Saint. The whole structure was built on a low, truncated cone, so the defenders had a clear, downward slope on all sides.

Hadrian himself had laid out the fortress, and it'd been as well planned for defense as any fort Scarface had ever seen. The walls weren't high, but were immensely thick and weren't, unlike those of most castles, stone curtains stretched between towers. Instead, they jutted out in angles like elongated pentagons with their bases open, so archers at the points and sides could launch arrows to any place on the facing wall. Any attackers approaching any part of the wall but the points would have to defend against missiles from every direction. The points themselves mounted siege engines; ballistae, towers for skins of burning oil, and catapults.

The road he followed was clearly marked by a border of rocks and he had no wish to ride off the road, although it ran at an angle that exposed anyone on it to the castle defenses. He suspected leaving the road would make life interesting but brief and unpleasant. Approaching the wall, he noticed trenches that followed the lines of the wall. The trenches would provide cover for archers far forward. At the bottom of the trenches, behind the walkways, stood sharpened stakes. All the ways from the wall to the trench ran under the rock on which the fortress was built. The gate on the near side was located between two of the jutting sections of wall, so that assaulting the gate would draw the untoward attention of troops manning the sides of the angled walls.

Above a central tower fluttered a flag bearing a gold circle on a field of blue; the flag of the empire. Above the gate flew the clan flag, with its winged dagger on its field of red, and hanging on the wall was Damon's banner, a black raven on a silver circle of moon, on a field of black.

Approaching the gate, he could see the walls were about three times his height, and he could clearly see guards, clad in clan livery, marching along the walls. One of them looked down behind the wall and spoke, gesturing, and, as Scarface rode through the gate, he saw a white-haired figure step out of the base of the central building and stride toward him.

Scarface dismounted, watching Damon approach. Hadrian's son had inherited much of his father's boneless, feline grace, both parents' slender builds, and his mother's white hair. Unlike either of his parents, he was tall; as tall as Scarface. Despite the illusion of age caused by the color of his hair, Damon was hardly more than a boy. Scarface tried to remember his age, guessed it to be near twenty, short or long by no more than a year.

As each man gripped the other's right forearm with his own right hand, Damon said, "Greetings, uncle. You've a gift for timing. We were just sitting down to table. And anticipating an attack within the next day or so. I've already dispatched couriers to Ong Vaun."

CHAPTER 6

Scarface grinned ruefully. "The first part of your announcement was far more welcome."

"You've changed, then," Damon said. He'd also inherited his father's unreadable black eyes and soft voice. "We've some Shannan wine we've been saving. What flavors do you prefer?"

"Plum, or pomegranate." He followed Damon into the building, along a passage, down a flight of stairs, and along another hallway to a room occupied by a table large enough for a man to lie down on with his arms outspread. The floor was covered by a rug and most of the walls were hidden behind tapestries. Light from the many candles in candelabra gleamed on the table top and the ornately carved backs of chairs. As they entered one doorway, a young woman carried a platter in through another.

Damon gestured. "Have you met my wife, Jeshka?"

Scarface bowed to the young woman, who responded with a nod. She had Mendarian's coloring; a pale, freckled face and dark brown hair, but her gray eyes had no coldness about them, although she seemed cautiously polite. She was also much smaller than Mendarian, shorter by a head than her husband, and very slender.

"I haven't had the honor," Scarface said.

"Our son, Danyol, is napping." He motioned toward a chair.

Scarface sat. "What's the attack you were talking about?"

"That conversation can wait until we've finished eating. You know the custom."

Scarface nodded. He helped himself to mutton from the platter, and bread. He was largely unfamiliar with the other foods on the table but sampled them and found them to his taste. "An excellent meal," he said to Jeshka, then turned toward Damon. "Have you seen your father of late?"

Damon had brought a flask of golden wine from the kitchen and poured some of it into three cups. "Hadrian last visited about six months ago. He's been here—" he thought a moment, "—three times in the last three years. As a matter of fact, when he last visited, he left a message for you. He said you'd find what you were looking for in Ong Vaun."

Scarface tried to guess what Hadrian could've anticipated his wanting in the empire. Perhaps Hadrian had already reached the conclusion Scarface had reached; that he needed an alliance with a god to be able to battle the church of Mordach. He finished the food on his platter, accepted a slice of some sort of melon with orange flesh. He finished the plum wine in his cup, and leaned back in the chair. "I hope Hadrian was well."

"He appeared so. He only stayed two days, then left to take ship to Porcash. He said he had some unfinished business there."

"I can guess its importance," Scarface said drily. There'd probably be a number of fresh corpses found in Porcash. That had been a Union stronghold. Forgren and several of his lieutenants had been from Porcash, and the Union had drawn reinforcements from there several times. "Did Hadrian speak the language?"

"Without an accent, I suspect. He said you also had a gift for languages." He poured another cup of wine for each of them, emptying the flask.

"That's one of the reasons I'm here. I need to speak Thani reasonably well, and I'd like you to ask the *Etrong Uven* for an audience for me."

"Both are easily done. Most of our troops here are native to the empire."

"Which brings us to the earlier question. What's this attack you anticipate?"

"Are you familiar with Myslan and its leaders?"

Scarface shook his head. "Only enough to know that I don't want a closer acquaintanceship with them. They say each village and hamlet has its own deity, most of them loathsome, fearsome, or both, and many of the local rulers dabble in the darker forms of The Art."

"Then you have the most important—" Damon was interrupted by a high-pitched scream of pure terror.

Scarface was on his feet and racing out the door, toward the sound, just behind Damon and Jeshka. He followed them down the corridor, his right hand gripping the hilt of his sword. They rushed into a room with a large pallet in one corner and, across from it, a smaller one on which a boy, hardly more than an infant, sat screaming. Jeshka swept the boy up and, after murmuring to him and rocking him, finally calmed him.

After a quick glance around the room, Damon signaled for

Scarface to return with him to the table.

Scarface stared at the lad, white-haired like his father, and the mother comforting him, then followed Damon out of the room. If he were looking for omens, he'd take this as a bad one.

Damon fell into a chair and sipped at his wine, staring at nothing. Suddenly his eyes focused on Scarface. "I keep spies and scouts across the border. They've been bringing me word that the *Alman* of Rikili is gathering an army. The *Alman* rules a province directly across the border from here. He's one of those who's dabbled in necromancy."

Scarface suppressed a shudder. He'd studied some forms of conjuration and thaumaturgy, but he firmly believed the dead were best left undisturbed. Those dead who deserved respect should be left with their secrets and their rest. Others were best left dead; he'd known several men he regarded as far better dead than alive, and he'd had no inclination to wake them.

Damon nodded, as though following Scarface's unspoken thoughts. "Myslan is ruled by a council of lords. If the *Alman* can successfully invade the empire, he'll gain prestige in the council and could gain a following among enough of the other lords to field an army to endanger the empire. We must stop him, here and now.

"I don't know his plans, but I've heard he's very powerful and has a brother who's also a necromancer, and mad. That makes him—them—doubly powerful and so, doubly dangerous."

Scarface finished his own wine, and noted the child had stopped whimpering. "Perhaps a thrust into Rikili could spoil his attack."

Damon shook his head. "All I know of his preparations is that his raid was set back by a plague in the province to his south, but he's gathered his forces. I'm sure he'll use the magic he and his brother know, perhaps to expand his army. I've considered a spoiling attack, but any attack that would do enough damage to upset the *Alman's* plans would require two or three times the number of men I have here, and would leave The Shield of The Saint unprotected."

"How many men do you have?"

"Two hundred fighting men, and another sixty people to defend. Most of the fortress is underground so, with luck, the *Alman* won't know the size of the garrison here."

Scarface rose and began to pace. "Don't count on having any secrets. Nothing known by more than one man is a secret." He stretched. "With your permission, I'll rest today and tonight, and tomorrow I'll do some scouting. I prefer to know exactly what I'm facing, and the best scouts are your own eyes. You haven't the freedom to do it, but I'm not commanding this fortress." He paused. "I presume you issue orders to your men in Thani?"

"Yes, Thani, horns, and a hanging steel bar."

"How do you keep the enemy from confusing your men with false orders?"

"The Shield of The Saint is important enough to the empire that almost all the men here are veterans. The thirty men the clan provided are also veterans." He stood. "I'll show you the defenses and the pass. First, let me show you to your room. It's two doors from the library."

At the mention of the library, Scarface grinned. "I've an addition to your collection of spell-scrolls in my saddle pouch. Something I picked up in Donradé. And would it be possible to bathe? I haven't had a real bath since I left Linistia."

A rare smile flickered across Damon's features. "I was beginning to wonder when you'd notice. The air down here tends to become stale quickly."

Together they walked to the stable, where Scarface took his saddle pouches, his cloak, and his blanket from the stablemaster.

His room in the keep was almost as small as his cabin had been on the Sazian ship, although it held a rope-bed for the pallet, and a chest stood in the corner. As they carried the scroll to the library, Scarface said, "If you know a magus powerful enough, you might have him copy this. It's very old, and it's been handled roughly."

Damon nodded and placed the scroll in a bin by itself. "I should be able to have that done. Perhaps because of the proximity to Myslan, the *Etrong Uven* isn't fond of magi, but keeps a few. I believe The Voice of The Faith regards them as necessary nuisances."

They climbed the stairs until they stood atop the keep, the imperial flag snapping in the chill wind from the pass. The passage through the mountains was slightly downslope from the base of the fortress and beyond the extreme range of a bow from the point of the trench nearest the pass. The pass opened before the holding like the mouth of a funnel.

"What's the chance of blocking the pass with an avalanche?" Scarface asked.

Damon shook his head. "Those mountains might be scaled, but trying to start an avalanche would be tricky and dangerous. There's little loose rock up there."

Scarface asked for the Thani translations for the most common orders, as well as the signals used by the men with the horns and by the man who pounded the steel bar that hung atop the keep.

As Scarface practiced his pronunciation, they made their way down the stairs and through one of the tunnels that ran out to the trench. In the tunnel, Damon pointed out a lever, set well out of the way, that would cause the tunnel to collapse if it were moved. They followed the light ahead until they stepped out onto the bridge to the walkway. At the mouth of the tunnel, he looked down and saw the stakes set in the pit. The pit was three times as wide as he was tall. That, decided Scarface, should discourage cavalry. The bridge to the walkway could be drawn up if retreat were necessary.

The walkway on the other side of the trench was just high enough to let a man on that side of the trench expose himself to the waist; enough to let a man use a bow. Listening to the hollow sounds of their footfalls on the wooden span, they trod across the bridge.

Scarface studied the terrain from this new position, then turned to look back at the wall. A smile touched his lips as he saw his banner with its sunburst red eagle on a field of black flapping beside Damon's pennon.

He glanced at the young man. "Thank you. I wasn't sure you'd still have it, or if you'd fly it."

Damon gazed at the banners. "We're born into the clan. We only leave it when we die, and then our banners are burned." For a moment his features took on a bleakness Scarface hadn't expected from one so young. "I've had to burn six banners. It wasn't a thing I want to do again."

Scarface felt a sudden sense of kinship with Damon. He bowed at the mention of those who'd died at High Rage. The silence lasted long enough that it became uncomfortable. The question that occurred to him was also uncomfortable, but he was curious. "Were you attacked here?"

"The Union didn't have enough people in the empire for a real attack. Runa tried to assassinate me. He failed and we fought. He wounded me, but I was able to kill him." He paused. "We burned the body. I sent couriers to High Rage, Northhome, and Aerie, as well as to Ong Vaun. I heard about High Rage from Gisli."

Scarface led the way back to the walls, then to the library. There was a spell he'd used many times in the past. In the library he found the proper scroll and studied it closely.

When he'd replaced the scroll in the bin he nodded to Damon. "Show me where you have traps off the road," he said. "I don't know how many traps I can cast, but I may be able to improve the defenses."

Damon first stopped in his room and buckled on a second sword and took a bow and a quiver of arrows, then the two of them strode out the gate and to the area bordering the road. The field was covered with a fine gravel that concealed several kinds of traps.

Scarface collected some slightly larger stones and placed them carefully. As each stone was set in place, he scratched a design on the rock while murmuring the incantation and drawing power from his scars. He'd expected to be able to set perhaps half a dozen traps before he felt the power in his scars begin to weaken, but he laid over two dozen spell-traps without feeling drained.

He sat back on his heels after finishing another spell-trap. He hadn't expected to expend so much power—or to have it to spend so prodigally. It were as though his power had been augmented, multiplied. He tried to guess at the source of the power, but nothing occurred to him. He felt he should be able to remember any event that had increased his power to such a degree, but he could pinpoint nothing, although he felt, vaguely, that the greater power was appropriate, as though the answer were in a dream he'd forgotten.

He stood. A bath, a meal, and sleep would all be welcome. He could cast more traps tomorrow. The sky was already turning rose and mauve with, in the west, a thin band of that breathtaking blue that can only be seen in sunsets. He nodded to Damon, feeling an urge to put an arm around the younger man's shoulder, and they walked, together, back to the fortress. Scarface realized he'd never truly appreciated family until he'd begun his own.

Scarface again dined with Damon and his family. He savored the food and the rich pomegranate wine, and the conversation turned toward kin. Both Gisli and Eagle had married. Pal and his brother Gatrin had established a holding in Shatilla.

"What of your mother and your sisters?" Scarface asked Damon. "Are they well? I'd heard they weren't at High Rage when it fell. Your sisters should be about ten years old now."

"They're in Sin Garlef, and were well when they sent their latest message. I've invited them to the empire, but Vornarei is waiting for Hadrian."

Scarface realized he'd touched an open wound, one Damon tried to hide. If the tales Scarface had heard were even half-true, Hadrian seemed to have become something both more and less than human; he'd become the personification of vengeance. From Damon's manner, Scarface guessed the warmth Hadrian had only shown his family had all been burned—or frozen—by a cold fury. "Has Hadrian done anything but hunt down the last of the Union and execute them?"

"When he was here before, he said he'd—" Damon paused, as though trying to remember the exact words, "dealt with other clan responsibilities."

"Pardon my asking, but—do you know what he thinks, what he feels?"

"I thought I did once. Now…." Damon shrugged.

"I'm sorry. I'm probably the one most responsible for what happened."

"I once thought that. I even mentioned it to him. He said events are sometimes like an avalanche, and you were only another stone, falling with the rest."

Scarface sipped at his wine. He suddenly felt as though his feelings stood naked. "I regret I didn't get to know you better, years ago."

"I'm glad to be able to know you now," Damon replied. "I'm not sure I could've said that five years ago."

Scarface grinned at the honesty. "Much has changed in five years." He stood. "I'm afraid I'm too weary to be good company. If I may, I'll have that bath, and then to bed."

In his room, Scarface stripped, then sank into the tub of warm water. The warmth was almost soporific.

His nephew had grown into a man he could trust at his back in battle. He'd also, apparently, grown into the responsibilities of command. Damon had obviously wanted to scout into Myslan himself, but had realized the leader wasn't necessarily the first man to face the enemy, but his was the mind that brought together all the elements of battle and tried to shape them into victory.

He didn't know whether to be pleased his nephew seemed to have matured so quickly past the stage in which Scarface had lived for so long, or to be sorry the boy hadn't experienced the wild excitement of being able to hurl himself headlong into the maelstrom, to seek the thrill of glory. Hadrian had taught his son wisdom, but learning wisdom through committing errors and surviving the consequences gave depth to life.

If the battle went badly, Damon would have a chance to fight, but there were too many lives depending upon him for him to be able to enjoy the struggle for itself. He'd be fighting with fear at his back; the fear that, if he fell, his wife and son would die.

Scarface would do what he could; not only because his nephew was part of the clan, but because he found himself liking the too-serious young man, and his family as well.

As Scarface had said, he had the freedom Damon lacked. Tomorrow, he'd ride through the pass and see what lay on the other side. Perhaps there was some way he could take the battle to the enemy. If he could catch them outside their defenses, create confusion, perhaps he could draw their fangs.

The back of his head struck the edge of the tub. He'd dozed in the warm water. He hurriedly washed and rinsed himself and levered himself out of the tub. Rubbing himself dry with an old blanket, he stumbled to the pallet. He hardly had time to tell himself how good the pallet felt before he was asleep.

~ * ~

A voice called his name, and he stepped out of the cave. Forgren stood waiting for him; men at his back, a bell in his right hand, and death in his eyes. Each word they spoke seemed to ring in the clear mountain air, a preliminary to the duel that would be the final struggle for one of them. Forgren's arm swung down, ringing the bell. Scarface thought the chime was too sweet a sound with which to announce a death.

With the ringing of the bell, darkness rushed at Scarface from the edges of his vision, and a baleful light glowed in Forgren's eyes. Scarface drew on the magic in his scars to keep the darkness at bay, could feel the power being drained from them, but the blackness retreated, although he could sense it lurking, waiting for him to weaken.

The strain of holding back the end began to tell on him. He could feel the sweat bead on his face and body, and his muscles began to cramp as he crouched, concentrating every trace of his will on fighting the blackness and turning it back on the one who'd called it. His eyes began to burn, but he knew if he blinked to rest them, he'd never open them again.

Forgren, in a voice choked by his own exhaustion, ordered his men forward and Scarface knew his life could be counted in heartbeats. If he turned to face the men, he'd die, and if he continued his battle with Forgren, one of the hirelings would plunge a spear or sword into him.

Unable to watch them, he saw the men falter and begin to struggle among themselves. Still he focused all his power on fighting away the darkness and forcing it back on Forgren. As if from a great distance, he heard a voice he recognized as Hadrian's. Hadrian was leaving Forgren and Scarface to finish their battle.

Forgren's strained voice demanded Scarface's true name of Mendarian. She hesitated, then replied, "Morgan."

With that name, Forgren wove a spell, even as he confronted Scarface. Suddenly, Scarface found himself in a void. Panic seized him as he realized his eyes had been closed and his heart stopped, and the darkness would claim him.

He found himself sitting on the pallet, struggling to breathe, his heart racing, his breath coming in shallow gasps, and he was drenched in fear-sweat.

From the room down the corridor he heard again the shriek of terror and, after a moment, Jeshka's voice, trying to sooth her son's fears, although her own voice was ragged with fear. The screams receded, and Scarface lay back down on the pallet.

He hadn't had any nightmares about his final confrontation with Forgren before, although, when he thought on it, it'd been a near thing. If Mendarian had actually given Forgren his true name, that struggle would've ended as it had in the nightmare. He supposed it was inevitable he have such a dream, and the real mystery was why it'd taken so long.

Forcing himself to relax again, he thought of Topaz. Her absence was no less painful for being a familiar ache. That pang stiffened his determination to return to her, if he had to defy all the gods to do it.

He saw her before him, opened his arms to her, then her blond hair darkened, her emerald eyes changed to brown, her features subtly shifted, and she'd become his cousin Martina. Martina stepped toward him, then her eyes brimmed with tears. As he reached for her to comfort her, her flesh began to dissolve, as though she were rotting. The body, already beginning to resemble that of a long-dead corpse, collapsed, but the head remained, impaled on a pike. The head continued to decay to a skull with strands of hair clinging to the bony scalp.

The skull changed. The hair became shorter and tightly curled, the canine teeth in the gaping jaws became longer, half again as long as the other teeth. Slowly, the jaws closed and features grew over the skull, although it remained on a pike. The black eyes opened, and Scarface was staring at the severed head, still alive, of Poker.

"Why did you abandon us?" The eyes and the gentle voice were filled with reproach. "You left us to the mercies of a creature without mercy."

Scarface writhed in the grip of that accusation, but it held him firmly, forcing him to look at his dead cousin's accusing face.

"You begin to suffer as we suffered, and you find it hard to bear. How much pain do you think you caused us? Could you bear that?"

Scarface experienced a sudden doubling of view. He realized this was a dream, yet he was trapped in the dream. He knew the real Poker would never have spoken as the dream-Poker had, but the truth of what the figment was saying was unavoidable.

He tried to change the dream, to shape it. He raised a mist between Poker and himself, tried to shroud himself in the fog, armor himself in ignorance, but the mist thinned.

Topaz lay at his feet. She was naked, her abdomen swollen with pregnancy, her legs drawn up. Her body gleamed with sweat and her face was twisted in agony. He could hear her ragged breathing, the keening that escaped her, and he wanted to reach for her but couldn't move. Her eyes opened and she seemed to stare up at him, then her eyes rolled back in her head. Her body twitched and spasmed, and blood began to run from her nose and mouth. It began as a thread of bright red, then began to flow more heavily. Her nostrils were rimmed with blood and a gout of it escaped her lips.

He screamed but could do nothing, not even close his eyes. A bloody claw appeared, thrust up from inside her belly, then other claws shot out. He screamed louder as the talons tore Topaz almost in two, and a head forced itself out of the wound. It had Forgren's face, but with five black scars on its upper face. It stared at him and grinned, displaying jagged teeth, then laughed maniacally.

He woke himself with his own screams, heard other screams from Damon's family's room.

Staggering to his feet, unable to stay on the cursed pallet any longer, he fumbled for his clothing, found his pouch where he'd left it, atop the chest. At first his fingers seemed numb, totally without feeling, then he found his flint, steel, and tinder. He groped for the candle that had been on the chest, cursed as his leaden fingers knocked it to the floor. Finally, he managed to secure the candle and light the wick.

The dim, flickering light was enough to let him find his clothing and draw on his shirt and leggings. Gripping the candle, he lurched toward the door. A presence seemed to brood in his room, and in the corridor as well. The impression of evil was so strong he could almost taste it, and it seemed to make the very air as thick as water.

His coordination began to return, although the candle flickered in his trembling hand. Staggering down the corridor, leaning, each step, with his right hand pressed against the wall, he made his way to Damon's room.

Suddenly Damon stumbled out of the door ahead of him and stood staring at Scarface, one of his swords in his hand. Even at four paces' distance, Scarface could smell the young man's fear-sweat. Damon's eyes and hair were wild, and the sword was drawn back for a thrust.

Again Scarface experienced that doubling of vision, although it wasn't just a vision of the eyes. For a moment, he seemed to see a fiendish shape crouched on the young man's shoulders, its taloned hand reaching into his head. The image faded in a blink.

Both men became aware of other cries from the corridor that led to the barracks. Damon seemed still stunned, as though drugged, and Scarface shook his arm and shouted. "It's an attack!"

Damon stood, undecided, for long enough to draw a deep breath, then he shook himself, growled an oath, spun, and dashed for the stairs leading to the roof of the keep.

Scarface followed and they reached the top of the stairs only a pace or two apart. Their sudden rush up the steps had shaken the guard, who almost thrust his spear at them, but, in the moonlight, they could see the area around the fortress was bare of visible enemies.

Scarface leaned on the stone parapet and tried to make sense of what he'd seen and felt. "It's either some form of attack," he said, "or we're sensing the power and the evil of your enemy."

The night air chilled him, but it helped bring him fully awake. He tried to remember the elements of his nightmares, then realized they were his own nightmares; that they sprang from within him, from his own feelings of guilt and self-doubt. Each person, he realized, carried his or her own ghosts, and something had goaded his unlaid ghosts to avenge themselves. While he understood the problem, he wasn't sure of the cause, and he had no solution, although he thought he could find someone who could help them. "Do you have a priest here?"

"Of course." Damon stared at Scarface and his tone took a note of certainty. "Of course!" He caught up a torch lying by the guards' fire, lit it from the blaze, and clambered down the stairs, Scarface at his heels.

Ianno's priest was a younger man than Scarface had expected, but he had an air of authority and mission. He'd emerged from his cell to comfort the men waking screaming, terrified, clawing for their weapons.

"We need Ianno's blessing," Damon said.

The priest ran a hand through his dark hair and stared at the men, almost all of whom were stumbling around the barracks as though struck a stunning blow, or sitting on their pallets with their faces buried in their hands, or waking the few who still cried out in their sleep. "I'll do it now."

He trod back to his room to soon return, wearing his ceremonial tunic of green, bound with a broad pale blue sash, and reverently carrying his Book. Holding The Book to his chest, he chanted several phrases in Thani, then held The Book aloft, as though it were a beacon. He lowered The Book, and each of the men stepped forward and kissed the green leather cover.

When the last soldier had completed the act of veneration, the priest faced Damon. "I'll bless your family next, then see to the others."

Scarface looked around the room at the warriors. Most of them were lying down again; a few had already gone to sleep. He stepped forward and kissed the cover of The Book. It might be only superstition, but, in a fight, a man seized any weapon. He nodded to Damon. "I'll be in my room, but if you need me—"

Damon rested a hand on his shoulder. "Only if I need your help more than you need your rest."

Scarface paced back to his room, already beginning to relax. He stripped again, blew out the candle, and lay down on the pallet. As his back touched the pallet, he felt a pang of doubt, then relaxed. If the blessing didn't work, he could always draw on the power of his scars.

Whoever their enemy was, he was a cunning bastard. If the priest hadn't exorcised the evil presence he'd felt before, the men standing sentry would be tired and the rest of the garrison exhausted tomorrow. Sleeplessness could be a debilitating weakness. He guessed the enemy's army would attack tomorrow, and he hoped the magus directing tonight's magical attack was unaware that his spell had been countered.

Almost fearfully, he thought of Martina and Poker, and he could almost see them smiling at him, then he thought of Topaz. She was well, and she also smiled. He drifted easily into a restful, dreamless sleep.

He rose a full hour after dawn the next morning and enjoyed a leisurely breakfast. The empire provided the garrison with fruit and melons as part of their provisions, and he was sampling different flavors than those available on the western continent. Even the bread was flavored with strange, sweet spices and dried fruits.

Jeshka joined him at the table and he asked her about the empire and the church, learning nothing Poker hadn't told him long before, but enjoying the conversation. Finally he leaned back, sated, and she said, "You have a fearsome reputation."

He smiled. "Was that why you were afraid of me yesterday? Or was it disapproval?"

She smiled back. "Perhaps a little of both. I hadn't realized you were so sensitive. I just wanted to tell you I'm glad you're with us."

He stood, hoping he gave no sign of the surge of warmth he'd felt. He bowed and strode from the room.

As he trod up the stairs he smiled to himself. Either the world had changed, or he had. He suspected the latter. Perceptions changed, and so did the things perceived. Sometimes, perhaps, the perceptions changed the things perceived. As he reached the parapet, he found Damon conferring with a soldier he didn't recognize. The younger man dismissed the soldier and turned to Scarface.

"Our scouts began to return last night. That was the last. He came through the pass just after dawn. The Myslan cavalry should be here at any time.

"I'd expected as much." Scarface stared down into the fortress. Men were preparing the ballistae and the catapults. Others were emerging from other doorways near the walls, carrying sheaves of arrows. All the men were armored.

"We have more armor. Why don't you go below and find a hauberk that'll fit you?"

"No hauberk will stop an arrow, and my leather's some protection. I may take a helmet and a shield. You seem to have your men well disposed." Scarface paused. "With your permission, I'll join the men in the trench. You need to remain here to direct the battle, but one of the clan should be in the forefront of the fight."

Damon frowned, then, reluctantly, nodded. "Be careful."

Scarface grinned. "I always am."

He followed a soldier down the stairs and through a corridor to a huge chamber. Mail hung on simple cruciform frames, and shields hung on the wall. He selected a shield with a faintly curved face, flat on top, with curving sides that met in a broad point at the base, and a helmet with a fixed visor to protect his face from the sun. He also picked up a short steel bow similar to Damon's and a quiver of arrows, then allowed the man to lead him through a maze of passages that ended in a long tunnel to the trench.

In the trench, he looked back at the fortress, could just recognize Damon atop the keep. A few more men stood behind the walls. He noticed one man standing on top of the wall, shading his eyes with a hand. The soldier looked down behind him and seemed to say something to someone out of sight, then jumped from the wall to the walkway behind it.

Immediately, the clangor of steel striking steel alerted the garrison and a horn winded three notes.

Scarface turned to face the mouth of the pass. Three men on horseback had just ridden out of the pass at a walk. They sat staring at the fortress, then began to ride wide around it, staying close to the rock wall behind them. Someone launched an arrow that fell perhaps twenty spear lengths short. Scarface glanced at the men with him, saw another man nock an arrow.

"Wait," he told the man, then repeated it in Thani.

The first three horsemen had gone less than a quarter of the way around the fortress when they all heard the clatter of horses' hooves on stone, and a large body of cavalry trotted their chargers out of the pass. As they cleared the mouth of the pass, the line of riders stretched out, and Scarface guessed their number at about two hundred.

Suddenly one of the catapults creaked and crashed, and hurled a load of flints. Most of the riders had already passed the point where the flints struck, but two men and their horses, apparently at the edge of the storm of stone chips, went down. One of the men clambered to his feet, but both horses were obviously dead.

Another catapult's arm swung up and another load of flints was flung, this time at the last quarter of the line.

Even at that distance, he could distinctly hear the screams of men and horses, and nearly a score of the animals fell. Less than half their riders scrambled to their feet, and many of those moved like wounded men,

Another mangonel crashed, throwing more death. Scarface saw one of the men who'd been unhorsed run forward into the next barrage and fall, kicking, to the ground. Another dozen men died with him, then the only sounds were the screams. The rest of the horsemen shot spurs to their mounts and raced around the periphery of the defenses until they were out of sight behind the fortress.

He heard one more catapult arm slam into its crosspiece, but couldn't see the engine or where its flints struck, and it was impossible to tell if there were more screams.

Damon would want to keep most of his siege engines ready, for it cost precious time to load them, and the cavalry weren't there to attack but to cut off their retreat and intercept couriers. The couriers had long since been dispatched and the garrison had no intention of retreating. The first moves had ended in stalemate.

Scarface found a place to lean on the side of the trench and made himself comfortable, glanced up at the clear blue sky. From the position of the sun, it was only a little after midmorning. Further along the trench, a man stood at the lip. Sunlight turned the shaft of his glaive to gold and the blade, like that of a heavy, curved sword, looked like a flame.

A man scurried down the trench with a bucket and a cup, He stopped beside Scarface, who dipped up a cupful and savored the cold, sweet water. The watercarrier continued down the trench.

Near noon, they heard the steady throbbing of a drum, or several drums pounded in unison, then a ragged line of marchers appeared. The steel alarm rang again, and the horn called.

The downed cavalry jerked themselves to their feet and began to walk toward the fortress, while the figures issuing from the mouth of the pass didn't form ranks; they simply continued to advance on the fortress at a walk.

A mangonel hurled more flints.

Scarface could see the stone chips striking near the middle of the line, but only a few of the marchers were knocked down, and all of them rose again and resumed their march.

"Prepare arrows," Scarface shouted in Thani, and suited action to words. None of the figures advancing on them except the cavalrymen appeared to be armored, but none of them wavered. From the sizes of the figures, he guessed that women and children followed the men. As they approached, he noted their skins were ashen or mottled and most of them were clad in rags. The marchers from the pass appeared to be armed only with clubs or sharpened stakes.

He drew the bowstring to his cheekbone, took aim at a large figure in the front rank, and shouted, "Release!"

The first flight of arrows arched up, then swept down into the marchers. Four arrows hit the big man Scarface had chosen as his target. Two of them drove completely through the figure, while Scarface's arrow buried itself to the fletching in the man's chest.

The man never changed the cadence of his advance.

Scarface would've sworn, but the breath had caught in his throat. Many of the marchers wore several arrows through their bodies, but not one had fallen.

He wanted to tell the men with him not to waste any more arrows but didn't remember enough Thani to give the order. It was unnecessary. The man nearest him had dropped his bow and was clutching his halberd with white-knuckled hands. The soldier beyond him was shooting arrows as quickly as he could nock and draw them, but only a few arrows rose from the trench, as most of the soldiers had observed the futility of trying to stop the enemy with archery.

The nearest marchers had reached the road. In another dozen paces they'd be among the traps. Scarface tore his gaze away from them to try to see the overall shape of the battle. He estimated nearly a thousand of the ragged infantry and over two score cavalry were marching toward them, all to the cadence beaten by the drummers. The only relief was that no more issued from the mouth of the pass, but he and the sixty or so men in the trench were hideously outnumbered, and their best weapons for evening the odds had been taken from them.

A marcher had lurched forward, his leg caught in a trap. He tried to tug his leg free, pulling and relaxing in time to the beat of the drum. Scarface again looked toward the pass. He still didn't see the drummers, who must be hidden in the cleft.

Another of the marchers fell into a trap and worked to free himself with the same mindless, passive determination as the first to be caught. A sheet of flame shot upward as another stepped on one of Scarface's traps. The shape engulfed in flame shriveled to a blackened skeleton and fell. The rest of the marchers continued their advance.

Scarface stared, horrified, at the figures still moving like an irresistible tide toward the fortress. Those were corpses, animated by magic. The plague Damon had mentioned hadn't slowed the invasion; it'd been an opportunity for their enemy to recruit. Those mindless, soulless bodies were a nearly perfect army; they were impervious to pain, they were utterly fearless, they didn't need to be fed or paid, and it seemed the only way to stop them was to burn them or dismember them.

More flames shot upward, and one or two of them claimed more than one marcher as the dead strode forward, even into the flames. One, caught at the edge of a trap tripped by the corpse beside him, continued to march, even as he burned.

Scarface did manage to curse then.

The burning thing took half a dozen steps before it fell. Scarface watched the marchers intently. The magic seemed only to drive them. If a muscle or tendon were cut or burned, the corpse was maimed. He had no idea whether cutting off their heads would stop them, but he resolved to find out. Within moments the nearest of the invaders would be beyond the traps, and he'd have to lead a charge against them; the defenders couldn't afford to lose the trench. Fortunately, the marching corpses were widely dispersed, in no sort of formation, so they couldn't attack *en masse*.

"Ready!" Scarface roared in Thani, and sprang to the top of the trench wall. Other men leapt up after him, most of them clutching glaives, halberds, or bills. He gripped sword and shield tightly, let the nearest damned thing take three steps beyond the traps, then shouted, "Charge!"

He raced downslope, his sword raised. As he reached the corpse he'd chosen, the thing thrust its sharpened stake at him. He parried with an overhand slash, then, on the backhand return stroke, he decapitated it. The head, its face as devoid of expression as before, fell, but the body repeated the thrust. He blocked the stake with his shield and slashed downward, taking off its left arm and left leg at the knee. Finally, the obscenity toppled, although the body writhed on the ground as though it were still trying to march forward.

No enemy faced him but, to his left, a man with a spear had lunged, driving the point of his weapon through the chest of the dead thing before him. The corpse shoved itself forward on the spear shaft, then thrust. The soldier doubled over and Scarface dashed to the enemy, swinging his blade in a series of circles that sheared off the corpse's left arm and both legs.

He became aware then the drumbeat had quickened and the bodies were now rushing forward in a shambling run. He stood astride the fallen man to protect him and almost missed deflecting the stake of the next body, then began to hew.

The battle became a thing out of nightmare. Some of the rushing corpses set off more fire-traps, adding to the ghastly scene of dead eyes in passive faces, and maimed bodies still pressing forward to attack. Their assault had no skill, but hacking the bodies apart still cost precious time, still drained him and the men with him.

Greater horrors were yet to come, as dead women flung themselves at the defenders, then the children rushed forward. Scarface knew he wasn't killing; one can't kill what's already dead, but rending those frailer bodies cost more in determination.

He noticed the man he'd protected was gone, looked around, saw him to the right, laying about him with a falchion. A blow to the edge of his shield drew his attention back to the enemy before him. His blade took off the arm that'd swung the club and swept the legs off the little girl.

Time became less than a notion as he hacked and chopped, felling a bitter harvest, although this crop was trying to kill him and his friends. It seemed he'd been slashing and cutting for hours. The only sounds were the infrequent roar of flames, the sounds of blows falling, his own breath whistling in his throat, and that damnable drum. He could hardly raise his arms to use his blade, and the left arm, holding the shield, had began to shake. Then there was nothing more to fight. Two or three corpses still struggled in traps, but the rest were dismembered.

He looked around. The number of men with him had grown; Damon must've sent reinforcements.

For the first time, he became aware of the stench of the long-dead, and he vomited. When he could trust his body, he stumbled back to the trench. He lifted his sword to return it to its scabbard, then decided he'd wait until he'd scoured the blade. He and his clothing were spattered with gore, and he felt a desperate need to wash.

At the trench, he found a man waiting for him with a bucket of water and a cup. He let the man give him a drink, not wanting to raise his gloves to his face. He drank greedily, then trudged across the bridge and down the tunnel.

The stairs to the keep seemed to go past forever and he had to stop on the steps to rest. When he gained the roof he stood beside Damon and looked down at the troops disposing of the bodies. Some of the fresher soldiers dragged the parts of corpses around to the side of the fortress so the wind from the pass wouldn't carry the stench into the holding. The men were using polearms as farmers used pitchforks, to haul and toss the dead things into heaps.

Other men had thrown bottles of oil onto the bodies caught in the traps and were using flaming arrows to incinerate them, and Scarface could guess the other bodies would also be burned.

"You might also have your priest bless the bodies," Scarface said. "It wasn't their fault their rest was stolen from them. I'm also worried about contagion,"

"There's nothing we can do about plague but pray. It'd seem our priest is going to be as busy as any warrior," Damon observed. "You and the men with you did well. If those things had reached the trench, we'd be bottled up in the fortress."

"I believe I'll join you here for the next attack. The spell I brought can do more good than another twenty warriors, but I must be above the battle to use it."

Damon, having caught the odor clinging to Scarface, edged up-wind. "What will you need for the spell?"

"The use of your signal brazier, kindling, pine, blackwood, and something of value to sacrifice."

"The brazier, pine, and kindling will be no problem, and I'm willing to sacrifice a ring given me by The Voice of The Faith, but we'll have to search for blackwood." He leaned over the parapet and shouted several phrases in Thani to a soldier below, then faced Scarface again. "I've ordered what you need for the spell, and also some soap, water, and rags."

"Do the same for the soldiers with me," Scarface said. He grinned crookedly. "At least this should help the provisions last longer, if there's a siege. I doubt any of us will be interested in eating for a while."

As they waited for the things Damon had ordered, Scarface gestured at the men below. "Did we lose any men in the attack?"

"Four. I'll have the priest bless them." Bitterly, Damon added, "Then I'll cut their tendons so that, if they're somehow magicked by the enemy, they can't harm us."

"A hard decision," Scarface replied, "but a necessary one. You're the right man to command here."

"That's no consolation."

"You learn very quickly. One thing you have yet to learn is that command offers no consolations, only hard choices. It's harder on good men, the ones who care about the people under them. The only reason, besides to preserve your family, to continue to command is because if you fall, the next man may not care as much."

Damon's face worked as though he were swallowing something bitter. "Go below and wash. And change clothing."

Scarface took the stairs to a room below, where he found two buckets of water, a tub, soap, and a number of rags. He peeled off his gloves and tossed them onto one of the larger rags, then washed his hands and face. He next cleaned his sword with the same care he'd given himself, and wiped it dry with another cloth before he returned it to its scabbard.

He undressed, cleaning his leather as best he could and tossing his shirt and leggings onto the rag with the gloves. Those could be burned. He stepped into the tub and poured water on himself, scrubbed vigorously with the coarse soap, then rinsed himself. After drying himself, he donned a fresh pair of leggings and a leather gambeson, drew on a pair of boots and tied them in place, then strapped on his weapons.

He'd seen men climbing the stair, carrying wood. When he returned to the top of the tower he saw the brazier had been filled and a torch burned beside it. Ignoring the men around him, he studied the mouth of the pass, but nothing moved there. The bodies of the horses still lay at the base of the cliff face but, save for the billowing smoke that rose from the burning bodies, nothing moved beyond the trench.

Damon had been talking with the priest and a soldier Scarface remembered as a captain. Damon and the priest had apparently just arrived at an agreement, and the priest and the soldier turned, walked to the stairway, and disappeared down the steps.

"Bronyak was hard to convince," Damon said. "One of the troops had suggested to the captain that the priest bless the flints to be used against the dead marchers. Bronyak was opposed, since it's anathema for a priest of Ianno to sanctify war in any way. I had to point out to him the blessing wasn't to kill but to grant rest and peace to the dead."

"Do you think it'll work?"

Damon shrugged. "I'd load the catapults with every gold coin in the place if I thought it had a chance." He turned to face the pass. "I'm surprised we haven't already been attacked again."

"That first attack was a probe," Scarface replied. "They wanted to see how we'd fight. It also disarmed most of our traps. I'd guess they're giving us time to fret, hoping we're passing fear around like cups of mulled wine. They may not come again until tonight. If their leader's a patient man, that's what he'll do."

"The moon will be almost full, tonight."

"That's in our favor. Unless they use assassins using a spell of concealment."

Damon frowned. "I don't like it, but we can fall back to the fortress, close the gates to the trench, and spread fine sand about. That'll let us know, in the morning, if anyone approaches at night."

"That should work very well—if the attack fails. If it succeeds, we'll have dead guards and perhaps a dead garrison. But the only suggestion I can offer is to post guards, in pairs, at each entrance to the keep and to strew sand around each post. With luck, the guards will see footprints where there shouldn't be any and sound the alarm before they're attacked.

"If I'm right, we'll be warned of an attack by the dead things by the sound of drums. I think the bodies move to the drums, but we can't be sure of that. We'll need to change guards often. Staring too long into the darkness can make you see things where there aren't any, or not see something you should. Have the sentries watching in pairs, so they can relieve each other. You also need some men to sleep now, so they can watch tonight. Most of the men who fought won't be able to sleep, so I suggest you have at least eighty of your rested soldiers try to sleep now."

"What about you?"

"I'll take command of the night force, but I'm going to eat first, and try to learn more Thani from you. I'm no good to any of us if I can't make my orders understood."

Scarface forced himself to eat while Damon taught him a rudimentary vocabulary in Thani, then he returned to the library, where he studied the spell again.

He had to master the spell, to make it a part of himself, so he could cast it even half-asleep. He knew the need would be certain to come at the most awkward moment, and it was necessary to prepare for that. When he was certain he'd absorbed the spell, he returned to his room and lay down.

Battle did strange things to a man. It burned a warrior's energy at the same time it stole his appetite, and it exhausted him until he could hardly raise an arm, but left him too anxious to sleep.

Experience helped. He'd learned to eat, whether he wanted to or not, and he'd taught himself to relax. He flexed each muscle, then relaxed each, and forced himself to breathe slowly, drawing each breath in through his nose and exhaling through his mouth.

He was glad Damon hadn't asked him how he'd known about the harsh truths of command. He, himself, hadn't been a particularly good man. He'd generally cared about the men under him only as another set of arms that could wield weapons. He'd thrown away troops to win a victory with no more regret than he'd felt when he spent coins in a market to acquire some item that'd caught his interest.

He wasn't sure he'd changed greatly. They'd lost four men in the attack and he hadn't even asked their names; not that knowing their names would make them any less dead. He had more sympathy for Damon, who had to mutilate the bodies of his own dead. Damon was paying a high price, and Scarface could only hope his family wouldn't have to pay it as well.

Thoughts of Topaz came to him; his family. The only price this battle might cost her was a husband. Perhaps, if Damon survived this war, his family wouldn't have to pay for the victory. If they won.

He'd learned from the younger man, too. No matter how obnoxious a child might seem to someone else, that child was beautiful to its father. Perhaps he could learn to be a father. That would take more learning, but it was pleasant to look forward to learning. He only hoped they'd all have time in which to learn.

~ * ~

Someone called his use-name, and a hand shook his shoulder. A candle shed enough light to let him see it was Damon waking him.

He groaned and rolled off the pallet, twisting to light on his feet. "Another attack?"

"No, it's sundown. I thought you might want to have time to eat and come fully awake before you have to go on watch. Jeshka has a meal ready for you."

After nodding his thanks, he poured water into the basin and washed his face and hands, then dressed, belting on his weapons, and strode to the room where he'd eaten before. Jeshka and Danyol sat at the table but the only food was on a platter set before an empty chair.

Scarface sat. "Thank you." He supposed they'd eat with Damon.

Jeshka observed the custom of only making pleasant conversation during a meal but, as soon as he'd pushed himself away from the table, she asked, "Will we be able to hold this place?"

"Yes," he said, hoping he was telling her the truth. "It won't be easy, but we can hold it."

He climbed the stair and visited the latrine, then took the stairs the rest of the way to the roof of the keep, actually beginning to feel better. Damon waited for him beside the brazier. Scarface clapped him on the shoulder, watched him light a candle from the nearby torch, and march down the stairs.

It hadn't been full dark when Scarface had mounted the keep, but he grew uneasy as the gloaming deepened until the moon rose and he could see the pass was as still and empty as it'd been earlier. He tried to force all thoughts from his mind, to become only a set of eyes and ears.

In the third hour after midnight, he heard again the throbbing of drums, and the man at the steel bar beat the alarm.

CHAPTER 7

Scarface lit the beacon. He wanted to look, to see how near the enemy had advanced, to be able to estimate their numbers, but now his concentration on the flames was vital. He started the incantation, calling forth whatever might take shape in the flames.

Again, the scaled neck was the first feature to appear. Again he watched and was part of the struggle of birth, as though watching—and being—a chick fighting free of its egg. With a roar, the dragon unfurled its wings and shot skyward.

Turning his head slowly, Scarface directed the dragon up and out toward the trench. Watching the fire so closely, he'd lost his night vision, so all was darkness except the area immediately around Lashastur, the dragon. Scarface saw nothing. He willed the dragon to spring out over the traps to the road.

At the edge of the circle of light a shape moved, and the dragon sprang on it, claws tearing at the ragged figure. For a moment the corpse continued its silent advance, then seemed to merge with the flame-dragon as the dry body caught fire. In the larger globe of light, Scarface spied another marcher and the dragon pounced again. Another shape melded with the fire.

In the glare of bright-burning bodies he could see more attackers, and the dragon struck at everything Scarface could see. Another marching corpse stepped over the first to burn and also caught fire. Scarface directed the dragon to create a barrier of burning corpses, a barrier that quickly grew. He became aware of the awful stench of burning flesh, but continued to attack.

The scene before him became another nightmare. Many of the bodies continued to march ahead, even as they became walking torches or candles, until the flames ate away sinews and tendons. Somehow, it seemed all the more horrible in the near-silence; the only sounds were the drumbeats and the roar of the flames.

Despite the distance from the wall of fire to the wall of the fortress, he could feel the heat, which quickly became more intense.

The drumbeat's tempo increased, as though the leader hoped to bury the fire under a wave of bodies, but the flames only burned higher and hotter, then the drumbeat changed again and the bodies turned.

Scarface couldn't allow the dead to withdraw to be used another time. He willed the dragon into the air again and sent it as far into the cleft as he could see, starting another wall of fire, lashing marchers with his tail, wrapping his bright wings around them, leaping after them like a mastiff. Again the flames spread from one body to another, and the drumbeat stopped.

Making the dragon rise, he noted the beast was smaller, hardly more than a firefly at that distance. "Feed the beacon," he shouted, and called the dragon back to the brazier. This time there was no contest of wills, as though the dragon perceived its own danger. Its return was like the flight of a flaming arrow and it crouched in the brazier, no bigger than a large cat.

He fumbled for wood, fed what he found into the flames. More hands tossed wood into the brazier until the fire leapt Scarface's own height into the night air. When he was sure it was strong enough, he again called Lashastur forth and sent it questing.

The nearer wall of fire had already begun to sink, and he sent the dragon to prowl between the two masses of burning dead. When the drums had stopped the marchers had fallen and he had to search to find a body, at first mistaking a corpse for a rock. He curled the dragon around the dead thing, then rose and sought more prey.

With the dead wearing drab rags and lying motionless on the field, they were hard to find in the darkness. He searched out over a score of them and set them alight, then drew Lashastur back to the brazier. By then, the fire had begun to dwindle again and the dragon didn't resist. For a moment the fire-beast rested in the brazier, then it was only a fire.

The corpses near the mouth of the pass still burned fitfully, while the ones near the road had become only a dark mass with an occasional flare, and glowing red points. The stench was thick in the air, and smoke billowed past the fortress and across the plains to the west. The attack had crumbled.

Finding a wineskin, he drank deeply, trying to wash the taste out of his mouth. His hands shook and he was bathed in sweat. Beyond the fear and excitement of the struggle, he'd learned a different sort of fear; some part of him had been out there with the dragon. It was he who had embraced the dead with fire and anger. If he were to call Lashastur up again he was afraid to find out which part of him was the master.

He noticed one of the men staring at him with something like awe. "Do you speak Gasgoran?" he asked, in that language.

The man babbled something in Thani and Scarface waved a hand in dismissal, then leaned over the parapet, peering into the pass. A quarter of an hour passed before the faint light of moon and stars were enough to let him distinguish the pass and the bodies. The fires had finally, one by one, faded into darkness.

A great rage began to grow in him. He drew on his cloak and gathered it about him as the wind from the pass chilled the sweat on his body. He wanted to face this enemy with a good steel blade in his hands. The *Alman* was a monster to use bodies the way he had, stealing even the peace of death to build an army. But Scarface's fury was tempered by caution. The *Alman* might be a coward, hiding behind a barricade of corpses, but he had enough men, living as well as dead, to threaten Tong Shavath.

Scarface paced, following the curve of the parapet, from one side to the other, watching the pass, wishing for a way to drag the *Alman* out where he could taste the death he was so willing to inflict upon others. He could see no way. He considered using a spell of concealment and stalking the bastard in his own camp, but attacking two such powerful magi with such a simple spell was worse than futile.

He contemplated the situation, trying to find anything he'd overlooked or taken for granted. Both sides had certain advantages. The *Alman* undoubtedly had a numerically overwhelming force. Damon and his men had the advantage of position in their fort: the *Alman* couldn't bring his entire force to bear. The fortress also had the advantage of well-planned defenses. Its siege engines were almost as good as scores of archers.

The greatest obvious danger was that the *Alman* would overwhelm the defenses. The mangonels required so long to reload they could only be used twice, three times at the most, before the enemy would have a massive force under the arc of the missiles. Most of the traps had been exposed or used and the few that remained would hardly slow a major assault.

He returned to the section of the wall he'd leaned on before and rested on his forearms. It would help if he were to set more fire-traps, but placing himself so far in advance of the defenses was more foolhardy than courageous.

An idea occurred to him then. The fire-trap spell required the sign for the spell be scratched into the dirt or onto a stone. If he were to cast the spell on stones in a catapult, he might be able to spread more traps before the enemy. He wasn't sure what would happen if one of those stones were broken when it hit the ground, but the only way to find out was to try.

The sky was beginning to lighten. With the mountains in the east, sun-up would be well over two hours away, but he could already see a few bodies he'd missed in his prowl in the dark. If the *Alman* were intending to attack, rather than simply putting the fortress under siege, there'd soon be more than enough light.

Glancing about, he sought the nearest mangonel and noticed Damon standing against the wall a few paces away. He nodded to the younger man. "I regret the stink. You're going to need to scour this place with rosewater for months to get the smell out."

Damon grinned. "I'd rather smell them than fight them. I've been up since the alarm rang. That was a most effective spell you cast. You'll have to tell me, sometime, how you got it."

Scarface realized, with a shock, that he hardly remembered, himself. "I've had another idea. By the way, how did the blessed flints work?"

Damon shrugged. "They seemed to have no more effect than the others."

"Do you know how many bodies they sent against us last night?"

"Hard to tell, in the dark, but I'd guess about twice as many as in the probing attack. Make it near two thousand."

Scarface had trod to one of the mangonels and began to dig among the stones that lay in a pile beside it. He chose stones carefully and placed them in the catapult's cup, then, with his knife, he scratched the sigil on them, chanting the spell. He was surprised to discover his power wasn't drained, even after he'd enchanted two score stones. He glanced up at the brightening sky, then stepped to the side of the engine, found the release lever, and launched the rocks toward the pass.

"What did you do that for?"

"That idea I spoke of." Soldiers rushed, grumbling, to the engine, drew the arm back, and, using shovels, reloaded the scoop. Scarface enchanted another dozen stones, then grinned at Damon. "That fire-trap spell I cast yesterday; I cast it on some of the stones. That should give the enemy pause, or keep a few bodies farther away from the walls."

"Very good. How soon do you think they'll attack again?"

"I'm surprised they haven't done it before now." He glared at the pass. "You said you'd sent couriers. How long must we hold before we can expect help?"

"Bhun Nahbi's a little over a hundred leagues from here. With remounts from the stations the empire maintains, a messenger can be there in three days. Bhun Nahbi is the nearest major city where an army can be mustered. Ong Vaun is almost another hundred leagues beyond that. If an army can be gathered in two days, they could have their vanguard here in twelve days from the time they set out. I dispatched the couriers five days ago."

Scarface scratched on the rock, calculating. "So, we hold for another fortnight." He smiled with half his mouth. "Optimism is an engaging quality—most of the time. Given the circumstances, I rather wish you'd erred on the side of pessimism."

Damon's answer was lost in the clangor of the alarm being beaten and, a few heartbeats later, the bawling of the horns. Skirmishers had dashed out of the pass and trotted toward the fortress. Two of them vanished in sudden fires and several others wavered, but most simply quickened their pace.

"I'm going down to the trench," Scarface shouted. "Those bastards have made me eager for a little honest killing." Without waiting for an answer, he raced to the stairs and clattered down them. He paused at the armory to seize a bow and a quiver of arrows, then ran down the tunnel, and the flickering patch of pale daylight in the distance showed that men ahead of him had already opened the gates to the trenches.

Once across the bridge, he crouched, surveying the area before him. One of the skirmishers had reached the trench, only to be speared by one of the soldiers.

Unlike the nearly silent struggle with the dead things, a cacophony beat at Scarface's ears. The Myslans had charged to the thin, high-pitched wailing of pipes, but the sound was almost indistinguishable from the shrill ululation of their war cries and the screams of the dying. Arrows hissed and struck with a sound like a blow. Catapults thumped against their crosspieces and the rocks fell with a clatter, exacting a terrible toll. Flames roared as more fire-traps were set off, turning their victims to charred skeletons. The skirmishers had been followed by other troops, all advancing as rapidly as possible.

Scarface nocked an arrow and aimed it at a man who'd reached the line of skeletons from the earlier battle. He aimed at the round plate on the man's chest and released. The arrow struck low and the man went down, screaming and kicking and clawing at his belly. The man behind him leapt over the wounded man and managed to run another dozen paces before Scarface's next arrow took him in the throat.

Scarface missed the next man, who almost reached the trench before another soldier drove a glaive into him. There was no time for cursing, and no satisfaction, since even he couldn't hear the words. He stopped ten more men before he'd used all the arrows in his quiver.

Soldiers rushed out of the tunnel with more arrows, Scarface snatched another dozen shafts, and invested them wisely.

He prepared to leap out of the trench but flinched when a crossbow bolt whined off the rock by his left hand and a stone chip nicked his little finger. As he ducked, two arrows swept past him to fall among the stakes in the pit.

The man beside him staggered back, then collapsed, an arrow in his chest. Scarface immediately grabbed the arrows by the man's foot and, kneeling on one knee, looked over the lip of the trench. He watched as one of the attackers with a bow was suddenly impaled by the heavy missile from one of the ballistae. He saw another enemy pause in his rush to nock an arrow and he took aim at the man. His arrow jutted from just below the Myslan's right eye.

Another enemy gained the lip of the trench but before he could raise his crossbow, the man with the glaive swept his legs from under him. He toppled, screaming, rolled across the walkway, and fell among the stakes.

The man with the glaive sprang to the lip of the trench and lay about him, using the shaft as well as the head of his weapon, until he seemed a living symbol of battle-fury, driving the enemy back with his skill and his power. An arrow burying itself in his thigh caused him to stumble, then he killed the last two Myslans within reach of his blade before he limped back to the trench.

The noise slackened and Scarface chanced another look down the slope. The Myslans were falling back. He aimed at one of the few still charging the trench. His arrow struck the man in the lower leg. The man howled and halted, stood undecided for a fatal instant, then fell with another arrow in his chest.

Scores of wounded and dead men littered the slope from the edge of the belt of traps to the lip of the trench; scores more lay within the belt of traps, and hundreds lay from the road to the mouth of the pass.

Scarface crawled out of the trench, stood, and thrust at the nearest body. The man's back arched, then relaxed. He used the corpse's own short, curved sword to dismember the body, then stalked forward. None of the wounded or dying were able to defend themselves.

They had to dismember the dead, so the *Alman* couldn't send them against the fortress again. More soldiers clambered out and Scarface directed them to haul the corpses around the trench to the place where they'd burned the dead the day before.

The bodies among the traps presented a different problem. Most of the snares had been sprung but Scarface was reluctant to risk soldiers by sending them among the traps for bodies. He considered casting more fire-spells, but if Damon were to direct his men through the maze of traps, the new spells would do more harm than good. Besides, his lack of sleep and food and his exertions were beginning to slow his mind as well as his body.

He trudged back to the trench, across the bridge, and through the tunnel to the fortress. Damon stood, leaning over the parapet, shouting orders, gesturing to make his commands clear. He finally turned to Scarface, his face grim. "I suspect we've done the *Alman* a favor, though I wouldn't count on his gratitude. This sort of attack doesn't smell much like his work. Probably he has some petty lords eager to show their prowess. They've learned discipline on that field." He gestured at the bodies. "Could you conjure another fire-beast?"

Scarface frowned. "There's danger in that." The sun had risen above the peaks and it was near mid-morning. He squinted at the heaps of dead. Those bodies wouldn't burn as easily as the long-dead corpses, but the petty lords had provided the *Alman* with another army; more warriors than he wanted to face again. Resignation sat as heavily on his shoulders as a coat of mail. "Get me something to eat, and water, but no wine. You know what's needed for the spell."

While Damon issued new orders, Scarface sat down, his back to the wall. This battle had left a bad taste—several bad tastes—in his mouth. He'd been denied the chance to come to grips with the enemy. He'd fought battles when he'd been reluctant to get his blade wet. There'd been nothing of himself in those battles; they were only tactical necessities. This struggle was different: it was personal. He'd learned to hate the *Alman* as he'd rarely hated before. He'd despised Forgren and his lackeys, but contempt wasn't hatred. It was hard to hate someone so petty, who only strove to fill his own purse and gain some power.

The *Alman* seemed utterly evil, something that deserved hatred, and hatred demanded confrontation and blood.

"The brazier is ready," Damon announced.

Scarface hauled himself to his feet, using the wall to help draw himself erect. At the brazier, he spoke the incantation slowly, afraid to mispronounce a single syllable. He hoped to see some different shape in the fire, not sure he was capable of commanding the dragon in his weakened state. The flames leapt up, forming wings, and he released a held breath. The wings were bird-like rather than the jagged bat-wings of the dragon. A head emerged and the firebird sprang up, trailing a long tail of flame.

He recognized the stylized eagle of his pennon.

He sent the eagle out over the plain and it hovered, as though reluctant to become a carrion bird, then it struck at one of the bodies nearest the pass.

The fresh body was slow to burn and Scarface willed the eagle to tear at the tendons of the inner elbow and at the backs of the knees. He slowly worked his way through the bodies toward the fortress. He'd just ignited a mound of bodies mowed down by flints from the catapult when he heard the drumbeat begin. He attacked another dead man as its limbs began to twitch and it began, jerkily, to rise. He burned it down before it could reach its feet, then drew the eagle back. The firebird flew as though drawn by the clangor of the alarm, and wrapped itself around the knee of one of the newly risen dead.

The figure tottered ahead four steps, then fell, still trying to drag itself forward. He left it burning and attacked another.

Only vaguely aware of the clamor about him, Scarface crippled one body after another. Shambling corpses, some of them still afire, began to reach the trench and he could only continue to attack, to try to cut the strings that held those lethal marionettes together.

Desperation made the anger hotter, but the flame he wielded was finite, while the number of enemies they faced seemed nearly infinite. The eagle grew, and he guessed kindling had been added to the fire. The figures continued to march and to burn.

Someone seized his shoulder and screamed in his ear, and he sent the bird toward the pass. Archers had rushed from cover at the mouth of the pass. Many had already been felled by flints, but others nocked arrows and prepared to unleash a flight. Scarface willed the eagle to attack faces and bowstrings. Killing them would only add to the host of marching dead they already faced, but inflicting pain could break them.

He could almost hear their screams, then the attack faltered and crumbled. Men rolled on the rock, thrashing, and those less badly burned stumbled back the way they'd come.

As soon as the new threat was ended he turned back to the field. Most of the dead were down, and he harried the few left far enough away from the trench he wouldn't endanger their own troops.

Blackness began at the edge of his vision and he wondered if the *Alman* and his brother were casting a death-spell. He called the eagle back, met little resistance, and saw it discorporate into the brazier. He desperately needed all his power and all his concentration to meet this fresh attack. He couldn't fall now; the fortress might fall with him. And the most bitter pain of all was to never again see Topaz, never know whether she survived the birth of their daughter.

He stood and glared at the pass, tried to scream defiance. He refused to die at the magic of evil cowards, but his vision swam, and the darkness rushed in from all sides.

~ * ~

The surface on which he lay was yielding. He heard a voice, faint with distance, couldn't understand the words it spoke. His eyes shot open and he saw a dim light above his head. A face leaned over him and he would've struck it away but he could hardly raise his arms, then he recognized the priest of Ianno, and he sighed.

An arm slid beneath him, helped him up, and the priest pressed a cup to his lips. Something sour and faintly astringent had been added to the water. He drank as much as he could, then took a deep breath. "Then their last attack didn't carry?"

"I am sorry, brother," the priest said. "I speak only little Gasgoran. Water?"

Scarface nodded and drank again. He tried to remember when he'd last had a drink of water. Sometime between the early morning

attack and dawn, he supposed. He drained another cup of the flavored water and, when the priest handed him a biscuit, ate ravenous-
ly. The biscuit tasted as good as any meal he'd ever enjoyed. The
priest chuckled, handed him a piece of fruit. He bit into it eagerly,
felt some of the sweet juices run down his chin and into his short
beard. When he'd finished the fruit, he said, in Thani, "More water."

The priest babbled something in Thani as he poured more water
into the cup and handed it to Scarface.

Scarface was able to accept the cup. "I speak only a little Thani,"
he said in Gasgoran, then, in Thani, "How does the battle go?"

"We still stand."

This ignorance of what had happened was maddening. Scarface
tried to struggle up but the priest placed a hand on his chest and
shoved him back onto the pallet. "Rest now," he said, then his hand
described a circle above Scarface's head and he murmured a phrase
in Thani.

Scarface's eyelids grew as heavy as his arms, and he sank back
onto the pallet. His last conscious thought was that, whether it was a
blessing or a spell the priest had employed, it worked very well. He
went to sleep with Topaz's face before him. She was smiling.

~ * ~

When Scarface woke again he was alone. The candle, or another
one, cast its dim light and he could hear voices. He drew himself up,
realized he was still armored. Grunting, he sat up, and groaned as he
stood. His body was as stiff as an old man's, and his upper arms
were sore. On a low table sat the ewer and the cup. He poured himself another cup of water and gulped it down, refilled the cup, drank
more slowly.

Three steps carried him to the corridor. He saw no one, but followed the passage to the room where he'd eaten breakfast, and dinner the night before. That room was dark. He turned and strode toward the sound of voices, reached the stairwell, and followed it
down to the barracks.

Half a dozen men lay on pallets, four of them talking softly
among themselves. All had apparently been wounded. He thought
one of them was the warrior who'd wielded the glaive to such effect.
One of the soldiers looked up at him and greeted him in Thani. He
returned the greeting, then, in Gasgoran, asked if any of them spoke
that language. All four who were awake shook their heads.

Scarface nodded and mounted the stairs to the tower. At ground level he looked out, saw it was dark. That answered one of his questions. He climbed the stairs to the roof, saw Damon leaning on the parapet, looking to the east.

Scarface leaned on the wall beside his nephew. "What happened?"

Damon started, looked at him. "We broke the attack at the trenches, but it was a near thing. If they'd attacked again, it would've carried."

"But they didn't attack again," Scarface reminded him. "Perhaps they couldn't." He stared out into the dark. "How many men did we lose?"

"Fourteen more died, and six were wounded. For a time, I thought you were one of them."

Scarface chuckled. "For a time, I thought so, too. I was afraid the *Alman* had cast some sort of death-spell."

Damon nodded. "You went down as though you'd taken an arrow. The priest said it was exhaustion." He looked quickly at Scarface. "I tried your fire-trap spell. It's in the library. By the time I'd enchanted three stones, I was as tired as if I'd fought a battle."

Scarface considered the implied question. "I'm not sure, myself, how I do it. I know the scars have something to do with it, but I'm not sure what part they play, except that I can draw power from them." It suddenly occurred to him that he had, for years, relied upon a process he didn't truly understand.

His stomach growled. "Where can I find some food?"

Damon jerked a thumb at the moonshadow cast by the stairwell roof. "There's food and a waterskin by the stairs."

Scarface carried the basket to where the younger man stood. "You'd better have some of this with me."

"I'm not hungry."

"Do you want to be the next to drop?" Scarface looked up at the sky. "What time is it?"

"Nearly midnight."

"Then you'd better eat and rest. I can watch for a few hours." He began to devour the provisions.

Damon gnawed at a piece of bread, washed it down with water, ate some meat and a piece of cheese. Scarface ate voraciously, and they watched the pass.

Scarface gestured, indicating the soldiers. "I hope you have some of the men resting."

Damon nodded. "There are three rooms for barracks below. I'm using one of them for the wounded. We'll have the rested men come up a little after daybreak."

"Don't come with them," Scarface said. "Sleep a little late. Spend some time with your family to remind you what you're fighting for. It'll make you a better leader than if you prowl the battlements until you fall. You might send up one of your warriors who speaks both Thani and Gasgoran, and order the brazier readied again."

"I've already loaded the brazier. If you weren't up before the next attack, I was going to try the fire-beast spell."

Damon opened his mouth to tell Damon the risk was too great, closed it without speaking. If the need had been that great, the danger to the garrison might've been even greater than had he not used it. And a quick death to a failed spell might be preferable to what probably waited for them if the *Alman* won.

"Use it only if you must," Scarface said, "and not unless I'm unable to cast it."

He walked with Damon to the stairwell. As they passed near the torch, he saw the young man's face seemed that of a man twice his age, and his features were almost as pale as his hair.

"I'll stand watch until noon," Scarface said. "Get some rest. If you can't sleep, ask the priest to use on you the spell he cast on me. And don't forget, send up a man who speaks both languages."

He strode back to the wall and peered into the darkness. Nothing moved from the pass to the wall. Scarface leaned over to stare down at the trench. Damon had apparently drawn his men back to the walls for the night. He could see soldiers below, most of them lounging, perhaps a third of them on watch, the rest looking after their weapons. Damon had said they were veterans.

Booted feet scuffed the stone steps and a soldier walked toward Scarface. "Damon said I was under your orders. I'm Jocile."

Harma, the Union's master magus, had been the ugliest man Scarface had ever seen, but Jocile was at least a contender for that dubious honor. He seemed to have been born without a neck, and his head seemed shaped to break down doors. His nose was short and up-turned, his eyes were small and as rounded as a pig's, and his mouth was a lipless gash. Had he had a lower lip, it would've been thrust forward, as was the lower jaw, giving him the appearance of truculence. Whatever beauty he might've been left had been obscured by the pockmarks.

Scarface gestured at the man who stood beside the hanging steel bar. "Tell him not to beat the alarm unless I give the order."

Jocile spoke to the other man in rapid, sing-song Thani, then faced Scarface. "He understands."

Scarface grinned. "I wish I did. I need to learn again some of the language."

As the soldier taught him the basics of Thani, Scarface remembered the sing-song quality was because the tone rose or fell at the ends of some words; possessives, for instance, always fell at the end of the word.

After an hour's study, they were interrupted by skirmishers with bows, who dashed out of the mouth of the pass. The man by the bar leapt to his feet, but Scarface snapped, "Not until I order it."

One of the enemy stepped on a fire-trap and disappeared in a glare. The rest of them released a flight of arrows that didn't even reach the trench, then scurried back into the pass.

"I thought that'd be their next trick," Scarface said. "They want us to react to every feint: they want to wear us down. Let the other soldiers get their rest. The real attack will come soon enough. I just hope we'll recognize it and know how to defeat it."

He knew almost nothing about necromancy. It might be a very limited form of magic, leaving their enemy with only a single string on his bow, but it would be a mistake to assume that. He wondered again if the nightmares before the first assault had actually been the first attack or whether they were a sort of shadow of approaching evil. The child had been the first to suffer, perhaps because children were more sensitive. That still left unexplained his vision of the demon on Damon's shoulder. He shrugged. He'd seen things before that hadn't existed. The disguise he'd worn into Donradé was an example of sight being tricked. Whatever the cause, the blessing had apparently removed the curse.

He suddenly realized he was hungry again. "Get us some food," he said to Jocile, then, almost idly, began to remove stones from the cup of the mangonel. He drew his knife and began to cast more fire-traps. He stopped to eat when the soldier returned with meat and bread and a wineskin, and learned the Thani words for the foods.

After eating, he cast more fire-traps. He soon lost count of the number, carefully removed more stones to make room for ones he could enchant. He felt the power strongly, as though he'd been branded again only a month or so earlier. He finally stopped, only weary, not drained. He wondered again at the source of power, hoped it wouldn't desert him when the need was greatest.

He heard the drum begin its beat again, but the rhythm was different. Still, he launched the stones in the catapult. Nothing issued from the pass. He grinned. He'd put their feint to his own use. It was always a victory when one gulled the enemy while sending another weapon against them.

After the man with him had cranked the arm back down and locked it, he seized a shovel and helped the soldier load more flints into the cup. They were beginning to run low on flints, at least for the engine atop the keep.

The power still sang in his veins. He mistrusted it; it seemed unlikely he'd still have such power, but the spells hadn't exhausted him. He'd be pleased to use any weapon that came to his hand, still, he distrusted it.

The sky brightened. Another squad of skirmishers rushed out. Three of them burned and half of them didn't even release a futile arrow against the fortress. The rest of the squad launched arrows in the directions of the walls and dashed back into the pass.

A thought occurred to Scarface. "How close is the next nearest pass?" he asked Jocile.

"Twenty leagues south. There's another twenty-five leagues to the northwest."

If the *Alman* had the use of those passes, and if he'd been intelligent enough to dispatch his men early enough that they could all strike at nearly the same time, the garrison might be facing more Myslans in no more than a day or so. Relief for the fortress probably couldn't arrive for another seven days or more. Poor odds, he decided.

Perhaps some thought should be given to retreat. He saw the folly of that idea almost instantly. He'd visited the stables, knew they contained no more than a score of horses. The enemy certainly had more cavalry than the screen they'd sent around the fortress. He supposed Damon's warriors could defeat cavalry, but even killing cost precious time. Escape wasn't a real possibility and, if it fell, The Shield of The Saint would become the empire's bleeding wound.

He wasted a quarter of an hour trying to plan an apparent retreat that could draw the enemy out where they could be killed.

He understood both the wisdom and the folly of considering such matters. Any fighting man would prefer to consider every possible move by either himself or the enemy. At the same time, such thinking could cause one to lose focus on the immediate problem. He watched the sun rise over the mountains. The drums began again, and the enemy marched a few dead only far enough out of the pass to be seen, then marched them back again.

Grinning, Scarface refused to rise to the bait, not allowing the man by the steel bar to beat the alarm nor launching more flints, which would've been useless, even had it been an attack.

Fresh troops filed out of the keep and relieved the men who'd watched through the night. Jocile glanced at him, stifled a yawn, and continued to watch.

Scarface tried to understand the *Alman*. His tactics were crude. He'd wasted a probing attack, since he hadn't really profited from the beating his army had taken; he hadn't learned. Scarface suspected that, until now, marching a sea of corpses over an enemy had been the extent of the *Alman's* war experience, and it galled him to think a man with such little skill wielded so much power. He began to doubt the *Alman* had dispatched armies through the other passes. He chuckled. If the other passes were nearly as well defended as the one here, the *Alman* wouldn't accomplish anything by splitting his army except to throw it away more quickly, piecemeal.

He looked up at the sky, guessed it'd be perhaps two more hours until noon. With nothing else to do, he found a good stone and began to whet the edges of his sword, then his knife.

The enemy came again in the hour before noon, and this time Scarface ordered the alarm be sounded. A handful of the first wave of skirmishers burned. Two catapults hurled their loads of death but Scarface shouted for the rest to wait. When the first wave reached the road the second wave broke from the pass. A few vanished in sheets of flame but the rest rushed forward, driven by desperation.

The archers in the trenches began to pick off Myslans, but cautiously, as some of the Myslans also carried bows. The ballistae creaked and crashed and killed a few more.

Scarface allowed two mangonels to throw their flints at the second wave, then the ballistae and the archers began to reach into the second ranks.

A third mob of Myslans trotted out of the pass, and Scarface ordered the crews of the last catapults facing the pass to fling their stones. The men tending the first mangonels to be used signaled they were ready again, but he held those engines in abeyance.

A few of the third wave still set off fire-traps but the rest broke from a trot to a dash. Scarface could guess they were desperate to face Damon's warriors while they were still alive: they knew their dead bodies would fight again if their rush failed to carry.

Scarface ordered the men at the reloaded mangonels to stand ready, in case the *Alman* ordered more archers out to support the assault, then he looked down into the trenches. Bodies had begun to fall before the trenches in heaps. The second wave faltered behind the corpses, some to use their dead comrades for cover behind which they could rest for the final rush, or to duel with Damon's archers.

While the archers on the walls were too far from the enemy for accuracy, they arched enough arrows over the wall of bodies to flush the Myslans, and the enemy rushed, screaming, toward the trench. From where he stood, Scarface watched as the battle became a series of hand-to-hand combats. Archers in the trenches shot their last arrows at enemies almost near enough to reach out and touch, then dropped their bows to seize swords or polearms. A Myslan reached the lip of the trench, only to take a glaive in the belly and be hoisted over the trench to fall, still shrieking, among the stakes in the pit.

An angular figure with white hair, wielding two swords, charged from the trench, leaving a trail of dismembered enemies. Damon had been one of the soldiers to answer the alarm.

The drumbeat began and Scarface looked to the brazier, casting the spell again. The eagle, Comarr, rose from the bowl and arrowed into the melee. Scarface hurled the eagle at the few Myslan bowmen still alive. He used his earlier tactic; burning through bowstrings and searing faces.

He soon saw his efforts partly wasted as the marching dead had begun to kill every living thing before them. Eddies appeared in the tide, as some of the live Myslans fought back, but they were overwhelmed. Scarface started another wall of fire on the far side of the road, but that line was breached, again and again. Finally he stacked the burning corpses high enough and thick enough that the dead things were unable to clamber over or through the wall before they became a part of it.

Smoke stung his eyes and the stench became unendurable. He felt his concentration fading and he drew the eagle back, now no larger than a falcon, and let it again become only fire.

Damon and the other men in the trench had stopped the rush and were flinging severed arms and legs into the inferno. Movement in the pit drew Scarface's attention to the body among the stakes. It still moved its arms and legs, as though to crawl to the wall.

Scarface hauled himself up to sit on the parapet and waited for Damon to join him, then twisted on the stone wall to stare out at the pass. The drumbeat had finally stopped, and he glanced down at the figure in the pit. It'd also stopped. Somehow it seemed especially horrible that, had the drum continued to throb, the corpse would've moved until its tendons had rotted away.

Scarface's mouth and throat were parched. He noticed the waterskin by the stairway and, after debating with himself, whether his thirst or his weariness were the greater, shoved himself off the wall and walked to the waterskin, drank until his belly felt full.

Damon climbed the stairs and stepped onto the roof. His face was grim, but the appearance of age and exhaustion had disappeared. He gripped Scarface's forearm as his own was gripped, and they stared into each other's eyes. "I'm grateful you're here," Damon said, then released Scarface's arm and looked away. "If you hadn't come, The Shield would've buckled."

Scarface grinned. "Let's not forget I'm fighting for my life, too. Consider your luck middling. If Hadrian were here, he'd already have hung the *Alman's* head on the tower. And I don't believe you'd have fallen so easily. You're your father's son, and you'd have devised something." He paused, reluctant to broach the subject. "How many men did we lose in that last rush?"

"Nine dead, six more wounded." Damon swallowed. "Migal was a new man. He'll never become a veteran now. And Joniv was one of the men I brought from High Rage. They were all good men."

Scarface rested a hand on Damon's shoulder. There were no words to use as a balm. "The enemy's made a series of feints. They may try it again. You'll have to watch closely and sound the alarm if an attack develops, but if you try to parry every feint, you'll wear out your sword arm."

He let his hand fall. "I'm going below. I'll eat something as soon as I can get past that stink." He gestured to where the smoke still billowed from the mound of dead. "Then I'm going to rest. I'll be back here about midnight." A thought occurred to him. "Keep a watch on the other side of the fortress, too. If I were the enemy, I'd try to use the distraction of a battle to mount another attack from a different direction."

Damon nodded. "I'll keep that in mind."

Scarface took the stairs down to the now-familiar passage and his room. He found fresh water in the ewer, and the basin had been cleaned. He washed the odor of death, as best he could, from his hands and face, then strode to the room where he'd taken meals before. Candles lit the room, and Jeshka sat at the table.

She glanced up from her sewing, then stood. "May I bring you something to eat?"

"Please." He sat at the table.

She disappeared into the kitchen and returned with a meal that might've fed a squad. Scarface decided it was sufficient. There were slices and buns of several kinds of bread, three kinds of cheese in colors running from bright orange to pale gray-green, two fruits he didn't recognize, mutton, and a cup and carafe of red wine.

Jeshka paused and he gestured at her chair. "Please, sit. Do you want any of this?"

"Damon said you were noted for your appetite as well as for other qualities." She sat down in the chair. "I like watching someone eat who enjoys their food, but I wasn't sure you didn't want to be alone."

"I've had more than enough of that." He ate about half the food on the platter, but found the silence uncomfortable. "You aren't from Gascolin, are you?" he asked. "Your Gasgoran is accented."

"I was born in Sazian Glangurra. My father was a silversmith there. He moved to High Rage when I was five. I guess I've kept my family's accent."

"Do you speak Thani?"

"A little, but not very well. I'm not adept at learning languages."

Scarface sampled a piece of fruit. "You've been here in the empire for about three years now, haven't you?"

"Nearer four."

"Forgive my asking, but, do you miss your family?"

She said nothing but her nod was eloquent. He supposed Hadrian was now head of the clan, since all the elders had died at High Rage. "Have you asked Hadrian to send you to some outpost nearer Gascolin?"

"No. Most of the others are bound to their holdings by birth or friendships. Damon was sent to The Shield of The Saint because

Poker had established the outpost but was needed for a time in Gas-colin."

"Did you know Poker?"

"I never got to meet him. He left the empire just as we arrived."

"I'm sorry. He was well worth the knowing, and I think you'd have liked each other." He leaned back in his chair. He perceived the incongruity of the conversation taking place so soon after he'd left a slaughter-pen, but the conversation also seemed proper, somehow, and he remembered what he'd told Damon; one needed some meas-ure of closeness to remember why one fought. It also provided a perspective, kept one from seeing the world as nothing but a charnel house. "Have you heard from your family at all?"

"Hadrian brought a message from them the last time he visited us, and he let them know I'd had a son."

Scarface raised an eyebrow. Since High Rage had fallen and was no longer a clan stronghold, Hadrian had risked his life to carry those messages. If he were so sensible of the feelings of kinship, perhaps he was beginning to heal. There might be some hope for him to be more than the embodiment of vengeance. "Perhaps the clan could help bring your family out of High Rage. Gisli might be able to help."

Jeshka had an attractive smile. "We were thinking of asking him, or Hadrian."

"Then ask, and do it soon. And if they can't do it, send a mes-sage to me. I have one or two small resources." Cerco was near enough High Rage a few Senshenni should be able to escort Jeshka's family to Cerco, and he could have them sent to Eagle, in Ianesk, to take ship to the empire. "You need family." His chuckle was self-deprecating. "No one is a firmer believer than one who's learned late and harshly."

Jeshka had picked up her sewing again. She looked up from the stitch she'd just taken. "Do you have a family—besides the clan?"

The question caught him unprepared, and he paused before he replied. "There's a woman—her name is Topaz—she's carrying our child."

"Why are you worried?"

Scarface looked down at the nearly-empty platter and moved the morsels left as though they were game pieces. Finally, he murmured, "Her mother died in childbirth."

"I'm sorry. It's obvious you care for her very deeply. I'll wish you both well." Her tone was warm and sympathetic, then she grinned at him. "From what I've heard about you, Topaz has worked a fine magick on you."

Grinning back at her, he rose. "I'll rest now. Thank you. For the food and the conversation." He paused, then added, "Damon's chosen well."

He returned to his room and stripped off his weapons, his boots, and the leather gambeson. Sighing, he laid down on the pallet. Making sure that flint, steel, tinder, and a candle were all ready to hand and his sword was in hand's reach, he snuffed the candle and stared up into darkness.

He'd been reluctant to speak of Topaz, perhaps because it revealed to another his vulnerability. Still, sharing vulnerability with someone you could trust strengthened the trust, and it seemed to ease the soul. He'd always been uneasy at sharing part of his life. He smiled into the darkness. Jeshka had chosen the proper words. Topaz had truly worked a fine magick on him.

~ * ~

He rose, lit the candle, dressed, slid the sword in its scabbard to ascertain it moved smoothly, then climbed the stairs to the roof. He found Damon sitting on the wall, and he could hear, from beyond the trench, the sound of metal against stone.

Damon glanced at him and grinned. "I took your words to heart. You said I'd have devised something, and I realized that I'd come to rely upon your power. It's an easy mistake to make, but one I shouldn't have made."

Scarface climbed onto the parapet and sat down beside Damon. By the light of torches, he could see work crews planting spears and pikes in the stone between the traps and the trench. The spears were set at an angle, so their heads were at the height of a man's waist, and the upper shafts were bound with cloth and connected to each other by a web of rags.

"The enemy were generous enough to provide us with a number of spears. It seemed ungracious not to use them. The rags are soaked in oil. One man, using a fire arrow, can set the entire web aflame. I've also issued each man fire fire-arrows."

"Very good." Scarface clapped his nephew on the shoulder. "How many of them do you think we've destroyed, and how big an army do you think the *Alman* has?"

"We've probably killed nearly five thousand of them, most of them twice. Our scouts estimated an army of five times that number, counting the dead things. With some luck, the *Alman's* facing reluctance among the petty nobles and the troops themselves. Our best hope is to make them more afraid of us than they are of him. That's difficult, when your enemy can use the dead to fight his battle."

Scarface raised his head, pointed at the pass with his chin. "Have they tried any more feints?"

"Not since the battle. Whether they really fear us or not, we've made them cautious."

"Good and bad," Scarface muttered. "They're less likely to repeat their mistakes. It remains to be seen whether they can learn. Is there any chance the troops will mutiny, or the *Alman* will decide his army could more profitably—and less disastrously—employed elsewhere?"

Damon ran a hand through his shoulder-length hair. "A mutiny isn't likely. As long as the *Alman* can control the dead, he can control the living. If there were a mutiny, it'd serve his purposes; any man who fell in the fighting, whether defending the Alman or in revolt against him, would become another loyal dead soldier, making more men loyal dead soldiers.

"As for the *Alman* abandoning his attack; he can't do that without losing allies and prestige. He won't run that risk. Not willingly." He turned around on the wall and dropped lightly onto the roof. "I'll send Jocile up, along with something to eat."

"Thank you."

Jocile carried another basket up the stairs and Scarface ignored the food, learned more Thani. Use helped him remember the language, and he was soon able to construct proper sentences. He'd need to absorb the finer points of grammar from someone whose language was more polished, and the words Jocile used were not, he was sure, the ones with which to discuss theology with The Voice of The Faith.

After Jocile had eaten, they stared out at the pass, which remained quiet and empty. Jocile dozed, and Scarface let the man claim an hour's rest before he woke him. While Jocile took his turn at sentry duty, Scarface used the opportunity to speak more Thani.

The night passed without an attack, or even a feint. Conversation added to Scarface's verbal skills so that, as the sky brightened, they were able to exchange crude jokes. He hadn't relearned the language well enough for wit, but soldiers' humor was less demanding.

When the sun appeared they ate more rations from the basket. The enemy still hadn't made a move and Scarface found himself growing impatient. He quelled the feeling, knowing it played into the enemy's hands.

Damon stepped out of the stairwell as the sun reached its zenith. The rest had obviously refreshed him, restored his composure. Scarface greeted him in Thani.

"There've been no alarms. Has it been as quiet as it seems?"

Still in Thani, Scarface replied, "Yes, and it makes me uneasy. When I can't see an attack, I wonder what it is I'm not seeing."

"Perhaps we've forced the *Alman* to take time to think of another approach." Damon sat on the wall beside Scarface. "You speak Thani fairly well, but you're still weak on the inflections."

For almost a quarter of an hour they conversed in Thani. Scarface still suffered some annoying gaps in his vocabulary, and occasional lapses. Verb tenses in Thani were more regular than in some languages he'd attempted, but enough irregularity remained that he still stumbled too often on words that sounded similar but with very different meanings. Finally, he went below.

Jeshka had a meal waiting for him, and Danyol was trying to escape her lap. Scarface forced himself to eat slowly. He had to keep a firm rein on his impatience and the irritability it created. The contest of wills between Jeshka and her son helped. The child was the aggressor. He squirmed first one way, then another, even attempted an occasional feint. Every move, every sound, was aimed at gaining his freedom. Jeshka was at a disadvantage, having to counter every move and maintain control without confining him too closely.

Scarface finished eating and decided to give her some rest. He held out his arms and took the boy. At first, it was like gripping a snake, then Danyol realized he was in the hands of a stranger. The child's face reflected fear, awe, and curiosity, all these emotions moving across his features like cloud shadows over a plain. The curiosity turned him into a whole nest of snakes as he wriggled closer to put a damp, sticky hand over the black scar on Scarface's right cheekbone.

He tussled with the boy for a few moments, feeling awkward and afraid he'd harm the fragile thing he held, then handed him back to his mother. Learning to be a father seemed harder than learning a language. He bade her a good day and, in his room, found water and a tub waiting for him.

The water was lukewarm and he gave himself a soldier's bath, then stretched out on the pallet. After an hour of staring into the darkness he growled a curse, rose, and dressed and armed himself.

He found his way to the tunnel and paced around the perimeter. Most of the traps faced the pass, but the enemy cavalry still lurked to the west, outside the range of the mangonels. The *Alman* would have to use those cavalry soon, or they'd have to run the gantlet again just to feed their horses. He doubted they'd carried enough provisions for more than a day or so, and the land was too barren for grazing. While the *Alman* seemed disposed to throw away parts of his forces, he'd need to reinforce those men or, at least, supply them, if they were to keep Tong Shavath surrounded.

He spent three hours creating a barrier of fire-traps in an arc on the western side of the fortress, then returned to his pallet.

Sleep still eluded him, but he forced himself to rest.

~ * ~

He rose unrefreshed and anxious, with a sense of impending doom. When he reached the tower he found Damon drawing his swords a hand's length from their scabbards and clashing them back again, glaring at the pass and at the rock walls flanking the northern and southern sides of the fortress.

Scarface peered out past the trenches and, as his eyes grew accustomed to the darkness, he saw furtive movement. "What is it?"

Damon pointed to some of the moving shapes. "Nearly an hour ago the enemy started sending out groups of four or five men. That's too few to waste a load of stone chips on, and they're beyond the reach of our bows. A few of them set off fire-traps, but most of them got through. He's been sending out the groups for the last hour. The *Alman's* started to think."

CHAPTER 8

Scarface sipped water and nibbled at a biscuit as he made the circuit of the keep. The enemy continued sending small groups around the fortress.

Damon had remained on the roof for over an hour after Scarface's return and had only gone below when Scarface reminded him that, as lord of the fortress, he must be rested enough to think clearly and command effectively.

The defenses had been prepared: the piles of stone chips had been partly replenished and skins of oil had been placed by the cranes along the points of the wall.

Scarface began to pace, muttering to Jocile. He'd already dismissed the idea of a sortie. The curve of the road and the belt of remaining traps around Tong Shavath would make mounting a raid difficult enough the enemy could prepare, could trap any raiders outside the walls and cut them apart. It'd simply deplete the garrison without hurting the enemy.

He had only one weapon left, and he was prepared to wait before using it. The fortress was beginning to run low on supplies. The pine and blackwood had been all but exhausted, and even common kindling was becoming dear. Most of the meat left was dried, as was the fruit. Only water was plentiful; Hadrian had made sure there were at least two wells within the area protected by the walls.

Scarface grinned to himself. He'd know when they'd eaten the last of the dried meat, and he wondered if he'd recognize the horse he'd ridden to The Shield.

An hour after dawn, Damon mounted the stairs, emerged onto the roof carrying a pallet and a blanket. He tossed the pallet into the shade of the rampart, went below, returned with a glaive, a bow, and a large quiver of arrows. "Since I can't seem to sleep below, I'll rest here, where I may be of some use if you need me. I've left orders for the men from the night watch to do the same, as soon as they've eaten."

"I'm glad you're here," Scarface said. He pointed to the northern cliff face. "Now the Myslans are trundling small carts around us."

He led Damon to the western side of the keep, indicating the line of Myslan cavalry drawn up just beyond the reach of the mangonels. They'd obviously been reprovisioned and, while they were few, were arrayed as a threat. "I'm prepared to call up the dragon. We can upset them, perhaps spoil their attack, and certainly teach them respect." Some of the infantry marching past the fortress were shouting and gesturing, and the cavalry had begun to make mock charges, advancing until they were just beyond the range of the catapults, then falling back again.

Damon frowned. "The last blackwood I could find is in the brazier, and I hate to waste it before they charge..." He stared out at the Myslans and his face hardened. He gripped Jocile's arm. "Get him whatever he wants, and make sure the fire doesn't go out. Feed fresh kindling as long as he commands it or we have a stick of wood in the place."

Jocile nodded and turned to Scarface. "How soon?"

"As soon as you're ready to give me all the fuel I need."

Jocile nodded again and pounded down the stairs. He returned with a brush, a bucket of pitch, and a length of rope slung over his shoulder. He placed the brush and the pitch beside the brazier, then tied one end of the rope around the base of the flagstaff and tossed the other end over the wall. "If we need wood quickly, it'd be best to have another way to get it up here than the stairway," he explained.

He tugged at the rope to make sure it was secure, then went over the wall and slid down the rope to the base of the keep, ducked back inside the building. When he returned, up the stairs, he dropped an armload of wood beside the brazier. "There'll be more when you need it," he panted.

Fixing the dragon in his mind, Scarface began the incantation. He dipped the torch into the bowl until the flames rose and he called forth Lashastur. It seemed appropriate the dragon, all power and anger, be the weapon he chose. The head rose on its neck and regarded him, and his vision suddenly seemed doubled as he stared at the dragon and gazed at himself through the dragon's eyes.

With a roar of flames, the dragon flung himself skyward, and he sent it against the cavalry. Lashastur drove the horses into a panic, whipping them with wings and tail, snapping at the riders with glowing jaws. He pursued them as they turned and ran, setting cloaks afire, making flambeaux of the riders. He harried them until they rode over the crest of a rise and disappeared down the other side, then he assailed the men on foot.

The Myslans scurried like rats, trying to escape him, but he sprang after them. Their bravado had turned to terror, and he ran them down or struck from the air like a bird of prey.

He stood atop the tower, roaring laughter as he drove them before him like chaff before a wind. Lashastur attacked the Myslans along the northern cliffs next. It wasn't necessary to kill them; it wasn't their deaths he required, but their pain and fear. He found himself feeding on their terror as the flames fed on the pitch-coated wood.

He drove the last few of them back into the pass, then, striding around the keep, attacked the men on the southern flank. The anguish and panic he caused delighted him; he—both of him—roared with pleasure. He roared and stalked and tormented them until he'd marked every Myslan in sight. Several of them lay among the rocks, still burning, and the dragon devoured them to the bones.

He took care to burn each wagon and cart in sight. Let the bastards eat rocks or starve. He caused the dragon to spring into the air, then called it back. The dragon fought the command as a spirited charger fights the bit or a dog the leash, but he raised his fists and repeated the command, shouting it so that his voice rang among the stones, and Lashastur lowered himself into the brazier, became only flames.

Scarface turned to Jocile. "You may extinguish it now."

Jocile scrambled to obey, and Scarface grinned at Damon. "They've learned respect—and fear. You wanted them more afraid of us than the *Alman*. We've made a start."

Damon's face was as impossible to read as Hadrian's had ever been. "So it would seem."

"What's amiss?" Scarface demanded.

Damon stepped within arm's reach of him. He spoke softly, and in Sinn. "You didn't see yourself. I think you've made some of the garrison as afraid of you as the Myslans are. In some ways, you *were* the dragon." He stared at the brazier, where the flames had sunk below the level of the lip of the bowl. "I think I'm glad we have no more blackwood."

"Say that again when the drums beat, and you face a sea of dead faces," Scarface snapped, then turned on his heel and strode to the stairs. He had to press his back against the wall to avoid a line of women and older children, some still passing up bits of wood to the next in line. As he moved past them they began to turn and descend the stairs; they'd apparently begun to learn the wood was no longer needed.

A turn above the outside door, he recognized Jeshka among the women. She opened her mouth, perhaps for a greeting, then her face paled so her freckles stood out and she turned her head away.

Scarface clenched his teeth until he could feel the muscles in his jaws stiffen. By the time he could relax them, he'd reached the familiar passage and stalked toward his room. Taking a candle from an alcove, he lit it from duty candle and, once in his room, thrust the candle into a holder. He picked up the ewer in both hands and drank deeply, spilling some water into his gambeson and feeling the shock of the cold water as it ran down his chin and his chest.

His thirst slaked, he sat on the edge of the pallet and forced himself to breathe slowly and steadily, trying to snuff the fury he felt. He'd learned that to pretend control of oneself was, in some measure, to have control. When he felt his body relax, he stood, picked up the candle, and walked to the dining room. The place was empty. He wanted company more than food, and he paced to Damon's room.

That room was also dark. For a moment he stood undecided, then made his way to the infirmary, the barracks used by the wounded. Several men lay on pallets, and several more sat in a group. Jeshka and two other women were examining wounds and changing dressings. Scarface approached Jeshka, the glow of his candle lost in the stronger light of the room's oil lamps.

"Could you please bring me something to eat?" he asked Jeshka.

She glanced up at him, them down at the arm she was dressing. "In a moment."

He waited patiently, then followed her to the dining room. She moved as though under orders and said nothing, placed a platter of food before him.

"Please, sit down," he said.

He stared down at the food on the platter, selected a bit of dried meat and sampled it, knowing it'd sit in his belly like lead. His body was still outraged at the tensions and demands to which he'd subjected it, and his emotions still roiled beneath the still surface he'd assumed.

"Why are you afraid of me?" he asked her. "I've held your son. Damon and I are kin. Why do you treat me like a stranger with a knife at your throat?"

"When I saw you on the stairs, you looked like a stranger." Her gaze couldn't meet his eyes. "You frightened me. Your eyes burned everything you looked at, and you looked as though you wanted to kill."

He sighed and leaned back in his chair. Words were useless. Misunderstandings grew like weeds, and nothing he could say could change what they'd seen, or thought they'd seen. He also felt some disgust. Commanded company was worse than no company at all. "I'm sorry I interrupted you. The wounded need your attention." He gestured dismissal.

As she left the room he glared at the food before him, then shoved it away. Did these people think you set a sheep to watch over the rest of the flock? Had he not the power and the rage, he'd would not have been able to make the Myslans run.

After a moment's thought, he picked up the platter. If the siege lasted long, food would be too scarce to waste. He carried the platter to the infirmary and handed it to the first man who looked at it with hunger, then mounted the stairs to the roof.

Scarface ignored his nephew, glowered at the dead still lying where they'd fallen. More wounded and maimed crawled away or groped and stumbled aimlessly. He took a grim satisfaction in the carnage he'd wrought. There'd be fewer enemies to have to kill twice.

When the sun stood overhead he drank water and a little sour wine, ate bread and dried meat, then lay down on the pallet Damon had carried to the roof. The wind from the pass was cold enough he was grateful for the blanket, and used it to cover his face. Half-listening to the few remarks of the soldiers, he dozed.

He was dimly aware when Damon ordered the men to retrieve as many enemy shields as they could reach, but he drifted into and out of slumber.

He woke at sunset and lay staring at the sky, picking out the brighter stars as they appeared. Despite the distrust and fear obvious in the men around him, Scarface knew he must and would defend The Shield of The Saint with every trace of power he had. More than his own survival was at stake. He wanted to live to return to Topaz, wanted it with aching intensity, but it was even more important Damon and Jeshka and their son live. A brief misunderstanding and a flash of anger shouldn't be allowed to affect what he knew and deeply felt.

The men were quiet; the fiercest battle any of them had ever seen was approaching. It was like watching the clouds gather, feeling the wind grow, seeing the lightning begin to stalk the heavens. Closing his eyes, he tried to relax, failed.

Levering himself up, he rose to his feet. Damon leaned against the wall a few paces away. His hair stirred in the wind from the pass, else he could've been taken for a statue. Scarface hesitated, then stood beside him. The pass was in moon shadow, but he could sense the Myslans in the darkness, creeping around the fortress.

"When do you think they'll come?" Damon asked.

"If it were me, I'd attack a little before dawn; get the first rush in while it's dark so they can try to close before we can use our defenses, then push the attack. If the battle's going to be long and bitter, it's best to have daylight for as long as possible."

"And how would you defend against such an attack?"

"I'd use the fire-dragon spell again. It's still our best chance."

"But we have no more blackwood. I fed the last of it into the brazier for the last spell."

"I still have my scabbard. And something of very great value, if it's needed."

The silence seemed longer in the darkness. Finally, Damon said, "Are you sure you want to cast that spell again? It seemed to have…untoward effects on you."

Scarface laughed softly. "That's a delicate way to say it seemed to make me go mad. We need that spell. With Jocile standing ready to kill the fire, there shouldn't be much danger."

Damon turned to face him, although his expression couldn't be read in the darkness. "You'll need to be up here to cast the spell. I'll be with the men in the trench."

Scarface wanted to argue, but it'd be useless. Damon strongly felt his responsibility to his men.

Damon seemed to have heard the unspoken thought. "I won't waste any lives, including my own."

Scarface studied the defenses Damon had added. Captured shields lay in overlapping rows along sections of the lip of the trench and along the wall, providing overhangs as protection from arrows.

Damon gestured. "I'd have tried putting some on the keep, but there's not enough wood left to build a frame. Every captured spear we could find is planted beyond the trench."

"I'll try to keep them from getting that close."

"Do you want me to wake Jocile?"

"Not yet. I'm confident they're not going to attack before midnight. They aren't prepared. They haven't moved enough men around us for an attack from all sides. They've learned we can block the pass and slow their attacks. They probably won't be ready until an hour or two before dawn." He shoved himself away from the wall. "I'll cast fire-traps on some of the stones in the mangonels facing the pass. That'll be the source of the main attack."

He cast the spell on a dozen stones in the keep's catapult, then took the stairs down to the ground level. The catapults nearest the pass would fling their stones farther, and he wanted to keep the enemy as far away as he could.

After casting the spell on a score of the stones in each of the scoops of the three catapults facing the pass, he still felt the power, but he guessed the time near midnight, and he returned to the roof of the keep.

Damon had already wakened Jocile, who's gone below to wake the women and older children, and some of the wounded. In a short time he'd set in place a chain of people to pass wood up the stairs, and Scarface had seen a man with one arm in a sling and a hatchet in his good hand enter the stable. Almost immediately he could hear steel ring against wood and guessed the man was breaking up stalls. Soon, wood was being hauled to the base of the keep.

Scarface himself painted pieces of wood with pitch, heaping them high in the brazier, then slid his sword out of its scabbard. He unbuckled the sword belt and removed the scabbard, laid it carefully atop the piled wood, then donned the belt and thrust the sword in it. From his purse he took the message he'd received from Topaz, so long ago in Donradé. He'd read it often; it always provided him peace and warmth.

For this spell, because so much depended upon its power and success, he needed to sacrifice something of tremendous value. He weighted the parchment down with a piece of wood, then struck flint and steel and lit one of the torches.

The chill wind from the pass was numbing his fingers, and he drew on a pair of gauntlets. When he was able to see again in the darkness, he stared out to where he knew the enemy crept. The moon had risen to its zenith and the pools of moon shadow had shrunk; he could see the Myslan soldiers slipping from one scrap of concealment to the next, using every rock and dead body to hide themselves. They were moving again, but he and the dragon had taught them discretion.

He tried to anticipate any disaster, but nothing more could be done. Now the initiative passed to the enemy. He enchanted more stones. He paced, sipped water, nibbled bread, paced again, then grinned at himself. If this were a contest of patience, the *Alman* was ahead.

Suddenly he realized the pattern of surreptitious movement had changed. Some of the Myslans were still flanking the fortress, but he'd seen two figures slipping toward the trench. He waited, watched other Myslans, saw several figures crawling toward the fortress.

Snatching up the torch, he thrust it into the wood in the brazier as the soldiers began to beat the alarm and the horns blared. He called on Lashastur, and the dragon sprang upward as though he'd been waiting for the opportunity to attack again.

From the trench came the music of bowstrings, and a scream. At least one Myslan had been hit. The rush became more general, and Scarface flung the dragon at the Myslans.

He couldn't afford to take the time to kill or maim each Myslan he attacked; he could only inflict fear and anguish, and burn through bowstrings. It was most important to keep them from smothering the defenders under flights of arrows.

Catapult arms slammed into padded crosspieces, and stone chips rattled on the rock. Men screamed and some fell. The bowstrings hummed and sudden flames roared, and the dragon roared in reply.

Scarface concentrated on the attackers on their northern flank, attacking archers first and foot soldiers only if they reached the trench.

The attack was quickly turned and he strode to the western side of the keep. The cavalry remained out of sight, but hundreds of infantry had rushed forward. Bodies already hung on some of the spears, and other corpses lay in the burning web of rags. The traps and other defenses, after the stones and arrows had taken their toll, had slowed the attack, and it'd begun to stall. Myslan archers had drawn near enough arrows had begun to fall in the trench, and Scarface punished the archers as quickly as he could find them.

The noise had become almost deafening. Men were shouting and screaming in defiance, rage, pain, and terror. Pipes skirled and trumpets brayed, and all the siege engines were flinging death as rapidly as their crews could arm them. Orders were shouted in Thani and Myslan, arrows struck flesh or stone, and the humming of bowstrings had become almost constant.

Lashastur had pounced on another archer and snapped through the Myslan's bowstring, just as an arrow from the trench took the man in the chest. The dragon instantly sought another victim.

The attack was faltering when a sergeant, or perhaps a petty noble, strode forward, shouting and driving men onward with the flat of his blade. Lashastur sprang on the Myslan, savaging him. Howls turned to shrieks, and the dragon tore at the body until he knew it couldn't rise again.

The Myslans to the east fought under the command of the *Alman* and his brother, and there was no retreat for those caught north or south of the fortress, but the Myslans in the west could escape. They pressed their attack until the bodies lay almost to the trench, then staggered away.

Scarface rushed to the southern side of the keep as the first Myslan to reach the trench fell with a spear in his belly. Lashastur hovered above the trench, darting at the nearer enemies, then sought out the remaining archers. When he was sure Damon's men had that part of the battle in hand, he turned to face the east.

Bodies lay in clumps, but the Myslans continued to attack. He pounced on the nearest archers, but a man no sooner fell or was disarmed than another drew bowstring to jaw and released. Scarface crouched, exposing himself at little as possible, while the Dragon cut a swathe through the attackers. Two of the crew of the keep's mangonel were already down and another had taken an arrow through the arm, but the rest of the men rushed to draw the weapon's arm to lock and refill the scoop with stone chips.

The ballistae groaned and crashed, casting their heavy javelins and, one after another, the mangonels hurled their loads of stone chips, but the first rank of Myslans had already reached the trench.

Again, Scarface could only try to disarm the archers; it was impossible to stem the flow of warriors, many charging over their own dead and wounded comrades.

The dragon moved with the speed of thought, but the *Alman* had decided to flood the defenders with an ocean of arms. The sky grew lighter as the battle raged, and the struggling figures seemed darker against the paling sky, the dragon more vivid now than in the full darkness.

Damon led a rush from the trench and wielded his glaive almost like a scythe. Blades rang against blades, battered shields, shrieked through armor, and hacked flesh. The screams of the wounded and dying grew louder until they almost buried the clash of weapons. Damon's counter-charge drove the Myslans back almost to where the traps had been, and Scarface protected his nephew as best he could, attacking more archers.

The Myslan pipes changed from a rapid series of notes to a single shrill, ear-piercing squeal, and the Myslans began to retreat. Some fell back facing the fortress, still fighting, but most broke into headlong flight, seemingly hoping to outrun any arrows shot at them.

It was easier to find the archers now, and Lashastur disarmed them, burned a few down, then began to consume bodies. At the edge of his vision, Scarface could see Damon and his men dismembering the bodies of men they'd killed, making sure they wouldn't have to fight them again.

The dragon began to prowl among the mounds of dead, setting entire heaps afire, trying to make them useless to the *Alman*.

Damon and his men had regained the trench, maiming the corpses they found, when the drums began their throbbing and many of the bodies began to jerk and twitch, and some, beyond the ones maimed by Damon's warriors, to rise. They advanced on the fortress, hardly slowing to kill their own wounded and add to their number.

The marching dead seemed not to see—they made no moves to protect themselves—but they seemed dimly aware of the living, and death was truly the enemy of life. When death and life clashed, death always won, although life might sometimes fight a delaying action.

The drums increased their tempo and the advance of death became quicker. Damon and his soldiers had bought a brief respite, and some of the planted spears slowed the first ranks as the dead things impaled themselves and had to tear themselves free or to break the shafts.

Scarface was barely aware more men had replaced the dead and wounded at the siege engines and the weapons were being readied. Those moments to rest and to shift their defenses were all too fleeting.

More archers dashed from the pass, prepared to try to force the defenders into hiding from the flights of arrows while the dead things marched on relentlessly. The stone chips rained among the archers, and missiles from the ballistae claimed more victims. The dragon leapt and spun among them, harrying them, but still more charged forward.

Scarface drew the dragon back to the line where the planted spears had been. Damon led another counterattack and at first he'd flung the enemy back with the sheer ferocity of his attack, but now he and his men were being pressed back by the overwhelming number of the enemy. Lashastur turned as many of the corpses into moving torches as he could reach, but the assault never faltered.

Damon's men had begun to fall back across the bridge and into the tunnels. Damon still led the rearguard, but Scarface wondered how long he could stand. He'd lost his glaive and was now fighting with a sword in either hand. His bright armor was now dulled and scarred and stained with gore, but he fell back grudgingly, retreating only a single step at a time, then fighting desperately to hold.

Scarface threw Lashastur into the melee, and he screamed for Damon to retreat. At last, Damon gave ground to the trench, and from there he hacked at legs until he stood alone, holding the line of retreat for his men, then he fought to the bridge.

The bridge was already being drawn up as Damon ducked into the tunnel. The dragon fought on, but the dead advanced even as they burned, falling into the trench and then the pit, among the stakes. The tide was irresistible, and Lashastur spread his wings and soared upward, searching for enemies he could affect.

Scarface felt as well as heard the rumble as the tunnel was blocked, saw a gout of rock dust billow from around the raised bridge.

Fresh attackers swarmed from the mouth of the pass, ready to follow the dead into the fortress. The corpses had broken the defenses by their sheer numbers; all the traps had been sprung, the spears broken or torn away, the trench had been taken, and the pit was rapidly filling with bodies. The enemy was determined to take the fortress, less heedless of the losses than calculating uses for their dead.

Scarface realized then the sun had risen and he could see the Myslans attacking, saw scores of them fall before the stones and dozens falling to arrows, but hundreds more still ran toward Tong Shavath. A few arrows began to fall on the roof of the keep; one glanced off a stone beside him and skittered away.

Something else appeared in the pass. It seemed to be a small, dense cloud, hugging the ground but moving at the speed of the breeze that ran from the pass; about the speed of a running man. Someone screamed, "The Deathwind!" then he heard the thing. It seemed to be the keening of the wind, but it was something felt as well as heard; felt in the soul. It felt cold.

Lashastur stooped like a hawk at the cloud and Scarface seemed to see it through the dragon's eyes. It seemed to be made up of hundreds of faces, all twisted in agony, and it was from the mouths of the faces that the sound issued, a noise like the wailing of lost souls. As the cloud passed over the massed troops it grew, as more tormented faces became part of the cloud, and the bodies below fell, to rise again.

Scarface didn't know the spell, had never heard of it, but knew it was death and, like death, might be slowed but not stopped. He could feel its enormous power, and hesitated. It seemed useless to sacrifice the dragon, and painful—like sacrificing himself, or someone he cared for—but they had nothing else. He seemed to feel a sudden chill of fear in the dragon, then it became all flame and rage, and hurled itself at the cloud.

The two magical entities were fire and ice and, for a moment, they mingled, then both disappeared in a flash like a near lightning stroke. Thunder momentarily deafened him, and Scarface reeled as though dealt a mortal wound. He fell, face-down, onto the roof of the keep.

For some moments he was unconscious, or might have been, then he tasted blood in his mouth, felt the stone cold against his face.

Lashastur was gone, snatched from existence, and he felt as though there were a hole in his own chest; some part of him was also gone.

But his body still lived. He struggled for a moment, then got his hands under him and shoved himself up onto his knees. His legs, like his arms and hands before, seemed as though they were no longer a part of his body, then he lurched to his feet and staggered to the wall.

Bodies lay in heaps across the plain, but some Myslans still rushed toward the wall. And all was silent save for the sound of flames.

He'd given nearly everything to defend The Shield of The Saint. The only thing he had left to place between his kinsmen and the enemy was his own body.

He remembered the rope hanging over the wall, found it, snatched it up, climbed across the top of the rampart, slid down the side of the keep. A pace or two from the ground, he let himself fall, dashed across the bailey, drawing his sword as he ran. The howl from his throat was no human sound.

Racing up the steps to the wall, he looked down. Dead men lay from the trench to the wall and, two dozen paces to his right, the bodies lay piled at the bottom of the wall into a heap that reached almost to the level of the top of the wall. The defenders had dropped burning oil onto the heaps of corpses, which writhed like a mass of maggots.

Below him lay only bare stone. He climbed atop the wall, crossed it, sat on top of the outer face, and shoved himself off. He fell twice his own height, struck with his feet together, rolled, sprang to his feet, his sword in his hand.

Myslans pounded toward him. More crossed the trench and the pit on a bridge of bodies and scaled the mound of dead to gain the wall. Driven by frenzy and a sense of loss, Morgan hurled himself at the nearest Myslan. The man thrust at him with a spear.

Morgan parried, spun, hacked off the Myslan's left arm and buried his blade in the man's chest. He had to kick the body away while twisting his sword to free the weapon, and almost missed parrying a lunge by another enemy. He side-stepped, struck where neck met shoulder, and threw himself at another Myslan.

An arrow swept past him and the next man fell. He ducked a halberd stroke that would've beheaded him, and chopped off the Myslan's right arm at the shoulder.

Sound was returning to the battlefield, growing louder. He heard shouts behind him but pressed ahead. He'd become a living weapon. The struggle appeared to him only as a series of impressions and re-actions. Faces snarled or screamed, blades flashed, and everything seemed flecked or spattered with blood. His body fought on as it'd been trained, though his mind was numb.

The Myslans who'd been stumbling across the heaps of bodies filling the trench and the pit began to struggle to escape. Morgan turned to face the growing roar behind him and saw that much of the garrison had followed him.

Damon parried a spear-thrust meant for Morgan and cut down a Myslan who'd preferred to die fighting than be killed running.

Morgan acknowledged with a nod and rushed ahead, pursuing the fleeing enemy.

He killed two more Myslans before he stumbled over a corpse and fell. He rolled with the fall, struggled to regain his feet, then sat, leaning on his sword, gasping for breath. Damon knelt on one knee beside him. "Are you all right?"

Morgan tried a grin, found he didn't have the energy for lying. "No, but there are more important matters."

Damon appeared to be studying Morgan's face, then looked away. "One is that a few more paces would've carried you nearer the pass than the fortress. We don't want to be beyond the protection of our archers."

Morgan tried to consider the information. Either he was unable to grasp it, or he simply didn't care. His body began to tremble, then his breath came in a sob. His emotions were in turmoil and he was unable to even feel them. He looked around at the waste of war.

Damon clapped a hand on his shoulder. "Rest. You've done your part." He turned to the men with him. "Dismember every body you can reach."

The soldiers fell to the task with grim efficiency. Blades rose and fell and, sometimes, a scream told them a body had still been alive. After a time, Morgan stood. He found a body wearing a scabbard that would hold his sword, buckled on the booty sword belt, cleaned his blade on the dead man's shirt, and sheathed the weapon, then found an ax and joined the others in the gory duty.

As they neared the trench they were forced to circle around. The men at the wall had poured more of the burning oil on the bodies against the wall, and the oil had flowed in burning streams downslope to the trench.

They circled farther north until they reached a section of trench the defenders had been able to hold, staggered across the bridge and through the tunnel to the fortress. Morgan and Damon laboriously climbed the stairs, both having to stop twice and bring their breathing under control and gather energy for the next few steps.

When finally they reached the roof of the keep, Morgan saw bloodstains where men had been wounded or killed. Jocile wasn't on the roof, and Damon told Morgan that the man had been wounded by an arrow through the shoulder.

Morgan stared out at the devastation and wondered why the drums remained silent. Another attack like the one they'd just survived would overrun the garrison. Their defenses had been depleted, the garrison had lost men, both dead and wounded, and the survivors were so weary they could hardly raise their arms. He saw men gazing out at horrors only they could see or, with their faces in their hands, weeping like heartbroken children.

No one stood. The most active among them leaned against walls. The others sat, or even lay, on the stones. A woman brought them a waterskin and each man drank sparingly, knowing his comrades were as thirsty as he.

"When do you think they'll come again?" Damon finally asked.

"I'm surprised they broke off the attack, and that they haven't attacked again already." He remembered what he'd seen when the *Alman* and his brother had raised the deathwind. "What did you see of the end of...?" He found himself unable to pronounce the dragon's name.

"Very little. I saw the cloud that's the manifestation of the Deathwind spell—"

"Did you see any faces in the cloud?"

"No, did you?" At Morgan's dismissive gesture, he continued. "I saw the dragon pause, then attack the cloud. Then a flash and what sounded like a clap of thunder, and the sky was empty. What happened to the dragon?"

Morgan turned his face away to hide the sudden tears that started in his eyes, but his voice broke when he said, "He died."

When he looked at Damon again the younger man seemed to have found his own hands fascinating, as though he were reading his own palms. Morgan knew he'd spoken the truth. If he ever cast the spell again, he wouldn't be able to call up Lashastur. The dragon was gone forever, and he felt an aching loneliness and as acute a sense of loss as if he'd lost an arm or a leg.

"Go below," Morgan said. "You need to eat and rest."

Damon nodded but continued to sit, his back against the wall. He seemed to have lost the energy even to rise to his feet.

"You also need to see Jeshka and Danyol, find out how many men we lost...." Morgan's voice faded.

Damon hauled himself to his feet, trudged to the stairway. Morgan watched him leave, dragged himself up. The mangonel held only half a load and no more stone chips lay ready. He crawled onto the battlement to sit facing the pass.

Even from the top of the keep he could feel the heat from the flames, and the stench of burning flesh was gut-wrenching. The fire had spread to the trench, and he supposed it might burn for days.

The wall near the pile of bodies had been abandoned as the heat had driven the defenders back. The two nearest ballistae and one of the mangonels had burst into flames. Arrows, most of them broken, lay everywhere, and he was amazed there were still unwounded men in the bailey. The rows of captured shields bristled with shafts and he guessed they'd been the salvation of much of the garrison. A few skins of oil still lay beside the cranes, but he saw few piles of stone chips, and those that remained represented no more than a load or two.

If the *Alman* attacked now, the fortress was lost, but there were still rituals to observe. Some of the soldiers had gone below, probably to eat. The others had begun to move again, looking to their weapons. A few gathered unbroken arrows, and sentries began to pace along the walls.

Morgan gazed out at the dead Myslans, trying to estimate their number. He'd visited cities that held less people than the Myslans had left at Tong Shavath. He guessed the dead at ten thousand or more.

Perhaps the *Alman* couldn't mount another attack. Perhaps he'd been weakened when his death-spell had been broken. Perhaps the Myslans had finally had enough.

The roar of the flames had subsided enough he could begin to hear the plaintive wails and occasional screams of the wounded.

In less than an hour Damon returned, his face and hands cleaner than they'd been when he'd left. "They've bread, stew, and wine in the barracks. Go eat. It's my watch anyway."

"What were our losses?"

"Sixty-two men dead, twenty-four wounded. Four of the wounded are probably dying."

Morgan gestured at the Myslan dead. "Our men sold themselves dear. It's not much consolation but, sometimes, it's the only one a warrior has. How's Jocile?"

"He'll be back at midnight. As soon as he'd had his shoulder dressed he wanted to come back, but I told him to rest unless the alarm is rung. Another sixteen of the wounded could also fight, if they're needed."

"If they're needed, they won't make any difference," Morgan said. He groaned as he pushed himself off the top of the wall and hobbled like an old man to the stairway. His muscles had stiffened. Once he could've fought a battle and run two leagues to fight another. Now, he limped.

In his room, he washed the blood from his hands and face, then trudged to the barracks where he sat at the foot of a table of soldiers and ate lightly and alone. He sampled the heavily spiced stew and fresh bread, and drank almost a full pitcher of water. Many of the soldiers were still lost in the last battle. The rest, like Morgan, anticipated the next one and listened intently for the alarm.

After he'd eaten he decided to return to the roof. If the alarm were rung, he might not be able to climb the steps quickly enough, and a leader was most needed when the battle was lost.

He thought of Topaz. He yearned for her, and the thought of never seeing her again pained him, but he had no regrets. He'd done what was needed: neither of them had reason to be ashamed of him. That was another soldier's consolation.

Atop the keep, he lay on the pallet and was almost instantly asleep, although he woke often. The frequent passage into and out of exhausted sleep gave his perceptions an air of unreality. The one constant was the sound of Damon's pacing. Morgan came awake once long enough to see the last bit of rose fade from the evening sky. Twice more he woke, and, the second time, he sat up. It was near enough time for his watch that the difference wouldn't matter. He climbed to his feet.

Damon handed him a waterskin, then collapsed onto the pallet himself.

"Have the Myslans done anything?"

"Nothing."

Morgan walked a circuit of the top of the keep. He saw nothing that looked like a prelude to an attack, heard nothing but the sighing of the fire, which had sunk to a sullen glow, and the cries and entreaties of the wounded Myslans. Perhaps a tenth of the men beyond the road were still alive, though some could count their lives in less than a score of heartbeats.

Morgan couldn't guess how many times he'd stood watch. It seemed a part of himself as much as a soldier's duty, but it seemed he'd never stood a watch as long. He'd had to hear the sounds all too often; the moans, the screams, the calls for water or for a loved one.

The acrid smoke still stung the eyes and the throat, while the stench could be endured, although one never became inured to it.

He could see occasional small movements, as the wounded and dying drew up a leg or flung out an arm. Besides the gruesome aspects of standing guard over a place where men had died and some were still dying, he was waiting for the first signs of inevitable disaster. It wouldn't take more than a force the size of the one the *Alman* had thrown away on the first probing attack to storm the fortress.

Finding a cloak beside the waterskin, he wrapped himself in it to ward off the chill. That dry, cold wind would finish many of the wounded before morning. He found, with some surprise, that he didn't hate the Myslans. All the anger seemed to have been leeched out of him, taking hatred with it. He'd have given water to those who begged for it, would've tried to give what little comfort he could to the dying, but he had to wait for their comrades to attack.

There'd been more pleasant watches. Guarding the flocks of Stag Mountain had almost been a pleasure, had been a real pleasure on those occasions when Topaz had visited him. He thought of her again, caressed her memory.

Footsteps plodded their way up the stairs, and Jocile stepped onto the tower, his right arm in a sling, his usual jaunty manner replaced by a taciturn grimness. Morgan nodded a greeting and made another circuit of the keep, saw nothing he hadn't seen on previous rounds.

While the fortress had few resources left, he could use what remained to keep the coming battle interesting. Among the stones in the mangonel's scoop he could find only half a dozen that were suitable for enchanting. He laid those down on top of the heap, drew his knife, and began to cast the spell. He could immediately feel power draining from his scars. Because it was dangerous to stop in the middle of a spell, he continued until he'd enchanted the stone, then leaned against the wall to think.

It seemed obvious that when he'd lost Lashastur he'd also lost most of his power. The power had come at about the same time he'd acquired the spell, and losing the spell had cost him the power. He could appreciate the symmetry, but not the loss of power when it was most needed.

There was something he could do; he picked up a shovel and began to scoop the ashes out of the brazier. With no other place to put them, he piled the ashes by the wall. Jocile grunted, then began to lay wood in the bowl. After he'd put in all the scraps from the floor of the tower, he asked, "Do you have what's needed to conjure it again?"

Morgan grinned. "No, but the Myslans don't know that. We've worked too hard to earn their respect to simply throw it away."

Jocile grinned back. "I'll go down and see what wood I can find."

Morgan struck flint to steel and lit the torch from the tinder, then dropped it into the brazier. The hardest part was enduring the vulnerable time it took for his eyes to adapt themselves again to the darkness, Except for the blind, each man trusted his own eyes best. He'd heard moans and sobs from the wounded when he lit the brazier, but the enemy still made no move.

Jocile had returned with another load of wood. "I wish they'd hurry up and get it over with," he grumbled. "It's easier to die well than to wait."

"Don't waste wishes on the inevitable." Morgan replied.

They didn't speak again until the sky had begun to brighten, with impossibly high wisps of cloud glowing gold shot with crimson. Morgan began to pace, partly to use some of the nervous energy with which he was afflicted. The *Alman* was either confident or a fool. Given the tactics the Myslans had employed, Morgan wasn't prepared to wager the price of a cup of cheap, watered wine on which was the greater likelihood, but the *Alman* had thrown away his best chance for an easy victory.

Damon woke with a start and extricated himself from the blanket. He stretched and yawned, then said, "At least we'll live to see another sunrise."

Jocile found a bottle of wine and the three of them shared part of it. They'd handed what was left of the wine to one of the men tending the mangonel and were drinking from a waterskin when a single Myslan walked out of the pass. He seemed armed only with a spear, which he carried in both hands, arms raised above his head.

The man approached to just out of bowshot, drove the spear into the gravel, then advanced again, slowly, both hands raised, open, and empty.

"I'll go see what it wants," Damon said.

Morgan slid his sword in the scabbard. "I'll go with you."

"If there's treachery, who'll lead the garrison?"

"If there's treachery, it'd be best to have both of us there to deal with it."

Damon paused, nodded, and strode to the stairway. By the time they'd reached the gate, the Myslan had halted between two of the jutting ramparts of the fortress protecting the gate. The man was staring up at two heads mounted on a single tripod made of spears.

"I hadn't seen that before," Morgan murmured.

"Neither had I," Damon said softly, "but it's impressed him, so we'll wait to look at it until after he's gone."

The two of them advanced to within a pace of the Myslan. Morgan observed the man was pale-skinned, with black hair and very light gray eyes made all the more striking by the dark pouches of skin under those eyes. He looked no more rested than Morgan felt.

The Myslan bowed, and his upright arms bobbed with his head and shoulders. "I've come to request that we be allowed to send messengers to the men to your west, to inform them the *Alman* and his brother are dead. We also ask you to allow those men to return to Myslan."

Damon hardly hesitated. "You may send your messengers and your men may leave, but they must do it single-file and out of range of our bows. You may also send two hundred men to take your wounded. If you wish to take any of your dead from beyond the road, do so. But tell your men that if we see them stealing from the dead or killing any wounded, we'll see how much farther a ballista can shoot than a bow.

The Myslan bowed again. "As you say." He seemed to study Damon and Morgan for a long moment. "I will remember the two of you."

"Why tax your memory?" Morgan snapped. "You and I are both here now, and my nephew has enough swords to be able to lend you one."

Damon gestured Morgan to silence, then said to the Myslan, "My uncle doesn't understand Myslan custom. He mistook what you said for a challenge."

Once more the Myslan bowed, then turned and walked toward the pass, leaving his spear point-down in the gravel.

"The Myslans believe that when you die, you can only live on in memory," Damon said. "Telling someone you'll remember him is like telling him you consider him immortal." He turned to look at the heads impaled on the spears and Morgan joined him.

"Who are our guests?"

"That might be the *Alman* and his brother," Damon replied, looking up at the dead faces, but I hadn't heard they were so tall—or so thin."

The faces were ashen, and the pale, glassy eyes of one of them bulged. Damon gestured toward that one. "He looks as though he was surprised to find himself dead."

Morgan shook his head. "He was strangled. You can still see the marks of the garrote on what's left of his neck. It doesn't look like Hadrian's work. He'd simply have killed by striking off the head—unless he's become more vengeful."

"I believe," Damon said, "this is the work of our relief. Besides the army, they must've sent *Etrong Filteth*." He turned and paced back to the fortress.

Morgan walked beside him. "Who's this 'Blade of The Faith'?"

"Only The Voice of The Faith and a handful of others know. When it's necessary that someone die, they send The Blade of The Faith."

Morgan felt the hairs stir on the back of his neck. "It discourages heresy, I suppose."

"The Blade of The Faith is never used in disagreements of faith, only when the empire is threatened with arms."

Morgan shrugged. "If The Blade is as sharp as he appears, how would anyone know?"

"Because there are always disagreements over interpretations of The Book." Damon stopped and they both listened to the sound of a horse galloping around the fortress, its rider keeping as far from the walls as the cliffs would permit. "Why don't you eat and rest? The battle seems to be over."

"I'll do that, but first I'll wait to see the Myslans pull out." He climbed the stairs to the roof of the keep. The climb seemed much easier than it had before.

From the roof, they could observe the Myslan forces returning to the east. The Myslans walked, single-file, along the base of the southern cliff. Another two hundred had issued from the pass and were moving among the bodies and carrying some of them away.

Morgan looked again at the tripod of spears and the heads, and tried to guess how someone could've set them up without being seen. A spell of concealment, probably, he decided. Whoever The Blade of The Faith might be, he had nerve, using such a simple spell to enter an armed camp and kill at least one of the leaders. He suspected the *Alman's* brother might've died when his death spell had been countered, but taking the head from the corpse still would've been difficult.

This Blade of The Faith troubled him. He'd known not all Ian-nists were as pacific as Poker, but he hadn't realized the church kept an assassin. Perhaps forming an alliance with the church of Ianno wasn't the solution he'd thought it might be.

Most of the Myslans were already out of sight, and he was sure the siege had been broken. He nodded to Damon, then said, "I'll take your advice now about the food and rest."

The water in his ewer and the basin was clean. He washed his face and hands and strode to the dining room, where he was sur-prised to see Jeshka waiting for him with bread, cheese, stew, and a bottle of Shannan pomegranate wine. He seated himself at the table and began to eat and drink, finding that even the odor of the burnt dead couldn't destroy his appetite.

"You've changed," Jeshka said.

Mildly surprised she'd speak to him, he finally asked, "How so?"

"There's something different about your face; something miss-ing. There was always an anger that hid just below the moment. It's gone."

Morgan paused, a piece of bread halfway to his mouth. Putting some of the bread into his mouth, he bit off a morsel, chewed. He was struck by the insight Jeshka had put into words; the connection he hadn't made himself. The dragon had been, in part, his own an-ger, the force that had driven them both, and when Lashastur had died, his simmering anger had died with it. The loss seemed, on its face, a benefit, but he was sure there must be a penalty. That rage might've warped him in some ways, as being born with a club foot might've caused him to limp, but it'd also given him much of his en-ergy, much of his raw power. Without it, he might be crippled in some subtle way. Perhaps that loss had drawn most of the power from his scars.

"You're very perceptive," he said, then smiled. "I'll hope your discretion matches your sensitivity."

"You can't hide what your face reveals."

"Most people see only what they expect to see."

"But why do you want to seem worse than you are?"

"Because some people in power, especially those who've risen to power by force, confuse anything but ruthlessness with weak-ness." There was something about her that invited confidence. "If the church of Ianno employs an assassin, then it probably also uses spies. I'd prefer not to be perceived as weak. It'll probably be hard enough to convince The Voice of The Faith to lend me support in Donradé. If I'm seen as weak, I'm afraid I'll fail."

She shrugged. "I don't believe you'll have to play any parts with The Voice, but it's your decision to make."

Having finished the meal and finding his body almost too heavy to keep erect in a chair, he stood. "We'll talk again." He picked up a candle from the table and returned to his room.

~ * ~

He woke feeling very alone, with fading dreams of a dragon still clinging to the shreds of sleep. He heard, faintly, the clangor of metal against metal and stone and, when he placed his hand against the wall, could feel a faint vibration.

The message from Topaz, his greatest source of solace, was gone, fed to the flames. Rising, he lit a candle, washed the last of the sleep from his face, dressed, and paced to the dining room. No candles lit the passage and the dining chamber was empty. He tried to guess the hour, but inside the fortress it was always night.

An unwonted listlessness afflicted him. He had ample reason for feeling disappointment; the death of the dragon, the unexpected end to the siege after he'd prepared himself for a final battle, and the discovery the church of Ianno might well be only another clique of ruthless old men who added to their shame by mouthing hypocritical platitudes.

He realized then he was mourning Lashastur. It was absurd, he told himself, to feel the loss of something that was only his own rage given form by magic, but knowledge is always prey to emotion. Whether or not he should feel as though something outside himself had died, he did feel it, and he understood that all mourning was, in the end, for oneself; for being left alone without something or someone on which one had lavished care.

He found his way to the barracks. It would've been easy enough to find it by following the sound of snoring. A few men sat at the tables in the front of the room, the rest sleeping as though dead, although many of them were far noisier. Stew simmered in a pot and he helped himself, took a handful of biscuits, and poured a cup of wine from the cask. Dragging himself to one of the empty tables, he ate alone. One by one, the men at the other tables finished eating and staggered off to their pallets.

When he'd broken his fast, he rose and climbed the stairs to the roof of the keep. The ringing grew louder as he ascended the stairs and he stepped out onto the roof to see Jeshka holding Danyol, and Damon and another man feeding out rope over the wall, from whence came the sound of pounding.

Curious, Morgan returned to the stairs and paced down them to ground level. Little could be seen from the bailey, so he crossed to the stairs on the wall and climbed to the top to look back. A man in a makeshift seat of rope and wood hung suspended, chiseling a chalked design into the western face of the keep. The shape he was hammering into the stone was Lashastur's. Morgan's eyes stung as he realized Damon was creating a memorial to the dragon. He seemed to not be the only one mourning the passing of a part of himself. The loneliness he'd felt was banished, and he realized he'd found closeness here.

He returned to the keep's roof, after he'd composed his face and wiped away the tears.

CHAPTER 9

Five days after the Myslans had limped away from Tong Shavath, the alarm was struck once, announcing the appearance of a dozen men on horses riding toward the fortress from the west.

Damon and Morgan, directing the disposal of bodies, met the riders on the road. Damon and the leader of the riders bowed to each other, then Damon smiled and said, "Either you didn't believe my message, or you and your men are more dangerous than you seem."

The horseman grinned in reply. "Each of my men and I are worth a thousand Myslans." He dismounted, letting the reins fall to the ground. "The courier who passed us three days ago told me the siege had been lifted, so I sent the rest of the cavalry and all but two hundred foot soldiers back to Bhun Nahbi and the other garrisons. The foot soldiers and the provision caravan should arrive the day after tomorrow."

At the mention of a courier sent after the Myslans had retreated, Damon glanced at Morgan, who replied with the slightest shake of the head.

"What did the courier look like?" Damon asked.

"A short, stocky lad. He impressed me as being a bit heavy for a courier, but he rode his horse well. Nothing remarkable about him. Why?"

"No reason, except I believe you met The Blade of The Faith."

The leader stepped forward for a ritual embrace. He paused almost in mid-step, and Morgan admired the man's attempt to hide his surprise, then the rider and Damon hugged each other. After he'd released Damon the man turned to Morgan.

"Tuman, this is my uncle, Scarface. The empire owes The Shield of The Saint to him and to The Blade of The Faith."

"Then I'm honored to meet him." Tuman spread his arms and Morgan exchanged an embrace with him. After the hug, Tuman stood with his hands on his hips and gazed at the field and the fortress, at the mounds of bodies and smaller heaps of bones and ashes, at the smears of smoke on the wall, and at the tower with its bas-relief of a dragon and its rows of names, some carved in the flowing

Gasgoran script, the rest in the curving slashes of Thani. "You seem to have exceeded my hopes. I feared The Shield of The Saint was lost, or, at best, I'd still be facing a Myslan army besieging a shattered garrison."

"The price was high," Damon admitted, gesturing at the names, "but the Myslans won't attack this place again for generations."

Tuman stroked the short, pointed moustaches at the edges of his mouth. "The fresh soldiers I'm bringing in are to relieve you and your garrison. You deserve to visit Bhun Nahbi, perhaps even Ong Vaun."

"My uncle wishes to meet with The Voice of The Faith."

"I'll give him a message to present at the city." He watched the fortress' horses being hitched to piles of bodies to haul past the fortress for burning. They'd cleared the dead away to the trench and had removed almost all the corpses from the pit. The cold, arid wind from the pass quickly dried out the bodies, making them easier to burn. Tuman gestured at the dead and at the smoke rising from one of the fires. "You can smell this place a good ten leagues away."

"There's much more work to be done," Damon said, pointing. "Three of the tunnels to the trench will have to be re-opened after the bodies are cleared away, more traps will have to be set between the trench and the road. We have hundreds of spears that can be set in the rock to force attackers into trapped areas. The skeins of the ballistae should be replaced and the mangonels should be refurbished. If you expand the storage tunnels, the stone chips are needed for the catapults."

"Also," Morgan interjected, "no one should approach the pass until you've cleared away the fire-traps that may be left. I'd suggest you drive herds of sheep or swine ahead of you to do that."

Tuman laughed. "From what you've said, there's time enough for all that. He finally caught sight of the heads on the spears. "The *Alman* and his brother?" At Damon's nod, he said, "I'm sure they've never looked better."

~ * ~

The journey to Bhun Nahbi was a long hundred leagues, the first twenty of which led through a desert of gray and rust-red stone. When they finally saw green in the distance, it was a relief to the eyes.

They'd spent two days at the fortress after the provisions had arrived, letting the men rest and eat well, and when they'd set out, only the women, the children, and the wounded had ridden.

The first green they saw were shrubs and stunted trees growing along the banks of a stream, but within another two days' march they'd found grass enough to let their horses graze. They'd reached the Kathan plains, where wandering bands raised sheep and goats, and three days later they marched through a small town set in the midst of fields and orchards.

By noon of the eleventh day of the trek they saw Bhun Nahbi, near enough to reach before sunset. The city's name was Kathan for "Traveler's Rest," so called because it was a crossroads for several traders' routes. These Kathans had found trade far less strenuous than farming or herding, and acted as middlemen for several tribes between the coast and the northern mountains.

The walls and spires of the city were built of a tan stone, and all the visible roofs were the turquoise shades of patina-coated copper.

Word of their victory had preceded them and, as they reached the great bronze gates of the city, they were cheered by people lining the streets, who threw flowers and offered them delicacies and wine. The soldiers strutted like caricatures of the warriors they were.

Morgan knew the qualities that made men worthy soldiers seldom survived the fame success brought. If the town still treated them as heroes for more than a day or two, it'd be because the soldiers exercised unlikely restraint or the townspeople exhibited uncommon tolerance. It's almost impossible to see a hero in a man who drinks till he pukes or takes liberties with the daughters of the townspeople.

They were herded like celebrated sheep to the city's plaza, where they were greeted by the *fali*, who exaggerated their virtues and expressed a gratitude Morgan supposed would last only slightly longer than most hangovers.

The *fali* extended his hospitality to Morgan, Damon, and Damon's family. Morgan seized the opportunity for a hot bath, and almost fell asleep at dinner, as the *fali* delivered another round of speeches.

Early the next morning he sent a courier to Ong Vaun, requesting an audience with The Voice of The Faith, then shopped for clothing and a new scabbard, and had his boots, belts, and jerkin cleaned. He'd had to borrow clothing from Damon, and would be relieved to be able to wear his own color again.

As befitted a city of successful merchants, Bhun Nahbi supported numerous tailors, many employing exotic cloths. Black hose,
black silk shirts, and a cloak were all he required, although it cost him
much of his patience and most of his civility to resist the tailors' at-
tempts to dress him in the latest fashion. On most of the western
continent, such clothing would have him mistaken for a court fool.

Once he felt himself again, he visited the local temple. If he
were to persuade The Voice of The Faith to aid the Donradans, he'd
need to know far more about the church.

Bhun Nahbi contained several temples, including the governing
church of Kath. Since one sees farthest from the highest peak, Morgan strolled to the cathedral, an imposing structure built of the same
tan stone as the city walls.

The interior of the church was cool and dim. Windows of narrow sheets of pale, translucent glass set in the walls admitted enough
light one could read, and glowing candles flanked The Book on its
pedestal. A pulpit stood to the left of the altar, which was heaped
with flowers. The altar itself was more elaborate than a simple table,
its back a white-painted wood edifice that soared upward in a series
of arches and peaks, drawing the eye—and, Morgan supposed, the
mind of the believer—up to the great golden circle at the apex.

He recalled the circle was the symbol of the completeness of
Ianno. Everything else in creation was represented by a tiny arc and,
even drawn together, those arcs didn't comprise a complete circle.
Ianno was needed for completeness.

He became aware of a figure standing at the base of the altar,
regarding the great circle. The man slowly turned to face him. "May I
help you?"

"I'd like to speak with the high priest of Kath."

"I am he."

Morgan studied the man, who had a broad forehead and ascetic
features and manner. Most of his hair was still dark, although the
temples were silver-gray. The priest asked, "How may I help you?"

"I'd like to know more about the church."

The man gestured toward a door beside the altar and Morgan
stepped through it into a small room which held vestments and articles of veneration he didn't recognize, the priest at his heels. Without
speaking, the priest led the way out another door.

In the harsher light of noon, Morgan could see the priest's robe,
which he'd taken to be black, was actually dark green and bound, of

course, with a broad sash of pale blue silk. The priest paced slowly toward a stone grotto and Morgan had to force himself into a more leisurely pace than his customary stride.

The priest took a seat on a stool in the grotto and Morgan sat on another stool across a small table from him.

"What do you want to know?"

"My…brother…was a convert. He seemed to believe the church of Ianno was a source of peace. I've recently learned the church keeps an assassin, and I wonder how much more about the church I don't know."

"Were you and your brother close?" The priest's gentle voice reminded Morgan of Poker's voice.

"Yes," He hesitated. "I thought we were."

The priest nodded. "Your brother may have been unaware of The Blade of The Faith. Or, perhaps, he knew but didn't consider it important. You must bear in mind the church is an institution of men. We trust that Ianno guides us, but it would be too much to suppose that, even guided by Ianno, fallible men could create a perfect institution. But The Voice believes, and I concur, that in an imperfect world the church must be capable of defending itself and its believers."

"Perhaps I had unrealistic expectations," Morgan said. "I understood the church of Ianno preaches the ideal of peace. Ideals are worth preaching, but if the church only gives them lip service but practices the same deception and raw power games as any petty lordling, why should I have more respect for the church?"

"You seem too concerned with the church, and not enough with The Faith. The central questions are; why are we here, what should we do, and what becomes of us?"

Morgan smiled. "Admittedly I'm of a pragmatic rather than philosophical bent, but it seems to me that stated ideals should be related to the policies of the church. A cynic might suggest that the church's answer to those questions might be—" he held up a finger at each point, "the church is here to gain power and wealth; as good worshippers we should buy the golden promises the church is selling us; and, finally, that we should become shorn sheep."

The priest's eyes and mouth narrowed with disapproval and he drew a deep breath before he responded. "The Blade of The Faith exists only to protect the church against those who raise weapons against it,"

"It's hard to believe a church—or anyone else—that has such a weapon to hand would have the restraint to use it only against unbelievers."

"As I said, The Blade of The Faith only defends the church against those who attack it, or the empire, with arms. The church would, for instance, wish to convert all the world to The Faith, but the church has taken no steps beyond preaching the words of The Book to any who will listen. You admit, yourself, that you know little about the church or The Faith. I'd advise you to take the time to learn something about both before you reject them."

Morgan considered that. It was, after all, what he'd asked for. "Fair enough."

For over two hours they discussed The Faith, but when Morgan took his leave he was still dissatisfied. He had no doubt Timyan, the priest, was a very good man, but he was too intellectual, too bound to abstractions to be able to appeal to Morgan. Theology might sound significant, but it was too insubstantial to move him.

Theology seemed a contradiction in terms. One could study a language, or magic, or swordsmanship, but how did one study a god, particularly one whose name, in Thani, meant "The Unknowable?" If theology were too intellectual and abstract, Morgan was even more suspicious of those religions which appealed primarily to emotion. He'd seen some of the Marked Ones whip themselves, sometimes literally, into a religious frenzy before an attack. He'd also heard of sects, in several countries, who chanted until their throats were raw or danced until they fell.

He'd seen that kind of religion once, in Doss, and had no desire to see it again. He suspected that sort of fervor had less to do with worship than with blood-lust and self-gratification. He accepted that Timyan believed he loved Ianno, but Morgan was uncomfortable around men who wasted their emotions on the impossible.

At least the church of Ianno had a coherent set of beliefs. The Prophet claimed to have been inspired by Ianno, and it was widely accepted that The Saint had, too, although apparently he'd never made that claim. The Book was written partly as a history rooted in myth. According to The Prophet, the Thanitur were the chosen ones. The Saint had written that the Thanitur had lost that favor by their own conquests, and the destruction of the first empire was seen as proof of Ianno's disapproval.

Much of The Book dealt with the proper way to live. The Iannists recognized no devils or demons. They believed evil was the result of man turning away from Ianno, while good was the result of man in harmony with Ianno. They believed death was the Great Sleep, that one who died in harmony with Ianno was blessed with dreams of joy and peace, but if one died guilty of unexpiated evil the Great Sleep was disturbed by nightmares without end and from which one couldn't wake.

One thing that surprised and impressed him was that the Iannists distinguished between evil and misfortune. He recalled, with sardonic amusement, one of his journeys through Ghiblein, when he'd seen the execution of a horse that had kicked a groom to death. He'd heard Ghiblins had "executed," by burning, a ladder from which a man had fallen and broken his neck. Whatever the church's faults, it avoided that sort of stupidity.

Evil, to the Iannists, required volition. For that reason, only men and gods could be evil. Evil was an action that caused unnecessary harm, especially if that harm were to people. They'd also tried to discriminate between accident and culpability. According to the church, reckless actions which endangered others were inherently evil.

Moderation, rather than abstention, was the blessed way, although abstention from one's soul's fatal weakness was necessary. He'd learned that from Poker, who'd abstained from physical union with women because he'd feared that to love a woman would distract him from his devotion to Ianno and, thus, to his mission.

Morgan was inclined to accept the church at its word, if only because it could inspire such devotion in a man like Poker, but the lurking shadow of a church assassin stood between him and the church.

He grinned crookedly at himself. Perhaps he was becoming naive in his old age. He'd come looking for more than just an ally in a war with a god, more than just another powerful deity to use as a weapon. He'd been expecting much from a deity, and just as much from a church, especially in light of most of his experiences with churches.

He returned to the *fali's* residence. Although the march from Tong Shavath to Bhun Nahbi had been almost leisurely compared to most of his travels, he hadn't yet recovered from the battle or its aftermath.

A large lunch, rest, a larger dinner, and a long night's sound sleep left him feeling refreshed and a little bored. After breaking his fast he visited the barracks where the garrison from The Shield of The Saint was housed. He learned Jocile was to be given ten lashes for drunkenness and brawling, and that Bronyak was staying at the temple he'd visited the day before.

Nothing could be done about Jocile, but Morgan felt the need to speak with Bronyak. He'd spoken, briefly, with the priest after the battle, but the man had been too busy tending to the wounded and the dying to discuss The Faith with Morgan and, on the march to Bhun Nahbi, he'd still been responsible for the wounded, as well as bone-weary from his duties.

Morgan found Bronyak strolling through the garden of the cathedral's residence. For the first time, seeing the priest among the foliage that was turning red and yellow, he realized it was autumn, and he'd been away from Stag Mountain for over three months. Nearer four, he corrected himself.

He greeted Bronyak, who responded with a grin. Morgan bowed to the priest and said, "I spoke with Timyan yesterday, and wanted to talk with you about The Faith."

Bronyak's grin broadened. "Timyan mentioned the conversation, probably the same way you'd talk about the battle at The Shield of The Saint. He despairs of converting you and said he'd rather be a missionary among the Myslans."

Morgan tried to conceal the urge to grin, fought it to a draw. "Actually, he would've been very convincing—had I been more like him, but we're too different. I can sense his devotion but I can't emulate it."

Bronyak began to walk again, his hands clasped behind his back. "Perhaps you're too concerned with what you think you should be feeling. One of the tenets of The Faith is that 'faith is action.' How you feel—whether you experience the peace and love of Ianno—is less important than the decisions you'll make."

"What's the difference, then, between faith and hypocrisy?"

"Faith is when you continue to strive to live as you should, and not just when it's convenient to do so. Those who feel the comforting hand of Ianno must continue to live properly, and continue to do so, even if they feel Ianno has deserted them. That's the true test of faith."

Morgan mulled over the statement and its ramifications for a full circuit of the garden, then asked, "What sort of faith, or Faith, requires an assassin?"

"Tell me, Scarface, do you think it wrong for The Faith to maintain the garrison at The Shield of The Saint, or other outposts at the borders of the empire?"

Morgan smiled. He saw the direction Bronyak was leading. "No, they're needed to defend the empire and, by extension, the Faith. I'll agree the *Alman* was evil and his brother mad, so what The Blade of The Faith did there was no worse than what we soldiers did. Better, in fact, because it saved lives. But it requires restraint to have a weapon and not use it. How can The Voice of The Faith be trusted to always show that restraint?"

"Your argument lacks consistency," Bronyak replied. "First, you're disappointed in the church because we aren't much more idealistic than you are yourself, then you doubt us when we attempt to practice idealism. The reason I believe that restraint will be practiced is because the force of tradition is very strong. Lively debate is part of the church. I don't know if you realize The Book is a living, growing part of The Faith, rather than a completed work. If three Voices declare a writing to be inspired by Ianno, that scripture is added to The Book. Some scripture now part of The Book were once considered heretical. With such debate so crucial to the church, using The Blade of The Faith to stifle the debate would be for the church to cut out its own heart.

"Of course, the church, like any other institution, will use every weapon to defend itself against armed insurrection. That's a very real distinction."

Morgan stopped, leaned over a bush covered with late-blooming purple-blue blossoms and inhaled deeply. He enjoyed the strange but pleasant scent. "Granted, for the sake of argument, that The Blade of The Faith isn't used within the church except in cases of armed revolt, what about unbelievers? I can see a blade being used as a tool to pry into places closed to you."

Bronyak picked one of the blossoms and handed it to Morgan. "The same prohibitions apply; only when violence is threatened is The Blade to be employed.

"We wish, of course, that all would accept the words and the blessings of Ianno, but unbelievers must accept His message willingly, without coercion. Centuries ago, the church was spread by the sword, and the church almost died with the Thanitur. Only when The Saint preached the love of Ianno was the message heard and accepted. Only then did the church begin to flower." He gestured at the bush. "This is only a nettle-bush. Without the flowers, it's only a weed, fit only to be burned. The church, without the love of Ianno, would be like that bush without flowers.

"Besides, the belief Ianno chose only one people has been shown to be an error."

"Was that error stricken from The Book, then?"

"No, because it's better to keep our errors before us, to avoid repeating them. As I said, we've learned that belief was an error. I've met many unbelievers who seem to follow the words of Ianno, even if they haven't heard them from the church. You may not know the prayers, or recognize the hand of Ianno in your life, but you still practice faith in action."

"Interesting," Morgan said. "That's a more tolerant view than I'd have expected."

Bronyak smiled. "That's because you haven't read The Book or the writings of The Faith. One belief that hasn't yet been make part of The Book, although I expect it to be added within the next generation or so, is part of folklore. The story is that The Saint, as he was dying, said he'd be reborn in each generation. Because it's the spirit, not the mind or the body that's reborn, the reborn Saint wouldn't realize that he—or she—is The Saint. He's supposed to have said that he might return as a *fali* or a beggar, a woman, a priest or an unbeliever, even as a foreigner. This is an important article of faith, because it requires us to treat everyone as though they might be The Saint, and to seek that part of Ianno within each of us."

Morgan, following the Kathan custom, embraced Bronyak. "I believe you've given me enough to think about for one day. I wish Timyan had the same answers."

Bronyak shrugged and smiled. "What would be the use of a church with only one set of answers, or which appealed to only one sort of person?"

Morgan left the garden feeling more at peace than he had since leaving Stag Mountain. Perhaps it was the conversation, the garden, the time of year, or the burning away of his rage, or even all these things together, but, whatever the reason, he decided to enjoy it. As he returned to the *Fali's* residence he took a way that led him through the market.

The Kathans were a demonstrative people. Their market was a noisy place, with customers and sellers haggling, often at the tops of their voices, and active, as they gestured broadly. Friends embraced each other, lovers walked together holding hands, and all the faces were animated.

The soldiers at Tong Shavath had been Gascolans and a few men from Doss on the western continent, or warriors from the mountain tribes of Kesh and Shun. Even the Gascolans weren't as expressive as the Kathans. Morgan doubted many of the Kathans would make good soldiers, but they gave richness and color to life.

Reaching the *fali's* residence, he borrowed a horse and rode a wide circle around Bhun Nahbi. He found the ridge where the stones for the walls of the city had been quarried, and rode through harvested fields of stubble. He returned greetings from groups of gleaners who picked among the stubble like birds, salvaging the grain missed by the harvesters.

North of the city, he passed through orchards and groves. The day was pleasantly warm and the season was golden. The creaking of the saddle was a soothing sound, and the swaying of the horse lulled him into reverie.

Had Topaz been with him to share it, the day would've been perfect. As it was, he tried to memorize the colors, the sounds, the rich scents of the fields and orchards to share with her another time. In his present mood, worry seemed an affront and an invitation to trouble.

By late afternoon he'd almost completed his circuit of the city and he noticed the wind had picked up and smelled of storm. The gleaners were leaving the fields. Turning his face to the wind, he saw dark clouds roiling on the horizon and by the time he'd reached the city, lightning was flickering about the hems of the clouds.

He ate dinner listening to the crashes of thunder and the pelting of rain, and later the storm lulled him to sleep.

~ * ~

When Morgan paid for the clothing he'd purchased, the scabbard, and the cleaning of his leather, the merchants recognized him as one of the heroes of Tong Shavath and scarcely overcharged him. He had another conversation with Bronyak and came to realize his answers were actually essentially the same as Timyan's. When he mentioned that observation to Bronyak, the priest chuckled.

"Of course, but you and I are more alike, so I can couch the answers in a way you can appreciate. Timyan's a good man and a good priest, just different. As I said, the church's importance rests in its ability to show us the value of differences.

"Furthermore, I suspect you're resisting Ianno more for personal reasons than philosophical ones. I suggest you take the time to think and feel those through."

Morgan embraced Bronyak and left the church garden to stride to the infirmary, where Jocile was lying on his belly, his back covered with poultices.

Morgan drew up a stool. "I'd have thought you'd seen enough of combat at Tong Shavath."

Jocile raised his head, rested his chin on his crossed forearms. "Fighting's what I know. I'm good at it."

"I've also heard you're good at taking stripes. You didn't scream, they say. So. You have two skills." Morgan leaned forward. "If you can keep yourself out of trouble, I know a place where you can get your fill of fighting."

Jocile's eyebrows arched. "How soon?"

"As soon as I return to Donradé."

Jocile shrugged, then winced as the movement pulled at the scabs. "That may be a long time. You expect me to become another Saint until then?"

Morgan stood abruptly. "If you want a battle that means more than a spilled cup of wine, yes. I know what kind of soldier you can be. I'll need good soldiers, and that means those who can follow orders, men who can bide their time, then strike a killing stroke. You can be a warrior or a cheap brawler. I need warriors I can respect. I've no use for brawlers." He leaned forward and rested his hand on Jocile's left forearm. "I'd very much like to have you with me in Donradé, but you'll have to decide whether it means enough to you to be worth some sacrifice."

Leaving the infirmary, he paced back to the *fali's* residence. He'd known men like Jocile. They were cripples, in a way. The only closeness they could appreciate was the camaraderie of the battlefield. Had Jocile had a woman, he'd probably have beaten her or driven her away. There was something dead in him. For such men, only struggle let them feel really alive.

The best Jocile could hope for was to die fighting for a good cause. Morgan shook his head at the waste.

Damon and his family sat in the courtyard, watching the play of water in the *fali's* fountain. Morgan sat with them, listening to the rushing water and watching the shapes in the water rise and collapse.

While watching and listening to the fountain was intended to be restful, he was growing impatient. He stared at Damon until the young man glanced at him, then jerked his head to indicate a corner of the courtyard.

Damon spoke to Jeshka for a moment, then sauntered to the corner Morgan had indicated. "Is something wrong?"

"Nothing of importance. I'm just impatient," Morgan leaned against the wall, his arms crossed. "As soon as Jocile is well enough, I think you should train him. He needs to use a sword, even if it's only a practice sword. The only way to keep him out of mischief is to work him until he's too tired to look for trouble.

"Also, I'm leaving for Ong Vaun tomorrow."

"Is that wise?"

"I'll take the same route as the couriers, so I should be able to intercept a reply. You have your family here," he gestured at Jeshka and Danyol, "and I'm glad for you, but I miss someone and it's important that I get back to her as soon as possible."

Damon glanced at his wife and son beside the fountain, then back at Morgan and nodded once, a sudden declination. "Is it important enough to perhaps fail at what you've set out to do and waste the time you've already spent?"

Morgan raked his lower lip with his teeth. Damon's point was well-taken. It'd already been over two months since he'd first boarded the Sazian ship, and he had a sense Thienn and the church of Mordach were building power; time wasn't his ally.

"And if you leave too soon for Ong Vaun, you'll look too eager," Damon pointed out. "I don't remember whether it was you or my father who taught me that too much eagerness can spoil a bargain."

Morgan began to pace, only a couple of steps one way, then the other, as though he were establishing the dimensions of the cage he felt himself in. He forced himself to grin and to keep his voice mild. "You're right, of course, but it rankles. Time's an enemy, and it won't grant quarter."

"Would you help me with the training? We can start this afternoon. There's a practice field by the barracks. I have more men than just Jocile who need to be kept busy."

"And an uncle who also needs to be kept busy, eh?" The only apparent alternative was to sulk, which would accomplish less than nothing. "I'll see you there."

He still faced an empty hour, and he left the residence to aimlessly wander the streets of Bhun Nahbi. He'd learned there were two forms of patience. One was when you had mastery of a situation and had only to wait to let an opponent learn that truth. The other sort was when the situation was out of your hands, when you could do nothing to manipulate the circumstances. The second sort was the harder to practice.

He thought of what Bronyak had told him; that he was resisting the church for reasons more personal than philosophical, and dug at the reluctance to find out what lay under it.

It was difficult to submit to the authority of the church. He'd lived his life by his own code and now he might have to live by rules established by others. He'd respected Poker enormously, partly because the man had lived by a more demanding code than Morgan was sure he could practice himself.

He'd tried hypocrisy, found it wasn't something he wore well, and it seemed the height of hypocrisy to claim to accept a church and then ignore its standards. This, however, led to the important question; would the church assist an unbeliever? And would he, to get what he needed—what Donradé needed—give up himself?

If The Blade of The Faith were a believer, then the code might be less demanding than he thought. Suddenly he stopped in the middle of the street and laughed, ignoring the people around him who gawked at him. He'd been concerned the church lacked morality, then feared he'd not be able to accept a more stringent code than his own, then felt relief the church might be less demanding than he'd hoped. He'd best make up his mind what he wanted.

Returning to the residence, he ate only a light lunch, then walked with Damon to the barracks. There they chose a dozen men Damon felt needed to improve their skills or needed the work. All donned heavy leather leggings, gambesons, and gauntlets, bucket-like padded practice helms with T-shaped openings for vision and breathing, and carefully-dulled practice swords.

Damon selected two men and the rest of them watched as the two sparred with sword and shield. Both men were Gascolans. They saluted each other, then fell to the task like a couple of woodcutters. Morgan finally stopped them to show how they'd fallen into a rhythm, and had only fought from the waist up, as though they'd taken root.

For the rest of the afternoon Damon and Morgan watched, instructed, and occasionally dealt bruises to assist memory.

Morgan observed that some of the Keshti fought with swords in a totally foreign style. One of them, in particular, began from stances that looked awkward to Morgan, and used slashing attacks that kept his blade in constant motion, frequently shifting his sword from one hand to the other. Morgan glanced at Damon, saw Damon looking at him. They both grinned, then Damon indicated Morgan should teach the first lesson.

Morgan interrupted the man's contest with another Keshti. They saluted each other, then the soldier took up his stance. Morgan feinted, drawing a slashing parry that missed, then lunged. His thrust, delivered with just enough force to bruise, caught the man in the right armpit.

Morgan stepped back, raised his sword in another salute. "That sort of drill with a sword is impressive to watch, and it builds familiarity and confidence with the blade, but in a battle, unless you're both skilled and very quick, the best you can hope for is to be remembered with admiration by the man who killed you. The only things worse than having your blade out of line of your opponent is to miss a slash, leaving you out of line and with the momentum taking you away from him, or to have your opponent's blade inside your own."

After the man had recovered, Damon practiced with him. The first time Morgan had been able to observe Damon's fighting skills had been in the battles at Tong Shavath, when the young man had shown himself a most efficient harvester, using swords for scythes, but practice allowed more opportunity to exhibit skill.

Damon toyed with the Keshti, easily adjusting to each shift in the other man's attack, then, as the Keshti tossed the sword from left hand to right, Damon beat the sword loose. The move had been so smoothly executed it almost looked like an accident. He stepped back and let the Keshti recover his weapon, then parried the next attack to the outside and tapped the man on the inside of the elbow.

He saluted his opponent, who'd clutched his injured arm and was apparently trying to rub feeling back into it. "It's as Scarface says. If you rely upon quickness, you'll always find a quicker man. Also, the more you move your blade the sooner you'll wear yourself out, and the more complicated your attack, the more things can go wrong."

They kept the men at practice until sundown, then, like farmers who'd spent a day working in the field, he and Damon returned to the residence.

For almost a week, Morgan helped Damon put a fresh edge on the soldiers, fighting his own impatience more than any other opponent.

Twice they practiced with each other. Damon had most of his father's skill, and only a shade less than Hadrian's speed. With sword and shield, Morgan was able to draw out the match until both men were hardly able to raise their swords and both their shield arms trembled with fatigue. The other bout was less even. Armed with sword and shield, he faced Damon using two swords, and felt as though he'd been in a hailstorm.

During that time they also found other quarters. Damon and his family moved to a small cottage near the barracks, and Morgan took a pallet with the soldiers.

Morgan had almost despaired of receiving a reply and was composing a second request when a messenger brought him a sheet of parchment bound with the seal of The Voice. He broke the seal and tried to read the message, then cursed. He now spoke Thani well, if not entirely fluently, but the written language still looked like nothing but a series of slash marks to him.

Damon had just arrived and was still picking the men who most needed either training or a drubbing. Morgan approached him and handed him the parchment. "The most I can make out from this is that their chicken is either angry or hungry."

Damon read the message silently, then said, "You're to carry this with you to Ong Vaun. If you wish to take the couriers' route, you may exchange mounts along the way, and rest and eat at the stations. When you reach Ong Vaun, present this to the priests in the cathedral. It says, 'At your convenience,' suggesting you might want to bathe and refresh yourself before you present yourself to The Voice." He handed the parchment back to Morgan. "Good fortune. Do you want a companion for the journey?"

"Thanks anyway. Besides what I can pack in my saddle pouches, all I need take is my leave."

Damon unbuckled his belt, slid his purse loose, tossed it to Morgan. "This sort of company's always welcome, I suspect. I'll hope to see you again."

Morgan smiled. "As someone remarked some time ago, counterfeit coins always have a way of turning up. You seem to be throwing good money away on bad."

He gathered his possessions. Anything he couldn't wear could easily fit into his saddle pouches. With the bags slung over his shoulder, he strode to the stable, saddled and bridled the black mare he'd ridden into Tong Shavath, and set out for Ong Vaun, leaving the dust settling in his passage. He left Bhun Nahbi at a trot, occasionally kicking the horse into a canter or letting it slow to a walk, if only as a relief from the bone-rattling bouncing of the trot.

Most trees were changing their green crowns for those of red or rust or brown or, occasionally, gold. The day was crisp and clear, with the sky a vivid blue, and cloudless. By the time he'd reached the first station, seven leagues from Bhun Nahbi, his horse was well-lathered with sweat.

At the station he displayed the message with its seal, then put his bridle, saddle, and saddle pouches on a steeldust gray.

The road he traveled ran near the center of the most fertile crescent of land in the empire. Cattle grazed on the stalks of harvested grain and the cloth crops. Small towns lay along the road like beads on a string, and he supposed that nowhere on the western continent was as populous.

At the next station he snatched a quick meal of sausage and bread and indifferent wine as the stableman transferred his gear to a liver-colored bay. The animal had spirit and endurance, and maintained a canter for most of the ride to the next station. Full darkness had fallen by the time he reached the fifth station and he was barely able to wolf down a quick meal before he collapsed on a pallet.

He rose again before dawn, still stiff from the previous day's hard riding, but eager to continue. Being able to finally take action seemed to relieve some of his aches, despite the chill in the air, and he seemed to become more limber as he rode. His first day's ride had covered over a third of the distance to Ong Vaun, and he rode with the air of a man beginning a journey home.

The morning was cold enough that he was grateful for his cloak but the day aged into unseasonable warmth. With towns clustered along the way he rode, he was seldom out of sight of tilled land, with stands of trees barely visible in the distance, except for occasional hedgerows. He stopped only at the stations, to change mounts, and reached the day's fifth station as the sun set behind the spires of a city.

Shang Vaul was only thirty leagues from Ong Vaun, and almost as venerable, constructed almost entirely of dark red brick, most of its walls covered with vines which had turned pale and brittle with autumn.

Morgan had arrived early enough that, after eating, he had time to lie awake on his pallet and consider his meeting with The Voice. He'd dealt with religions before; he'd managed to buy the church of Mordach for a ridiculously small sum, with the real price paid by others. It was important he impress upon The Voice the urgency of his mission and the need of the people of Donradé and Glangurra for relief from Mordach's church.

Without a qualm, he set aside concern for others and selfishly indulged in thoughts of Topaz. His image of her lacked clarity, as though he were seeing her through gauze. He tried to remember if she had fine lines running from the corners of her eyes. She smiled often enough that he couldn't remember if her warm humor had left its mark on her face.

~ * ~

Dawn was gray and cold, and he rode through Shang Vaul before all but a handful of traders had begun to set up their wares in the bazaar. Near the center of the city a bridge spanned a wide river, the banks of which were white with rime. For over a league past the city the road ran beside the river, and he stopped to let his horse drink where the river curved away.

The day grew no warmer, the wind had become bitter, and he smelled an impending storm. The sun continued to hide; at its brightest it was only a patch of wan light in the dense clouds creeping past. He drew his cloak tighter and kicked the horse into a canter. At the next station he allowed the stableman to transfer his gear to another horse while he sat by a fire, holding a cup of mulled wine in both hands, letting the cup's warmth seep into his icy fingers.

Snow began to fall before he'd covered less than another league, driven by a cold wind so it struck his face like needles of ice. Afraid his horse would slip and fall on the slick surface, he left the road. The towns through which he passed could've been taken for deserted but for the smoke rising from the chimneys.

By the time he'd reached the next station the storm had passed and the sun made a belated appearance, although it still seemed to begrudge any warmth. He devoured a quick meal and purchased gloves, a woolen smock, which he donned over what he wore, and a leather cloak lined with fleece, which had a cowl that could be tied close around the face.

In the late afternoon he could make out the tallest spires of Ong Vaun, glinting like bronze spears, and the sun was still an hour from setting when he crossed a great bridge to the city.

Ong Vaun was divided by a river that emptied into a nearby lake. The city, at first, seemed constructed of metal but as he drew nearer he could see that the walls were actually glazed brick, most of them bronze-colored, but with occasional patterns of jet black, turquoise, forest green, or gold.

He presented the sheet of parchment to a guard at the gate, who provided directions to an inn near the palace of The Voice and the couriers' station where he could leave his mount.

After he'd seen to the comfort of the horse, and carrying his saddle pouches, he entered the inn, which was dim and warm and had a low ceiling. The common room was apparently popular and, sampling the food, Morgan learned why. He studied the other people in the room, found no one with whom he wanted to speak. He finished the meal before him, luxuriated in a hot bath, and lounged on the inn's pallet.

He was still uneasy about his interview with The Voice, but it'd soon be over and he'd be returning to Donradé. Unless something disastrous had occurred in his absence, he should be able to ride to Stag Mountain and return to Donradé before the spring. A spring campaign was risky, but represented the best chance for a quick victory. The peasants would only reluctantly leave their fields, and spring in Donradé was a time of uncertain weather and sudden, torrential rains. Without enough audacity or the loyalty of his petty lords, Thienn probably wouldn't be prepared to field an army before summer.

He couldn't regret burning the message from Topaz; the need to sacrifice something of great value had been desperate, but he greatly missed that note. As sharp as his memory was, it was a comfort to actually hold something real that reminded him of her. He closed his eyes and visualized Topaz saying the words she'd written.

~ * ~

Dawn was clear-eyed and energetic, and Morgan rose feeling much the same. He dressed in fresh clothing from his saddle pouches and chose the lighter cloak, dressing with the same care he'd exercise in armoring himself before a battle. By habit, he half-drew his sword from the scabbard, then slid it back before he left his room.

Outside the inn, he faced a huge open square. From a street or two away he could faintly hear the hawking of the merchants in the bazaar, but here the area was quiet, with small groups of men garbed like priests or in gray robes, moving slowly across the open area, some in quiet conversation, the rest silent, perhaps meditating. The palace of The Voice stood diagonally across the cobblestones from the inn. The facing diagonal was occupied by an immense building with many windows.

Walking across the square and nearing the palace, he studied the huge iron-bound doors, made of some dark wood and intricately carved in a pattern incorporating the design of the black iron hinges and handles.

The iron handle of the door was so cold that touching it almost seemed to burn his hand, but he opened the door, closed it behind him. An old man with ascetic features sat at a table, writing, apparently copying the page beside him. Morgan approached the table, handed the priest the parchment that had brought him so far.

The priest motioned toward a stool near the fireplace, then rose and walked out a tall double door. Scarface stood staring into the fire, his right hand clutching his left wrist behind his back. He remembered how he'd faced battles in the past and he put himself into the same state; he tried to clear his mind of everything, every thought, so that he simply existed, an integral part of the scene in which he found himself.

Hearing soft boots on the tiled floor, he turned. The priest held out his hand. "You may speak with The Voice. And you may safely leave your weapons with me, my lord."

Morgan recognized the priest's words as an order, not a suggestion, however deferentially phrased. As for the clan law that one always have a weapon within reach—he'd broken it before for matters far less important.

Unarmed, he strode to the ornate double doors through which the priest had passed and returned. Both doors swung open with little more than a touch to one of them, and he faced a corridor.

As he stepped into the passage he glanced back to see two guards standing in alcoves, not visible until one had stepped past them. Ignoring the soldiers, he strode ahead. A fine blue carpet covered the floor, and the tan plaster walls were plain, but paintings in heavy frames and tapestries were hung at intervals along the wall. The hallway ended at another tan wall, in which was set a single very plain wooden door not much taller than he was. He entered.

The Voice of The Faith looked up, then rose from a heavy chair, stepped around a low table, and approached Morgan. He was dressed very plainly, like every other priest of Ianno Morgan had seen, but his presence was commanding. Morgan couldn't have guessed the man's age with any hope of certainty. His dark blue eyes bespoke a finely-honed intelligence without any trace of the fanaticism Morgan had half-expected, and the fine lines around his eyes revealed both care and humor. The Voice's face was otherwise unlined and his hair, worn loose and shoulder-length in the Kathan manner, was still dark brown, but the face also displayed a serenity that usually only appeared in the elderly.

The Voice motioned toward a couch. "Please, sit," he said, and seated himself on a matching couch across the low table. "May I offer you something with which to break your fast?"

Morgan, recognizing a ritual offer of hospitality and the necessity of ritually accepting it, took a biscuit and a cup of tea. The bun was filled with some very sweet dried fruit and the tea, judging by its fragrance, was apparently made of some sort of flower.

Morgan ate and sipped, then leaned forward on the couch. "I'm here as a petitioner for the peoples of Donradé and Glangurra. They're being oppressed by the church of a god of war, and desperately need the blessings of Ianno."

The priest smiled. "Your brother, Poker, spoke of you. He said that for someone so devious, you had a very frank manner and a habit of speaking directly to the problem. I presume you seek some more martial expression of Ianno's blessings than, say, words or gestures."

"Actually, I've come to ask for priests, teachers, perhaps healers. I quite understand that it would be sacrilegious to ask Ianno to sanctify a war."

The Voice leaned back on his couch and stroked his chin. "Interesting. I'd expected a request for an army. Don't you intend to resist the war-god's priests and the renegade king with arms?"

Morgan nodded, surprised by the knowledge The Voice had revealed about a struggle across the world from the empire. "I'll take what help is offered, but from the empire I hoped for only one ally—its god."

"To what end? If the priests of Ianno aren't accepted in Don-radé, or worse, are accepted but side with the man who loses the war, what have we gained?"

"What would you have lost? I've been told your Faith is spread by reason and persuasion. If reason and persuasion fail in southern Donradé, who can blame you? And if we become Iannists and die, who can hold you accountable? But we need a god to oppose a god. I need something for the people to fight for as well as something to fight against. What sort of victory could I achieve if we win the battle but Mordach's church still rules? The war-god and his priests will extort everything but blood, which they'll take at their whim."

"What's your part in this? Do you intend to rule in Donradé and, perhaps, in Glangurra?"

Morgan was careful to keep his features from revealing his surprise. The Voice was much more well-informed than he might've guessed. "I'm paying a debt; nothing more."

"But the kingdoms will need a ruler. If your acknowledged bastard is unfit, and Mordach's church is broken, who'll rule? Did you expect us to try to govern a nation of foreigners half a world away?"

Morgan grinned. "No, and that's another reason I turned to you. If the church of Ianno were to try to oppress the Donradans and the Glangurrans, it could be thrown out much easier than the church of some more local deity."

The Voice grinned in response. "As your brother said, you have a taste for directness. I applaud your honesty, if not your diplomacy, but who will rule? Don't you have other children? Don't you want them to rule after you?"

Morgan sank back into the couch and considered his daughter, growing up among the Dieri. And if Topaz were to live and bear him a son, would the boy be content being a shepherd? "I've learned something about the costs of power. One is that power can turn a good man into a bad king. Being a good ruler is difficult; harder la-bor than farming. But being a bad ruler means having to sleep with a dagger in your hand and still not knowing you'll wake. If any child of mine were so ambitious or deluded to want to rule, they'd earn it as I did. To be honest, I rather enjoyed the way to the throne. It was the duties once I'd put on the crown that became onerous."

"What of your responsibility to the people of Donradé and Glangurra? Don't you owe them a ruler?"

Morgan pursed his lips, examined his reluctance. "I detest slavery. It's no less slavery when a whole people force a single man to do something he chooses not to do than for one man to force another to do something against his will. Besides, a man can't be forced to rule. That's something he must decide for himself."

"Very good. And Ianno wants those who serve him to do so because they choose to do so. I must carefully consider your request, and you need to learn more about Ianno. You'll need to spend at least a month at the seminary."

CHAPTER 10

Morgan felt as though he'd been struck in the belly. He'd been counting the days until he could see Topaz, and now the time seemed impossibly far away. "That's impossible. I must return to the western continent as soon as possible."

"But it won't be possible for over a month," The Voice replied. "Any sailor can tell you that for another month the Interland Ocean is too storm-wracked for any vessel to make the voyage to the western continent. Even some coastal towns are being abandoned for the next twenty days." He sipped at his cup of tea. "Also, you've decided the church can be of temporal use to you. It's only fair to allow the church to determine whether you can be of any use to us. And you don't seem to have given much thought to whether we can be of spiritual use to you."

The man's face seemed open and his tones were steady, and he was probably telling the truth. It would do no good to rage at the unexpected delay, although Morgan was having to fight down his frustration.

The Voice seemed to read him with uncanny accuracy. "I'm sorry you're disappointed but, since you must remain here yet awhile, wouldn't it be best to use the time well?"

Morgan stood and bowed, beaten by circumstances. "As you say. I'll return to the inn for my belongings."

"Kiartan will assist you and take you to the seminary, where he'll share a cell with you."

A man, dressed all in black, stepped forward, and it was as though a chair or a table had moved toward him. Morgan's hand swept to where his sword's hilt would have been and he took a quick step back, then composed himself and studied the figure. The man was clad all in dead black, with a cloth wrapped around his head and face, hiding all but a strip of pale skin and blue-green eyes. He was a little more than a hand's span shorter than Morgan but with a stocky build. Morgan knew that "Kiartan" was Thani for "the foreigner."

Morgan bowed to him. "I'm pleased to meet The Blade of The Faith."

Kiartan nodded to him, waited with a familiar patience.

The Voice rose from his couch. "You're very quick. If you have any questions, especially in regard to The Faith, Kiartan will answer them for you. It's been a pleasure to meet you. I can see Poker's regard was well-placed."

Morgan felt a flush of pleasure and warmth at hearing Poker's name. He bowed again to The Voice and strode back to the antechamber where he retrieved his weapons, donned them, then, followed by The Blade of The Faith as by a shadow, crossed the square to the inn. It was the work of mere moments to gather his few items of clothing and stuff them into his saddle pouches, then he gestured for Kiartan to lead the way to the seminary.

As he recrossed the square, two paces behind the church's assassin, he was able to recognize the sense of familiarity about the man, and differences as well. Kiartan had Hadrian's stone patience, but Kiartan's extended further. He had the air of a man who practiced parsimony in all things, even to the economy of motion; he was still until he chose to move, and no effort was greater than required by the purpose.

They entered the immense building diagonal to the palace. Inside the great double doors, similar to those of the palace, they passed through a large chamber where priests and men wearing simple gray robes stood, or sat on couches, and conversed in hushed tones. Morgan could guess the gray robes were the garb of novices.

No one stopped them, or even more than glanced at them, despite both being armed. Kiartan wore a sword in a broad scabbard thrust into his sash.

The Blade of The Faith led Morgan up a flight of stairs, down a corridor, then opened a door, standing in a manner that invited Morgan to precede him.

The small room was illumined by daylight slanting through a small window set high in the wall, with dark wood walls and polished yellow hardwood floor. Two pallets with blankets lay on opposite sides of the room and a small chest rested at the foot of each pallet. The room was chilly in more than temperature; it had about it an air of austerity.

Morgan glanced at the other man, then chose the right-hand pallet and chest. He emptied his saddle pouches into the box, stuck the pouches into one end of the chest. After a moment's hesitation, he unbuckled his sword belt and left the weapon between the chest and the bedding. He stood. "What now?"

Kiartan, still at the door, removed his own scabbarded blade and placed it as Morgan had, then opened the door again and waited. Morgan stepped through the doorway and followed the man through the corridor and back down the stairs, followed another passage to a room similar to theirs, but lacking pallets and chests. An elderly priest, who reminded Morgan of Timyan, sat on a stool fingering a string or fine chain of bright, varicolored beads.

Morgan entered and sat down on the other stool, facing the priest. He'd seen Poker pray on the beads, and so he waited. The priest finished his devotions and slid the beads up his sleeve, looked at Morgan. "Are you here to listen?"

Morgan smiled. "I'm here to learn."

"I can't promise you'll learn. If you listen, perhaps you'll learn." For over an hour the priest told him of the struggles between Ianno and the other gods. Ianno had created the world and the lesser gods: Romshaku, the god of the sea; Venestra, the god of the earth who was sometimes male and sometimes female; and Tirdan, the sun god. Gods, like men, sometimes turned from Ianno and then He had to use His power to remind them that He'd created them to live in harmony with man.

When Romshaku rose in revolt, his rage and their struggle set the seas in turmoil. Romshaku rebelled every year, and their battle lasted for over a month. When Venestra became Venist, a male, the change made the earth flinch and shrug, and the struggle caused earthquakes and avalanches. More often, Venestra was in harmony with Ianno and bore fruit and grain. Tirdan sometimes turned his face away, but he rebelled more often by inciting his three servants, Khalsin, the hot, dry wind; Fadra, the rainstorm; and Talak, the icy blizzard.

These deities and their servants weren't evil, only rebellious, and harmed men only by carelessness. Venestra was a loving mother, who fed men. Romshaku provided fish and a way to trade with faraway lands. Tirdan provided light and warmth, and when he and his servants served Ianno, they gave warm breezes, gentle rains, and the snow that left new life when it melted.

Morgan had no questions to ask of the priest and, after the priest had finished, returned to his cell. He did have questions for Kiartan, but the man was nowhere to be found, and the room felt empty. Then a short, olive-skinned man with gray eyes, his black hair and beard braided like a Keshti, appeared, as Kiartan had in the palace.

"Interesting spell," Morgan observed. "I've never learned that version of the spell of concealment. How does it make the room feel empty?"

"It's not a spell. Part of the art of concealment is to assume a form that doesn't seem human but fits with the place. The rest is a matter of concentrating on void. When you think or feel, you radiate presence. By concentrating on void, you don't radiate."

"That's a trick worth knowing. Will you teach me?"

Kiartan stared at him a long moment, then said, "There's a price. You'd have to forswear magic. Now, you have more important things to learn."

"Why did The Voice put me in your care? To me, that's of some importance."

"Perhaps he thought you'd learn better if I were one of your instructors."

Morgan sat on the edge of his pallet and wrapped himself in his cloak. "Then teach. Let's begin with why you're called "the foreigner.""

"Because I wasn't born in the empire." When Morgan only stared at him, he added, "I was born in Myslan."

"Have you a name?" Morgan decided not to ask what the name might be. He'd no intention of giving this man his own name, and it seemed only fair to respect the other man's secret, but he was curious.

"No, I was consecrated from birth to a deity called Tavisi. I was his tool. You don't name a tool."

"What sort of deity was this Tavisi?"

"He was a death god. Since I served death, I was taught to deal it." He paused. "Tavisi was, of course, a fraud. His church wasn't about death. Like most churches, it was about power and wealth. When I converted to the church of Ianno I realized one needn't make sacrifices to death. True death requires no one to take lives for him; he takes them all, in his own time."

Sensing a story, Morgan asked, "How did you come to convert to Ianno?"

"The *Zaisi*, the chief priest of Tavisi, dispatched me to kill The Voice. It was, of course, necessary to learn the language and the customs of the empire. Pretending to be mute, I spent several months in the mountains of Kesh. Then I presented myself to the seminary as a

Keshti eager to become a priest. From the seminary I could watch the palace, and, as a novice, I could move freely, learn those things I needed to know to finish my mission and escape. I also learned other things I needed to know, which had nothing to do with killing The Voice.

"I converted, and confessed myself to The Voice. I expected to be executed. He told me I should become a priest. I decided it was best to become The Blade of The Faith. Just as you don't plow with a sword or weave with a spear, I, as a tool, should be properly employed. My first act as The Blade of The Faith was to kill the next assassin sent to murder The Voice, then I killed the *Zaisi*. Since then, I've been used five times."

"You have no compunctions about killing, I presume?" Morgan stood and stretched.

"None. I'd killed for Tavisi more than I ever have for Ianno. Why should I shrink from protecting the empire or the church, both of which are blessed by Ianno?"

Morgan's belly rumbled, reminding him it'd been hours since he'd eaten. "When are meals served?"

"When you hear the great bell rung. It's rung for rising, meals, and sleep."

Morgan studied the other man. "What do you really look like?"

"I took an oath never to show my face. Like a name, my face has nothing to do with what I am, so I'm always either masked or disguised."

Morgan barked a laugh. "There we differ. My face, or, more properly, these scars—" he touched them with his fingertips—" is central to who and what I am. They're the repositories of my power, and they influence the actions of others. Which, of course, affects me."

They heard the bell sound, almost felt it, as the great bronze-tongued bell tolled, and Kiartan led Morgan to a huge hall containing lines of tables running lengthwise. A number of tables, set end-to-end ran crosswise along the front of the room, and a very elderly priest stood at the foot of the tables. Kiartan stopped beside a bench flanking the table nearest the door and they waited until the room filled with priests and novices.

When the flow of churchmen stopped, the elderly priest began to chant a prayer and the rest intoned a response. Morgan listened closely and was able to join the others in their responses.

The prayer ended, Kiartan indicated Morgan should rise and approach the head table, on which lay platters, cups, spoons, and bowls of food. Morgan chose two small loaves of bread and sampled three of the foreign dishes, took a cup of water. He returned to the table near the door, sat on the bench, and ate and drank, observing that the novices and priests had formed a queue. The novices preceded the priests and the younger priests went before their elders. He glanced at Kiartan, who made the sign for silence.

After the meal he followed Kiartan to a tub, where they washed their utensils. When the last of the priests had cleaned their platters, cups, and spoons, the elderly priest again led a chant giving thanks to Ianno for the meal.

Back in their cell, Morgan sat on his pallet. "I assume silence is observed in the corridors and halls?"

"That's correct. You may speak only in this room, the rooms where you receive instruction, in the antechamber, and in the square outside."

"Perhaps you should show me more of this place. I have no idea how to find the latrines. And is there a place I can practice the use of weapons?"

"I'll show you the toilets and the well. We each draw our own water. All the rooms in the seminary, except the dining hall and the kitchen, near it, are either cells or rooms for instruction. As for arms practice, I'll arrange for us to practice with The Voice's guards. After I show you the toilet, I'll lead you to your next instructor."

The latrines, behind the seminary, were large enough for a score of men to relieve themselves at once. "I hope there's no outbreak of diarrhea or trouble with the food while I'm here," Morgan said.

Kiartan only made again the gesture for silence and led Morgan back into the seminary, to the room of his next instructor, a young priest with a very deep voice and dark, piercing eyes.

"Sit," the priest said, motioning toward a stool in front of him, and when Morgan was seated, continued. "I understand you've been learning about The Faith. You already know, I believe, about the rewards and punishments to be expected by a follower of Ianno."

Morgan narrowed his eyes and answered quietly, "It does neither of us any honor to suggest I'm studying The Faith because I've been bribed or threatened."

"Very good. Reward or punishment should be incidental. One should live one's life properly as a sign of respect for oneself and for

Ianno."

"What aspects of The Faith do you teach?"

"I usually instruct those who will become *falis*."

"I've been curious about how the church governs the empire."

"By governing, not ruling. Each region has its own Fali. Those are chosen by each nation according to its own traditions. The *falis* are brought here to learn their duties. Then they return to their region to rule. If they rule badly, if a complaint is made to the church, the *fali* may be tried for heresy."

"What would constitute heresy?"

"Favoring one nation or its people over another, for example. It's essential a citizen be treated fairly any place in the empire, otherwise the empire will collapse into squabbles among the different peoples. A *fali* is expected to follow the precept that sanctity is service."

"Is that why the novices eat before the priests?"

"It is."

Morgan cast about for other questions. "Why do you all speak Thani in the church?"

"Because it's a dead language. All the Thanitur who'd survived the revolt were absorbed by other peoples. Since the language is dead, it doesn't change, so an Ibari can speak with a Kathan or a Keshti or a Batian, and each understands precisely what the other is saying. Also, by making the common language Thani, we prevent any of the nations from gaining ascendency."

Morgan shifted on the hard stool. "What about The Voice of The Faith? With his power, he could tip the balance."

The priest shook his head. "The Voice serves for five years. Each nation in the empire, in turn, chooses The Voice. Usually, they choose a priest from among their own people, although it's often happened that a priest widely known for wisdom or sanctity—they amount to the same thing—may be chosen by another nation. Had he remained in the empire another two years, Poker might've been chosen The Voice of The Faith."

"You knew him, then?"

"Yes. I even know you a little, through him. He studied here, and established a small seminary at The Shield of The Saint. He taught many of us; taught us as much by the way he lived as by what he said. Some of us thought he might be the reborn Saint."

Despite the chill in the room, Morgan felt a warmth that his cousin was so well and fondly remembered, and it gave him a sense of kinship with this priest.

The statement also raised another question. "If Donradé were to accept the church of Ianno, would it become part of the empire, and eventually be able to choose The Voice?"

"Such a thing has never happened, but it could be. The church council and The Voice would have to discuss the matter, but if another nation were to accept Ianno, and if their ruler were educated by the church, I see no insurmountable obstacle. That nation's people would, of course, have to learn Thani."

"All of them?"

"Not all, but many. How many would be another issue for the council and The Voice to decide."

Morgan considered the church's form of government. "It all sounds very good, but I've learned that nothing more sophisticated than a club ever works as well as it's intended."

The priest smiled. "True. There are always disputes and alliances, but the church and the empire have thus far managed to survive being governed by fallible men."

Morgan had begun to wonder if Topaz might not embrace the church, but the priest's last words made him realize he'd seen no women at the seminary. If Topaz chose to join, would there be a place in the church for her? A church that had no place for Topaz also had no place for him.

This could create another problem. If he were to find Ukena, would the church oppose her ascension to the throne of Glangurra?

He shifted on the stool again, but it wasn't the seat that was uncomfortable. "Could a woman become a *fali*, or a priest?"

The priest's face betrayed surprise, then concentration, and he answered slowly. "It's never happened. None of our peoples teach our women to read. Among some of us, few men can read, and one must be able to read The Book to embrace it. I can recall nothing in the canons or in The Book itself to forbid it, but tradition makes no provision for such a thing." He grinned. "You have the makings of a great heretic."

Morgan laughed. "Does that mean you're throwing me out of the church before I've decided to join it?"

The priest's grin broadened. "No, it means you might someday become The Voice." He fought his grin into submission. "That's the church's greatest strength, and its reason for existence; to ask questions and to inspire debate. In the third book of The Saint, Dahlman states the way of The Faith must never be easy, that contentment rather than contention would be the death of the church."

He seemed lost in thought for a moment, then said, "While no woman had ever been a priest or a *fali*, some of our finest herbalists and healers have been women. It appears we've given each other things to think about. I'm grateful for this unanticipated gift."

"You have wood for fire and food to eat. How does the church support itself?"

"The church receives donations from the faithful and a tithe of the taxes, and the seminary nearly supports itself. Elderly priests and priests who've been called by Ianno but who are indisposed to minister still have valuable skills. This seminary sells books, for example, and has an herb garden and a bee farm. All these things provide income, and our expenses are small; firewood, robes, and foodstuffs. The meals are cooked by priests."

For another two hours they discussed the history of the church, until Morgan swallowed a yawn. "You still have two hours before dinner," the priest said. "Why don't you walk in the square, or perhaps read some of The Living Book?"

"I don't read Thani."

"The Living Book is written in a number of languages. It contains the writings that may someday be part of The Book."

"Will you show me?"

The priest rose and led him to a small room, not much larger than the cells, off the antechamber. The room contained only a pedestal, flanked by tall candleholders, on which rested a great book bound in green leather. A couple of stools completed the room's furnishings. As they entered, a novice standing behind the pedestal looked up from the book, then returned to his reading. Morgan had many more days in which to read, and no desire to either hurry the novice by his presence, or to wait for the other to finish. He nodded to the priest, then strode out into the square.

The air was dry and cold, with the smell of the city less intense than he'd have thought.

Ong Vaun seemed to him to be the most civilized city he'd ever visited, although he'd actually seen very little of it. The wind was still and he was able to stride twice around the square before the chill drove him back inside.

When he entered their cell he found Kiartan lying face-down

and spread-eagled on the floor. Before he could shape an inquiry, the man raised himself from the floor by the tips of his fingers and toes. Morgan realized he was gaping like a yokel at a fair and closed his mouth. It was an impressive display of power of the shoulders and arms. The man lowered himself slowly and smoothly, then rose again, repeating the exercise a dozen times while Morgan watched.

Finally, with an agile maneuver Morgan hadn't seen before, Kiartan flipped himself to his feet. He still wore the appearance of a Keshti. "I've arranged for us to use the practice room by the barracks for an hour each morning and another hour each evening, after the evening meal. We may begin tomorrow morning." He glanced to where Morgan had laid his sword. "May I see your weapon?"

At Morgan's nod, Kiartan bent, picked up the weapon, drew it from the scabbard, then turned it in his hands, studying it and acquiring a feel for its balance.

"May I look at your own sword?" Morgan asked. Kiartan picked it up and handed it to him, still in its scabbard. The weapon had a plain pommel and a crossguard with arms a little longer than usual and with a pronounced hook at the ends. The dull blackwood hilt was long enough to wrap three hands around it between guard and pommel. As he drew the blade from its sheath, Morgan saw the entire weapon was black except for a thread of brightness along the cutting edge of the blade. The blade was a hand's span shorter than Morgan's, single-edged, with a straight back and an edge that tapered to its greatest width a hand's length from the pointed tip. It could be used for thrusting but was primarily a cutting weapon, with its balance nearer the point. Such a weapon was harder to control precisely but had more authority when it struck.

Morgan slid the sword back into its scabbard and returned it to Kiartan, who handed Morgan's weapon back to him. "Good steel," Morgan said.

"You may repay anything you learn from me by teaching me your language," the assassin said.

"Gasgoran?"

Kiartan nodded. "If I teach but don't learn, something I may offer Ianno is lost."

Within a dozen words, Morgan noted Kiartan was a natural mimic, and he had a gift for languages.

The lesson was interrupted by the pealing of the great bell, and they walked together to the dining hall. After the prayer and the dinner, one of the priests read a passage from The Book, then delivered a homily based on the reading. Morgan listened with only one ear, although he joined in the chanted responses.

After the service, Kiartan left the seminary and Morgan, with time to himself, decided to visit the room of The Living Book. The chamber was empty but for the book and the furniture. Feeling a little self-conscious, Morgan stepped behind the pedestal and opened the volume.

The first page was filled with the Thani slash marks, while the facing page was written in thickly-drawn shapes and dots. Each successive pair of pages bore different forms of writing. He recognized a few, including the blocky ornate shapes of Ghiblin, though he couldn't read them.

Finally he found a page of the flowing Gasgoran script and, facing it, the intricate patterns of Sinn, which seemed to have been written in Poker's distinctive hand. He read from the pages, realized they both bore the same meaning. A passage near the bottom caught his attention in particular.

Know that all who live are a reflection of Ianno, seen in a flawed mirror, In our folly we reflect, if poorly, the wisdom of Ianno. To think on a kindness is to recognize in man the love and compassion of Ianno. To reflect on immortality is to look into the eternal, the lifetime of Ianno. To perceive beauty is to accept the grace of Ianno, and to aspire to perfection is to pray. One need not achieve perfection to have one's prayers answered. One is blessed in the attempt.

~ * ~

Morgan and Kiartan rose with the first toll of the bell, dressed themselves, and, with Kiartan in the lead, made their way across the square to an annex of the palace of The Voice.

They entered a large room, one corner of which was occupied by what seemed a number of smaller rooms, and Morgan could see a corridor, with flights of stairs leading to upper levels, among the doorways. To the left of the door through which they'd entered stood a bench littered with practice armor and blunt swords made of some sort of dark wood.

Morgan removed his cloak, robe, and tunic, and dressed in the heavy padded leather leggings and gambeson, drew the practice helm over his head and buckled the strap under his chin, then accepted and donned the metal gauntlets Kiartan had handed him.

Among the wooden swords leaning against the wall stood one

near the dimensions of his own weapon. He hefted it, found that with its thicker blade it approached the balance of his sword.

Kiartan had also donned armor and around the waist of his gambeson had wrapped and tied a sash, into which he'd thrust a practice sword. Morgan faced him, his own weapon held loosely. "Are you ready?"

He'd barely gotten the words out before Kiartan had taken a step toward him, his right hand drawing his sword. Instead of drawing the sword across his body, Kiartan had drawn it almost straight out, slamming the pommel into the pit of Morgan's belly. As Morgan doubled over, trying to recover his breath, he felt The Blade's weapon tap him lightly on the bottom of the helm.

Kiartan stepped back, lowering his sword.

When he could breathe without pain, Morgan dropped into a crouch, his right foot pointed at Kiartan, his left far back and pointed at an angle, his sword's pommel almost touching his right knee, the blade slanted slightly forward and in a vertical line with his opponent's body.

Kiartan still stood, his legs spread not much wider than the width of his shoulders, his knees slightly flexed. His left hand, near the pommel of his weapon, was at about the level of his navel, the right hand near the guard, holding the sword so the blade angled down, its tip almost touching the floor.

Kiartan seemed to be daydreaming, his eyes hardly focussed.

Morgan tried a tentative cut and Kiartan's blade swept up, caught his, deflected it, and continued up and around in a partial figure 8 that ended in another light tap on the bottom edge of his helm.

Wasting no time in a salute, Morgan dropped back into his crouch. Kiartan faced him in a similar posture and the tip of his practice sword began to slash from the upper left. Morgan swung his weapon to parry but Kiartan's blade had slipped away and, as his own blade was drawn out of line, he heard and felt The Blade's weapon ring against his gauntlets, then rasp as the dulled edge was drawn across his knuckles. Had the blade been edged steel, it'd have sawed his fingers off.

For almost an hour he tried to defend himself and, occasionally, to try to attack Kiartan. He failed at both. He hadn't been so thoroughly humiliated at practice since he'd been the rawest recruit in the Marked Ones, except those times when he'd practiced with Hadrian.

When their hour of practice was ended they stripped off the

practice armor and again donned their robes. Despite the coldness of the room, Morgan was sweating heavily.

After they returned to the seminary and Morgan had broken his fast on tea, bread, and fruit, he sat in the cell, digesting the meal and the lessons.

On the western continent, an opponent would've attacked his legs, especially his knees. Here, the style was apparently to cut at the wrists and fingers. He'd noticed that, after the initial strike, the technique was to draw the edge of the weapon across the fingers or the arm. He'd also observed the pommel could be as much a weapon as the blade of a sword, and that because an opponent didn't have a sword bare in his hands didn't mean he was defenseless. He'd need to practice more, perhaps learn the advantages of the open stance Kiartan seemed to favor.

He'd begun to wonder if he weren't being left to meditate when Kiartan entered the room, gestured for him to follow, and led him to another cell for more religious instruction.

~ * ~

During the evening practice, Kiartan instructed. The first thing he taught was the stare into the middle distance, which had looked so much like daydreaming to Morgan.

"If you focus your attention on one thing—an opponent's eyes, his hands, his blade, you may miss seeing something of importance."

"But the eyes will usually tell you where your opponent will strike next," Morgan protested.

"If a fighter's so obvious that he tells you with his eyes where he'll strike, you'll beat him anyway. But a man who can keep his eyes fixed, or lie with his eyes, will leave you as bad as blind. If you look at your opponent, but stare through him into the middle distance, you'll 'feel' his every move; where and how he places his feet, the movement of his blade, all of it will be yours.

"Another thing to remember is that one must always attack."

"What if your opponent has you overmatched?"

"Then it's even more important to attack. If he's better than you, his attack must eventually beat your defense. Your only hope is aggressive action. And, if you lose, would you rather die attacking or defending?"

Morgan stared at the assassin. "Have you met my clan brother, Hadrian?"

A nod.

"You remind me of him."

For all the response the remark received, Morgan might've told Kiartan the evening was cold. And that was another similarity. Kiartan was the second man Morgan had met that he couldn't read.

As they returned to the seminary, Morgan reflected on the many meanings of black. Mendarian wore black, he supposed, for the same reasons he did; it was the color of mystery, of intrigue, and of power. Authority was gold, but it was a weak reed next to power. Also, black was a dramatic color. Hadrian wore black because he was death. Kiartan wore it because he was void.

Morgan's religious instructions turned to the history of the church. He found it difficult to respect and impossible to feel affinity with Thegan, The Prophet. Thegan had apparently been a vision-seeing preacher who'd screamed exhortations and warnings at the Thanitur. From what Morgan could see, he'd been narrow-minded and vengeful. He'd apparently been one of those who'd whipped the Thanitur into a fever for conquests.

Morgan did, however, become fond of Dahlman, The Saint. Perhaps it was a measure of the man's greatness that one could feel affection for him although he was four centuries dead. While he hadn't claimed to have seen visions, he'd clearly been a visionary. Unlike The Prophet, who wrote little—most of the stories of The Prophet had been written by others—The Saint had written as well as traveled and tended the needs of the people. He'd been instrumental in forging the second empire although he'd never become The Voice of The Faith. He'd been chosen for that honor three times, and three times had declined.

Morgan had a low opinion of false modesty and a scarcely better one of the truer variety. It'd generally been his experience that those who displayed modesty had earned it, but The Saint had been one of those rare men who seem to appear only once in half a dozen generations, one who'd changed a nation, had breathed life and something finer into its soul. He'd actually been the soul of the empire.

When he'd asked what The Saint had looked like, the priest had smiled. "He looked like you or I—although I hadn't heard he was scarred."

"That wasn't what I meant."

"In the days of The Prophet, it was considered a sacrilege to make any representation of Ianno, because He is The Unknowable.

That's when the symbol of the circle was chosen, because man requires something he can see. But representations of men were also considered sacrilegious, because some feared others would worship them, as they had the effigies of false gods.

"By the time of The Saint, that had changed, but The Saint asked that no likenesses of him be made. He believed that one saw most clearly with the eyes of the soul and the mind. He's supposed to have said everyone who read his words saw him, that they saw in him a part of themselves, which is as he wanted it. He wanted to remind everyone he was only a man, like ourselves, and we could also achieve sanctity. He felt many were saints."

~ * ~

His instructions with Kiartan also progressed. Kiartan introduced him to fighting with sword and buckler. The buckler was a tiny, round shield not much bigger than a man's spread hand. The only way to use it effectively was to use it to crowd the opponent's weapon hand.

They also began using the stairs and rooms set in the practice chamber. Corridors limited the room to use a sword or ax, and favored polearms. He was reminded winding stairs always turned to the right because it kept the defender's shield between him and the enemy and forced the opponent to expose his weapon arm.

He enjoyed a few successes. Once, using a polearm, he bested Kiartan on the stairs. He'd lunged, dropped the weapon's head below the parry, and managed to catch Kiartan's leg with the hook on the back of the head. He'd felt a real satisfaction in seeing Kiartan fall on his ass.

Such times were rare. Kiartan was a master, and he was the teacher. The assassin taught him how, in close fighting, the left forearm could be used as a shield, to sweep aside a thrust or even a weak slash, though always using the outer arm. He also showed a sword had other uses than as a weapon.

Kiartan's strength and agility were remarkable. Once he showed how, by holding his single-edged weapon by the back of the blade, he could leap up, hook an arm of the sword's guard on the sill of a second-level window, then climb the blade.

He also showed how, inserting the blade upside-down in the scabbard so that it only entered by a hand's breadth, and with one end of the thong normally wrapped around the scabbard in his teeth, he could use the extended sword and sheath as a probe to feel his way through a dark room while remaining out of sword's reach of any opponent hiding there, but still able to free his own blade with a sudden twist.

The days of training and instruction and his teaching Kiartan Gasgoran seemed to fade, one into another, until only knots tied in a cord let Morgan realize he'd been twenty-five days at the seminary, when Kiartan informed him, after the morning practice, that The Voice of The Faith wished to speak with him after he'd broken his fast.

In the dining hall his response to the prayer was habitual; his mind was occupied with why The Voice had summoned him before the thirty days had passed. It was possible the storm season had abated sooner than expected, but he held little hope. He'd experienced so many setbacks in his plans he'd become almost fatalistic about delays.

After he'd eaten he treated himself to a quick bath and dressed in clean clothing, partly out of respect for The Voice, partly because it gave him a trace of confidence. Kiartan accompanied him to the palace, where they were immediately ushered to the living quarters of The Voice.

Again The Voice rose to greet him and offered him a seat. "The priests tell me you're very quick; a rapid learner."

Morgan smiled with half his mouth. "I've little to do but learn."

"Still, you've been applying yourself." The Voice sat down in a chair facing Morgan's. "Have you considered the question I asked you earlier?"

Morgan frowned. "Which one?"

"Do you still renounce the throne of Glangurra?"

"That throne isn't mine to claim or renounce. It belongs to Queen Ukena. As for the throne of Donradé—I've already abdicated, and nothing has changed my mind."

The Voice leaned forward and rang a small bell on the table between them. "The reason I've asked to speak with you earlier than I'd intended is to tell you I've decided to aid you. I'm also sending Damon and his family with you, along with any of the veterans of Tong Shavath who choose to go to Donradé."

"Does this mean the Winged Dagger Clan has exhausted its welcome in the empire?"

"Not at all. The Shield of The Saint will always be regarded as a clan holding, but I believe there are good reasons for letting Damon and his family accompany you. I've found thirty priests, most of them teachers, who speak Gasgoran well enough to work in Donradé. I'm also sending half that many healers. And The Blade of The Faith will also sail with you.

"The first ten priests will sail with you. The rest will follow within three months."

"Will Bronyak be one of the priests?"

"Unfortunately, no. He wanted to go but he hasn't the ear or the tongue to learn Gasgoran well." He glanced past Morgan.

Morgan turned his head, saw a curtain in the doorway twitch, then it was pushed aside, and Queen Ukena entered the room.

Morgan was almost paralyzed by astonishment, then he scrambled to his feet and bowed deeply. He stared at the woman. Whatever hardships she'd endured had given her strength of character, had tempered her. Once a plain woman, she'd become stately.

"How—?"

"Hadrian brought her to us a few months ago. He said she needed our protection."

So that was what Hadrian meant when he'd said Morgan would find what he was looking for in Ong Vaun, Morgan reflected. He studied the queen closely. She'd been abused by a man Morgan had claimed as a son, and he was almost afraid to look at her face, afraid he'd find contempt or hatred there.

"No need to bow, Lord Daign," she said. "We're equals. You've abdicated a throne and I've had to run away from one. Neither of us is what once we were."

"No," The Voice said, "you aren't. I think you've both been changed by more than the loss of a crown, and you appear to have gained more than you lost." He gazed at Morgan. "Are you willing to offer your protection to the lady?"

"More than that. I offer her my support to reclaiming the throne of Glangurra."

"And what will you take as your portion?"

"Knowing I've paid a debt and corrected some errors."

"The reason I've called you here early is to give you time to make preparations for the journey. I've already sent a messenger to Bhun Nahbi, although I fear recent storms have slowed the message. I'd hoped your nephew and the others would've arrived by now. You'll go to Bayang Lon, where you'll meet a Sazian ship. It's been trading in the lands south of Myslan and will be returning to the western continent."

Morgan grinned. "I hope it's not the *Zarin Hestaprin*."

The Voice raised an eyebrow, looking a question at Morgan, then shook his head. "It's a ship called *Vinig ni Litat*. We're still trying to arrange passage on other vessels for the rest of your party."

"Unless you wish for me to leave immediately, I'd as soon remain at the seminary until Damon arrives." He smiled at The Voice. "You haven't asked me if I've converted."

The Voice returned the smile. "It wasn't necessary that you become a priest, only that you understand and respect The Faith."

"I've long since learned one needn't believe in a god to be used by one, and I'd already decided if I were going to be used by a god, I'd prefer it be Ianno."

The Voice poured tea into four cups and offered one to each of his guests. He picked up the remaining cup in both hands, apparently warming his fingers. "I'm sure your continued presence at the seminary will please several of the priests. They appreciate the challenge." He sipped at the tea in his cup. "I'll send a messenger as soon as Damon and his party arrive. For the present, however, I'd like to learn more about the western continent. We have, of course, some knowledge of the place, but I'd like to learn more from you."

For nearly two hours The Voice listened, often asking probing questions. Queen Ukena had obviously spoken with him about Glangurra, and he might've interviewed Hadrian. Morgan concentrated on Donradé and, to a lesser extent, on Cerco. His most recent information on the Sazian empire was limited to what he'd absorbed from Jonfré.

Finally The Voice rose. "It's been enlightening. I'll send for you as soon as the party arrives from Bhun Nahbi."

Morgan stood and bowed, returned to the seminary.

It'd become customary for him to visit the room of The Living Book after the evening meal, and it was there one of the priests found him. The man beckoned and Morgan followed him to the antechamber. "The Voice wishes you to know your nephew has arrived. He'll meet with you again in the palace tomorrow, half an hour after the hour of rising."

"Thank you," Morgan said, "Please tell him of my gratitude and that I'll see him then."

The priest nodded and left.

Morgan found Kiartan waiting in their cell. "I'd prefer to forego the practice tonight."

"You may do so," Kiartan replied, "but I'd remind you that battle seldom waits for our convenience."

Morgan mentally shrugged. "Very well. Let me get my cloak."

The wind was bitterly cold as they walked across the corner of the square and Morgan shivered almost uncontrollably as he stripped and donned the cold leather armor.

Kiartan held out two staves to him. "Choose one."

Morgan took a staff, holding it as he'd learned to hold a spear in the Marked Ones. Kiartan held his with each hand about a third of the distance from the ends. They went through a drill in which Kiartan's skill and quickness allowed him to tap Morgan with his staff almost at will while defending himself. Suddenly, Kiartan shook his staff, then swept the lower end around. A weight attached to a fine chain wrapped around Morgan's ankles and, with a tug, he was jerked off his feet. As he lay stunned, Kiartan twisted the upper end of the staff and a blade shot out.

Kiartan pressed the point against the stone floor until he'd forced the blade back up into the staff and twisted the end again, locking it in place. "Never assume a weapon is only what it seems." He showed Morgan how to use the weapons hidden in the staff; how to shake free the weight and chain at one end of the staff and how to release the blade so it would snap out and lock, making the staff a spear.

Kiartan laid aside his staff. "Now, use your weapon."

Morgan feinted a lunge, then shook the weight free and tried to sweep Kiartan's feet out from under him. Kiartan leapt over the chain and, as Morgan tried to regain control of the weapon, Kiartan whipped loose the sash he'd donned over his armor and lashed out with the end of it. The cloth wrapped around Morgan's right arm and Kiartan jerked him off-balance. Suddenly the sash was around Morgan's neck and Kiartan pulled him down.

Kiartan stood and unwound the cloth from Morgan. "Remember that anything can be a weapon." He showed how he'd sewn a few coins into the ends of the sash to give it weight.

Finally, Kiartan led him on a run around the room, up and down the stairs, pausing only to use ropes to climb or descend. At the end of the hour, Morgan was panting and sweating.

When they returned to the seminary they drew and heated water and bathed. Morgan was afraid he'd be too excited to sleep, too eager to return to Cerco to be able to rest, but the activity and the warm bath had prepared him so he hardly had time to think of Topaz before he was asleep.

~ * ~

Damon, Jeshka, and Queen Ukena were already with The Voice when Morgan and Kiartan arrived. Morgan hugged Damon and Jeshka. Tea and a light meal had been left on the table, and The Voice invited them to eat with him. As they ate, The Voice said, "It's been a pleasure to meet you all."

Morgan nodded. "It's been mutual, but I'm curious why you're sending The Blade of The Faith to the western continent."

"He's responsible for protecting the priests and the healers. I realize you and your family will try to watch over them, but the church must ultimately be responsible for protecting its own." He stood and drew a circle in the air. "May the blessings of Ianno attend you, to guide and preserve you."

~ * ~

Kiartan, dressed as a Keshti soldier, took the lead to the stables. Morgan was pleased to see Jocile among the soldiers. A grin made the Gascolan even uglier, if possible. The men saddled mounts while grooms hitched teams of horses to two coaches for the women and children and a wagon for supplies.

The day was cold but clear and still, as though the storm had been wrung out of it. Ong Vaun was about a hundred twenty-five leagues from Bayang Lon. The road showed the marks of traffic but most of the fields and lines of trees were covered with an unmarked blanket of white that glared in the sunlight until it seemed to blaze.

On the evening of the fourth day a storm rolled in from the west, and a day was spent at an inn in a small Ibari town. On the ninth day, a dispirited storm delayed them for only a couple of hours.

A fortnight's travel from Ong Vaun, they rode through the cobbled streets of Bayang Lon. They found a large inn near the docks and, in the morning, Morgan, Kiartan, and Damon searched among the ships riding at anchor. The *Vinig ni Litat* was a sleek vessel, half again as long as the *Zarin Hestaprin,* with four masts, and the lateen sails favored by the Sazians. More of the afterdeck was devoted to cabins, and the hold was lined with hammocks.

The church had already paid passage for the travelers, and the ship's master informed them he could carry a score of them, that the rest would be carried in other ships.

Damon glanced at Morgan. "I'll be on the last ship, to make sure everyone else has boarded. You need to return to Donradé as soon as possible." He looked meaningfully at Morgan. "And Queen Ukena and the Crown Prince should be first back as well. Choose the rest of the party for the first ship."

Morgan looked his gratitude at Damon. "Queen Ukena and her son, of course, and Kiartan. Five of the priests, three healers, and nine of the soldiers. I'll take Jocile and eight others."

~ * ~

By the early afternoon they'd moved the passengers and their trunks aboard the ship and had found berths for another dozen of the party on another, smaller, Sazian ship. The captain of *The Pride of the Sea Goddess* took advantage of the tide and the wind, and the port had fallen out of sight before darkness fell.

If Morgan entertained any doubts about Jocile's docility on a sea voyage, the man turned out to be an even worse sailor than Morgan. He was never strong enough to practice with Morgan and Kiartan and spent most of the journey lying in his hammock, eating seldom and little, unable even to vomit.

Ukena was obviously uncomfortable with the motion of the ship and the confined quarters, but she maintained an air of stolid determination that inspired respect. The prince, Terralyn, was too bold by half and the second time Morgan had hauled him from the rigging he appointed himself the boy's caretaker, keeping him constantly in sight whenever he was on deck.

It was hard for Morgan to consider the lad his grandson, although that was the accepted fiction, and he was constantly concerned the prince had inherited his father's less admirable qualities. He watched closely for evidence of selfishness or arrogance. He tried to teach by example, showing respect for the other men and women on the vessel.

He wondered, if he had a daughter, whether it'd be easier or more difficult to deal with her, and he developed a new-found respect for parents who brought up their children well.

As much as possible, he fasted and meditated, reviewed all the spells he could remember, trying to reinforce the depleted power of his scars.

He learned from the captain, who spoke passable Gasgoran and better Ghiblin than Morgan did, why the Sazians regarded the sea as a woman. "She has her moods," the man said, gazing at the horizon, "and she often changes her mind, and she's subject to sudden rages. How could she not be a woman?"

Apparently, referring to her with such familiarity didn't deeply offend her, as they were only lightly buffeted by the edge of a gale in the Interland Sea.

As they ran along the coast of Porcash, north of Sin Garlef, Morgan discovered his anger at his father, like most of his anger, had vanished. He had no desire to see the man, but he realized the man's fears and weaknesses were probably beyond his mastery, and that most of his other flaws were born of those. He could wish the old man well, if he were still alive, and an easy death if he were gone. He suspected that, dead or alive, his father had, at some time, drank deeply the bitter brew of regret.

He also thought of Hadrian. His envy of Hadrian's apparently effortless mastery of everything he essayed had robbed him of the opportunity to truly be a brother. Strange, that even with the rivalry between them, he'd still felt a deep respect for the man, had trusted him as much as he could bring himself to trust anyone in those days. Now that he could appreciate Hadrian, the man was gone, perhaps dead, probably still dead in soul, and with no way to reach him.

~ * ~

The captain steered just out of sight of the coast of Bildesh. In the winter months, the reavers preferred to stay close by their home fires, and the captain was obviously confident of the speed of his vessel if they were pursued.

The first landfall was Wimarik, where they took on supplies. Morgan remained below deck until they'd left Pitlahsa behind. The prospect of returning to Donradé excited him and, from there, to Stag Mountain, but hope was mixed with dread. He ached to hold Topaz in his arms, to share with her what he'd seen and felt and learned, but he couldn't be certain she was still alive. He also wondered, if she lived, whether his return would be entirely welcome. He'd left her alone when he should most have been with her. And he'd become Scarface again, for a time, and now he was a different

Morgan than the man who'd left.

The return to Donradé was shorter by four days than the outbound voyage had been, although it still cost time Morgan felt he could ill-afford. When the ship docked at Sazian Linistia, he borrowed a horse and set out for Jonfré's palace at a gallop.

Jonfré looked even older than he had when Morgan had left, and perhaps a trace less steady. Morgan embraced him, then said, "I've brought allies. Queen Ukena and her son are on the ship I left at the pier. You'll want to accord them every honor. I've also brought a man called Kian. He's been away from Glangurra long enough to have forgotten some of the language. He's got some soldiers with him, as well as some priests and healers." Kian was a common enough name in Gasgoran, and close enough to "Kiartan" to be comfortable to the man, who'd displayed his gift for languages. "Hadrian's son, Damon, and more troops will be on other ships. They should all arrive within the month. Other priests will follow later."

Jonfré seemed to have to work at forming a grin. "I'm glad you bring good news. The raiding in the north is getting worse."

"Damon and his men should be able to make a difference."

"You sound as though you're not going to be here."

"I need to borrow some mounts again. I've another journey to make, one I've already delayed too long." He noticed the appearance of worry lines. "I'll be back before spring."

"Be careful, if you're going north. It's been a mild winter here in Linistia, but I've heard the snow's deeper than usual in the north. And you might as well wait until tomorrow to set out. There's only a couple of hours left in the day."

Morgan pursed his lips, finally nodded. "I'll go back to the dock with you."

Jonfré shouted for an escort. The two of them rode, together, with the honor guard, to the wharf, where Jonfré knelt before Queen Ukena and Prince Terralyn.

Ukena rested a hand on his shoulder. "You needn't kneel to me. I'm Queen of Glangurra, and this is Sazian land. We're allies, not ruler and subject."

"Your majesty is most gracious, but our countries were united."

"Perhaps that union was another mistake. But my son and I accept your hospitality."

Morgan rode back to the palace in the middle of the procession, with Kiartan and the priests and healers. "I've told Jonfré your name is Kian and that you're a Glangurran who's been in the empire for nearly twenty years. Jonfré's a good man. You can trust him."

"As much as I can trust anyone but Ianno."

"You know, you even sound a little like Hadrian."

"He's evidently a very wise man."

Morgan glanced at Kiartan but couldn't detect a hint of a smile. "I'm leaving tomorrow. There are matters to which I must attend in Cerco. I'll try to be back within the month."

"I'll wish you good fortune, then," Kiartan said.

It was impossible to tell from either his expression or his voice whether he was expressing concern or only reciting a social formula. Morgan chose to hope the assassin had some warmth. "Thank you."

~ * ~

During the night he often fell out of sleep into anticipation. Two visions visited him often. Topaz was waiting for him. He could see her, smell the sweet scent of her, could almost feel her. Their reunion would be like the first time he'd coupled with her, and the urgency he felt was more in his heart than in his loins; the coupling was an expression of something deeper, as words were an expression, however inadequate, of sentiments.

The other vision was of returning to Stag Mountain and being told she'd died. That image made him taste the desolation that awaited him, that enormous void that would devour him; the numbness and lack of purpose. All he'd have to live for would be duty. While duty could provide a reason for existing and even for fighting, it couldn't give a reason for living.

CHAPTER II

He rode a plodding, stumbling horse through the Wolf's Gate at Stag Mountain, leading two more weary and emaciated animals. One of them had carried supplies until those had been depleted, and yet another horse had broken a leg in a cleft hidden by drifted snow. Morgan had killed the beast, drank its blood for the warmth and strength he'd needed, and had taken meat from the carcass.

Three soldiers trotted toward him and he handed the reins and lead lines to one of them. "Is Ergun in his quarters?"

The man nodded and Morgan hobbled to the headman's rooms. Ergun's wife answered Morgan's scratch on the door hanging, and her face expressed shock. A cold fist of fear for Topaz formed in his belly, then Ergun stepped into the doorway. "By the Fang, man, you look like you died twice getting here. You might want to clean up so you don't frighten your own family."

Morgan felt pressure in his nose, and his eyes stung as relief overwhelmed him and turned to an unaccustomed happiness. Not trusting his voice, he saluted and hurried down the corridor. Ergun was probably right, he should wash himself, but he was desperate to see Topaz, and being so near made any delay intolerable. He broke into a shambling trot, ignoring the Dieri he dodged past in the hallways.

He finally reached the familiar hanging with its rose pattern, where he scratched at the wool and waited. A familiar voice said, "Come in."

Drawing a deep breath to compose himself, he swept aside the hanging and entered their rooms.

Topaz had looked up from the herbs she'd been pulverizing in a mortar. Her face was transfigured by a joy so strong and genuine it was almost painful to see, then she was on her feet, across the room, in his arms.

They clung to each other fiercely, and he could feel her tears on his cheek, mixing with his own, and neither found words adequate or necessary. When he could control his breathing he moved his head and pressed his lips against hers. The kiss communicated more directly and completely than anything else could have, and he learned from her response that he'd been as sorely missed as he'd yearned for her.

A howl from another corner of the room caused them to end the kiss, although they couldn't, or wouldn't, release each other. Morgan looked for the source of the sound, saw Saril holding a small bundle of cloth and trying to hush the baby hidden in the blanket. The woman grinned at him, carefully gathered her legs under her, and rose, still holding his daughter. She walked carefully across the room until she stood before him, then folded back the blanket from over the baby's head.

He looked down at a red face not much bigger than his fist, a face in which he saw no resemblance to Topaz or himself, hardly a similarity to anything human. "Take her," Topaz whispered.

He released Topaz to awkwardly accept the bundle, afraid of either dropping it or crushing it. Saril showed him how to hold the baby, supporting the head. The tiny face's eyes opened, then its mouth, and it howled again. He handed the infant back to Saril. "This may take some time."

Topaz brushed the hair back from his forehead with gentle fingers. "Are you all right? You look as though you haven't eaten or slept in a fortnight."

He wrapped his arms around her again. "I'm a little tired is all."

"And in desperate need of a bath," Topaz added, grinning.

"I'll take Cari to the room down the hall," Saril said. She paused to gather a few necessities, then ducked through the door curtain.

Morgan kissed Topaz again, felt it returned with equal ardor.

Finally she drew back. "You really do need a bath. Let me gather some things."

Reluctantly, he released her and allowed her to gather robes and blankets and they walked, arms around each other, to the baths. His hands, still clumsy with the cold that had seeped through to the bone, fumbled with the fastenings of his clothing and Topaz had to help him undress. His clothing they tossed into a heap, to be claimed and cleaned later.

Topaz's body had changed. Her belly seemed softer, not the taut, thin skin over smooth muscles, and her breasts were larger, but she seemed even more desirable than he remembered.

At first he only sat, bent over, beside the pool, letting the warm water take away the cold in his hands and lower legs, but at last slid into the pool. He had to make a conscious effort to stay awake as the heat relaxed strained muscles and tendons. When they'd finished bathing he could hardly haul himself from the water, and the walk back to their rooms seemed much longer than he remembered.

A meal had been laid out on their table and he managed to eat a bun and a morsel of venison before he realized that he must lie down or collapse. Too exhausted to do more than rest, he lay nestled beside Topaz and was almost instantly asleep.

~ * ~

He lay on a pallet, wondering where he was. A painful emptiness in the pit of his belly reminded him why he'd wakened. He drew a deep breath and knew he was home. The aroma of warm bread and spiced meat overlaid the smells of herbs and the faintly acrid tang of the lichen that provided light to the caverns. There was another strong smell, not entirely unpleasant, making him aware that a baby lived in these rooms. Near him, he could detect Topaz's scent where she'd laid beside him. He opened his eyes to stare up into the eternal twilight of Stag, then rolled onto his side and propped himself up on an elbow to peer around the room.

Topaz stood at the door of the sleeping room. "I'm sorry, I meant to be here so that on your first morning back you could wake up beside me, but I had things to do, and you obviously needed your rest." She approached the pallet, lay down beside him, and embraced him. "I've made something for you to eat."

For a moment he was caught between two hungers, then made a decision. "I'll eat that later." He learned again all the secrets of her body. The months of yearning were relieved in the next couple of hours. With his hands and his mouth he learned her again, even finding new ways to wring moans and indrawn breaths from her, and responding the same way to her rediscovery of him.

At last, their passions spent, or perhaps invested, they lay beside each other, tired and sweaty and sated. He said, "I don't think I ever want to move from here again."

She smiled. "We've talked about that before. You're likely to starve to death."

"Not for a while," he said, and nibbled at one of her nipples.

She stroked his hair and kissed his forehead. "Still, we must be up and about."

He kissed her again, then forced himself to rise and don his robe. "You'll have to tell me what happened in my absence."

She also rose and put on the robe he'd taken off her. "Three seasons. You know how life is lived in Stag. I'm eager to hear what's happened to you, and what you've made happen."

"I've got to go back to Donradé," he said. "I haven't finished it yet, but I'll tell you everything, either this evening or tomorrow." The other hunger had returned and his stomach was complaining. Although the bread and meat had cooled, he ate voraciously.

Topaz ate with him, though sparingly, watching him devour his meal. When his shrunken stomach could accept no more, he rose. "I'd best see Ergun." He ran his hand over his face. "And I need to shave. I'd forgotten that tending to my toilet was one of the things I neglected on my way here."

"I can understand that. Riding through these mountains in the dead of winter was dangerous. If I weren't so happy to see you again, I'd probably scold you for the risks you took."

He shrugged. "The mountains didn't frighten me as much as the thought of not seeing you until after spring."

She smiled. "You always knew how to avoid a scolding. You must've driven your mother to distraction."

He left their rooms and found Ergun in the practice chamber. He put on leather armor and practiced with the headman, found the training he'd given the Dieri inadequate. After having learned from Kiartan, he perceived his own previous weaknesses magnified in the Dieri. He knew he was gifted with weapons, but Kiartan was a master, one who'd taught him well.

Ergun signaled for a halt. "You seem to have learned a bit in your travels. How soon will you be returning to your duties? Although I suppose watching sheep will prove boring, now."

"I'm ready—no, I'm eager for that sort of boredom, but I have to leave again, and it'll be late spring or early summer before I can come back to stay. I'll need to leave again for Donradé in the next ten days or so."

He retrieved his razor from his saddle pouches and returned to the baths. The clothing he'd worn had all been washed and draped across rocks to dry. He shaved and bathed, then returned to his rooms, carrying the damp clothing.

A boy was visiting, and Topaz was treating his hands for the cold. Saril sat in a corner, holding Cari. Morgan carefully laid out the clothing near the fire, then, moved more by curiosity than any other feeling, he sat down beside Saril and asked to hold his daughter.

The infant stirred in her sleep but didn't waken, and he studied her face. Her lips, curled into a smile, reminded him of rose petals. Her fragility and vulnerability appealed to some part of his nature. He waited until the boy had gone, then grinned at Topaz. He'd largely ignored infants before; they had no conversation nor even mastery over their own bodies. The orphans he'd brought to Donradé from Glangurra had been older, and expressive enough to be interesting and endearing.

This was different. He'd almost become used to being a grand-father, but he'd never before been a father. This was his own daughter he held, and she depended upon him and Topaz. Cari's mouth opened in a yawn, then she sighed and drifted back into deeper slumber, and he smiled at the performance.

Eventually he smelled bread being baked, and spiced meat, cooked in sour wine. His mouth watered and his stomach grumbled, causing the baby to stir. Then he felt the blanket grow damp. When the baby began to fuss, Topaz took her and changed the cloths in which she was wrapped. "You're still new to this, so I'll wait until tomorrow before I teach you how to change her." As Cari continued to fuss, Topaz opened her robe and let their daughter nurse.

Morgan found himself fascinated, and only looked up when Saril set food on the low table.

"I'll take Cari again tonight," Saril said. "You two need one more night, or at least part of a night, to yourselves."

Topaz drank milk with her meal. Morgan had never acquired the taste and was grateful for the thin, sour red wine in his own cup. A thought occurred to him. "How were the harvests and the flocks?"

"It was a good year," Topaz said softly, staring down at the infant at her breast, obviously thinking of more than vegetables and sheep, then, "We should have more than enough for the rest of winter and the spring."

He turned to Saril. "I don't know if I've properly thanked you. I deeply appreciate your coming here, far from your own family, and helping Topaz through the birth."

She smiled. "You thanked me when you saw Topaz, and when you held your daughter."

After they'd finished eating, Saril gathered a few items and took Cari with her down the corridor to Meryem's rooms. Morgan lounged on the heavy rugs and pillows with Topaz wrapped in his arms. He lay stroking her hair and her hands as he told her what had happened since he'd left in early summer. Some of it was difficult for him to frame in words. When he told her how Renay had died he chose his words carefully, knowing she'd see through any attempt at understatement.

After he'd told of his meeting with Mendarian, Topaz turned her head to stare into his eyes. "If you face her over swords, will you be able to kill her without hesitation?"

He looked away. "I don't know."

"You must. I take her threats very seriously. Don't for a heartbeat think she wouldn't kill you in such a circumstance. It's the only way that woman can hurt Cari or myself—to kill you. So steel yourself, and strike. We depend upon it as you do."

Uncomfortable feelings and half-thoughts made him pause, trying to remember what had occurred after that. He recalled the rumor about Ukena being held captive and riding out to search for her, but could remember little beyond the facts that she hadn't been in Donradé, and he'd come awake with a spell scroll tucked into his shirt.

He related the tale of the sea voyage to the empire, of his fear during the storm at sea, and the other incidents aboard the *Zarin Hestaprin*. He mentioned the trip down the coast of the empire and finding kin at The Shield of The Saint. When he spoke of the walking corpses attacking the fortress, he could feel her shudder, and when he explained how he'd lost the dragon to the Deathwind, she finally spoke again.

"What else did you lose?"

"Most of the power I'd gained when I found the spell scroll. It seems somehow fitting that one gift be connected to the other. Also, the anger I'd used to drive the dragon."

"I hope that didn't hurt you. You've dealt with it for so long, held it so tightly reined, I was afraid you might be too passive without it, although I hadn't noticed much passivity."

"I haven't felt any loss of energy or resolve." He ran his hand gently down her spine, enjoying the feel of the satin skin covering the row of bony ridges.

She caressed his cheek. "Perhaps it's for the best. You've fought it so long—perhaps, if you think on it, you'll realize you have more energy. You've always had to use so much of your resolve to stifle the rage that now, without it, you may have more resources."

He mulled over the possibility, absently kissed her forehead, then finished the story of the siege of Tong Shavath. Explaining the church required more careful choices of words, and Topaz stirred and asked him questions. Most of her inquiries were the same as those he'd asked of the priests.

After a time, she said, "It's an interesting church. I'd almost consider converting."

He remembered what he'd been told, that unbelievers sometimes heard Ianno, even if they didn't recognize His voice, or The Voice. "Perhaps you already have."

As he finished his recitation of the time he'd spent at the seminary and the voyage back to Donradé, during which he'd restored some of the lost power to his scars, he tried to smile. "Sometimes I'm not sure who I am anymore. For a time, I was Scarface again. I thought that was who I needed to be to be able to return to you. Then I was Morgan again, but a different Morgan. Do you know who I am?"

She tightened her embrace and kissed him. "Yes, you're the man I want here beside me." She kissed him again. "What are your plans?"

His smile flickered like a candle flame in a breeze, then he said, "I presume you're referring to Mordach's church and the King of Glangurra?" His fingers toyed with the knot of her belt.

She grinned. "I was when I asked." She slid her hand inside his robe, running her fingers through the hair of his chest.

"I've decided we've worried far too much about Thienn, and it's past time for him to worry. When I return, I'll see to some alliances, then, as soon as the ground's fit for travel, we'll drive north and west. I doubt he'll attack in the early spring, so we'll do it."

He untied her belt and reached around her to run a hand down her back. "I don't think we need attack the church directly—we can just let it wither. After we've beaten Thienn, I suspect the church will fall like rotten fruit." He nibbled at her ear, then worked his way down her neck to bite at the muscle that ran from neck to shoulder.

She gasped, then her hand slipped around his back, where her fingers became claws.

They built their passion slowly, carefully, as though constructing an edifice in which to live.

~ * ~

Morgan spent most of his remaining time at Stag with his family, some of the rest of it training the men of the mountain. While few of the men were as capable as the veterans he'd met in the empire, they were still better than most soldiers he'd seen, and they learned quickly.

As the day neared that he must return to Donradé, he lived as though his horses were already saddled, immersing himself in each moment, storing up provisions in his memory for the lean times to come.

His first impression of Cari was fading, replaced by a deep and growing affection. It became a matter of pride that, if she were clean and fed and still fussed, he could always put her to sleep by holding her to his chest, her head on his shoulder, and gently patting her back.

His appreciation of Cari grew, and she seemed to not only accept him but actually seemed happier when she saw him. For her part, Topaz allowed Saril to deal with many of her duties, to share time with him and their daughter.

On the morning of his departure he woke before dawn, unable to sleep longer. Topaz lay beside him, staring at him, and he wondered how long she'd been awake. He held her. "If it makes it easier, I don't want to go."

She stroked his hair. "It doesn't. But it's a thing you must do. Be careful. For all three of us."

He nodded, then kissed her before he crawled out from under the blanket. After he'd eaten he visited Ergun, to take his leave and to pen a message to Orhan, one to be delivered as soon as the mountain passes had opened.

In the stables, he again examined the horses, as he had each day. The animals had largely recovered from the ordeal of reaching Stag Mountain, and he added another horse, a gray he'd taken from one of Forgren's men, so long ago. He saddled a dark red bay and packed provisions on two of the animals.

Returning to his rooms, he dressed again in the furs, leather, and woolen cloth he'd worn to Stag. "I'll say farewell here," he said to Topaz. He didn't say, nor did he need to, that it was hard enough to leave, and her presence and that of Cari would make it even more painful.

They embraced and kissed each other, then Topaz handed him a scarf of pale blue. "To remember me by, or to use, if the occasion demands."

Cari began to cry, and Morgan wondered about omens. He held

her and patted her back and, after a time, she fell asleep. Carefully, he handed her to Topaz and kissed her cheek, then left while he could.

For his return to Donradé, he chose to ride west, then south, a route that would take him out of the mountains quickly. In the mountains, when the winds were still, he was almost deafened by the silence, as though even the sounds had frozen.

Once in the foothills, he crossed occasional meadows, and at the edge of one of those he found a Senshenni winter camp. He'd almost missed seeing the camp; the snow-covered leather domed tents were almost invisible and he saw no one outside. He'd have ridden past it but his horses caught the scent of the herd picketed in a small pine wood nearby.

He approached cautiously and the guard who stepped from behind a tree with bow drawn recognized him and pointed out the headman's tent. He spent the night with the Senshenni, and told the headman he'd be hiring warriors in the spring.

From the Senshenni camp he rode south, counting on the cold to keep any of the locals from observing his passage. He gave any settlements a wide berth, and sited each night's camp with concealment as his first consideration. His animals had almost exhausted the fodder he'd brought for them, and he guessed it time to turn west again. With but a rough knowledge of the landmarks, he could only estimate distances based on the number of days he was in the saddle, the depletion of his supplies, and the general character of the land.

If he guessed correctly, the hardwood forest through which he rode was the eastern fringe of the Forest of Omaire. He made his way through the trees, heading southwest, and a day's ride from where he'd entered the woods he found a river he supposed to be a major tributary of the Bromron. Following the river, he topped a rise near midafternoon and found himself in the outskirts of a town.

Staring at the collection of buildings, he shrugged. He'd rather have approached the place nearer the fall of darkness, but, unless everyone here were blind, he'd already been seen, and anything he did to leave would simply attract more attention. He rode to the largest building, which seemed to be a communal stable and barn, and drew rein.

A balding, thickset man with an eight-pointed blue star on each cheek was trimming a draft horse's hooves when Morgan slid from the saddle. "I'd like to put my horses up for the night."

The man hardly glanced up. "That'll cost. For the four of them, it'll be five marks of silver." At least the man wore tattoos and spoke Gasgoran, and his accent wasn't too thick.

"Five marks of silver's steep," Morgan said. "Are you having a famine hereabouts?"

"Not with four horses to add to the larder." The man guffawed at his own wit.

Morgan pulled off a mitten and dug the money from his pouch. "Is there a place I can get a meal and a drink and rent a pallet for the night?"

"Inn's across the road." The stocky man jerked a thumb in the general direction. "I'll tend your horses."

Morgan removed the saddle pouch from his mount, then took off the saddle and its blanket, laying them across a beam. By the time he'd finished, the stableman was lifting the pack off the gray.

Leaving the man to feed the horses and rub them down, Morgan strode across to the inn, a building too low to have a loft. He halted just outside the door to test the draw of his sword; it slid easily in its scabbard. Pushing open the door, he glanced about. After his eyes had adjusted to the dimness, he saw two men sitting at a table, apparently absorbed in a game involving moving pale and dark pebbles around a pattern scratched into the table top, similar to a game he'd seen some men from Doss play. He approached the table. "How much for a meal and a pallet?"

One of the players, who appeared to be the stableman's younger and plumper brother, and with the same star tattoos, looked up. "A mark and a half of silver."

Morgan stared at him coldly. "I've already been hideously overcharged for the tending of my horses. Neither my purse nor my patience are infinite. Eighteen marks of copper are too much, but I'll pay that. Not a copper more."

Apprehension and anger wrestled each other across the innkeeper's face, but the man glanced at his companion for support, then snapped, "A mark and a half, silver."

"Since you don't seem to like outlanders," Morgan said, "you won't miss any foreign money, either." He turned to leave and the other man at the table rose and stepped in Morgan's way. He was obviously the big brother, and appeared displeased with the direction of the conversation.

Kiartan's lessons had been well-learned. Morgan's right hand leapt across to his sword hilt, and he drove the pommel into the man's belly, just under the breastbone. Morgan spun, then, clearing the blade from its scabbard, to see the innkeeper standing as though petrified, his hand grasping the hilt of his knife.

Morgan brushed the man's knuckles with the tip of his blade. The man squealed and flinched as though branded, and blood flowed from his hand. "You've already annoyed me," Morgan said softly. "If you make me angry, I'll turn this hovel into your pyre."

The big man had fallen to his knees and was still struggling to draw breath. Morgan stepped past him and out the door. Outside, he sheathed his sword, drew his cloak about himself, and stalked to the stable. When he entered, the stableman was leading one of his horses to a bin of oats.

"Just put the oats in a bag and add it to the pack. I'll be leaving."

"You can't leave before you've paid me." The self-satisfied smirk announced the stableman's opinion of his craftiness.

Morgan untied the thong that held his hood tightly around his face, revealing his scars, then tossed the left side of the cloak over his shoulder, displaying his sword. "I've paid you once in silver. If I have to pay again, it'll be in steel. You can return four of those marks of silver before you've readied my horses, or after."

The man's face went pale to the lips. "Yes, my lord."

"I'm not your lord. If I were, you'd be branded for the thief you are and whipped out of town. If you delay me any longer, I may do it anyway. Put the saddle on the sorrel and the pack on the roan." He leaned against the door and watched the man prepare the horses for travel and, after he'd hauled himself into the saddle, extended his hand for the money. The stableman handed him the coins with the reluctance of a man giving up his children, and Morgan rode away, following the river.

He'd need to discover the name of the baron who either didn't know or didn't care his subjects were stealing from travelers, and he wondered how many lone travelers rode into town and failed to ride out.

It seemed not to matter who sat on the throne; thieves and bullies would always exist, and even thrive. It hardly seemed worth fighting a war when such reptiles and rodents would prosper.

He reminded himself he wasn't fighting for them but for others more worthy. Queen Ukena, he was sure, would be an excellent ruler, even though she couldn't rule in her own name—the Glangurrans were too bound by tradition to accept a woman as ruler—she'd rule as regent. He could only hope that when the time came for Terralyn to ascend to the throne he'd inherited far more from his mother than from his father.

~ * ~

The ride south was like a trip into spring. Winter was indeed retreating to its stronghold in the north, and the climate around Linistia, moderated by the ocean, was always warmer than the hills and plains of northern Donradé. Morgan had removed some of his wraps and bundled them in the pack. He'd discovered his last campsite had been but half a league from a Sazian-built fort, and he could simply follow the line of forts back to the port city. He exchanged his animals for a fresh mount and acquired remounts at each fort, stopping each night for a meal and a pallet.

Near noon he spied the towers of Linistia and the sun was going down somewhere over Glangurra when he dismounted in front of Jonfré's palace and handed his horse's reins to a guard. Saddle-sore, he walked painfully into the palace. A servant brought him a pitcher of water and a basin in which to wash his hands and feet, and a guard led him to the dining hall.

Torches blazed in sconces and candles gleamed along the table. Ukena sat at the head of the table with Terralyn to her right and Jonfré to her left, a space between them. Damon and his family sat to the right of the crown prince. Kiartan sat beside Jonfré, and the rest of the places at the table were taken by priests of Ianno, healers, and men Morgan guessed to be petty nobles.

Jonfré waved Morgan to the empty seat. "We've been waiting for you." He grinned. "You cast a long shadow."

Morgan limped to the chair, sat down with a sigh. "I hope it's been quiet in my absence."

Ukena sipped at her cup and her eyes shifted to Damon, who said, "One of our ships was wrecked in a storm. Three priests, two healers, and five soldiers were lost, along with the ship and its crew."

Morgan looked a question at Kiartan, who nodded. "Yes, it was the same storm that touched us. Also, two of Ianno's priests were attacked here in Linistia."

"Are they hurt?" At Kiartan's shake of the head, he asked, "Their attackers?"

"Dead."

Jonfré grinned. "The matter inspired some conversions. It seems that when followers of a god of battle are bested by followers of a god of peace, people draw some obvious conclusions about the war-god's power.

"Also, the archpriest of Mordach here in Linistia has asked for another meeting with you. I told him you were considering his request. It seemed more politic than to tell him you were gone. Now that you're back, I can tell him the only way you want to see him is with his head on a pole."

Morgan sipped at a cup of wine. "Actually, I rather think I'd like to hear what they have to say. Tell him that another man and I would be pleased to meet with two of them." He cut a bit of the meat on his platter and ate slowly. It'd been long enough since he'd eaten a meal cooked by Topaz, and he was hungry enough, the Donradan cooking didn't seem objectionably bland.

Damon leaned forward. "May I accompany you? I've never seen one of these priests."

Morgan swallowed the meat he'd been chewing. "I appreciate the offer, but I believe Kian should be the one to attend me. It's a struggle between gods, and he can best represent Ianno's side."

Kiartan nodded. "I'll look forward to the discussion of theology."

Jonfré finished his bit of meat and tossed the bone onto his platter. "How was your journey?"

Morgan told him of the unpleasantness in Donradé, and Jonfré scowled. "That's another score to be settled with a northern lord. I'll send a messenger to the temple of Mordach in the morning." He ate the last of his bread and leaned back, then slapped the table top. "I almost forgot. The guards said a man with a peg leg had asked about you. Said he'd served with you in the Das wars."

"Everyone I served with there either died or got out with all their parts," Morgan said. "He must've lost the leg since the wars. What did he look like?"

"No one's mentioned anything but the wooden leg. I can ask them."

"Please do so." Besides the brothers and sisters of the clan, most of the people he'd known then had been natives of Doss or members of the Union. He paused in his chewing. Perhaps one of the Union was looking to avenge Forgren, but even members of the Union weren't so dense as to warn him. He washed down meat with another sip of wine and set the cup down. "I'd also like you to request an audience for me with the Sazian governor."

Jonfré raised an eyebrow. "Is that wise? Some Sazians still haven't forgiven you for taking half of southern Donradé from them. He's dealt with me, but I'm not the one who took a quarter of a kingdom from them."

His meal finished, Morgan leaned back in his chair, his fingers laced across his belly. "I've got to deal with him, either directly or through you. When establishing an alliance, it's always best to deal directly. If he'll see me, I'd like to talk with him. Also, I'd like to meet with the southern lords and the lords from the north who've joined us."

"How soon?"

"Yesterday." He glanced around the table. "We need to take stock of all our assets and resources."

"We've the contents of the clan library from the empire," Damon remarked. "Magic is somewhat out of favor in the empire, so the soldiers who replaced us at Tong Shavath had no use for the books and scrolls, and there was always the danger someone suffering a bout of misguided fervor might've destroyed them. That would've been too great a loss."

"You've done well. I don't see any immediate use for them, myself, but I'm an indifferent seer. You've also brought—what?—fifty warriors?"

"About that many."

Most of the petty nobles at the table claimed between two score to two hundred men apiece.

Kiartan said, "My duty is to protect Ianno's priests and healers, not to join an army in the field."

"You're still a resource," Morgan replied. "All I asked of Ianno was his blessing. That should be enough. Everyone who converts to Ianno is a man less to fight for Mordach."

"The lords under me can, together, provide about twenty-five hundred men," Jonfré said. "If I strip all my garrisons and call out the peasants, I might have another three thousand men."

"We'll count on half that many. Dispatch a courier to Anjular, have him send word when the ground is fit for marching. There's no sense in marching men into a morass to drown."

"All Terralyn and I have is our royal blood," Ukena said softly. "We have no army."

"Not so, my lady," Jonfré replied. "All of us here are your army."

"Agreed," Morgan said, "and every man who deserts Thienn's forces is another man we don't have to fight. And if nobles refuse to serve him because of your name, you'll have added scores to our army." He turned to Jonfré. "How many men can Thienn field? I need to know the worst."

Jonfré's fingers stroked his beard. "Southern Glangurra is still lightly defended. They took heavy losses taking the place from the Sazians. The best guess I can make is twelve, fifteen hundred men from there, perhaps three times that number from northern Glangurra, and another fifteen hundred to two thousand from northern Donradé. More men are available, but most of them will either take no side, or they'll side with Mordach's church and try to fall on a crippled victor."

"We faced worse odds at Tong Shavath," Damon observed.

"We haven't the advantage of position we had there, or siege engines, nor can we count on Thienn or his advisors being as incredibly stupid as the *Alman*." Morgan tried to hide a yawn. "One step at a time, and right now, I'm too tired to walk." He rose.

"I'll have a guard show you to your room," Jonfré said, "and I'll send couriers to the temple, to the governor, and to Anjular tomorrow." He gestured for one of the men standing by the door to lead Morgan to his room.

While having a guard standing watch outside his door offered some assurance, Morgan again set a chair against the door before he undressed and laid his sword and knife beside the pallet.

It'd seemed to him, despite the space between their chairs, Jonfré had treated Ukena with more than the deference accorded royalty, and Ukena hadn't discouraged it. They could both do far worse, as could the kingdom. Or kingdoms. Their marriage could reseal the bond Thienn seemed to be trying to tear apart.

That was in an uncertain future, after the demise of Thienn, an occasion which he was anticipating with a certain satisfaction,

~ * ~

Trying to hide his trepidation, Morgan rode into the walled compound that contained the residence of the Sazian governor. The man's name, Jonfré had told him, was Tregarin, and he'd once served as a commander of the Elites. Scarface had led the army that had wrested half of southern Donradé from the Elites, and he suspected defeats were rare enough for them that they were unlikely to forget.

The residence was plain enough, though well-guarded by squads of Elites. He'd seen the place before, briefly, after he'd taken Linistia during the war. Then the walls had been smoke-stained and everything that could be broken had been shattered. He noticed the decapitated statue that had stood in the courtyard had been replaced.

Vesparin, the general commanding the Elites, hadn't been an enemy but an opponent, and had won Scarface's respect. Later, after Vesparin had made himself emperor, Scarface had warned him of a Union plot to assassinate him. Morgan hoped Vesparin had a good memory for such things.

Tregarin met Morgan at the door of his palace. The Sazian's tunic and boots were richly decorated but the sword he wore wasn't merely a bauble worn for appearance's sake. The man was as tall as Morgan, and strongly built, with dark red-brown hair and a beard that was almost black, but for the gray streaks beginning to appear.

Morgan dismounted and handed the reins of his black horse, the largest in Jonfré's stables, to the servant who approached him, and bowed to the governor. "I'm pleased to have this opportunity to meet you. You've impressed Earl Jonfré."

"I thought the meeting would be...interesting." The Sazian waited until Morgan had reached the doorway, then turned and led him to a small room, bare but for a table littered with scrolls, a pair of backless chairs, and a simple but elegant rug on the floor.

"I appreciate your courtesy," Morgan said, "particularly in not asking me to take off my weapons."

"That would insult us both." Tregarin said, as he sat in one of the chairs. The other stood a little over an arm's reach away, and the Sazian gestured at it.

Morgan sat. "We'll be starting our campaign soon; as soon as the ground's fit for an army. I understand you're willing to provide ten *seymana*, five of them from the Elites."

"Yes. Vesparin seems inclined to favor you. Just be sure you use our soldiers well. Don't throw them away, as you did your own petty nobles in our war."

Morgan inclined his head. If the man had misgivings, they wouldn't be dispelled by mere words, and if the Sazian were simply protective of his troops, he was too good a man to annoy without reason. "That's something for which I owe you my gratitude. Those lordlings were a contentious lot, and killing them cost you enough time that the better part of my army could escape. I'll regard your soldiers as the better part of this army."

Like Vesparin, Tregarin had pale blue eyes. They seemed to have a blade-like sharpness but Morgan thought he read grudging approval in them. "Where do you want our soldiers to join your army?"

"At the bridge, five, six days march north on the Bromron."

Tregarin looked as though he'd bitten into a bitter fruit.

"There are still too many memories of the war—on both sides—for us to march them through Donradan Linistia," Morgan said. "This alliance may help bury some old angers."

Tregarin surprised Morgan; he laughed. "I begin to see why Vesparin seems inclined to deal with you. It's safer to be standing beside you, if only to make sure you're not pissing on my boots. But I'd check first to make sure the wind wasn't blowing in my direction. I believe we understand one another. For the present, that'll suffice."

Morgan shifted on the chair. "I've agreed to meet with priests of Mordach's church. With your permission, I'll see them the same place I met with them before."

"Very well, but I suggest you be sure which way the wind is blowing."

Morgan grinned. "I'll try to come out of it with dry boots."

Tregarin stood, and Morgan understood their meeting was ended. He rose and they walked back to the entrance together.

Outside the palace, Morgan accepted the reins from the servant and sprang into the saddle. Tregarin still stood in the doorway, hands on hips. Morgan nodded to him, turned his horse's head, and rode past a nearby inn.

A scarred man wearing the well-used armor of a veteran warrior rose from the bench beside the door and caught up the reins of a scrawny nag. The beast bit at him as he snatched the reins, and the man avoided the teeth with uncommon dexterity or long practice.

Morgan never slowed, nor did he look back to see the rider behind him. He rode northward, to the edge of Sazian Linistia, to a hollow in which stood a cottage and he halted at the rim of the depression. The cottage stood nearer this edge than the others, and was still more than a bow-shot away. The stand of trees in which he'd hidden his mount on his previous visit overgrew the cleft that provided runoff and kept the place from becoming a bog.

The copse and a lone ancient oak in front of the cottage were beginning to show buds, but neither offered much concealment. From where he sat he could see a number of other dwellings and, beyond the hollow, open fields.

The scarred man drew up his horse beside him. "If they intend to ambush you, they'll have to do it inside the cottage."

"I suspect Tregarin will have the area cleared and guarded until just before the time of the meeting."

"You put a lot of trust in a man you've just met."

"I trust myself, and my sense of people. Tregarin's a capable man, who leaves as little as possible to chance. He's swallowed the bitter draught that Donradans rule half of Linistia, but he doesn't want Mordach's church as a neighbor any more than he wants Thienn or one of his bootlickers."

"You rely heavily on others."

"Unlike you or Hadrian, I have to. But just as I wouldn't presume to tell you the quality of a weapon or the best way to use it, I trust my own ability to judge the character of those around me; to know what they'll do, and how much I can trust them."

Kiartan's eyes narrowed. "And you've never been wrong?"

Instantly, Morgan was reminded of Mendarian and his madness for her. He laughed. "Only once, but it was enough for a hundred mistakes." He considered what he'd known of Mendarian, and what he'd thought he'd known. "Perhaps I knew that person better than she did. Or, perhaps, she gave up on herself before I was ready to give up on her."

"Do you trust me?" Kiartan's eyes, as gray and hard as the steel of a blade, stared at Morgan's face.

"Of course. I trust you to risk your life to protect me—unless I were to try to betray the church of Ianno. Then you'd kill me without a qualm."

Kiartan's eyes returned to their study of the cottage and the grounds around it. "Perhaps you're right to trust that ability."

Morgan turned his horse and rode through Sazian Linistia, across the bridge, and to Jonfré's palace, knowing Kiartan rode somewhere behind him.

Jonfré, wearing full armor, beat at a pell with a dulled sword, feinting, covering himself with his shield against imaginary attacks, and lashing out again to make the courtyard ring. He stopped when he noticed Morgan, tucked his sword under his left arm, pulled off his helmet, then mopped the sweat from his face with an old cloak. "I'd almost forgotten how heavy this is." He held up his arm and turned it so the mail jingled. "And how boring the practice is."

"Perhaps Kian would practice with you. Or I could teach you some of what he taught me."

Jonfré rubbed his damp hair vigorously with the cloak, then re-adjusted the set of the patch over his missing eye. "I'll wait until I'm sure I can defeat a pell before I contend with more active opponents. One of Mordach's priests arrived while you were gone. Said they'd meet you at noon tomorrow, the same place they met you before."

He raised his helmet, then lowered it again. "Oh, yes. I asked about the man with the peg leg. The guards could remember nothing about him save for the wooden leg. He seems to have been remarkably unremarkable." He raised the helm again, ducked into it, and turned back to the pell.

Morgan stared at the ground, as though looking for an answer written there. If the man were an enemy, he'd have to wait his turn. He shook his head, trying to clear out fancies that might distract him. The air seemed thick with suppositions, while certainties were scarce. It'd be several days before the courier could return from Anjular's fortress, and any plans he might make were at the mercies of the weather.

~ * ~

Morgan studied the cottage. He doubted Mordach's priests would come from the north; they'd probably be riding from the temple in Donradan Linistia, unless Mendarian intended to appear again. Having cast the spell of concealment, he stood near the oak where he could watch the cottage, the cleft with its stand of naked trees, and the ridge nearest the city. Kiartan had vanished into the copse and Morgan assumed he'd found a vantage place there.

Two riders topped the ridge, just where he'd expected them. They stopped at the crest to stare at the dwelling, then urged their mounts forward. One of riders carried a staff across his saddle but Morgan observed that he dismounted easily and his companion, who wore a short sword under his cloak, uttered a few words before the man with the staff limped to the door.

He'd have expected priests of a war god to be armed, but the fact these two bothered to hide their weapons suggested they planned a surprise attack.

Morgan looked for Kiartan in the copse. The man had been clad all in dark blue, and Morgan would've thought it easy to find the color among the trees but, if he were still in the woods, Kiartan was invisible.

Returning his attention to the cottage, he noticed Kiartan crouched by one of the windows. The assassin looked toward where Morgan stood and nodded.

Morgan allowed the spell of concealment to dissipate and strode toward the door. Kiartan raised two fingers, then signed to indicate he'd seen the short sword, and that the staff probably held a hidden blade. When Morgan signified he'd noticed both weapons, Kiartan immediately turned and stepped into the doorway.

One of the priests had just risen from the bench behind the table as Morgan strode into the room. "I'm surprised you asked for this meeting," Morgan said. "I thought we'd irritated each other enough the last time we spoke. Or are you an optimist?"

The two priests stared at Morgan and Kiartan for half a dozen heartbeats, then the one who'd risen, the man with the short sword, sank back onto the bench. "When last we spoke, you mentioned the church might hand you Mendarian on a chain. Was that a bargaining point?"

Morgan sat down on the bench across the table from the seated priest and Kiartan stepped forward and sat on a stool to Morgan's left, facing the priest with the staff. "What do you want in trade?"

"An understanding. You've dealt with the church before, and we can also deal with Ukena, if you'd like. We'll take up arms with you against Thienn. For your part, you'd agree Mordach's church is the church of Donradé."

Morgan pressed his index finger against his lips in exaggerated imitation of some scribes he'd met, apparently contemplating. From their offer, he guessed the church supposed he was contending for the throne, that perhaps he intended to marry Ukena to again join Donradé and Glangurra. He lowered his hand and steepled his fingers, his forearms resting lightly on the table.

The priest with the staff started to turn, as though to walk behind his companion.

"Don't do that," Kiartan said softly. As the man hesitated, he added, "If you move behind him," he indicated the sitting priest with a nod, "I'll have to kill you both."

The priest's hands tightened on the staff until his knuckles turned white, but he said nothing and remained where he stood.

"Let's see if I've reached this understanding you mentioned," Morgan said. "You're offering to betray an ally if I'm unscrupulous enough to do the same. In view of the treachery of that sort of arrangement, why should we deal at all, since both sides would've already shown their word's good only as long as they're forced to keep it? Or perhaps I'm insufficiently versed in theology to appreciate that sort of double-dealing. Could you explain it to me, since you're obviously more experienced?"

"You owe the outland god and his church nothing."

"Except respect, which is a far greater obligation than I feel to you or to Mordach."

"You owe them nothing," the priest repeated. "They're preparing to betray you and I have proof." He leaned forward, his hand in his robe. He spoke a phrase Morgan couldn't understand, then tossed something onto the table. "Be bound, Morgan."

Morgan had seen a flash of movement and turned his head toward it as the spell suddenly seized him. His arms and legs were held fast, as though his body had turned to stone.

The movement he'd seen was the second priest drawing the concealed sword from the staff.

Morgan felt as though he were trapped in a nightmare; unable to move and with the movements of those around him slowed, as though they were all under water.

The priest made a side cut at Kiartan, who'd partly drawn his sword with his left hand, holding the hilt blade-down. The blades rang as Kiartan's weapon, still partly in its scabbard, parried the slash, then steel rasped as Kiartan seized the pommel of his sword with his right hand and drew his blade.

Using the leverage of his spread hands, Kiartan snapped his blade up, tossing the priest's sword up and to the left.

As he'd drawn his sword, Kiartan had dropped forward onto one knee and, as he whipped the priest's weapon aside, he rose. He swung his blade through a quarter-turn and drove it into the priest's chest.

There was no scream, only the sound of steel tearing flesh and grating past bone, then a ripping sound as Kiartan cut upward.

Morgan desperately wanted to see the priest he'd been facing, but he'd glanced away as the spell was completed and it was as impossible to turn his head as to move any other part of his body.

The priest must've long since drawn his sword and Morgan, trapped, waited for the blow.

Kiartan freed his blade from the dead man with a twisting jerk, at the same time driving his hip into the table and, to Morgan's ears, the scraping of the legs against the floor sounded like a drawn-out groan.

Kiartan's blade swept over Morgan's head as slowly as a tree beginning to fall, then Kiartan side-stepped out of Morgan's view. He heard another ripping sound, as though a tailor were slowly rending a sheet of cloth.

After what seemed an interminable delay, something heavy struck the floor.

Morgan could see nothing, do nothing, so he waited. He felt something hard pressed against his body, moving up from the backs of his ankles to the back of his head, and suddenly he could move again. He turned to look at what Kiartan held out to him. It was a carving that resembled him, and he could see the cords Kiartan had cut away from the simulacrum. "What do you want to do with this?" Kiartan asked.

Morgan held out his hand, accepted the figurine, and pronounced a spell of release over it. He felt a draining of power from his scars telling him the spell had been cast by a lesser magus. He tested the efficacy of the release spell by pressing on the figure's arm with his thumb. He felt nothing.

"This is still dangerous," Morgan said. "Having been enchanted once, it has a residue of power." He carried it to the hearth, struck a spark into the kindling and, as flames grew, fed the wooden figure to the fire. As it blackened and began to burn, he stood and looked around the room.

Blood had been splashed and spattered over most of the room, and more lay pooled near the bodies. The priest who'd cast the spell lay sprawled across the floor, his sword half-drawn. His throat had been cut almost to the spine. The other priest lay in a heap, his face still twisted in agony. "I hate leaving a mess for the owner," Morgan said.

Kiartan's reply was delivered slowly and distinctly, as though Morgan might be slow-witted. "There wasn't time to poison them."

Morgan cast a sharp glance at the assassin, but Kiartan's face revealed nothing. "I'd have hated being the mess far worse than leaving this one. Thank you."

Kiartan moved to the door, stood just inside as he scanned the area, then gestured for Morgan to follow him. Once outside the cottage, he tugged loose the reins of the priests' horses and, after Morgan had mounted, sprang into the other saddle and kicked the animal into a canter, heading north. They made a wide semi-circle around the hollow and rode to the inn where they'd left their own mounts, tied behind an outbuilding. Leading their own horses, they rode into the city.

As Morgan rode, he considered what he'd learned. The first, and most obvious, lesson was that the church was more dangerous than he'd permitted himself to believe. The second was Mendarian had finally severed the last bond between them; the shared secret of his true name.

This pained him. She'd declared herself an enemy who must be destroyed if he were to defend himself and his friends, but he couldn't forget what they'd shared. He was having to raze a part of his life, tear down bridges on the road from where he'd come. Despite his regret, the attack demanded a riposte.

He drew rein before Jonfré's palace, dismounted, entered, and, as soon as he could find quill, ink, and parchment, penned a message to Tregarin. The priest's half-drawn sword was weak proof of a church conspiracy, but the sword-staff was almost a declaration of treachery. He finished with the observation that if his boots were wet, at least it wasn't piss.

Jonfré appeared at the door. "It looks as though it's been a brisk day in the blood trade."

Morgan glanced down at the brown spots that freckled him and his clothing. "A couple of his priests made offering to Mordach. They should probably have prayed more."

Jonfré hooked his thumbs in his belt. "The man with the peg leg's back. The guards are keeping him in the room at the end of the corridor."

"Excellent." Morgan handed Jonfré the message to Tregarin. "I'll see him immediately. Could you have this dispatched to Tregarin as soon as possible?"

"I'll see to it." Jonfré accepted the parchment and strode down the hallway.

Curiosity drew Morgan up the corridor and to the door. When he stepped into the room the two guards, who'd been leaning against the wall facing a bench, snapped erect. On the bench sat a nonde-script man with a peg leg. He was short and lean, with a wizened face and a scanty beard.

"I understand we served together in the Das wars," Morgan said.

"Yes," the stranger replied. "With Poker and a man named Morgan."

Morgan tried to keep his face from betraying his surprise. If the man had been one of Mordach's killers, he wouldn't have wasted using the name on anything but a spell. He turned to the guards. "You may leave us."

As the guards closed the door behind them, the man said a phrase in Sinn and his features flowed to become a saturnine face of indefinite age, with eyes as black and hard as obsidian. Hadrian un-strapped the wooden leg, then untied the binding holding his right lower leg tight against his thigh. "You've no idea how uncomfortable that was."

Hadrian stood, and it was like watching a weapons master draw-ing a sword; Hadrian's presence was as menacing as a naked blade. "Do you presume to rule the clan?"

CHAPTER 12

Morgan could only stare, not comprehending.

Hadrian went on, in his soft, dangerous voice. "I commanded Damon to remain in the Empire of The Book. How dare you countermand any order I've given?"

Morgan finally found his voice. "I didn't. The Voice of The Faith made that decision. But I'm glad Damon's here." If rage had driven Hadrian mad, it was dangerous to beard him, but Morgan refused to grovel. "Nor did I ask The Voice to change his mind."

Hadrian studied him through narrowed eyes. There was nothing Morgan could do; the decision was in Hadrian's hands.

"What do you intend to do with the crowns of Glangurra and Donradé?"

The question surprised Morgan, and he hesitated before he replied, "Glangurra belongs to Ukena. As for Donradé, Jonfré would make a reluctant king, but that may be the best kind." He paused again. If Hadrian had gone mad, mentioning Topaz and Cari might endanger them. On the other hand, Hadrian hadn't, so far as he knew, killed any innocents, and, mad or sane, Hadrian was too capable not to learn about them; probably, he already knew. "I've a family in Cerco, and flocks to tend there."

When Hadrian said nothing, Morgan walked to the bench, sat on the opposite end from his adopted brother. "What are you doing here? The last I heard, you were bound for Porcash."

Hadrian sat on his end of the bench, facing Morgan. "I've come from there, and I'm looking for a trade. We both have enemies, some of them in common.

"Almost all the surviving members of the Union went to ground in Porcash. When I began to hunt them down, the ones that were left formed a mercenary company and rode west. They say that if something can't kill a man, it makes him stronger. I seem to have made these vermin stronger. They never let down their guards for an instant, and there are too many of them to kill all at once. I've learned they've joined Thienn's army."

"That's two good reasons to wish them dead," Morgan said. He studied Hadrian, saw the man needed to shave and trim his beard, noticed the eyes were underlined with fatigue. Hadrian looked like the unlaid ghost of the man Morgan had known. "What'll you do after they're dead?"

Hadrian shrugged.

"Why not return to your family in Sin Garlef? Or bring them here? There'll be many lordless holdings before this is over. You've more than discharged your duties as the clan's avenger."

Hadrian shook his head. "I've become a creature of retribution."

"The Hadrian I knew was that, too, but he was more than one person. I think you should at least see your family."

"There wasn't the same kind of fire in me then. Before the fall of High Rage, I was a man who wore an executioner's mask when I had to. Now, I've become the mask. Mendarian and the Union burned that man. Now he's all scars and fire." He stared for a moment into Morgan's eyes. "Can you explain to me why you let her live?"

Morgan had folded his hands together. Now he looked down at them and realized he was rubbing one thumb against the other. "I doubt I can. I've learned it was a mistake, but I couldn't know that at the time. I was hoping the part of her I cared about would grow, but it seems to have been stunted. I was hoping she'd learned."

Hadrian stared at him as though he'd grown a second head. "You've changed, brother."

"Grown a little, perhaps. I'm really not Scarface anymore, although I'd prefer that in the presence of others you call me 'Daign.'" He flashed a brief grin. "Anything else is liable to confuse too many people." He looked back at his hands. "You may be pleased to learn Mordach's church and Mendarian are to be dealt with first. It's a matter of necessity, not pleasure, but I suppose it was inevitable."

Morgan stood. "I'll get you a room here, and order you water for a bath, and a razor." He suddenly realized what had struck him. "I haven't seen you out of your armor but once since the Das war, and you seem to be unarmed."

"I hope you wouldn't bet your life on that," Hadrian said, and slipped out a dagger that had been strapped to the back of his thigh, where it'd been hidden between his thigh and his calf when the leg was bound up. He drew another knife from a scabbard on his upper back, hidden under his smock.

"I'll see to it you get some worthy swords," Morgan said.

"I've a pair cached in the city, along with some other weapons. I'll retrieve them now and be back within the hour." He made the knives disappear again.

Morgan hesitated, then extended his arm to Hadrian, his hand open. For a moment he felt he'd been rebuffed as his clan brother seemed to ignore the gesture, then Hadrian wrapped his fingers around Morgan's forearm, let Morgan grip his own wrist.

Morgan released Hadrian's arm and said, "I'll assign a man to wait for you at the outer door, so the guards won't try to stop you or to disarm you. We've only a small army and have to be sparing of the men we have."

Hadrian almost replied, then nodded. They walked out the door with Morgan leading. "They don't follow the clan custom here. We'll be discussing the war at dinner."

Morgan introduced Hadrian to his guards as an old comrade and they walked together to the palace door, where Morgan left a guard to wait for Hadrian's return, and watched the other man leave. He'd need to tell Damon his father was here, although Damon probably knew his father well enough not to be surprised.

~ * ~

Washing down a bite of bread with a drink of wine, Morgan glanced around the table. As before, Ukena sat at the center of the head of the table, with Morgan on her left and Damon on her right. Morgan had invited Hadrian to sit beside him but Hadrian preferred to sit on the other side of Jeshka, and Morgan noted Hadrian and Kiartan had been surreptitiously studying each other since the church assassin had entered the room.

Morgan leaned toward Ukena. "I realize how important it is to depose Thienn, but I believe we must deal with the church first."

Ukena took a sip from her cup. "I rely upon your judgment. If you believe the church is the greater threat, then they should be beaten first."

"They may be dealt with at the same time. If our army lays siege to Hope, it may draw Thienn out to battle."

Jonfré had apparently been listening. "That sounds like dancing with a bear. You'd risk putting part of our army in jeopardy, with small chance of success. If Thienn takes the bait, part of the army could be trapped between the garrison of Hope and Thienn's forces. Since Hope is built on an island, the men caught on Thienn's side of the river will be facing Thienn's entire army, with a river between them and escape, and if you try to rescue them, the rescuers will have to try to cross a river in the face of the enemy. Even with bridges across the river, you'd be feeding Thienn and his army a few men at a time. That's a design for disaster."

Morgan had finished eating and drinking during Jonfré's objection. He glanced once around the table. "We can mount an attack on Hope and reduce it quickly, then hold both Hope and our side of the river. Then Thienn will have to come to us, try to cross the river to the bank we defend, or watch us supply Hope so it becomes a permanent thorn in his side."

"And what will you do if you fail to take Hope?" Jonfré asked.

Hadrian's quiet, precise voice cut into the conversation. "How large a garrison does the church maintain at Hope?"

Jonfré frowned. "We built the place to house three hundred soldiers. The church is made up of new men with pretensions to nobility, so the quarters for them will use up some of the barracks space. I'd guess a garrison of a hundred to a hundred twenty, with another score to thirty church leaders, along with their whores and a few sycophants. They could easily get another two hundred warrior-priests inside in a few days. Less than a fortnight, certainly. They could, within a month, gather a formidable army, probably near three thousand men, which is enough to defend against a river crossing and reinforce and supply the castle."

Morgan leaned back. "If we fail to take Hope in a few days we can draw all our men to one side of the river and wait for Thienn to attack us." He raised a hand as Jonfré seemed ready to voice another objection. "We'd best be to our pallets. Tomorrow will be a long day. We'll begin to gather our army. Within a day or two, we'll send a handful of men north to tell Anjular to assemble his forces, and our army should be prepared to march from Linistia within ten days."

Morgan looked first at Hadrian, then at Kiartan, and both men gave an almost imperceptible indication that they understood. "Lord Jonfré, I'll meet you in your room in a quarter of an hour." He rose. "I suggest you all spend the evening in either rest or meditation—all but the nobles. They'll have to decide what they need to prepare their forces. I'll expect them to submit lists to Jonfré in no more than two days."

The petty nobles stood and bowed, then walked from the room in groups of twos and threes. Morgan watched them disappear down the corridor, then turned to Hadrian. "It's been a long time. I'll walk with you to your room." He bowed to Queen Ukena. "With your permission, my lady."

She nodded and remained seated as the others all rose, bowed, and walked away.

Morgan strode beside Hadrian to his brother's room and closed the door behind them. Together, they waited most of a quarter of an hour, then Hadrian cast the spell of concealment and closely followed Morgan as he paced to Jonfré's quarters. When the guards at the door saluted him with a bow, Morgan told them to take their positions at the far end of the corridor, then he knocked at the door.

"Enter."

As Morgan entered the room, paused, then closed the door, Jonfré rose from behind a table on which lay an opened map scroll. "Scarface, you know better than to lead an army with hopes instead of plans."

"Of course." Morgan smiled, and Hadrian appeared beside him. "I also know better than to reveal my plans to a dozen men I don't personally know, as well as the guards at the door. I wouldn't be surprised if, by tomorrow morning, someone from the church knows what we all ate tonight, as well as every word uttered in that room. It's almost as likely someone else will be taking that information to Thienn. Even if everyone in that room can be trusted, the orders they'll issue and the time they'll allow to carry out their orders would tell a spy most of what I said tonight."

Jonfré sat down heavily, a smile spreading across his face. "I shouldn't have assumed you'd become less devious. What do you have in mind?"

"First, to wait for Kian, who should be here any moment."

"Who's here now," said a voice from outside the window, and the assassin crawled through the opening like a lizard.

"*Etrong Filteth*," Hadrian said. "Well met."

Kiartan responded with a nod.

Morgan studied the map. Hope was in northwestern Donradé, north and east of Glangurrach by about forty leagues. "A dozen men can move more quickly than a hundred and, properly used, can accomplish as much."

"Three or four men can move even more quickly, and with less chance of being noticed," Hadrian said, with a glance at Kiartan,

"Kian is here for his advice," Morgan said. "His responsibility is to protect the priests and healers of Ianno."

Kiartan looked down at the map. "I believe the best protection for them is to destroy Mordach's church as soon as possible."

Morgan grinned. "Then three men it is."

Hadrian moved his fingers across the map like a man walking stiff-legged, trying to estimate the duration of the ride to Hope. "Did you want me to tell Damon to prepare?"

Morgan shook his head. "I've got to ask him to do something more dangerous than ride to Hope. I want him to remain here, then lead the army north, disguised as me. I'll go north with you, disguised as Damon." He saw Hadrian draw a breath, and spoke before he could argue. "I'm the only one among us who's spent any time at Hope. You've only visited the place once, and then briefly. Neither Damon nor Kian have ever laid eyes on the place, while I'm the one who planned the fortifications. You'll need me."

Hadrian stared at him a long moment, then nodded, a single bob of the head. They both looked at Kiartan.

"Anyone else would share the secret, and would add little to our power," Kiartan acknowledged.

"Good," Morgan said, and dropped into a chair. "Tomorrow we'll announce that, the day after, we're sending Damon, Hadrian, and the men from the empire north to join Anjular and to help him gather his forces. Kian can ride along as just another soldier; he's been almost invisible till now, and won't be missed in Linistia.

"Damon knows me well enough to be able to carry out his charade, and if the church tries a magical attack, they'll probably use my name to direct the spell, which should actually protect him." He took a perverse satisfaction in recognizing a flicker of surprise in Hadrian's eyes when he'd admitted that some within the church knew his true name.

"We'll use tomorrow to cast the spells. With Hadrian's skill and knowledge and both his power and mine, we may be able to cast both spells in a single day. The day after tomorrow, we'll ride north."

He faced Jonfré. "The church has to know I'll strike back. They can even guess where I'll attack. The only secrets left are the timing and the means. With this subterfuge, I hope to gain at least a fortnight. I want them to watch our army slowly assemble and make its long, steady march and not notice the sudden attack until it's done. If we can crush the head of the church, the survivors will be forced to side with Thienn, which should further discredit them. When we form ranks for the great battle, I want as many of our enemies under Thienn's banner as possible.

"As for Thienn, I want to break him far closer to his capital than Hope. We must force him to fight or run, and if he runs, he'll lose all his power, like blood from a mortal wound."

Jonfré shook his head as though rousing himself. "I have but one question left. How do three men hope to attack a castle of a hundred and fifty warrior-priests?"

With a rare smile, Hadrian replied, "We each kill fifty."

Morgan stood. "While the plan is different, the need for rest is as great as before."

Without a word, Kiartan moved to the window and slipped out. Hadrian poured water from an ewer into a cup, dipped his fingers into it, then touched his forehead as he murmured the spell, and vanished. Morgan left the room with Hadrian following him. He ordered the guards to return to their station by Jonfré's door, then escorted Hadrian back to his room before returning to his own chamber.

He'd been mildly surprised and very pleased when Kiartan had offered to help attack Hope, but felt some misgivings about Hadrian. He remembered what Martina had once said about Scarface; that his shadow had grown darker. Hadrian was darker. He might've smiled as he said it, but he'd meant what he'd said about killing fifty men.

Hadrian had probably used the wooden leg as part of his disguise because the debility was so obvious anyone seeing him would remember the peg leg and notice less the man who wore it, but it also seemed appropriate Hadrian appear a cripple. He was crippled, although in a more subtle way than a missing limb.

In a way, he was using Hadrian's disability. That weakness wouldn't keep Hadrian from attacking Hope. In fact, it'd probably be an advantage, but Morgan still had misgivings.

~ * ~

They activated the spells just before dawn. Morgan had remembered how precious the gift had been; to be able to bid Topaz farewell in his own body, and he wanted to give the same gift to Damon and Jeshka.

Now he stood beside a horse that bore Damon's saddle and bridle and watched himself march down the stairs outside the palace. His bearing was confident, almost arrogant, and his walk was the same, but without Hadrian's feline grace or Kiartan's almost serpentine sinuosity.

He approached and stared at himself critically. He hadn't realized until he saw them worn by another how his lambent green eyes and black scars dominated his face, nor had he realized until now, seeing his body worn by another, how the years had marked him. He still thought of himself as a young man, albeit one with a few more aches and a trace less enthusiasm, but as he looked at the man on the stairs he noticed the crow's feet that had begun to form at the corners of the eyes, the lines across the forehead, the faint hollows beginning to shadow the cheekbones, the streaks of gray in the hair. The moustache was still black, but he knew if he hadn't shaved it away, there'd be white in the beard. He was nearer Jonfré's age than Damon's, and before long it'd be time for him to surrender these adventures to younger men.

He wondered if Damon were experiencing the same strange sense of dislocation. He stepped forward and clasped forearms with the strange self that faced him and Damon said, in Morgan's voice, "Good fortune."

His voice wasn't as deep as he'd thought, with a trace of accent he hadn't realized he had. He bowed to himself and strode back to the horse, forced himself to spring lightly into the saddle, ignoring the stirrups until he has astride the mount. With a last glance back to be sure all his men were mounted and ready, he set out for the city gate at a trot.

Half a league from the city, Hadrian joined him at the head of the column. "That was well done. You both played your parts well."

Morgan grinned. "Good. I wasn't sure I could manage the mount. I hadn't realized how much lighter my body was when I was younger."

They kept the horses to a steady pace as the morning's coolness wore away. Cloaks were flung back or removed and bundled on the fronts of saddles. Morgan felt a curious lightness of spirit, despite the appearance he wore like a tight suit of mail, and he attributed it to being able, finally, to take action. Months had passed in which he'd had to weigh each move, marshalling forces and reacting to the initiatives of others, but the waiting and the planning were past.

Near midday they halted briefly at a stream to eat and rest the horses, then pressed on until the sun rested on the western horizon.

They halted beside another stream and Kiartan led his horse into the water and let him stand there, resting. "The moving water," he explained, "is good for the horse's legs."

Morgan ordered that all the mounts be kept in the stream for an hour, then the men pitched a dark, quiet camp.

Dawn found them tying packs on the pack horses and saddling their mounts, and for two more days they followed the Sazian-built road north. Morgan observed the only patches of snow remained in shaded places where the sunlight never reached, and the mud near the road was growing firmer.

Sometimes they rode through small towns, and boys ran beside them, cheering and shouting questions. Morgan knew most of the boys and some of the soldiers regarded the visitation as an adventure.

On the fourth day out of Linistia, just after rising, Morgan called for Damon's sub-captain. He handed the man Damon's swords, then took a plain but well-made bastard sword from one of the packs and buckled on its scabbard. "I want you to lead the men to Anjular's fortress. Just follow this road north. Tell Anjular the army marches. My father and I," he glanced at Hadrian but his brother didn't flinch, "and that man," he pointed at Kiartan, "will ride northwest and scout for the army."

The man tried to hide his surprise, bowed, and secured Damon's weapons on his own horse.

Morgan left the sub-captain to bawl commands while he, Hadrian, and Kiartan rode away from the road, leading two pack horses. By early evening, they'd left the plains behind and made their night's camp in hill country.

"This part of Donradé isn't as fertile," Morgan said. "Consequently, there are fewer people living near here, but we should still be discreet." He stood and stretched. "Hadrian, since we're out of sight of all but badgers and foxes, may I dispel my disguise?"

"I wouldn't advise it. I've never done a reciprocal spell like this before, and I don't know what effect your dropping your spell might have on Damon's disguise."

Morgan stretched again. "Fair enough, as long as I can dispel it before we attack Hope." There remained enough light for the others to see lines scratched in the dirt, so, using a twig, he began to draw a shape like a boat, with a pointed prow and rounded stern. "This is the rock on which Hope is built." He drew lines for the walls, and a rectangle extending from one of the lines. "This is the main building, with the great hall." He drew circles at the points of the rectangle and halfway along the long sides. "These are the turrets."

~ * ~

Five days later they were hidden in the rocks and brush of the eastern bank of the Bluewater River, squinting at the castle itself in the fading light. The western bank was a more gentle slope to a lower floodplain where the monks of Mordach were already planting crops. The castle stood near the middle of the river on its boat-shaped spit of rock. The three of them studied the walls and towers, then drew back into deeper concealment.

Morgan smiled mirthlessly. He'd ordered a tower built at the "prow" of the rock, but the church hadn't finished the defenses he'd devised; neither the tower nor the walls that would've connected it to the rest of the castle had been built.

Hadrian tested the points and edges of his weapons and began honing one of his swords. "We wait. The moon should set a little after midnight."

Kiartan opened the pack he'd carried from where they'd left the horses, a league downstream. He handed each of the others a bundle. "Put these on, and keep only the weapons you intend to wear across the river."

Morgan opened his bundle, found that it contained a loose tunic and trousers made of dark wool, with boots and a head covering of the same material. "What's this for?"

"The water will be cold. This will help a little, and will help more when we take them off and put on dry clothes on the other side of the river." He disappeared into some bushes.

Morgan peeled off the light mail he wore and the thin leather under it. He debated with himself, decided to leave the mail behind and to carry only a knife across the river. If a guard saw them, no armor nor weapons could save them. He shivered in anticipation of the river's chill.

Kiartan returned within moments, wearing the same dark garb and with his sword slung across his back. He laid out a complete, treated hide. "Put your clothing, armor, and weapons into this." After they'd placed their articles on the leather, he drew it closed and lashed it tightly. "This should keep the water out."

The church assassin crouched in the shade of a bush, becoming all but invisible. "When we reach the river, I'll cross first, towing a rope. When I'm on the other side, tie the bundle to the rope and I'll draw it across. Scarface, you come next. Draw the rope back until I stop paying it out to you, then cling to the rope and I'll pull you across. Hadrian, you hold the other end of the rope. As soon as it's taut in your hands, come across."

Hadrian and Morgan murmured acknowledgements, and they waited.

Morgan felt a grim satisfaction and an appreciation of irony. They'd seen no patrols, nothing but the monks, who lived in a wooden shed beside their fields, and the church had stopped building the castle before they'd completed all the defenses Scarface had planned. They'd grown complacent, and seemed to have forgotten they served a war-god. Morgan was also forced to admit to himself that his defenses wouldn't have stopped men like Hadrian or Kiartan, but the lack of those defenses made their attack easier.

"When we're ready to go up the walls," Kiartan murmured, "I'll go first again. After I've silenced the guards on the northern wall, I'll lower the rope."

"It'll go more quickly if you take the eastern tower and I the western," Hadrian said softly. "We'll meet again at the corner and lower the rope to Scarface."

"Well said," Kiartan muttered. "After this is over, we'll have to swagger blades."

"I'm always pleased to learn." Hadrian's tone suggested he'd almost said, "and teach."

Each recited to the others his part in the plan until they were all satisfied that each understood what was needed of him and none of them could see a flaw in the plan. In the silence that followed, Morgan found himself becoming anxious. His companions were confident, but it was the confidence born of experience.

Morgan had fought battles, and even carried out assassinations, but never had he attempted anything like this. When he'd killed secretly, he'd depended as much upon speed as on stealth. It was relatively simple to slip into a place, kill one man and perhaps a guard or two, and escape. It was another game entirely to trap oneself in a castle with over a hundred mortal enemies, with no escape until the garrison was all dead.

He started when he felt a hand on his arm. Hadrian indicated the moon hanging low in the branches of the trees to the west. "Good hunting," he murmured, and Morgan and Kiartan repeated the wish.

Together they crept to the river's edge and Kiartan slid into the water as noiselessly as an otter. Morgan waited, felt the rope tugged twice, tied the bundle to the line, and fed out rope as the bag was hauled across.

As soon as the rope was tugged again, he drew it back across, tensing at the thought of the water's icy coldness. He drew a deep, shuddering breath, then slid into the river. It would've been easier if he could scream, he thought, as water like ice washed over his chest and his genitals. His hands gripped the rope with desperate strength, and he was grateful he didn't have to try to swim, because the cold seemed to have stolen all his strength but that in his hands. He felt rock beneath his feet and forced himself to crawl slowly out of the river.

He crawled on his belly up the rocks, fearing he'd freeze to them and be unable to move, then began to work his way out of the woolen clothing Kiartan had provided. By the time he'd stripped off the wet, frigid wool he was handed his own gear. He donned the supple leather tunic and leggings and light boots, strapped a knife to his right calf, and secured his sword across his back. Then, feeling his way over the rocks, he crept to the wall and waited.

Two figures moved up the wall as silently as a cloud shadow, and seemed scarcely more tenuous. He listened intently but heard only the river flowing past and lapping at the stones. Any guards above were silent, and the castle might've been deserted.

It was humiliating to allow other men to lead the attack while he waited at the base of the wall, but he realized he couldn't aid Hadrian or Kiartan, only hinder them. While he was capable, they were exceptional and, until the guards were silenced, he had no part to play.

He strained to hear, heard only the comforting noises of the water, then saw the rope being lowered. Wiping his suddenly damp palms on his tunic, he tried to ignore the tightness in his belly, forced himself to breathe slowly and deeply. He grasped the rough hemp, set his feet against the stone wall, and began to ascend. The rope was being drawn up smoothly, so he twisted his forearms in it, forming coils around his arms, and hung on, helping by using his feet to find purchase on the rough stone. His world narrowed to the rope in his hands and the wall before him, then his wrist was gripped and he was helped over the top of the wall.

He followed the more slender of the two shadows along the wall, to his left. They entered the tower and Morgan saw no bodies, only smelled them. Besides the salty, almost metallic, tang of blood he could detect the sewage stench from the relaxation of bowels and bladder. The odor seemed to turn the knot in his stomach, and he had to fight a wave of nausea.

The walkway turned a corner within the tower, and Morgan wetted a finger with saliva, daubed it on his forehead, and mouthed the incantation of the spell of concealment.

Advancing to the next turret, he tried to see Hadrian, saw nothing, heard only the river far below and the faint scuffing of his own boots on stone. When he reached that tower he pressed himself against the stone wall beside the entry, listened, heard nothing, then his sense of smell assured him these guards would raise no alarm.

He slipped through the chamber and to the next turret, felt his way through it, and advanced to the tower on the southeast corner of the wall. All remained quiet. In the tower, he glanced at the base of the duty candle that still burned there and noticed, lying near it, a bloody hand. The candle had perhaps half an hour to burn before it burned down to the next red ring. He couldn't guess whether the ring indicated an all's well or a change of guards. If it were the latter, the next group of sentries would soon be waking and arming themselves.

Hadrian moved past him and he followed. All the guards on the outer walls were dead, and he hadn't heard a scream, or even the sound of a body falling. He hurried after Hadrian, slowed at the stairs that led from the tower directly into the northern barracks. He could just make out a faint glow ahead and as he ducked through the barracks door he could see that a single candle gleamed. By its feeble light he could distinguish rows of sleeping bodies on pallets.

Three of the sleepers, at least, would never wake, and Hadrian had piled the corpses to block the door leading to the other tower.

Morgan drew his knife and scratched the sigil for the fire-spell on the top body, murmuring the incantation, feeling power drain from his scars. By the time he'd cast a third spell on the floor, the door through which they'd entered had been similarly blocked, and he cast the spell three more times.

Hadrian moved among the sleepers like the shadow of death. Morgan found two jars of oil for the lamps in the cabinet on which stood the candles, and he poured the oil onto the floor near the door to the bailey. The nearest bodies took no notice of the oil that soaked into their pallets, but Morgan expected the odor to rouse the others.

A man near the center of the room stirred, then a shadow fell on him and he thrashed a moment, then lay still, but others began to wake.

Morgan could spare them no attention. He again scratched the design on the floor, touching a tendril of the spilled oil. When he could look up, he saw Hadrian had drawn his swords and was cutting down a man who'd half-risen. The man had begun to scream, a sound that ended suddenly when his throat was torn out.

Hadrian sprang toward the door, cutting down another man as he moved, pausing only to give Morgan time to get outside before he killed one more man, then both were outside. Morgan slammed the heavy door shut behind them and they heard more screams, both from the barracks they'd left and the one that stood against the southern wall.

Even through the heavy oak door, Morgan could hear a roar as one of the traps claimed a victim, and more screams. A sentry in one of the main hall's turrets winded a horn. The alarm was an eerie, rising moan, and an arrow whispered past Morgan to thud into the barracks door.

Morgan saw Hadrian sprint toward the hall and dashed after him, but before they could reach the door, they heard a bar being dropped into place, and nothing less than a ram could force that entrance.

Hadrian cursed in Sinn, then flung himself at the wall and began to climb.

Morgan spun to scan the bailey, knowing his brother made an easy target, but saw nothing. Smoke had begun to billow from the chimneys of both barracks, but the doors apparently remained sealed, and he doubted a dozen men would escape the fire alive. The horses in the stable had begun to whinny and pound at their stalls. If the stablemen weren't in the barracks, they'd be too occupied with their charges to attack the raiders.

He looked up again, failed to catch sight of Hadrian. He suddenly realized he still wore the spell of concealment and turned to the wall, found crevices for fingers and toes, and started to climb.

The walls of the great hall were four times his own height, the tops of the turrets almost the same distance above that. He feared to look up or down and gave all his attention to finding the next handhold or testing cavities with his toes, both made more difficult since he couldn't see his own hands or feet.

He'd just reached the top of the wall when he heard a scream from one of the towers and a body fell with a crash of armor and a groaning of timbers. Morgan cleared the wall and trotted toward the tower to his right, drawing his sword.

Mounting the stairs, he climbed as rapidly as stealth and his stamina would allow. As his head reached the level of the tower floor he spied a figure peering over the parapet, a crossbow in his hands. Morgan gripped his sword with both hands and crept up the remaining steps, then lunged. The sentry howled as the point drove between the ribs on his right side, then he fell over the brink, and Morgan had to seize his weapon tightly to keep it from being jerked from his grasp.

Morgan glanced about the tower, trying to avoid looking at the candle, then, seeing no one else, descended the stairs. He passed the door to the walkway by which he'd entered the tower and kept moving down. Hadrian and Kiartan should already have reached the great hall, where the church would have its last line of defense.

A door jerked open below him, spilling light into the stairwell, and a shadow appeared, feet pounding the stone steps as the man charged upstairs.

The ceiling was too low, the stairwell too narrow for swinging a sword, so Morgan planted his feet and gripped his weapon in both hands. He let the priest run into the sword's point, then lunged. The priest shrieked and fell, almost taking Morgan down with him.

Morgan was spattered with blood, making the spell useless, since the blood was clearly visible. He dispelled the concealment and picked his way past the body, almost slipping on the gore lying thick on the stairs.

At the foot of the stairs he shoved open the door and saw two priests standing near another door, one cranking a crossbow. As he stepped out of the stairwell the man with the crossbow saw him. The priest blanched, the red lightning bolts and a blue bar across his forehead suddenly vivid, and he shouted a warning to the other priest.

Morgan rushed the two, his blade pointed at the second priest's face. The man swung his mace up, and Morgan lashed out while the mace was still moving away from him. The priest screamed as Morgan's blow caught him in the left ribs, tore his chest open, then Morgan sidestepped and slashed down at the crossbowman.

The other priest raised his crossbow, almost parried the cut, then lurched back, his head split to the upper jaw.

A leap carried Morgan through the door, into the great hall.

Torchlight flickered, so that shadows leapt and capered on walls and pillars. Chairs and tables lay tumbled about the floor, and the nearest table lay on its side. Men moved among the pillars flanking the center of the hall, vanishing and reappearing as they ducked and weaved through the chamber.

A priest leapt at Morgan, swinging back his sword.

Morgan had lowered his own blade and he whipped it up and around from the low guard position Kiartan had taught him. The swords clashed, then whined, as Morgan's stroke swept them both around in a bind. They both strained, their faces hardly the length of a dagger apart, each striving to press the other's blade aside, then Morgan drove his knee into the priest's groin. As the man grunted and lurched, Morgan hooked the guard of his sword under the other's guard and shoved upward, then freed his weapon and chopped in a side-stroke that caught Mordach's priest under the arm.

Morgan's blade was buried deeply in the priest's chest, and as the man spun and fell, Morgan was drawn after him. He rolled into the fall so he fetched up on one knee and whipped his sword up into guard before him. He rose slowly, casting about for more attackers.

He saw movement among the timbers supporting the roof, strained to make out who moved among the shadows. A low growl issued from the darker shadows and three priests spun at the noise.

Hadrian growled again, stalking them like some great, hungry cat, through the forest of pillars, then he was attacking with both swords. The first man fell to a slash that opened him from shoulder to belly, the second was cut deeply across the chest, and the third went down clutching a slashed abdomen.

Hadrian's laughter caused Morgan's hair to stir. The sound wasn't the shrill laughter of a maniac; it was even more disturbing. It was a deep, throaty laugh of satisfaction.

Kiartan suddenly appeared near the center of the room, away from the pillars. He was dressed as he'd been when Morgan had first met him; all in black, and with his face covered. Half a dozen priests rushed toward him and halted just out of reach of his blade, surrounding him.

The clash of steel told Morgan Hadrian was fighting another man and he gathered his muscles to rush to aid Kiartan when suddenly the assassin moved. He glided forward, then back, then turned and sidestepped, moving like an adder, his blade whipping about him as though it had a predatory life of its own, bodies fell until Kiartan stood alone.

They all heard the flat, lethal snap of a crossbow and Kiartan stumbled, the point of a quarrel protruding from his chest.

Hadrian tossed his right-hand sword into the air, caught it by the forte of the blade, and hurled it like a javelin. Morgan watched its flight, saw it bury itself a third its length into the priest with the crossbow.

The man swayed, gaping at the sword that had killed him, then raised trembling hands and began to push feebly at the guard.

Hadrian sprang over a table and reached the man in a bound. He snatched his weapon from the priest's body and struck with both swords. The priest fell as though boneless.

Another form in red rose from behind the fallen table in front of Morgan and vaulted over it. A chair lay near Morgan's right foot and, as the figure rushed toward him, he kicked the chair into its path. The shape stumbled and fell, rolling, and a sword clattered across the floor, then a pale, oval face bare of tattoos looked up at him.

Morgan's sword was raised for a killing stroke, but he simply gawked at Mendarian. Her features were drawn and her fear-stricken eyes stared at his face, all panic and entreaty mixed, and her fear touched him. He felt a sudden, unexpected fury at her helplessness and loathed himself for the rage.

He knew he should, must strike, but he couldn't bring himself to kill. Anger and compassion seemed almost one, and he wanted to turn away from his own fury in horror. He hesitated to cut down the woman he'd once loved, defenseless before him. It had come to this; Mendarian, facing death, seized by panic and unable to save herself, and he knowing he must end it but wanting, instead, to assuage the terror in her eyes.

Still wearing the expression of abject fear on its face, the head toppled, dropped to the floor, and the body jerked, bright blood jetting from the neck, then it lay still. Morgan stared at Mendarian's face, grief and relief mixed until he couldn't distinguish them.

Kiartan stood swaying, then sagged forward, leaning on his sword stained with Mendarian's life's blood. His mask and chest glistened with his own blood. His eyes were wide and wild, and he seemed to be trying to breathe through the rent in his chest. He sank to one knee, then pitched forward, his sword still clutched in his right hand.

Morgan scanned the room but saw nothing moving but Hadrian, who prowled among the bodies. Morgan reached out and laid his hand on the church assassin's neck, knew Kiartan was dead as soon as he'd touched him.

Morgan's curiosity about the face under the mask was strong enough he reached for the cloth, then, leaving the face covered, closed Kiartan's eyes. He picked up the body, which was heavier than he might've guessed, carried it to one of the tables, and laid it down.

Hadrian joined him, his features set. "He died well, doing what he meant to do."

A cough made them turn to face the motionless figure sitting in a chair like a throne. The chair was dwarfed by and seemed almost a part of a massive idol of Mordach, a muscular male figure with red lightning bolts on his face and with eight arms, each hand brandishing a different weapon.

As Morgan approached, he noted the chair was heavily padded with cushions, and he almost failed to recognize the reclining man as Cruach. He'd always thought of Mordach's high priest as a man of iron. Now he realized, could see, that even iron can bend and rust away. The priest had suffered a brainstorm, and the left side of his face sagged as though he were already half dead. He'd once been almost as robust as the statue, but his body had wasted. His left side seemed to be useless, and his right side had withered from lack of use.

"Kill me." Cruach's voice was hardly more than a croak.

Hadrian stalked toward the priest. "Do you grant him his wish, brother, or do I?"

Morgan gestured for Hadrian to step back. "No, we take him back with us alive. He's our best proof Mordach is a fraud and a liar. If any man deserved to die in battle, it should be Mordach's own high priest. Now, we can show that Mordach cheated even his own chosen leader."

"Kill me," Cruach rasped again, "or I'll raise all the church against you."

"That bolt's already been shot," Morgan replied. "All your real power lies dead on the floor."

Hadrian showed his teeth to Cruach and chuckled, then turned to Morgan. "Brother, I've seen your capacity for cruelty before. This time I approve."

They made their preparations, piling chairs and benches under the table on which lay Kiartan's body, then hauled Cruach to the antechamber. When they lifted the bar out of its mortises and swung open the doors to the great hall, they saw both the barracks smoking. The nearer building gave a groan as timbers gave way and the tiled roof collapsed. The fire, no longer contained, shot upward.

From the stables they could hear the screams and panicked pounding of fear-maddened horses. Hadrian returned to the hall, emerged holding a bow and a handful of arrows. "I'll release the horses. Watch yourself. We don't know if any priests are still alive." Then he stalked off across the bailey.

Morgan paced to the antechamber to see to Cruach, heard shrill screams, then half-drew his sword as the door to the hall was thrust open.

The two frightened women who stood in the doorway saw him and immediately ran back into the hall. Through the door, he could hear more women's voices. He strode into the great hall, to the center of the room, and roared, "Get out! Gather any other women here and get out. We're burning this place."

He'd forgotten the newer priests of Mordach weren't as abstemious as the priests had once been. He herded over a dozen women out the door, then seized a torch from its sconce and thrust it into the kindling under Kiartan's body. When the flames began to lick at the bottom of the table he laid other flambeaux at the bases of the wooden pillars, then rushed out the door.

Crossing the antechamber, he peered outside, looking for Hadrian. Frightened horses milled about in the bailey, their eyes rolling. He rushed, shouting and waving his arms, through the animals until he reached the windlass that raised the eastern drawbridge. Grunting, he drew down an arm of the windlass. He shoved aside the ratcheted stop and sprang back as chains rattled and the bridge ponderously swung down then slammed to the eastern bank with a crash.

Horses raced past, then women began to cross the bridge.

Hadrian had somehow managed to saddle one horse and hitch another to a cart, which he'd drawn in front of the hall. Morgan trotted across to help carry Cruach out and place him in the wagon.

With Cruach reclining on blankets and bags of grain, Morgan

climbed to the driver's seat, clucked to the horse, and shook the reins. With Hadrian following on horseback, he drove the cart out over the drawbridge and followed the faint trail that led eastward.

When the horse had trotted off some of its panic, Morgan drew rein and looked back at the castle. Smoke billowed up from behind the walls, and he heard another crash as another roof fell. There was no satisfaction in what he'd done. It'd been necessary—of that he had no doubt—but he was afraid when he closed his eyes he'd again see Mendarian's face, so terror-stricken it had provoked both pity and fury in him. Their relationship had been a volatile one, with love and hate mixed. It was a source of pain that it had ended on an unpleasant turn.

Then there was the fall of Hope itself. It was the only thing he'd ever built, and now he was leaving it a burning ruin. He seemed to be leaving much of his past behind him in flames.

Even worse, those ruins were a pyre. He was surprised to find himself mourning Kiartan; it seemed as strange as feeling the absence of a void. Still, Kiartan had been an ally and Morgan had come to regard him as a friend—to whatever extent one could be friends with that strange man. He'd been harsh in his training, but the lessons had been desperately needed.

Morgan glanced at Hadrian scouting well ahead of the cart and waving the directions to the best route through the broken country ahead. Hadrian had always seemed dark, but now he seemed touched by a deadly madness. He'd once been impersonal death, but during the battle at Hope he'd been driven by frenzy. The Hadrian Morgan had known had always maintained an iron control; that control was beginning to evanesce. Too many deaths on his shoulders, too many on his hands.

Hadrian drew rein, waited until the cart had drawn beside him. "I saw you looking back. Fearing pursuit?"

"No, although it might be a good precaution to take."

Hadrian's smile was predatory. "If it were you, would you follow anyone who could do what we did?"

Morgan, in spite of himself, grinned. "No, probably not, but then I'm not a deluded fool worshipping a war-god."

"Rest your horse. I'll go get the mounts we left upriver."

Morgan watched Hadrian ride into the trees and felt a surge of affection for the man he'd been. Once they'd been rivals, or at least Morgan had tried to vie with his brother for the leadership of the clan, but Hadrian had hardly seemed aware of Scarface's resentment.

Now, Hadrian was a doomed man. He was a body and a mind, but something vital was lacking.

Morgan looked again in the direction of Hope. The towers were hidden by the trees, but he could still see the smoke. He'd lost Hope. He had to find some way to save Hadrian.

CHAPTER 13

The same distance Morgan had ridden in six days with Hadrian and Kiartan required three times as long to cover in a wagon with Cruach. Once, a handful of bandits had tried to ambush them but Hadrian flushed them like quail and killed them all, and, once, Hadrian had remarked that they were being followed by a score of men wearing red. He'd waved Morgan onward and had remained behind with the bow he'd taken from the castle and a sheaf of arrows. By evening he'd rejoined Morgan and Cruach, carrying the bow and with three arrows left in the quiver.

Cruach's health had become a cause for concern to Morgan. The old man had once been a powerful speaker, and Morgan wanted the army to hear him now, his voice only an echo of what it had been. The weakened voice and ravaged body would give the lie to every word he spoke, but something seemed broken within him. He drank little and ate less, and seemed weaker each day.

Hadrian had noticed the waning, too, and on the sixth night he said, within Cruach's hearing, "It were just as well he died. Hauling his body back would be quicker, and showing his corpse without an honest wound on it to the army would be a more persuasive argument than any he could deliver."

Cruach glared at Hadrian, the hatred in his eyes strong enough to feel, but he began to eat again.

The slow pace also chafed at Morgan. By now, Thienn should've begun to marshal his forces. The time he spent gathering his army was a gift to Morgan, but the sooner his forces had assembled, the sooner they could march, and Morgan wanted their battle fought on the ground he chose.

A day's travel from Anjular's fortress, they were met by riders wearing Anjular's colors. The soldier who commanded the troops saluted Morgan. "Lord Daign, may my men and I escort you to the army?"

Morgan nodded a greeting to the man. "Have you heard any word of Thienn? And how near is Jonfré?"

"I've heard nothing about Thienn, but Jonfré should be at the fortress by the time you arrive."

Morgan gnawed at his lower lip. The scouting he'd take these men from might be crucial to his army. On the other hand, the sooner he reached the army the more quickly they could march, but if he rode on alone, leaving Hadrian to bring in Cruach, his brother wasn't so well-known that he wouldn't be stopped by every sentry. He and Hadrian could ride together, but he mistrusted leaving Cruach with the soldiers.

Hadrian walked his horse beside the cart. "Take a couple of horses and ride. I'll take two men from the patrol as escorts, and the rest of these men can continue scouting for the army."

"Done," Morgan said, and sprang off the cart. He chose two mounts, saddled one, and rode away at a canter, leading the other animal.

He passed more patrols. Anjular seemed to have dispatched all his cavalry to scout for the army and, as Morgan neared the fortress, he saw more footsoldiers. By midafternoon he could see the walls and squat towers and observed that a city of tents had sprung up outside the holding. He kicked his tired horse into a trot and slowed to a dignified walk when he reached the tents.

Men began to shout the name by which he was known in Don-radé and he rode through a mass of men clamoring the name and beating weapons against shields. The great gates of the fort stood open, and he rode through them to find men were crowded even more closely within the walls. Over the throngs of soldiers he could just see a man with an eyepatch and, beside him, a man with white hair.

He drew up before Anjular's quarters, dismounted, handed the reins of his horses to a soldier, and embraced Jonfré and Damon.

He turned to the mass of soldiers and raised his arm, and the shouting became louder, then he turned and strode through the door. Anjular followed Jonfré and Damon, and closed the door against the noise.

Turning to Damon, Morgan said, "Your father should reach the camp before this time tomorrow. He's bringing Cruach." He noticed a bottle of wine and a cup on the table. He poured wine into the cup and drank deeply, then sighed with the relief the drink brought. "The old man suffered a brainstorm, and I decided that, alive, he was far more valuable to us than to Mordach."

"You actually did it!" Jonfré's grin subtracted a decade from his face.

"We did it," Morgan agreed. "Unfortunately, it cost us Kian."

Damon bowed. "I feel as though I should burn another banner."

"He deserves no less. I'll tell the priests of Ianno. I'm going to ask them to appoint you their new protector."

Jonfré dropped onto a bench. "Will you see Queen Ukena soon?"

"She's here?" Morgan drained the cup.

Jonfré nodded. "She insisted on accompanying the army."

"I'll see her after I've talked with you. Who else has joined us?"

"Besides a few defections from Thienn's army—two more Donradan nobles and a Glangurran baron—the Sazians are marching with us. Both their commander and I felt it were best if they remained half a day's march from the rest of us. And the emperor of Cerco is sending six hundred warriors from among the Dieri and some other tribes, and the same number of Senshenni horsemen. They should arrive tomorrow, or the day after."

"If they arrive tomorrow, they can join us. Later than that, and they'll have to catch up with us. They move more quickly than most of our men. I want this army to be ready to march no later than tomorrow noon." He found a waterskin and refilled the cup. "Have you heard anything of Thienn or his army?"

"The last reports we received were from the Glangurran baron. He said Thienn was still gathering his forces." Jonfré chuckled. "Some of his lords seem reluctant to support him."

"Excellent. We'll drive straight at Glangurrach."

Damon walked to a large chest, returned carrying Morgan's sword and knife. "I brought these for you."

Morgan grinned broadly. The weapons he wore had served him well, but he'd missed the familiar blades, blessed by Topaz's wish. He removed the plain sword and dagger and buckled on his own. "I'll meet you here for the evening meal. Where's Queen Ukena?"

"She's staying in the quarters you used before," Anjular replied. "I'll walk with you. You may need help getting through the soldiers."

Morgan noticed then the shouting had continued. He strode to the door and opened it.

Anjular stepped in front of him and led the way, moving soldiers with his bellow and, sometimes, his arm, until they stood outside the door of Ukena's quarters.

Morgan gestured at the milling men and shouted, "Are they this confident, or this desperate?"

"Both, perhaps," Anjular bellowed. "They hate Thienn worse than the clap, and they're eager to follow you, but Thienn's lords don't fight for love of Thienn but to save their own skins and holdings."

Morgan rapped at the door and waited. He'd almost decided to knock again when a maidservant opened the door. She allowed him to enter, then closed the door behind him, shutting out some of the noise.

Morgan saw Ukena standing behind a chair, bowed to her. Terralyn sat on the floor, playing with bits of wood. After looking up to see who'd entered, he returned his attention to the wood scraps. Morgan smiled, appreciating the ability of the very young to understand what was truly important, then faced Ukena. "You could've remained in Linistia in greater safety and more comfort."

Ukena sat in the chair and placed her hands on the table. "I wanted Terralyn to learn, as young as possible, the responsibilities of royalty. You, your family but for Thienn, some of the Donradan nobility and some Glangurrans—even the church of Ianno—have risked all you have, all you are, to restore Terralyn's throne. All he and I have to offer are our lives. That's all we can give, so that we must offer."

Morgan studied her face. The self-effacing shyness from which she'd once suffered seemed to have been refined into what he could only perceive as nobility of spirit. "You inspire my respect, which isn't an easy thing to gain. Thienn isn't my son, but even if he were, I'd still be ready to fight him for you and Terralyn." He hesitated a moment, couldn't decide whether it was cowardice or prudence that kept him from admitting to her his responsibility for helping create the situation in which they found themselves.

He bowed again, more deeply. "I ask leave to depart. I have to tell the head priest of Ianno that Kiartan is dead."

"So," Ukena said, "the losses have already begun."

"Don't grieve," Morgan said. "You're a leader and you can't afford it. You may miss those who're gone. You should respect their sacrifices and be grateful for them, but you can't let the losses keep you from taking action."

Ukena nodded and Morgan trod to the door. He turned and said, "We march tomorrow," then he turned again and left.

Anjular still waited outside the door and he led Morgan to the inn in which he'd stayed before Anjular had offered him a room. Now the rooms were being used by all but two priests and two healers from the empire, although only two priests and four healers remained when Morgan rapped at the door of the senior priest.

Morgan bowed to Ianno's priest. "I bring bad news. Kiartan died at Hope."

"I'll miss him," said the priest. "I'll pray he finds a well-earned rest and dreams of joy."

A silence grew, then, to break the oppressive quiet, Morgan asked, "How well does the proselytizing go?"

"Always briskly in an army facing battle. We make it clear that we cannot pray for victory, only for the man's survival or for peaceful rest if life can't be granted. Men are more receptive to such a balm when they face pain and death."

"I'm pleased by your successes, but I'd rather you had less opportunity."

"I, also."

"You'll need another protector. I believe my nephew would be a good choice."

"I'll consult the other priests and healers, but I think he'd be worthy."

Morgan bowed again and returned to Anjular's quarters. As he walked across the sandy stretch between the buildings, he noticed that the noise had subsided to the usual chaos of men anxious for their lives, preparing to risk those lives in battle.

In the quarters again, he observed that, besides the pallet in the bed frame, three more pallets had been placed on the floor. "Which one is mine?"

Jonfré gestured at them. "You choose."

Morgan grinned. "Yours are the oldest bones, so you'll need the frame." He sat on the end of one of the pallets on the floor, unbuckled his belts, laid his weapons beside him, then pulled off his boots. He needed rest, but his mind was still wrestling with possibilities and concerns, and it was like wrestling with a nest of snakes. He thought of Hadrian, tried to remember what his brother had said about himself. He'd said that a different fire burned in him now, and that the Union and Mendarian had left him all fire and scars. Fire. A possibility occurred to him then. It was a gamble; it might save Hadrian, or destroy him utterly.

No, he corrected himself, Hadrian had already been destroyed.

The worst that could happen was that his body and mind might die. He considered asking Damon about the idea, then realized that sharing his notion with Hadrian's son was a form of cowardice, a desire to avoid accepting all the onus if it failed.

He did, however, need Damon's assistance. "Damon, did you bring the clan's library from the empire?"

Damon had been sitting on a stool, honing the edge of one of his swords. He looked up from his work. "Most of it. The scrolls are in that chest." He indicated the trunk with a nod.

"Did you bring the fire-beast spell?"

~ * ~

Morgan's horse stamped and shook its head, making the bridle rings jingle, sharing its rider's impatience. The Senshenni had arrived at midmorning and he'd given them time to eat and rest, then sent them ahead to follow the woodsrunners he'd dispatched as scouts. He'd ride with the Donradans and Glangurrans in the vanguard, with Ukena and Jonfré accompanying the Sazians in the center. The other Cercans, when they arrived, would be the rearguard.

He'd decided to strike north. The Forest of Omaire was a belt running across Donradé and most of Glangurra, stretching over a hundred leagues from east to west, but hardly more than seven from north to south. While the woodsrunners, the Donradans, and even the eastern Cercans could fight well in heavy forest, the Senshenni and the Sazians were almost useless where the Senshenni couldn't use their speed nor the Sazians their formations. Also, the forest slowed them all and the wagons would find few trails to follow.

He looked up at the sky, which was darker than it'd been earlier in the morning and felt the wind full in his face. The branches overhead shook and rattled with the force of the wind. One of the minor gods of Donradé was a weather deity, aptly depicted as a woman of mercurial temper. He hoped that, if she existed, she'd prove friendly, but spring in Donradé was a time of sudden, violent storms and soaking rains.

He'd been tempted to wait another day but he couldn't be sure a storm was inevitable or that tomorrow would be more promising, nor did it greatly matter. The army was too large to let everyone take shelter inside the walls of the fortress.

At last the signals that all was ready were shouted to the front of the line and he touched spurs to his horse. His standard-bearer kept pace with him and the great black flag with its red sunburst eagle snapped in the stiffening wind.

A few Senshenni had ridden back to guide the column along the overgrown traders' trail and Morgan hoped the passage of so many men would clear the way enough to make it easier to move the baggage train through.

Once in the dense woods, the darkening sky was visible through a web of boughs and twigs laden with buds, but the forest was as dark as if it were twilight, and after an hour's march they heard the rumble of thunder.

The trail they followed was seldom straight; it followed the features of the land and wound around massive stands of trees and outcroppings of rock. For a time, it followed a stream, then ran across it, and the swiftly running water threatened to overflow the banks. The rolls of thunder came more often, now, and from much closer.

Morgan twisted in his saddle to look at the men behind him, could only distinguish the nearer ranks; the others were lost in the gloom. He dispatched one of Anjular's men to the rear to tell him when the rearguard had reached the stream. By the time the courier would be able to reach him again, he could halt the column.

They pressed on and Morgan saw a flash of brilliance ahead, and a shower of sparks, and was almost deafened by the roar of thunder and so barely heard the crash as a tree top fell. His mount began to pitch and buck at the light and the noise. A firm hand on the reins and a steady voice finally soothed the frightened animal, but Morgan rode tensed for another fight with his horse, knowing the storm would worsen.

They advanced into the tempest. Morgan could do nothing but ride on. With the men behind him, he yearned to dismount and find shelter, but there was no shelter, only the trees naked but for buds.

Twice more he heard lightning strike trees within a bow shot of where he rode, sounding like the crack of a gigantic whip, followed by a deafening roll of thunder, then the thunder was behind him and the only ordeal was the frigid rain. He'd begun to shiver when the courier returned with word that the Cercans were crossing the stream. Morgan turned and shouted for the men to set up camp.

The camp was damp, cold, comfortless. Morgan drew another cloak from his saddle pouch, used it to rub down his horse, then hung his wet cloak on a low limb and wrapped himself in the slightly drier one. When he could control his shivering, he rose and began to trudge along the back trail.

Damon fell into step beside him and they walked together. Most of the men had drawn off the sides of the trail and sought the highest ground they could find. They stopped once when they found a healer attending a man who'd been struck by a falling limb, and again when they found half a dozen men lying dead. They'd been struck by lightning, and two of Ianno's priests were tending the bodies.

They were finally stopped by a Sazian sentry, who, after he'd recognized them, escorted them to the center of the Sazian camp, where Ukena and Jonfré waited. Another man stood with them and Morgan didn't recognize Ergun until the man muttered greetings.

Morgan and the Dieri struck the palms of their right hands together, and Morgan said, "I'm grateful to have you and your men with us, but I'm curious why you'd march to a war that isn't your own."

Ergun's shrug was almost lost in the dark. "Orhan didn't want to be outdone in generosity by the Sazians, and he'd heard they'd lent men to your army. Besides, you're one of us." He reached into his tunic and handed Morgan a rolled sheet of parchment. "Topaz asked me to bring you this."

Morgan had felt warmth and a sense of belonging when Ergun had claimed him as one of his own. He took the message, stood holding it. He wanted to read it immediately but the darkness was too deep, and he wanted to be alone when he read it. Carefully he slipped it into his shirt. "How is she? And Cari?"

"Both were well when I left."

The Sazian commander, Sestarian, joined them, and Morgan introduced each of the leaders. They'd need to know each other and be prepared to rely upon each other. The Sazian spoke Gasgoran, so now Morgan used that language. "We should reach the edge of the forest by noon tomorrow. I'll march the vanguard a bow shot beyond the trees, then keep them there. Sestarian, I want your men to march a bow shot past us, and the Cercans will stay at the edge of the woods. We'll remain in columns unless we're warned the enemy is near. If that happens, our response will depend upon the attack. I'm going to keep the woodsrunners in the forest. Any ambush will likely come from that quarter. The Senshenni will range north and west, ahead of and to the right of the Sazians."

He repeated what he'd said in Dieri, for Ergun.

The Sazian commander said, "I'll see to my men," and strode

into the night.

"There's one with a long memory for lost battles, and little affection for us or the Cercans," Jonfré remarked.

"But he'll fight well because it's his duty," Morgan replied. "I'll be pleased if the Donradans fight with only twice his enthusiasm and half his skill." He bade them all a good night and, with Damon, slogged his way through the mud to the van. As he reached his horse he touched the parchment in his shirt for reassurance, then tried to find a reasonably dry place in which to eat his rations and rest.

~ * ~

A cold, damp fog had formed during the night and the soldiers grumbled as they fell into their columns, hardly able to distinguish the man in front of them from the nearest tree. Morgan led his horse, unwilling to risk its legs on footing that could hardly be seen.

The sun, which had been only a dim glow in the east, finally burned through the mist and by noon, when they left the forest, the day was bright and clear.

He'd relayed his orders to the leaders of the woodsrunners and the Senshenni and after marching three hundred paces from the trees, he led his column only far enough forward to clear the way for the Sazians, then let his men rest while he rode another hundred paces forward and took out the message from Topaz.

> *Morgan,*
>
> > *Ergun is calling out many of the warriors to march with you, so I asked him to give you this message. Cari and I are well, but Saril has returned to Crown, so I find myself busy. I'm looking forward to your return. Somehow, the mountain isn't as warm without you in it.*
>
> > > *All my love,*
> > > *Topaz*

Morgan read the message twice, smiling through the second reading, then rolled it again, put it away, and looked around him. The Sazian column had begun to form to his right, and so he missed seeing Hadrian's arrival until he heard the padding of a horse a few paces away. He gestured to Hadrian, and both rode back to where Damon and the standard-bearer waited.

Morgan gave Hadrian enough time in which to greet his son,

then asked, "You delivered Cruach to Ianno's healers?"

Hadrian nodded. "The way they fussed over him, if the old devil has any vestige of gratitude, he'll become a convert."

Morgan smiled at the thought of Cruach embracing a god of peace. "It's too much to hope for, but a pleasant thought." He paused, then said, "Damon has something for you; a spell I acquired. I want you to have it now so you can learn it well, and, perhaps, prepare. I haven't the power to use it anymore, but you might. It seemed apt, since it's a way to destroy the last of the Union, and you can put your anger to use in casting the spell."

Hadrian accepted the fragile scroll from his son and scanned the parchment. "I'm impressed." He looked up at Morgan. "It's a very old spell. I'd heard of it, but thought it lost. Where did you get it?"

Morgan had experienced a flush of pride when Hadrian had confessed to being impressed, but the question disturbed him, for he couldn't remember, precisely, how he'd discovered it. "I think that perhaps I found it in a dream."

"Then sleep more often. This is worth slumbering for a decade."

The Dieri began to issue from the forest, and Morgan shouted for the columns to march.

For four days the weather remained fair. The troops gathered kindling and loaded it into the wagons to keep it dry. Morgan also gathered pitch and several kinds of wood, which he kept in the first wagon in the train. They passed several villages and marched through fields still waiting for the touch of the plow.

The Donradans, listening to the songs the Sazians used to mark cadence, began to create their own chants.

The songs and the spirits were drowned in the downpour that began on the evening of the fourth day. The fields turned into a morass and, while they'd covered thirty-five leagues on the four good days, they dragged themselves scarcely half that in the next six, although the provisions shrank at least as rapidly. A dozen more men died in the storms and nearly a hundred became too ill to march.

Fighting the weather was almost as dangerous as facing an opposing army, and much less satisfying, for there was no way to attack it. Morgan began to wonder if he'd erred. There were good reasons for not fighting wars in the spring. There were also excellent reasons for fighting as soon as possible. His forces would be difficult to marshal later, when they might be fighting with their backs to the sea. A single quick stroke now might stop both Thienn and the church of Mordach before many more lives were blighted.

Or, perhaps, he admitted to himself, he simply wanted his obligations ended. He had other duties, which offered greater rewards. He'd almost begun to wish there were indeed a weather goddess, so he could blame the fickle bitch for his problems and those of his army.

She teased them again with two more days of fair weather, and Morgan had begun to hope they'd be able to defeat Thienn before he and his men could be beaten by the rains and the dwindling supplies. He'd already ordered that, as each wagon was emptied of provisions, the draft horses be killed and fed to the troops.

The rain began again the next day. The scouts had reached the Bluewater River, now brown and flood-swollen, about twenty leagues south of Hope. Four of the Senshenni tried to cross the river and three of them succeeded. Morgan regretted the loss of a man, but his need for eyes to look ahead was desperate. He marched with the men, plodding forward, carrying what seemed to be his own weight in mud on his boots.

The army reached the river by late afternoon, and Morgan conferred with the Senshenni scouts. The men who'd crossed had strung ropes from one bank of the swollen river to the other, and more men had crossed, stringing more lines. By the time the army had reached the river, most of the Senshenni had crossed and many were ranging ahead, probing for the enemy.

Morgan paced beside the river, cursing. His army was groping ahead like a blind man, and crossing the river would be dangerous enough, but if Thienn and his army reached the river before Morgan's men had crossed, his force would be whittled away. Still, he had to cross. Glangurrach was no more then twenty-five leagues away. If neither army crossed, Thienn would win. His army could outwait Morgan's, with supplies much nearer. Under the circumstances, Thienn would be a fool to try to cross, and whatever else his "son" might be, he was no fool. No, he'd wait, let Morgan's men starve and begin to desert, then he'd cross and pursue, first overwhelming the rearguard, then cutting up the remnants.

The decision was a distasteful one, but it was already made. If Thienn were within striking distance of the river, the Senshenni in Glangurra would've given an alarm.

He gave the order to cross.

Two things favored them; there was little wind, and no lightning. With only the ceaseless rain and the swollen river to fight, Morgan led them across. Some of the wagons were broken up to build rafts, to ferry across supplies and the armor of the horsemen. They'd have to ride the horses across, but if a man fell or was thrown, Morgan wanted to give the rider a chance to survive.

He stripped off the helmet and mail he wore, saw them secured in the wagon with the wood and pitch Hadrian would need to cast the fire-beast spell, and urged his mount into the river. The horse slipped and scrambled in the mud at the water's edge, then forged ahead into deeper water. Morgan's belly tightened, but the river, though wide, wasn't as deep as it'd been at Hope. The horse swam forward until, near the midpoint, the animal lurched and Morgan felt a stab of panic. While horses were strong swimmers, he'd sooner trust his own arms and legs, and he prepared to fling himself from the saddle, but his mount struggled against the current and finally won to the far bank.

Morgan slid out of the saddle, then, and labored with the Senshenni, hauling line, helping pull out men exhausted by the crossing, and cursed the rain.

As soon as enough of the men were across, he established lines, the Sazians on the left flank, the Cercans to the right.

The weather seemed determined to wreck other plans. He'd counted on having an advantage in archers, as well as in the Senshenni, who could use their bows from horseback. The rain had caused the bows to lose their spring, the bowstrings their tension, and made horses all but useless in the mud.

Damon appeared out of the darkness, his white hair plastered to his head. "All but the last few wagons are across."

"Leave them. As long as the men have their armor and weapons and food enough for tonight and tomorrow morning, we have all we need but luck, and I doubt we have a wagon of that. I'd rather Thienn caught us hauling those last few wagons across. It might make him think we've just crossed and that the men are tired."

"You're going to fight here? With our backs to the river?"

Morgan gestured at the plain that lay beyond them in the night and the rain. "There's no better place. The rise on this bank is the highest point around. Do you see how the field ahead of us slopes? They'll have to fight their way through a bog to reach us."

As he paced along the line, a Senshenni drew his tired mount to a halt a spear's length away. "Thienn and his army made camp some two leagues west of here. They should be here by noon tomorrow."

"Very good. Do the rest of the Senshenni understand that we want to deprive Thienn of his scouts?"

The Senshenni chuckled. "We remember. I have two victory rings to paint on my lance. And Kiril took one of their sentries with a lasso. He should be here soon."

"Excellent. Eat and rest. You may have to fight on foot tomorrow."

"Nothing's perfect," the Senshenni said. "But it should be a glorious battle." He walked away, into the darkness, leading his horse.

Morgan shook his head. Once, he supposed, he'd entertained a similarly simple view of battles, although he doubted he'd ever been quite so carefree about them.

He trod further, noticed a dim shape in the darkness, and leaned against the wagon's wheel. He was still resting when another Senshenni appeared, a rope in his hands, leading a panting, moaning captive.

Morgan stepped forward and tried to look at the prisoner, but the darkness and the mud covering the man made him all but invisible. Half a hundred paces away, someone had coaxed a fire out of pitch-soaked wood, and Morgan dismissed the Senshenni, then caught up the rope and led the captive toward the light.

As he walked, he shouted for a bucket of water, then ordered it dumped over the prisoner. When they reached the fire he freed the man of the rope around his chest. The Glangurran seemed to be in fear of his life.

Morgan felt the man's hands. From the calluses, he took the man to be a farmer, and he seemed near middle age. One eye was swollen almost shut and Morgan guessed, from the coatings of mud, that he'd fallen and been dragged, probably several times.

He gestured for the prisoner to sit and, when the man had caught his breath, offered him a cup of watered wine. The man gulped it down and nodded to him.

"How many men are with Thienn?"

The man paused, then replied, "Over a score of hundreds."

Morgan watched the man closely. He suspected the man probably couldn't count past a score, if that high, and to him a hundred would be some nebulous number greater than "many." "Who marches with him?"

"Many of the lords of Glangurra, and a few from Donradé. Many of the priests and monks of Mordach. And hirelings. Someone said there were paidsoldiers from Shatilla—many from Shatilla—and some from Pitlahsa, and some other foreigners, too."

Morgan frowned, saw the farmer cringe and composed his face. He should've realized Thienn, unable to inspire loyalty, would try to buy it. They might be facing a bigger and more capable army than he'd feared. "Where do they plan to fight us?"

"I think they hoped to reach the river before you, or catch you crossing."

No more questions occurred to him. The prisoner sat stiffly, as though waiting for a sword thrust. Morgan was surprised to find himself feeling more kinship with this reluctant soldier than with the Senshenni, who saw battle only as a form of contest. He nodded to one of his men. "Feed him and take him to one of Ianno's healers. Let the drovers watch him, but tell them to treat him well. I'll expect to talk with him tomorrow." He grinned at the captive. "Unless you try to escape, you'll live to plow your fields again. Do you understand?"

The man nodded and let himself be marched away by the Donradan.

"You've changed, brother," said Hadrian's soft voice. A part of the night broke loose and walked into the firelight.

"I'd gain nothing more from him with harsher treatment. The ones we fought in Doss would've spit in my face. He was too afraid to have any spit."

"It seems we can settle a few old scores for the clan," Hadrian observed.

"The mercenaries out of Pitlahsa? If they'll fight. They don't like dismounting from their horses for battle."

"We can hope."

"Hope first to deal with the last of the Union."

"That's not a hope, it's a certainty. Tomorrow, they all die. If not by fire, then by my blades."

~ * ~

The rain had slackened to a steady misting that kept the ground boggy, and the sun remained hidden, although the darkness had lightened to the color of a pearl. Morgan rode down the line. The Sazians waited with the patience of stone, each man resting his large, rectangular shield on the ground before him, each wearing the leaf-shaped stabbing sword, each holding a pair of javelins and the short spear that was their favored weapon. They were arrayed in staggered ranks. At the end of the line stood the Elites; iron men in iron armor.

He rode to the end of the line, then returned to near the center of the Sazian formation where Sestarian waited, astride a white horse.

"They're good men," Morgan told him. "I'm glad to be on the same side with them. Tell your men to give quarter to none but common soldiers, and then only if they throw down their weapons. The rest of the orders I gave you stand."

Sestarian nodded and began to pass orders to his men.

Morgan rode toward the center of the line. Anjular's men held the left flank of the center. Morgan saluted Anjular and nodded to Aovalyn and Edou. Edou grinned and raised the sword Scarface had given him months before. *May it serve you well*, Morgan wished, and rode on.

Beyond Anjular's men were other Donradans and Glangurrans, the most suspect of the troops. Another reason Morgan had chosen to fight on the river's bank was to make flight impossible. The men began to shout his assumed name and his horse shied at the noise, but he brought it under control. He raised his right arm, fist clenched, and rode past the line.

Near the center stood the veterans from the empire. If the middle of the line were the weakest part, he wanted steel at the very center. Hadrian stood beside a covered brazier, helmeted and armored, Damon beside him, the younger man's white hair hidden in a battle helm. Jocile's ugly face was almost split by a wide grin, and he winked when he saw Morgan's gaze reach him.

Past the men from the empire stood more Donradans and Glangurrans under the petty nobles they served. Morgan recognized a man or two among them and nodded, then reached the contingent from Linistia, Jonfré at their head. Morgan saluted him and repeated the orders. There was no need to give orders to the center of the line; he was sure that, with mercenaries in Thienn's army, they'd attack in a spearpoint formation, and that point would be made up of mercenaries, the priests and monks of Mordach, and Glangurran nobles and their household bullies.

Past the men of Linistia, the Cercans readied for battle. They'd laid aside their bows and rested their large, round shields beside them. He recognized too many men to nod to each, so he raised his hand and saluted Ergun. He repeated, in Dieri, the order about sparing only common soldiers who surrendered or fled, then reminded them once the battle began, the Cercans were to move to their left to fill any gaps in the line while moving forward and around, striking Thienn's forces from the side and rear.

The Senshenni held the far right end of the line and Morgan reminded their leader he was relying upon them to break through Thienn's rear and complete a circle with the Sazians. The Senshenni shouted war-cries and beat on the faces of their small, round horsemen's shields with the flats of their weapons.

Morgan grinned, looked across the field to the Sazian lines. He'd taken advantage of a curve in the river to array his forces in a broad arc, a cup to hold the enemy spearpoint.

Watching the fields to the west, he returned to the center of the army. He'd dismount for battle but, for the moment, it was more pleasant to sit than to stand.

Within an hour, the first of Thienn's scouts appeared, clad in the drab homespun of peasants. Morgan ordered the drovers to bring the rest of the wagons across, with as much shouting as possible. He watched the first of the rafts ride on the current in an arc from one bank to the other, straining at their belaying ropes.

Some of the Glangurran scouts stood watching, while others hurried away. In no more than a quarter of an hour, a column of red and yellow appeared; the priests and monks of Mordach. As they approached, their formation changed to a triangle pointed at the middle of Morgan's line. The point of the formation was red, with the men in yellow making up the center of the triangle.

Behind him, someone hooted and shouted, "We'll give them all red robes today."

Morgan grinned, said nothing. It'd be done, but the doing wouldn't be easy. He suspected that those who'd joined the church as an alternative to learning a trade or hiring themselves out as mercenaries had all left the church in search of an easier way to fortune, and those who remained were the men he'd met three years ago. They'd fight with skill and a thirst for revenge.

As soon as the churchmen had formed their formation, two more columns appeared. The file to Morgan's right rode behind a gold banner marked with a green ring, and each man's cloak bore a green ring on the left shoulder. Morgan glanced at Hadrian, who was glowering at the riders like a great cat eyeing its prey, and he earnestly hoped no one jostled his brother.

Morgan gave his attention back to the enemy. The other column of men, clad mostly in pale blue, wore the high, peaked helmets favored by the Shatillans, and more men rode behind them.

Morgan guessed the remnants of the Union to number about two hundred men, while there were at least twice that many Shatillans. Soldiers wearing heavy plate armor advanced behind the Porcashians, riding massive chargers. Thienn must be paying the Pitlahsans well, Morgan reflected, to make them willing to attack on foot. Wearing that armor, they'd remain mounted for as long as possible, but he doubted they'd charge on horseback.

Still more Shatillans rode to the right of the Pitlahsans, and behind those Morgan could just make out the yellow and black livery of Thienn's personal troops. He'd guessed Thienn would be behind the mercenaries. When you paid men to fight for you, you made sure they earned their pay, but you kept your own men between them and yourself.

Morgan dismounted. He'd seen the best part of Thienn's army; the rest would add only numbers. He strode to where Hadrian stood beside the covered brazier. "Time to light a torch, brother. Have you put something of value in the brazier?"

"Not yet." Hadrian was still staring at the men under the banner of the green ring, his dark eyes smouldering. Morgan hesitated, but they'd need all the power they could muster, and he drew Topaz's scarf from his pouch and placed it under the leather cover. Hadrian lifted an amulet on a chain from around his neck and added it to the kindling, then took flint, steel, and tinder from his pouch.

He had to strike several times before a spark took hold, and he held a torch over the weak fire. A farrier's apprentice standing on the opposite side of the brazier from Hadrian stood ready, his bellows in his hands. Morgan, standing to Hadrian's left, turned again to watch the enemy. Most of Thienn's army had found their places in the formation and some of them had begun to dismount.

Hadrian whipped the cover away and plunged the torch into the wood. They both muttered curses as the wood only smouldered, then flames began to rise. Hadrian's muttering changed from oaths to the incantations, and a shape began to take form in the fire. The pitch flared and the apprentice pumped his bellows, making the flame burn hotter and brighter, becoming a blaze.

Morgan thought he could see a maned head, then wings shot up, spread, and a winged lion sprang into the air.

The flame-beast roared and bounded toward the Porcashians, moving almost at the speed of thought, leaving a trail of steam. The horses screamed and plunged, and the lion leapt, pouncing onto a man before he could draw weapon. The man disappeared in a mass of flames and dense black smoke, then another soldier writhed in the jaws of the fire-lion, wrapped in its embrace.

Men and horses screamed, and the stolid unit dissolved in pandemonium. Blades were drawn, horses reared and bucked, men fell from saddles, were trampled by their mounts. The panic spread. The Pitlahsan's heavy horses began to stamp and shake their heads, fighting the reins.

Drawn into their formation, the survivors of the Union were unable to escape, and they had no weapons with which to fight the beast among them. Hadrian continued to claim victims, leaving some afire, shrieking and scrambling in the mud.

Then the Pitlahsans were also being thrown from their saddles, and armor that could turn a blade offered little protection from shod hooves or the weight of their huge chargers.

The soldiers around both groups began to break away. The king's guard fought with a few Pitlahsans who'd tried to flee to the rear. Shatillans began to distance themselves from the others, less in a charge than in an attempt to escape the madness around them, and the priests of Mordach leapt from their saddles and surged forward.

Facing disaster, Thienn ordered the charge. The front of the formation was pushed ahead by those behind them who couldn't see what was happening and supposed the noises they heard were simply the sounds of the clash of armies.

Hadrian's face, normally placid and opaque, was contorted with fury and fierce exultation, and he was again growling like a hunting animal.

The last of the Union fell and was pounced upon by the lion of fire and rage, the man's shrieks lost in the roaring of the fire-beast.

Morgan signalled to the apprentice, seized one of the buckets of water beside the brazier, and dashed water on the wood and ashes.

Even at the distance of three hundred long paces, Morgan could hear the hiss as the lion was extinguished, and Hadrian staggered. Morgan took a step forward to support him, then the blade that appeared in Hadrian's left hand was sweeping toward his throat.

Morgan saw his death rushing at him, and there was no way to avoid it; there was no time to move, or even to think. Only Hadrian or Kiartan could've turned that stroke, kept it from killing.

Hadrian did. Somehow, he slowed the blade, swung it upward, and, at the last instant, twisted the sword in his hand so it was the flat of the blade that rang against Morgan's helmet.

Even turned, and delivered with the flat of the blade, the blow stunned Morgan, left him gasping for air and seeing black shot with red, then he focussed his eyes on Hadrian.

Hadrian glared at him, his face demonic in its rage, then he rasped, "We'll settle this later."

The warrior-priests of Mordach had almost reached the line of Donradans. Hadrian flung himself forward, through the defenders, and both blades became blurs. A priest went down, wailing, blood jetting from his severed leg; another pawed at the ruins of his face with red-stained hands; yet another doubled over, trying to hold his guts inside the gaping slash in his belly. The swords rose and fell, darted and slashed, and Hadrian rushed into the enemy's ranks, where they fell before him like wheat before a scythe.

Morgan forced himself to look to his left flank, saw the battle there was wavering, with his line beginning to fray. He shouted for the man with the horn to call for Anjular's men to move toward the center, then drove forward, his sword like a living thing in his hand, and helped throw back the masses of red and yellow.

The immediate danger dealt with, he drew back to study the field. He saw Hadrian even deeper in the enemy ranks, cutting down Shatillans and a few of the Pitlahsans who'd lived to advance. Hadrian had driven so far forward that the enemy were beginning to close the swath he'd left behind him. Then Hadrian was gone.

Morgan screamed Hadrian's name to Damon, pointed with his sword, but before he could join his nephew, saw a knot of Pitlahsans had broken through his left center. Protected by their heavy armor and fighting like madmen, they'd torn a gap in his line.

He signed to the trumpeter again and strode forward, leading the handful of soldiers who'd been around him.

The Pitlahsans were no longer fighting for gold, or even for victory; they were fighting for their lives.

Morgan feinted, drew one of the Pitlahsans out of his place in the formation, and caused him to strike off-balance. Beating the man's sword aside, he hooked the guard of his weapon under the other's and snatched back. Holding his sword in a grip born of panic, the Pitlahsan fell.

Morgan left the fallen man to the soldiers behind him and struck another Pitlahsan, his blow falling in the joint between the plate covering the forearm and the cop on the elbow. He felt his blade bite deeply, dragged it free, then struck at a third man who'd just become aware of him. His upward slash caught the man just below the bottom of his helm, and the Pitlahsan recoiled.

The men following him thrust their spears ahead, then the Pitlahsans were all down, and he could see the men on the left center fighting toward him.

He killed a Shatillan who'd already been wounded and realized the veterans from the empire had cut these men off from the main body of Thienn's army, and he fell back. He and his men drove to the right, taking over that part of the battle from Damon's men, then pushed the mercenaries before them into the river, killing them or watching them drown.

His left arm trembled with the weight of his shield, his right arm had hardly enough strength to raise his blade, and his legs seemed to have turned to lead. His mouth and throat were parched. He stumbled back to the wagons, dropped his shield, and took a dipper of watered wine.

Somewhat refreshed, he tried to see the battle as a whole, but the lines had dissolved into knots of battling men and he could distinguish no more than a few banners. The standards of the Sazian *seymana* seemed nearer, and one had moved to the right. He also noted that Ianno's priests and healers were as busy as the soldiers, dragging wounded men to safety and tending to the hurt and dying.

Even at a distance, the din of battle rang in his ears; the clash of steel on steel, the cries of the wounded, the shrieks of tortured metal, the orders and battle-cries shouted, all combined to make a sound like no other.

He spared a moment's regret for Hadrian, and that regret was tinged with guilt. He'd known the likely effect of extinguishing the beast before it'd returned, and so he was responsible for what had happened to his brother.

The enemy surged forward again in a desperate counterattack and Morgan trod back into the press, fighting his way toward Thienn's standard with its device of a three-headed and four-winged eagle. Most of the warriors of both sides had dropped their shields to use both weary arms to wield their weapons.

He continued to advance until he found himself among the royal guard. He beat aside an attacker's blade, then thrust past the man's shoulder, used the other man's own resistance to help whip the upper edge of his blade into the Glangurran's helmet, then he drew the blade across the man's eyes.

Shoving past the keening man, he confronted more men and fought on, his arms worn past ache to pain, his breath coming in ragged gasps. There was no artistry to this sort of fighting, only endurance and the execution of actions practiced often enough to become habit. He cut down four more men, then saw one of Thienn's captains crouched before him, sword raised. Before Morgan could attack, the man fell, cut from shoulder to breastbone, and Damon was working his blade free of the corpse.

Behind the dead captain stood Thienn, his armor flecked and spattered with blood. It was impossible to tell whether he was wounded or not, but he saw Morgan and snarled, "Win or lose, I'll have your head."

Morgan found himself calm, his voice steady. "If you want it, you'll have to come much closer to get it."

Mindless of the battle that raged around them, they faced each other, and it was as though Morgan were again training with Kiartan. He dropped his point and assumed the open stance he'd learned. Thienn's eyes narrowed, and Morgan's blade swept up. Thienn had made the mistake of announcing his intentions with his eyes and by drawing his sword back to strike. The tip of Morgan's blade gashed Thienn's left arm, then arced over his head and hacked through the tail of his coif and the shoulder of the hauberk.

Thienn sagged forward, his head down, seemingly held up only by Morgan's sword, which had buried itself to his chest. Morgan twisted and wrenched at the hilt, and the corpse of his "son" fell face-down into the trampled mud.

Damon and another man killed two more of Thienn's guards and Morgan stumbled back. Even without Thienn, his army would still coil and lunge, like a headless snake. He stepped back farther from the line, then a man pressed a wineskin into his hand and he drank deeply, relishing the sour wine's bite.

He began to see Sazians among the fighters then, driving their enemies before them with their great shields, then closing to stab with their short spears or their swords. Damon staggered away from the slaughter the battle had become, and Morgan handed him the wineskin. "I'm sorry," he said.

Damon shook his head, then set the wineskin to his lips and drained it.

The sounds of battle had diminished, nearly dying with the last of the Glangurrans who'd supported Thienn, leaving little noise but the moans and the entreaties of the wounded.

Morgan wiped his blade clean on the smock of a dead man and sheathed his sword, then, too exhausted to do anything more, he hobbled to the line of trees fringing the river the river to the ground there, only slightly less churned than the field, and dropped to his knees, then sat on his haunches.

He was aware of men around him, and an increase in the noise, but it cost too much energy to attend to them. There were a few cheers, but most of the soldiers were too drained in body and spirit to do more than follow his example and find a clear place in which to drop.

When his breathing slowed and became steady, he looked up. The Sazians had re-formed their ranks and begun to march down the river's bank, while some of the Senshenni were plundering bodies or collecting gory trophies.

He looked toward his banner, observed men had gathered about it. He worked his way to his feet, then trudged toward the standard. As he neared them, he began to recognize his commanders: Damon in stained red and black; Sestarian, his bright armor battered and blood-flecked; Ergun, looking as stolid as one of his mountains, though his shoulders sagged; Jonfré, with a fresh blood trail from the bottom rim of his helmet to his hauberk.

The man he most wanted to see was not, of course, among them.

When he reached them, he said, "You've all done well. Had any of you failed, we'd not be standing here. You and your men have won a victory." As if to remind him of the cost, the breeze shifted, bearing to them the charnel house odor of the battlefield.

Sestarian saluted him. "You've used my men well. I thank you for them."

Morgan bowed to the Sazian. "I'll visit your army's camp this evening."

Sestarian turned and walked away to where his men were pitching camp.

Jonfré tried to grin but the expression was little more than a rictus. "One more time you crawled into the shit and came out holding a crown."

"Then wash it off and award it to Queen Ukena." He put his hand on Jonfré's shoulder. "She'll need an advisor if she's to be regent to Prince Terralyn. Advise well." He turned Jonfré to better see the blood on his face. "What happened to your head?"

Jonfré ran the tips of the fingers of his right hand along the new scar on his helmet. "It kept the edge out, but left me reeling like a drunkard. It'll mend." Sensing that he'd been dismissed, then, he turned and made his way back to the wagons.

"Will you be needing us or the Senshenni?" Ergun asked.

Morgan shook his head. "With Thienn dead, I doubt there'll be anyone to garrison Glangurrach against us."

"Then we'll be back to our mountains."

Morgan smiled at the taciturn mountaineer, who never wasted words—or anything else. "I'll follow in a few days. If I don't catch up with you by the time you reach Stag, tell Topaz I'll be home soon."

Ergun bobbed his head in a nod and marched through the mud back to the Cercans. Like the Sazians, they'd move away from the battlefield to establish their camp.

Morgan turned to Damon, drew himself up like a man who is facing execution but was determined to meet it with dignity. "I'm deeply sorry. I wanted to bring peace to your father, but, instead...." His voice faltered as emotions long buried or denied racked him. Hadrian had really been a brother, in all but blood. Morgan had always envied his detachment, his skills, his closeness with his family. What he'd found with Topaz had made him appreciate more what Hadrian had achieved and lost.

Damon shook his head. "He's not dead. At least, not yet. He's unconscious, but the healers believe he'll live. Do you want to see him?"

Morgan could only nod, struck mute by relief, and he followed his nephew to where the wounded who'd been gathered lay, moaning or terribly quiet. Hadrian had been laid on a piece of canvas and covered with a blanket.

Morgan knelt beside Hadrian, studying him. A splint of broken spear shafts kept his right arm straight, and the side of his head was bruised to the cheekbone.

Somehow, he'd forgotten how small Hadrian was, until he saw him lying unconscious and helpless, seeming as frail as a child. Morgan carefully laid his hand on Hadrian's head, avoiding the bruise, and drew power from his scars. He'd once used a spell that could make a touch lethal, and he'd used the power, several times, to give himself strength. Now he concentrated on giving some of that strength to his brother. After a moment, he stood. "Tell me when he wakes."

Damon nodded.

A few paces away stood the wagon that had held the brazier. Morgan walked to it, stripped off his weapons and his mail, then buckled on his knife and sword again, and returned to the field. Many of the priests and healers of Ianno leaned over wounded men, helping them fight off death, or helping make their passage more peaceful.

All these deaths were his, he knew, and he had experienced regret to numbness.

The Sazians were beginning to carry away their dead and wounded, the dead to be burned. The Dieri and the eastern tribes would bury their men who'd fallen, while the Senshenni would build frameworks to let the bodies of their dead seem to stand, facing the mountains, their bodies offerings to Father Wolf.

The mercenaries and most of the Glangurrans with Thienn would be allowed to rot where they fell. They'd lost everything; no one here would mourn for them nor give their bodies the respect their doomed courage had earned them. They truly had given all.

Other men walked among the corpses, probably searching for friends or kin. Anjular limped along the line his men had held and Edou, his face pale and his eyes red, was using his sword to hack out a grave for Aovalyn.

Morgan made his features a mask of stone. That wasn't the only friendship being buried. He trod carefully, looking at the still faces or those racked by pain, recognized a few. Jocile's face was less ugly in repose, and he seemed to be smiling. There were a few here who'd met their ends as they'd wanted, but most had fought only from a sense of duty, and had wanted to live. Willing and unwilling, they lay heaped together.

Dragging himself through the mud back to the wagons, he found his horse tied to a wagon wheel. He tugged loose the reins, mounted, rode to where the Sazians had pitched camp. He finally noticed the rain had stopped, the sky had lightened; the sun would make a late but welcome appearance, even if it were brief.

He conferred with Sestarian. He'd send provisions to the Sazians and tomorrow they'd either capture Thienn's supply train, or they'd provide the Sazians with stores from Glangurrach, and the Sazians would march southeast, back to Linistia, within the next two or three days.

Returning to the wagons, he dispatched two of them to the Sazians, rode beside two more where the Cercans had assembled. Ergun had already decided to set out for the mountains in the morning. "There's game in the woods, and we'll pass through the holdings of nobles who chose not to fight here. They'll contribute cattle and grain to those who did fight."

Morgan grinned. Ergun was a hard bargainer, and all the trades would be to the advantage of his men. "I'm grateful for the sacrifices you Cercans made. Please express my gratitude to Orhan."

"Express it yourself. And it's 'we Cercans,' you're one of us."

"I stand corrected. I'll stay long enough to see my brother recover or die, and to make some arrangements. I believe I'll be carrying a new pact with Donradé and Glangurra for Orhan to sign."

Ergun extended his hand. "I'll see you in the mountains, then, if not before."

Morgan struck the palm of his hand against Ergun's, then mounted again and rode back to the wagons, which had become the center of the Donradan and Glangurran camp.

He tried to rest, but the battle, while it'd drained him, had also left him without appetite or the peace required for sleep. He stared at the moon, saw clouds drift across its face, tried to think of all that remained to be done. He had no part in what lay between Queen Ukena and Jonfré, nor between Donradé and Glangurra.

What was it a priest of Ianno had once told him? That a hundred years from now, people would still argue or fight or fall in love. The trees and mountains would remain, and the seasons would still come in their time.

Thunder rolled, off in the distance, and he drew out his cowled leather cloak. All the tents would be needed for the wounded. He rose. Not all the tents had been set up, and the priests and healers would need help.

~ * ~

Hadrian's eyes were open, but their opacity had deepened. His gaze was dull and lifeless, and he'd only glanced at Morgan before staring again at the clear morning sky.

Morgan understood perfectly Hadrian's feelings; the same as his own when he'd lost Lashastur. He sat down beside the wounded man. "That emptiness you feel is the void left by the loss of the anger with which you empowered your lion. What's left is more precious. It's you, without the rage. Your anger did its work; the clan is avenged and the battle's won. Now it's time for you to live. How you live, or if, is for you to decide."

Hadrian glanced at him again with unreadable eyes, then returned his gaze to the cloudless sky.

Morgan wanted to give Hadrian a reason for living, but neither he nor anyone else could do that. All anyone could do was to remind him of reasons he already had for living. "Have you seen Vornarei? Or your daughters? Don't they have a right to be heard before you choose death?"

Hadrian didn't even look at him again.

Morgan left, mounted his horse, rode to the front of the column with Jonfré and Anjular. Less than a thousand men, besides the Sazians, followed them to Glangurrach. Of the rest, those who weren't dead or seriously wounded were burying the dead. Most of the wagons remained behind. Among the few that followed the column was the one in which Hadrian rode.

The Donradan scouts captured Thienn's supply train at noon, without a fight, and evening found the remains of the army making camp less than six leagues from Glangurrach and enjoying fresh provisions.

Morgan sat beside a fire. His appetite had finally returned, and he'd eaten as well as any soldier in the field could expect. He'd drank water with the meal, hoarding his ration of wine until he could enjoy it. Now he sipped, appreciating the fruity flavor, and listening to Anjular's reply to Jonfré's offer.

"I'm pleased to be so well regarded, earl, but Linistia needs a lord who knows his letters. Besides, I'm happy at Omaire Garde."

Jonfré gazed into his wine cup. "I need a man I can trust in Linistia, a proven ruler." He cast a glance at Morgan. "Would your nephew accept?"

"Why don't you ask him? I think he'd be a worthy lord. He's ruled a holding before."

Jonfré smiled at Ukena, who returned the smile. "I'll be staying in Glangurrach, but Donradan Linistia is our most important holding." He paused. "I'll ask the lad, but he seems young to be an earl."

Morgan permitted himself a rueful smile. "Thienn was no older when he became king and ruined a kingdom. I think Damon has as great a capacity for building as Thienn had for destruction. Sestarian respects him, as do the men. If any lord of Donradé can claim to have done more in the battle, I'll dispute them myself." He sipped again at his wine. "If you have another holding that needs a capable lord, I'd suggest you offer it to Hadrian,"

"There are more lordless holdings than good lords. If you think there's a chance he'd accept, I'd be pleased to make him a noble. Has he spoken yet?"

Morgan stared at his cup, then drained it. "Not yet."

He rose to seek a place to lay his blanket and, as he moved away from the fire, Damon appeared, his hair yellow in the firelight. "Father asked to see you."

Morgan hesitated and felt almost as though he'd been stabbed with an icicle. The last thing Hadrian had said to him had been a warning. From anyone else, it would've been a threat, but Hadrian never threatened. He forced his face to smile. "Jonfré wishes to make you an offer. I suggest you accept it. I think it'd greatly please Jeshka."

As he made his way to the wagon, Morgan cursed himself for having stared into the flames, leaving himself night-blind.

He felt the crush of inevitability, something akin to futility, and the sensation was like being embedded in stone. Perhaps what was between Hadrian and himself was a sort of doom, the same sort of fate as between Mendarian and himself, and Thienn and himself. There seemed to be a cycle of death.

He tested the draw of his weapons before he climbed into the back of the wagon and lowered himself to the bed. By the light of the candle between them, he could see Hadrian was still pale, but sitting up, his back braced against rolls of canvas. He seemed as enigmatic as ever.

Morgan stared into the obsidian eyes. "I'm sorry, Hadrian, but if you're determined to settle something between us, I'll fight you. You have a right to be angry, but my life's become precious to me, and to others, too. My life isn't mine to give, so if there's to be a settling of affairs, I won't die easily."

Hadrian gestured at his right arm, held in a cast of sword blades and leather. "Do you think that would keep me from being able to kill you?" At Morgan's silence, he laughed, and seemed to have to fight to regain control over himself.

"I'll say one thing for you. You're the only man who's beaten me twice. You staggered me when you extinguished Hladon. No other single man can claim that. You beat me the second time when I realized you'd risked your life to give me mine back. I said that something needed to be settled later."

Hadrian smiled, and Morgan was astonished to find genuine warmth in the expression. "It's settled. I've decided to return to Sin Garlef."

Morgan exhaled, sat down beside Hadrian. "If you want, you can bring them back to Donradé, to your own holding."

Hadrian's smile broadened. "I may just do that. Sin Garlef is an austere place for my family." He looked at Morgan as though he hadn't seen him in years. "If you care for the company, I'll ride with you as far as Cerco. I'd like to meet the woman who's worked such a fine magick on you." He gestured again at the bound right arm, then extended his left.

Morgan grasped his brother's forearm, felt his own held in a firm grip. He'd soon be riding home, a brother beside him.

~ * ~

When they came to Glangurrach, the city's gates stood open to them.

About the Author

James K. Burk is a sometimes serious writer who enjoys a challenge. He has written five novels and many shorter works. His previous novels from WolfSinger Publications are THE TWELVE and HIGH RAGE, both fantasies. He's also written two science fiction novels: HOME IS THE HUNTER and REDEMPTION, and a weird western novella, "The Ghoul of Socorro" which is the fourth book in the Night Marshal series.

His shorter works were published in two chapbooks and several anthologies. One of his highlights was "The Trailer Park Vampire Meets the Bubba Yumbie" in THE INTERNATIONAL HOUSE OF BUBBAS.

He doesn't own any cats. His writing tends to be quirky.

Other Books by James K Burk
from WolfSinger Publications

<u>The Twelve</u>

Valtierra, a city-state, is governed by archetypes. Every two years they choose twelve men and women to wear the masks and to become the Wise Old Man, the Fool, the Mother, the Harlot, the Warrior, and the rest of the council. But now Valtierra faces hunger, decay, and an enemy on their border and, when the need for leadership is greatest, one mask is worn by a foreigner and one mask hides a traitor.

<u>High Rage</u>

Scarface, on his way back to a clan stronghold after assassinating a legate, meets and falls in love with a woman even more ruthless than he. To win her, he must reunite an empire and create a kingdom. His only allies are his wits, his sword, and the power in his scars—black marks like the taloned finger prints of a demon.

To achieve his goals, he must deal with old enemies, gods of dubious worth, and his own family—who may be the most dangerous of all.

Get ready for more adventures with these fantasy books from WolfSinger Publications.

Call of Chaos – Carol Hightshoe

The exiled daughter of a minor noble, Kyrianna Dalynne, finds herself trapped in a temple dedicated to Thynitic, The Lady of Chaos.

She and her companions, are charged with finding an ancient artifact before the ones guarding the portals out will allow them to leave.

As their search continues, Kyrianna begins to question if there was a specific reason she and the others were brought to this place.

The Hunters of Shadow – Jason J Sergi

The Battle of Delldoan is over; The Demon Saint Flesh is dead; the threat to Anfaria defeated; but, even with all this good fortune, Bathmal is left feeling lost and anxious.

His friend Sir Kasper is still among the missing long after The Battle of Delldoan has concluded, as is the vile dark-elf Zenlem Sidor. And, perhaps most troubling of all, Nojo-his trusted and faithful con-squire-continues to display signs of Dangerous Instability. If a solution to the problem cannot be found soon, Bathmal fears he may have to do the unthinkable…

Once more he will head into darkness, in hopes of finding Sir Kasper, and ridding the world of the dark-elf Sidor. But unseen forces will try to prevent him from doing both, and Bathmal will soon find out the taint of Hadez lasts far longer and doesn't go away just because he is no longer within the fell realm; but when the time comes, will he decide to fight against the taint, or will he embrace it?

The Golden Griffin waits for Bathmal…possibly forever…

Find out more about these and our other books at
www.wolfsingerpubs.com

www.ingramcontent.com/pod-product-compliance
Lightning Source LLC
Chambersburg PA
CBHW071853020726
47502CB00003B/735